I0822740

MIRROR, MIRROR

A Barbara Holloway Mystery

ALSO BY KATE WILHELM

A Flush Of Shadows
All For One
And The Angels Sing
A Sense Of Shadow
A Wrongful Death
Abyss
Better Than One (with Damon Knight)
By Stone, By Blade, By Fire
Cambio Bay
Casebook Of Charlie and Constance (Volumes 1&2)
Children Of The Wind
City Of Cain
Clear And Convincing Proof
Cold Case
Crazy Time
Death Of An Artist
Death Qualified, A Mystery Of Chaos
Defense For The Devil
Desperate Measures
Fault Lines
For The Defense (aka Malice Prepense)
Heaven Is High
Huysman's Pets
In Between
Juniper Time
Justice For Some
Kate Wilhelm In Orbit (Volumes 1 & 2)
Let The Fire Fall
Listen, Listen
Margaret And I
More Bitter Than Death
Naming The Flowers
No Defense
Not Dead Enough
Oh, Susannah!
Seven Kinds Of Death
Sister Angel
Skeletons
Sleight Of Hand
Smart House
Somerset Dreams And Other Fictions
Storyteller
Sweet, Sweet Poison
The Best Defense
The Clewiston Test
The Clone (with Theodore Thomas)
The Dark Door
The Deepest Water
The Downstairs Room
The Fullness Of Time
The Good Children
The Gorgon Field
The Hamlet Trap
The Hills Are Dancing (with Richard Wilhelm)
The Infinity Box (novel)
The Infinity Box (collection)
The Killer Thing
The Mile-Long Spaceship
The Nevermore Affair
The Price Of Silence
The Unbidden Truth
The Winter Beach
Torch Song
Welcome, Chaos
Where Late The Sweet Birds Sang
Whisper Her Name
With Thimbles, With Forks, And Hope
Year Of The Cloud (with Theodore Thomas)
Yesterday's Tomorrows

A complete bibliography may be found at katewilhelm.com.
Ebooks are available at infinityboxpress.com.

MIRROR, MIRROR

A Barbara Holloway Mystery

Kate Wilhelm

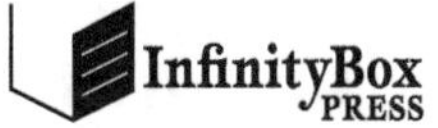

MIRROR, MIRROR
Kate Wilhelm

First edition

For more information, write to:
InfinityBox Press LLC
7060 North Borthwick Avenue
Portland, OR 97217
www.infinityboxpress.com

Designed by: Richard Wilhelm

ISBN-13: 978-1-62205-049-9

The Valducci's sign was obscured by rain and mist that cold February afternoon. Fronting River Road were parking spaces for a hundred cars close to the Valducci store, a large building with three overhead double garage doors. One of the doors was open. A few shoppers were picking up bare root trees and shrubs.

Glowing spots of light, some indeterminate distance away on the right and to the rear of the market building, seemed to be pulsing as mist and rain waxed and waned. That was the big Valducci house. To the left and rear of the customer area six greenhouses loomed, three of them lighted. Workers were preparing for the season, potting up early vegetables and ornamentals…

In the far-most greenhouse Gina Valducci was carefully cutting through a thin layer of gel with a newly-sprouted seedling centered in it. She cut a one inch square section from a shallow pan containing a layer of the same material. Moving with caution, she transferred the newly-cut square to a pot prepared with coarse sand and compost, sprinkled a bit of sand and compost over the square with the seedling, then drew back with a satisfied grin. She put the pot on the heat mat next to seven others just like it.

"Eight," she said.

At her side Jeff Cobbe was already making a note on a laptop. He was grinning as broadly as she was.

Heat mats on two long benches held tomatoes in every stage of growth from the newly sprouted seedlings to blooming plants, some with small green tomatoes, half a dozen with reddening tomatoes. Grow lights inches above the plants illuminated the greenhouse, along with overhead fluorescent lamps. It was as bright as mid-day in June.

Gina's glance over the thriving plants was automatic, swiftly done. If anything had been amiss among the many pots, she would have noticed and she would have sprung into action to correct the problem. But all was well. Her glance at the big wall clock over the entrance to the greenhouse was more purposeful. It was five minutes to five.

"I have to go," she said with a regretful look at the gel remaining in the pan. There were four seeds that had not sprouted, and she wanted to be on hand when and if they did.

"I'll hang out here," Jeff said. "But, hey," he added, "eight out of twelve is proof enough. Go on." His smile deepened, creasing his face, accentuating laugh lines at his eyes. He was twenty-nine and looked more like a happy sixteen-year old at the moment.

"I'll drop in later," she said, heading for the entrance. There, she pulled on a waterproof poncho that covered her head to toe and was ready to face the relentless rain. She turned to wave to Jeff who, engrossed with the computer, didn't acknowledge it.

The rain was coming straight down, hard and icy, and she hurried over the paved bare area where rows and rows of benches bearing starts of just about everything they grew would fill the space in a few weeks. Here, behind the store and office there was space for aisles for shoppers, room for the big garden carts bearing produce on the way to the store, room enough for an occasional truck. Now the space was empty, and dimly lighted. Every dip in the paving concrete had become a miniature lake, reflecting lights set adance by the falling rain.

Gina had been called coltish as a teen; long-legged, thin, edgy, with energy left over no matter how active she was. Now, at twenty-six, she was a slender, strong, athletic, self-possessed young woman, or so she told herself from time to time. Her long black hair was in a thick braid. Like all the Valduccis, she had a nose bigger than she liked, a wide, generous mouth, and she had the deep-set dark Valducci eyes, heavily lashed. When she made the effort, people said she was very handsome or striking. Pretty seemed the wrong word for her.

As she approached the house, she was planning the dinner she would make for her grandmother. Lamb chops, thawing in the refrigerator, minestrone left from the day before, sure to be better today than yesterday. It always was after a day. Salad. Baked potato.

She reached the house and continued around to the porch that led to the kitchen. At the kitchen door she took off the poncho and hung it on a peg, then she opened the door before removing her boots. She left them on newspapers on the kitchen floor and put on slippers.

"Gramma, I'm home," she called out. She walked through the kitchen, through a hall, and stopped when she came to the living room doorway. Her grandmother, her leg in a cast, was in her recliner, and opposite her in an easy chair was Gina's father.

"Gina," he said, rising. "Good to see you. Mother tells me you're her babysitter, nurse, companion, something. How are you?" He came across the room toward her with his arms outstretched.

Robert Valducci was tall, handsome, with a wide mouth, a high forehead, the big Valducci nose, dark eyes and enviable eyelashes. His smile reminded Gina of a politician's smile: easy on, easy off. A little gray at the temples emphasized his thick black hair and gave him gravitas, he liked to say. He was dressed in what looked like an expensive gray suit, a sparkling white shirt, and a bright red tie.

When he embraced her, she could smell his familiar minty aftershave.

"This is a surprise," she said, drawing back from him. "When did you get here?"

"This afternoon. I'm not staying for dinner. Mother says you're also her cook these days. Good for you. But starting tomorrow I'll take over the kitchen for a few days. Deal?"

"Deal," she said. He was a marvelous cook. All the Valduccis were marvelous cooks, including Gina, when she had time and the inclination. "You're welcome to have dinner with us," she added.

He shook his head and returned to his chair near the fireplace where a brisk fire was blazing. "Not tonight. I have an engagement. A colleague is in town. I'll take off in a few minutes and come back later tonight. Up to my old room. I already went up and opened a window to air it out."

Her grandmother had not said a word, but she looked strained and maybe a little anxious. Gina wanted to reassure her that she would not start a fight with her father, but it didn't seem appropriate to bring up the past when he was obviously going out of his way to be charming. He could be very charming when he chose, she had long known, and that charm was like his smile: easy on, easy off.

"Gramma, can I get you anything before I get started in the kitchen?" Gina asked, advancing a few steps into the room. It was spacious, the full width of the house, with French doors opening to the porch, and more French doors to a terrace at the other end. Big as it was, it was crowded with furniture, two sofas facing each other across a coffee table, the easy chairs by the fireplace, the recliner, end tables, a game table at one end. Some of the furniture was out of place, having been moved to accommodate a wheelchair and the recliner, giving the room a disordered appearance. Two worn Sarouk rugs carpeted wide plank floors that gleamed with reflections of light from lamps throughout the room. The wheelchair was near the game table, and crutches were more readily at hand by her grandmother's recliner.

Magdalena Valducci was seventy-four, and stood at five feet seven when erect. She had decided years before that long hair was a nuisance that she no longer had to endure, and now wore it in a short, almost boyish cut. It was thick, salt and pepper. Normally she would have been dressed much as Gina was, but with the cast, jeans had become a problem and she had switched to long skirts. That evening she was wearing a deep-red velvet skirt with a gray sweater.

She shook her head at Gina's question, reached around to pick up a wine glass from the end table at her side, and held it up. "Robert brought gifts of wine," she said. "And very good it is. You must try it."

"I will later," Gina said. "I'll get started on dinner now." She turned to leave the room then stiffened at the door when she heard her father's voice. His words addressed to her grandmother were meant to be heard, she well understood.

"Over the next day or two let's talk her into taking that job I offered last year. It's time she began acting her age and get started up the ladder."

Magda watched her granddaughter stop in midstride, then walk again in her loose, easy way on into the hall and out of sight. She sighed. What Gina had said about Robert's offer of a job the previous year was very much on Magda's mind as she sipped her excellent pinot noir.

"Your company, Halsey Enterprises," Gina had said in a furious and cutting voice, "is worse than Sherman's march through Georgia. Your guys leave a trail of toxic destruction behind. Fire and ashes are pristine compared to the poisons you spread."

After that, a lot of yelling had started. Magda drank deeper of the good wine her son had brought.

Two days after her father's unexpected arrival, Gina was sitting cross-legged on one of the greenhouse benches. Opposite her was Daniel Ito in the same position. The third member of the group, Greg Pollock, had taken a place at the open door where he stood gazing out, and Jeff Cobbe paced back and forth from the door to the bench.

"What does he want?" Jeff muttered, drawing near Gina.

"I don't know," Gina said through gritted teeth. "For the tenth time, hundredth time, thousandth time: I don't know!"

"I wasn't asking," he said almost as sharply as she had spoken. He ran his hand over his hair, turned and started back toward the door. "Thinking out loud."

"Think quieter," Gina snapped.

"Hey, guys," Daniel said, "cool it. Gina's having dinner with her father tonight. Tomorrow we'll probably all know what's on his mind."

Gina flashed a quick, scowling look at Daniel. He shrugged. He was her age, twenty-six, had been her class mate for four years, and had gotten his master's degree when she got hers. For a short time she had been in love with him, a secret love never acted upon or even acknowledged. She had fallen in love with his sculpted face with its high cheek bones. Then she had grown used to him and love faded and changed to the kind of friendship that allowed them to criticize and scowl at each other with no offense meant or taken. When they formed a real company, he would be one of the founding fathers. She toyed with the idea of founding fathers and a mother, but it didn't work, and she let it go.

"Tilsen's leaving," Greg said. He was the youngest of the group, twenty-two, although he looked like a teenager, and still retained an adolescent-like awkwardness and lightning-fast changes of mood. He was their computer guru. He had set up the program they used to keep track of everything they did, and what others around the world were doing with small farms. While he tried to take the same interest in the plants and seeds as the other three, his heart and mind lived in the world of electronics. Their records would be impeccable, they all felt confident. As far as the plants and seeds were concerned, he did exactly what he was told, did it well, and never went a step beyond his instructions. Where the computer was concerned no one questioned his expertise.

It made the biggest difference to Jeff, that their records be perfect. His doctoral dissertation depended on it.

Greg had looked up Donald Tilsen, a vice president in R&D at Halsey Enterprises, the same department where Robert Valducci worked as his assistant. Greg had assembled a long report about Tilsen, which he had read to them, but the important, maybe the only important item was Tilsen's position in the company. It had sent a message of icy foreboding throughout Gina. Two R&D guys had to be bad news.

"Your dad's heading this way," Greg said. His voice quavered and he ran from the door to the bench farthest from it, the one that held blooming and fruiting tomato plants. He pretended to be studying the labels. Gina's father, most men in expensive suits, terrified him.

Gina and Daniel scrambled down from the bench and hurried to the newest seeded pan. Nothing had yet sprouted in this one. Jeff joined them and they all waited for Robert Valducci as if they were on trial and he was a hanging judge, who had never doubted their guilt.

Robert walked a few feet into the greenhouse and stopped there.

"Hi, Dad," Gina said. "These are my friends. Associates," she corrected herself. She introduced them, and Robert looked them over coolly, nodded, and gave the rest of the greenhouse the same scrutiny.

"I can see that you're busy," he said. "I don't want to interfere. Dinner at seven," he said to Gina." He nodded again, turned and left.

What did he want? Gina knew he was after something, and could not dispel the sense of dread that had settled over her like a blanket.

When her grandmother was hit by a car in a parking lot, resulting in a broken leg and dislocated shoulder, Gina had left her apartment in town to move back to what she would always think of as her real home. She loved her grandmother and it pleased her that after so many years she finally had something to give back after receiving so much from childhood on. With Robert's appearance, the peace and harmony the two women shared had been shattered, and Gina had returned to her apartment, taking with her only a few necessary items from her bathroom. It was a temporary move, she had assured her grandmother, who had nodded in understanding and probably in relief. Gina and Robert were seldom in the same room longer than a few minutes before one or the other started an argument. Their arguments tended to get loud and involve a lot of gestures and hand waving.

It was not going to happen this time, Gina told herself, as she had done several times already. No matter what he said, she would stay calm and cool. She wiped her sweaty hands on her jeans.

Dinner was excellent, as expected, but beyond the veal Marsala, which was her favorite of Robert's specialties, Gina would not have been able to name another dish ten minutes after consuming it. Robert told funny stories about being a corporation man, how snow in Chicago came down sideways, about getting lost in Tokyo, "not really lost, just confused for a while," about how long it took to get from the airport to his wife's hillside house in Sherman Oaks, California. Debra, he said, was more beautiful than ever and twice as busy as ever. He spoke of her exactly the same way he might have spoken about a movie star or popular singer whom he didn't know personally. Still married, they had not lived together for the past eight years. Gina had not seen her mother since her graduation, rarely talked on the phone to her, and more rarely had a card or a letter. Debra was busy with her real estate business. She was a consultant, a go-between for rich clients and those eager to sell or lease mansions they no longer could afford.

With the dishes in the dishwasher, the kitchen restored to a state of neatness and cleanliness, Robert ushered Gina and her grandmother out. "Help Mother get settled by the fire," he said. "I'll bring in coffee and a little treat."

His treat was a plate of tiny imported chocolates. He passed out coffee and put the chocolates on an end table between Gina and her grandmother before taking his own seat across from them, smiling.

"You all may wonder why I've gathered you together," he said, then laughed. "Actually, I do have something on my mind. Something really big." He leaned forward, fixing his intent gaze on Magda. "Mother, the company wants to buy your land here, all of it. And they're offering a staggering figure. Four million." He raised his cup in a salute, took a sip, and put it down on his own end table. "And, Mother, I think I can talk them into increasing that by at least half a million."

Magda put her cup down and looked over the chocolates before taking one. "What in the world makes you think I'm interested in selling?" she asked. She popped the tiny candy into her mouth and closed her eyes for a moment after biting down on it. "Delicious," she murmured. When she looked at Robert again, she said, "I'm not, you know, interested in selling."

"Mother, look at you. You can hardly maneuver in this mausoleum of a house. You can't even go upstairs to your own bedroom. It's a mile from one room to another, and you're stuck inside, with cold, miserable rain nine months of the year. You should have retired ten years ago instead of sticking it out for God knows why. You've worked like a field hand as far back as I can remember. It's time for you to relax and live in the comfort you deserve. Hawaii, or Palm Springs, even Florida. Travel. Spend time in a villa in Italy or southern France. Take Gina with you, your companion, gofer. She can make all the arrangements so you won't have to do a thing. First class all the way, every day, the rest of your life."

She shook her head. "The answer is no, Robert. I have no desire to sell. I do exactly what I want, and if I want to go to Hawaii, I'll go. But when and if I want to."

"You'll never get another offer like this," he said. "You'll have to sell eventually and you'll get chicken shit, pennies on the dollar. I know what the market's like these days, what it's going to be in the foreseeable future. That offer is twice as much as this land is worth in the best of times, which isn't now."

"Robert," Magda said forcefully, "stop. I said no. That's enough."

"And I certainly won't let you assign me a role in your plans," Gina said. "Don't you even hear yourself telling us what we'll do? I have my own life, my own plans, and they don't include first-class travel as anyone's companion."

"You're content to sponge off an old woman, take over her property for some harebrained scheme you and your little playmates have cooked up."

"We have a business arrangement!" Gina said in a sharper voice. "It's settled between us and it's none of your business."

"It's my business. I see you taking advantage of my aging mother. I know how much those greenhouses cost, how much it takes to heat and light them, how much the supplies cost, the water, fertilizers."

"You don't know anything about what we're up to. We're starting a new company, plants, seeds, produce, plus some innovations we're experimenting with. And we work for the business to pay our expenses. I don't sponge off anyone! And I don't tell anyone else what they have to do."

"A seed business! My God! I knew you were naive, but I didn't think you were stupid! You're like a guy dreaming of a better horseshoe when Henry Ford was starting his assembly line! I offered you a good job. Nepotism? Damn right! Starting you half way up the ladder instead of letting you grope for the bottom rung–"

Gina jumped to her feet, both hands balled into fists. "I don't want your putrid job. I don't want to poison plants, poison the gene pool of plants, poison the land, poison the animals and people who need your poisoned plants to survive, only to die younger and sicker than they would have done."

"We're feeding the world! Someone has to! Your produce and seed company! Bullshit! You'll be lucky if you feed yourself and your puppy dogs!"

"You aren't feeding the world! You're poisoning the world! Turning farming back into serfdom, grabbing good land, destroying it..."

Gina's hands were flying in all directions as she yelled, and Robert, on his feet, yelling over her, was pointing to her, then to Magda. Pointing to God alone knew where, Magda thought, struggling to her feet.

"Gina! Robert! Both of you, stop this!" she shouted over their voices. "I won't have you screaming like children in my house! Stop it right now!" She was momentarily off balance and clutched the chair arm. Almost instantly Gina was at her side, supporting her, and Magda straightened and accepted the crutches Gina held for her.

"Robert," Magda said then, "I told you no. End of discussion. Gina has my permission to use the greenhouse and whatever it takes to make it function. Now, if you'll excuse me, I think I'll go to my room."

"Look at you," Robert said. "You can't manage alone any longer and you know it. What, you'll bring in a paid companion to help out?"

"In a week or so I'll be out of this damn cast," Magda said. "Then some physical therapy, and after that as good as new. That's all I need to know."

"I think you hit your head when you had that accident," he said furiously. "I think you scrambled your brain. As good as new! You're seventy-four years old! It's unreasonable for you not even to consider my proposal, just reject it out of hand. That's not how a rational person behaves."

Magda took a few steps, then stopped and looked at him over her shoulder. "What time are you leaving in the morning?"

"By nine," he said. "I'll come back on Friday. Give you time to think about all this." She shook her head, then turned slightly to say to Gina, "Why don't you run along now. And don't show up here until after nine in the morning. Good night, Robert, Gina."

Gina hurried to her side. "I'll walk you home," she said with a slight smile.

Magda smiled also. "In the morning come on in and I'll braid your hair."

"He's coming back tomorrow," Gina said to Sophia Mirano, Magda's neighbor. They were in the Valducci kitchen where Gina had started a pot roast. "I'll take off and stay in my apartment until he's gone again. I don't know how long he'll stay this time."

"I'll be around," Sophia said, patting Gina's arm. "I'll pop in several times a day and keep Magda company if he goes out at night. Don't you worry about it. I just wish she'd stop trying to do so much right now with that cast. Like going upstairs. I told her I'd get whatever she wanted, but no, you know her, she had to do something herself." She shook her head. "But, honey, something's on her mind. I've known that woman all my life and I know when something's eating at her." She gave Gina a searching look, as if debating adding to what she had said. She shook her head again, and pulled on her jacket.

"I know," Gina said. "I told her the same thing, that I'd fetch anything she wanted. Anyway, I practically ordered her to give a shout when she's ready to come down again. And she thinks I'm hard headed." They both laughed.

They were walking from the kitchen when Gina heard her grandmother cry out and heard a terrifying thumping noise on the staircase. With a cry she ran to the stairs in time to see her grandmother tumble down the last several steps.

"Call 911!" she screamed to Sophia. She was on her knees by her grandmother. “Gramma! Gramma!” she cried, afraid to try to move her, afraid to do anything except cradle her head.

Magda’s eyelids fluttered. She moaned, closed her eyes, then opened them and focused on Gina’s face. She moaned again and her eyes closed. She was trying to say something. All Gina could make out was, “The Lorax. Remember the Lorax.”

Those were the last words Gina ever heard from her. Magdalena Valducci died two hours later in the emergency room at Riverbend Hospital.

Five endless days had passed. People had come and gone. There had been a funeral. Debra, Gina’s mother, had come and Robert was there. Debra and Robert didn’t talk to each other, and neither had anything to say to Gina beyond the obligatory good morning, good night, you should eat something, did you sleep? Debra had arranged everything in an efficient way and she had said firmly that she had no intention of staying in the house. She was perfectly comfortable with a room in the Hilton, downtown.

“Robert will be going through everything, and I’ll help him, of course,” Debra had said in a cool, remote voice. “We’ll have an estate sale, and there are decisions to make, but I don’t want to be around when he starts going through her personal things. That’s a family matter best left to the immediate family.”

Gina felt that she could not bear to see her father coldly appraising, putting dollar signs on her grandmother’s beautiful garden prints, the lovely blown glass from Italy that she had treasured, countless books she had loved. She shook her head at Robert’s invitation to stay in the house, and moved back into her apartment where she could grieve in private, where she didn’t have to respond to inane comments, answer impossible questions, be polite to the two strangers her own parents had become to her.

Debra was a large woman, overweight, broad through the shoulders, with heavy, full breasts, and thick, sturdy legs, big hands. Her hair that year was long and platinum blond, with a little wave. She wore stage-like makeup, kept her fingernails perfectly manicured, that year pale pink with white, and she used a lot of scent, so much that on entering a room, she announced her presence without any need for visual verification. Sometimes Gina found herself examining her own mother as she might examine a complete stranger, searching for the reality behind the façade.

That day Gina was carrying some of her belongings down from her upstairs bedroom, bit by bit erasing her presence from the house. On her way to the front door, she could hear Debra and Robert in the den as she passed the partly-open door. Debra was talking.

"Of course, we'll sell as soon as possible. I'll do some research about land prices around here. Twenty, forty thousand an acre? I imagine it's something like that."

"It's going to take time," Robert said. "Probate, creditors, the plant stock."

"I'll take care of it," Debra said. "That's my field. I want half, Robert. I won't settle for less. My share will be something like four, five hundred thousand. That's my guess now, but it can change after I do a little research in county records. After that, the divorce. Not before."

"I thought you wanted it now, right now. That's all you could talk about this past month. I signed the papers and mailed them while I was in Chicago."

"I changed my mind."

He hadn't told her about the Halsey offer, Gina thought dully. She would find out, of course, and there would be a real fight. She shrugged. Let them fight. She walked on to the front door, out to her car parked under the portico. It was a Honda hatchback without a lot of room for boxes. She had made two trips already, slowly stripping one room, creating chaos in her apartment. Feeling little, thinking of nothing, numb with grief, it was as if she had slipped out of real time into some kind of personal void. She was hardly aware of how many days had passed since she had held her grandmother's head in her arms crying her name over and over.

She shoved the box she carried into the back of her car and only then became aware of Jeff standing under the portico watching her. She had refused his help earlier for no reason she could have named. It was better to maintain the distance she had established between them, a carefully measured privacy zone that neither of them was meant to enter. More than that, it just seemed to be her task to clean out her presence, to erase her past in her grandmother's house. Now she looked at him and, when he beckoned, she walked toward him.

"We have to talk," he said. "The guys are in the greenhouse. I said I'd bring you. Will you talk to us?"

She nodded and they walked across the empty space to the sixth greenhouse together, but not close enough to touch.

Greg Pollock and Daniel Ito were waiting. Greg looked embarrassed and shuffled his feet, but Daniel came to her and embraced her for a moment. He kissed her cheek before he backed away.

"Tilsen's back," Jeff said.

Gina nodded. She knew.

"We have to make some kind of plan," Daniel said. "Is there anyplace else where we can set ourselves up?"

He lived with his girlfriend in an apartment. Greg lived with his parents, and both Jeff and Gina had apartments.

No one answered the question.

"Maybe we can get a loan, rent some space and put up our own greenhouse," Daniel said, and again there was no response from any of them.

"I think Gramma left me a few thousand dollars," Gina said, breaking the silence. "I won't get it for weeks and weeks, maybe even months. Dad said there's probate to get through."

"If we can hold out," Daniel said, "we can make it work. Gina, would you use your own money that way?"

"It's my idea, remember," she said. She felt with a new rush of despair that her idea, her dream was the only thing she had.

Suddenly Greg looked frightened and took a step backward, his eyes large and staring. Gina turned to see Robert entering the greenhouse. As before, he stopped when he had come inside ten or twelve feet.

He looked them over, glanced at the tomato plants, then focused on Gina and said, "Tomorrow around noon an appraiser is coming down from Portland. I want you on hand to pick out any items you might want to keep. And I want you all to clear out everything from the greenhouse within thirty days. It will take that long to get paperwork done, and everything has to be gone by then." He turned and left.

Jeff was the first one to move. He picked up a clay pot and smashed it to the floor, then stalked out through the rear door.

When Gina entered the house the following day she found Donald Tilsen in the study with her father. She stopped at the doorway and involuntarily drew her jacket closer about her when she saw him. She had seen him making a tour of the property with her father, and talking to him a time or two, but always at a distance. He was a slender, sharp-featured man in his fifties, dressed in a pinstripe suit and button-down shirt with a maroon tie. With thinning hair, tanning-bed complexion, pale gray eyes that seemed to be open too wide, he looked like a well-paid accountant who had found an egregious entry in his books. He had a worried expression, as if in distress, on the verge of frowning. She knew it was unfair, but she couldn't deny that she had disliked him intensely on sight. He made a tentative movement with his hand toward her when Robert introduced them, but she simply nodded and he withdrew his hand and nodded in return.

The doorbell rang and Gina said, "I'll get it." Both Tilsen and her father followed her into the hall and to the door. A smiling woman was on the stoop. Robert stepped forward past Gina.

"Mrs. Chadwick? I'm Robert Valducci. My daughter, Gina, and this is Mr. Tilsen. Please, let me help you with that."

She was carrying a case, which she relinquished to him. She was about five feet five, trim, dressed in a navy pantsuit. Her hair was short and dun-colored, brushed back from her face in a careless way, and the only makeup she had on was a trace of pale pink lipstick. Her smile was wide and engaging. "Well," she said, "if I could have a glass of water, I'd appreciate it. The traffic was ferocious on I-5."

"This way," Robert said. "You might as well start in the kitchen as anywhere."

Mrs. Chadwick was eyeing the hallway, the walls, the carpet runner underfoot, and she was talking as they made their way to the kitchen. "What I'll do today is make a video of each room, the furnishings, paintings, art work, everything. Anything you can tell me in the way of provenance would be helpful, of course. Then I'll have to do a little research for some items. That's how it usually goes. As soon as I finish I'll send you an itemized list with my appraisal value."

Gina stopped listening as Mrs. Chadwick drank her water, opened her case and brought out a camcorder and proceeded to make her video, talking as she worked. This was going to be a long day, Gina thought, leaning against the doorframe, thinking about the new seedlings that Greg would be shifting to pots, wishing she were out there helping him instead of in here considering the worth of a twelve-year-old gas stove, or a fifteen-year-old refrigerator.

When they moved on to the dining room, to Gina's annoyance Tilsen tagged along. Mrs. Chadwick murmured that the cherry table and chairs were beautiful, not museum quality antiques, but lovely. When they got to the silverware, Gina said she would like to have it, and Robert made a note. They moved on to the living room and Mrs. Chadwick had to measure the Sarouk rugs and spend a good deal of time with them. Gina wanted them, too, but she had no place to put them and remained silent. The blown glass items from Italy got a lot of attention, and those Gina definitely wanted. Especially one of a fantasy horse, pink and silver with a blue mane and tale. Gaudy, beautiful. Her grandmother had brought the four pieces back with her when she and Grandfather had taken a vacation, their delayed honeymoon, four years after their marriage. Gina blinked, remembering how misty-eyed Gramma had been when she talked about that trip.

Gramma's pineapple-four-poster bed kept Mrs. Chadwick's interest, but the monogrammed comb and brush didn't. Then she caught in her breath when she saw the mirror on the wall. It was an oval, beveled-glass mirror framed with intricately-carved ivory about four inches wide all around, with a fluting crest on top. Twenty-six inches high, eighteen wide, it was fine art to Gina's eye, and had been fine art to her grandmother's eye. Gina claimed it and Robert made a note.

"I wonder if we could take it down, examine the back," Mrs. Chadwick murmured. "It could have the artist's name or something else identifying the artist."

There was nothing on the back to indicate the artist. Mrs. Chadwick sighed. "I'm almost certain that I read something, saw something… I'll do a little research on it. Oh, well, shall we move on?"

It was ten past three when Mrs. Chadwick finished.

"When your report is finished," Robert said, "send it here, to this address. He handed her a Valducci's card." He walked to the door with her, and as soon as he closed it, he turned to Tilsen. "God, what a drag! It's time for a drink." He nodded to Gina. "Join us?"

She shook her head. "Back to work for me."

"Keep in mind that you have no more than thirty day to wrap things up out there," Robert said as she opened the door.

Several nights later Gina was staring at the calendar she had placed on her coffee table in her apartment. Twenty-six days left, she thought as she drew an X, marking off another day with no solution. Thirty days, ninety, two hundred. It didn't matter. There was no solution. No one, not a single one of them, could come up with an answer. No money, no acreage, no greenhouse, no company. Her eyes burned and she felt fatigue in every muscle, every fiber of her being. She had put in another twelve-to-thirteen-hour day of physical work, many hours more of useless mental work, trying to figure out how much she could make if she sold this or that. Her car. She could ride her bicycle. A couple of thousand dollars, plus what she would save on gas. The mirror from her grandmother's estate. Maybe a thousand dollars. Wait for Mrs. Chadwick's estimate, she reminded herself. The blown glass. Again, wait for the estimate. She should have claimed the rugs. Maybe she still could claim them, sell them. Above all, keep working in the greenhouse, keep praying for a miracle. They were going through the motions, potting up starts, keeping records, pretending. Praying for a miracle.

She knew she should knock it off for the night, take a soaking bath, hope for sleep. Then face another day just like this day had been, like yesterday and the day before that. Pretending.

The phone rang, startling her. She found it under papers on the table, saw that it was Jeff Cobbe and mumbled hello.

"Gina," Jeff's voice was shaky, low-pitched. "Gina, something terrible has happened. Your father. Gina, he's dead. Your father's been shot. Your mother needs you out at the house."

Frank Holloway signed the letter Patsy had prepared. His signature was big and bold, and he resisted an impulse to add a squiggle, some kind of flourish, under it. He put the letter on top of a stack of papers and looked at Patsy across his immaculate desk. He was grinning broadly and her smile was equally expansive.

"We did it, Patsy," he said. "By God, we did it again."

"You did it," she said, but whenever she talked about his book, now two books, she always said *we. We're writing another book. That book we wrote is doing well. We're working hard on our book these days.* She had done the index for his books, this one on opening and closing statements in criminal trials.

"Well, box it up and off it goes. Then we sweat out a response from the editor. And while we're waiting, why don't you take off a few days? That's what I plan to do."

"We'll see," she said as she picked up the bulky manuscript. She had no intention of taking off unless he did.

After Patsy left his spacious office, Frank leaned back in his chair with his hands behind his head and gazed at the ceiling, still smiling. His editor would love it. He had no doubt. It was better than the first one on cross-examinations. He began to think of another book that had taken up space in his brain like a squatter and refused to leave. A book on the wiles and ways of attorneys, especially criminal defense attorneys. He had a lot of material stored in memory, and there was a mountain of material waiting to be mined. It would be another thick book.

His phone rang, interrupting his pleasant chain of thoughts. Patsy was on the line to say that a Ms. Gina Valducci had come to the office without an appointment asking to see him.

Valducci? He had read about the tragic death of Magdalena Valducci, followed within days by the murder of her son. He knew about Valducci's. Many of the plants in his yard had come from there, and he often frequented their store for seasonal fruit and vegetables that he didn't grow in his own garden.

"Bring her in," he told Patsy. He suspected that Gina Valducci was really looking for Barbara, but he could be a bridge if that turned out to be the case.

When Patsy opened his door and stepped aside for Gina, Frank's first impression of her was that she was an ill-treated child, almost haggard, pale, with deeply shadowed, hollowed eyes. When he shook her hand, it was trembling and cold.

"Patsy, maybe you could rustle up some coffee. And do you have any cookies around? I'm feeling a touch peckish." He well knew that Patsy always had a box of cookies on hand. He helped Gina off with a jacket and with his hand on her arm guided her to the sofa, not the client chair across from his desk. He took her jacket to hang on a coat tree near the office door.

Then, seated in an easy chair at the end of the coffee table, he regarded her and said, "Ms. Valducci, I'm very sorry about your losses. You have my deepest sympathy. I know this is a time of great stress for you. Please relax, take your time to get warm. Let's wait for coffee before you tell me what brings you here today."

She ducked her head and said, "Thank you," in a faint voice. She was clutching a big shoulder bag, sitting rigidly upright, about as relaxed as a rabbit facing a wolf.

He heard Patsy tap the door. She came in carrying a tray with the coffee service and a platter of the good Danish butter cookies that he especially liked. She placed it on the coffee table, smiled at Gina, and left.

"I find that around this time of day, a little something is appreciated very much," Frank said as he poured coffee. "The British have it exactly right, tea time, even if coffee is the preferred drink."

He put coffee in front of Gina, and sat back with his own cup in one hand and a cookie in the other. "Please, have at least one," he said. "That's my limit since my doctor frowns on my overindulging on anything that's good."

Gina helped herself to cream and sugar and watched her cup as she stirred the coffee. Frank finished the one cookie he intended to eat, put his cup down on the table, and said, "I understand that you're not going to relax until you tell me what I can do for you. Am I right?"

A tiny smile flitted across her pale face and she nodded. Paying no more attention to the coffee, she reached inside her big bag, drew out an envelope, and handed it to him. "I need to know if this is what it seems to be, and what I can do about it."

Frank extracted two folded papers from the envelope and read the handwritten pages carefully. "Your grandmother's last will," he said. "Hand-written and witnessed. Tell me about it."

"Is it good? Valid, I mean. There's another will that she had written years ago. This one's dated February 24, this year. Does it count if there's another will?"

"Let's start somewhere else," Frank said. "Where did this one come from?"

"I found it," Gina said. "She fell down the stairs and I was by her, holding her, waiting for 911, and she tried to tell me something. It sounded like nonsense, like she was out of her mind, saying things that made no sense. I thought she said 'The Lorax. Remember the Lorax.' I thought she was rambling. She died two hours later without speaking again. I forgot about it. Just forgot it. I've been moving my things from her house, back to my apartment, and I came to a box of children's books, and in my apartment two days ago, I was crying over the books, remembering how she used to read to me, how we laughed together, how much we loved the Dr. Seuss books. I picked up *The Lorax* and that fell out."

Frank read the will again. "Do you know those witnesses? Sophia Mirano and Ethel Juarez?"

Gina nodded. "Sophia is a neighbor." She bit her lip. "She was my grandmother's neighbor and best friend, and Ethel is Sophia's housekeeper."

"Did either of them mention anything about this to you?"

"No."

"Ms. Valducci, if that handwriting proves to be your grandmother's, and if the witnesses confirm that they did indeed watch her sign it, that will is as good as gold. Have you shown it to anyone? Told anyone about it?"

She shook her head. "It was late when I found it, and all day yesterday I kept going back and forth about what to do about it, who to tell, what it means. I started to go to her old attorney, but I thought if she hadn't gone to him, maybe I shouldn't either. Then I remembered reading about you, when you had a book published a couple of years ago, and how you worked with your daughter on cases, and here I am. I don't know what to do next."

Frank rose from his chair and went to his desk. "What you do next is drink some of that coffee before it gets cold, and eat a cookie or two, three if you can manage. I'm going to have my secretary make copies of the will and I'll keep the original in my safe. Then we will talk. I'm afraid I have a lot of questions. Fortify yourself." He rang for Patsy.

Moments later, seated again at the coffee table, this time with his yellow pad on his knee, Frank started. "First, tell me something of the relationships involved here. Yours and your grandmother's, where your mother fits in, your father. Just what comes to mind."

Gina kept her eyes downcast as she spoke haltingly about her grandmother. The picture that emerged was of a child, then a teenage girl, a young woman at her grandmother's side, being guided, educated, tutored by a loving grandmother.

"There's a general manager," Gina said, "but my grandmother really ran everything. They consulted always, of course, but it was her business and she knew every detail of what was being done. And she taught me along the way." She became silent and Frank waited without speaking.

Then she said vehemently, "She never would have sold out to the Halsey people! She hated what they represent, what they do. She loved that land with passion."

"Gina, did she show any indication of being confused, irrational?"

"Absolutely not!"

"All right. Now, about the old will. Do you know who drew it up for her?"

"Yes. Leo Barrasso. He's been the family lawyer as far back as I can remember. He was my grandparents' friend in addition to being their lawyer. He used to come out just to visit."

"Yet she produced a handwritten will instead of going to him. Can you speculate about why that was?"

Gina shook her head. "She was in a cast and couldn't drive. I don't know why she didn't call him and have him come out to the house. He would have done that."

"Okay. Let's leave that. What's going on now, today? You haven't told your mother about the new will, have you?"

"No. Two days after Father's funeral she flew to Chicago, to settle things there. She hasn't come back yet. There's insurance, a condo, a BMW, personal effects. She'll put what she can in the hands of an agent or an attorney or someone like that. But it will take a few more days, she said. She's the sole beneficiary of my father's estate, so even if she didn't sell the farm, she would still have a lot of money.

"She doesn't see it that way. She said that Tilsen, the Halsey man, offered to buy the house, furnishings, equipment, everything for five million dollars and he would liquidate it all himself, not make her bear the burden of having an estate sale. She's quite willing to make that deal with him. She'll probably give the go-ahead for that as soon as she returns."

This last was said with such a dejected tone that it appeared that Gina was once more near the tears that had glazed her eyes when she had talked about her grandmother. Frank poured more coffee for both of them. "It's still hot," he said. "Nice thermal pot makes it good to the last drop." He waited until Gina added cream and sugar to hers, then said, "Now, is anyone at the house these days? Where are you living?"

"I'm staying out there. Mother and I agreed that the house shouldn't be left empty. I told her that there are contracts, buyers waiting for plant starts, customers with orders to be filled. She could be sued if the company doesn't fulfill its obligations. I don't know if that's true," she added with a sidelong glance at him. "But she doesn't know either, and for the time being, at least, we're still acting like a business. It won't last long, though. She's the executor, personal representative, whatever it's called, and she can pay bills and other expenses. Everyone knows it's all up for grabs, and everyone's on edge, but Mike, our manager, talked most of the workers into hanging in there until things are straightened out. I don't know when we'll have to close shop and lock the doors."

She gave him a long examining look then and said, "Mr. Holloway, I have plans for the farm. My grandmother knew what I was going to do and she approved all the way. She was making it happen."

"Tell me about your plans," Frank said, and he leaned back in his chair.

It took another hour of listening to Gina talk before they both stood and shook hands. "Try to rest as much as you can," Frank said as he helped her on with her coat. "I'll talk to Leo Barrasso and we'll get started on the will business."

She looked ready to kiss him, but she simply said, "I think I might be able to sleep now. Thank you."

After she was gone, he buzzed Patsy and asked her to get Leo Barrasso on the phone. He knew Barrasso's office was one flight up the stairs in his own building and he fully expected to be invited to drop in for their chat. Instead, Patsy called him after a moment to say that Mr. Barrasso was out of the office and not expected back until after the middle of April.

Barbara had just poured her first cup of coffee that Friday morning when her phone chimed and a car horn sounded simultaneously. Todd ran up from the basement den slinging on his backpack, waved to her and Darren, and dashed through the house and out the front door on his way to high school. Darren kissed his finger, planted the kiss on her nose, and followed his son out. By then she had fumbled in her robe pocket for her phone.

"Hi, Dad, what's up?" she said and lifted her coffee.

"Are you up and decent? Free for the next couple of hours?"

"Yes and yes. Why?"

"I'll explain as we go," he said. "I'll be there in ten minutes. Enough time?"

"Barely," she said. "Just honk your horn outside and I'll come bouncing out in my usual top-of-the-morning fog."

He chuckled and hung up. She put a piece of bread in the toaster and went to the bedroom to get dressed. By the time she got back to the kitchen the bread had toasted and grown cold. She buttered it anyway, and was eating it when she heard the car horn and hurried out.

After heaving her briefcase onto the back seat, she slid in and buckled up. "It must be important to have rousted you out before noon," she said. She finished the last bite of toast and licked butter from her thumb.

"Could be," Frank said. "Last Friday, Gina Valducci paid me a call." He told it succinctly as he drove. Traffic was heavy at that time in the morning and got heavier when he reached River Road, giving him plenty of time to fill her in. "I hauled in Sal Menniger, our probate fellow. So the wheels are turning on the will matter. At seven-thirty this morning four detectives appeared at the Valducci house and told Gina they wanted to question her for the record and asked permission to conduct a search of the greenhouse where the kids do their thing. She called me. I told her to refuse permission for a search without a warrant, and to keep her mouth zipped until we get there. I expect we'll get there before they rustle up a judge to issue a warrant."

Barbara exhaled a long breath. "One thing's for certain, the girl sure does have a motive, doesn't she? A several-million-dollar motive apparently."

Frank snorted.

"How much push-back is Valducci's widow making about the will?"

"Debra Valducci? She claims she and her late husband were convinced that old Mrs. Valducci suffered head injuries when she was hit by a car in January. He, Robert, was prepared to start proceedings to have her declared incompetent in order to protect her interests. Debra Valducci has produced a statement from Donald Tilsen, the Halsey guy, in which he says Mrs. Valducci was incoherent and confused. Debra Valducci will go for incompetency, duress, undue influence. The usual."

"You've just reminded me why I don't want cases involving wills."

"Neither do I." Bumper-to-bumper traffic crept to the Beltline intersection and then thinned out. He drove faster. "It's just up the road a few miles. Green Briar Road."

Minutes later he made the turn, and after several hundred feet he turned again onto a concrete driveway that split with one section going to a garage and the other to a wide cobblestone-paved drive that dead-ended at a portico.

Two cars were on the cobbled driveway. Frank pulled in behind one of them. When they left the car and walked to the entrance of the house, Barbara could see a large terrace at the far end. The house, a wooden building, was in good repair evidently, painted a warm-sand color with green trim. Mature shrubs and some evergreen bushes looked like garden magazine props in their perfection. Fragrance from a blooming daphne bush was intoxicating.

The door was opened promptly at Frank's knock. "Good morning, Gina," he said, entering. "My daughter, Barbara." He took Gina's hand for a moment, then looked at a tall black man at her side. Barbara shook hands with Gina and studied the man.

"He's Detective Tracy Jackson," Gina said. She looked and sounded strained, but the hollows under her eyes were filling in and no longer looked so black.

"'Morning, Detective," Frank said and gave his and Barbara's names. "Attorneys for Ms. Valducci. Has the search warrant appeared yet?"

"It's coming," Jackson said.

"Well, I'll mosey on out to the greenhouse and meet your partners," Frank said to Gina. "I'll keep your boys company while they carry on their search."

And make sure nothing significant is damaged, Barbara thought, nodding to Gina, who looked confused. "Is there by any chance coffee made?" Barbara asked. "Dad hustled me out before breakfast. Why don't you lead the way to the kitchen and we can make ourselves comfortable and drink coffee while they ask their questions."

Jackson looked doubtful, then angry. He opened his mouth to say something, but Gina had already turned to lead them to the kitchen and he didn't voice whatever he had intended. He merely followed along.

The hallway was wide with folding closet doors on the right. An umbrella stand decorated with ducks was at the end of the closet near the entrance, and a few steps farther along they passed a closed door on the left. Another closed door was on the right. A dense, variously colored carpet with twining shades of blue and red muffled their footsteps. Many pictures hung on the walls: forest scenes, a snowy mountain wreathed in mist turned rosy by late afternoon sunshine, several large pictures of single flowers in exquisite detail. They reached a broad staircase on the left with a runner of the same carpet design as the floor.

Next to the staircase was another wide hall off to the left. Walking toward them in that hall was a heavy-set man, scowling.

"Let's get to it," he said. His voice was gravelly, baritone.

"He's Detective Hardesty," Gina said over her shoulder as she kept on toward the kitchen.

"How do you do, Detective," Barbara said pleasantly. "Barbara Holloway, representing Ms. Valducci. We're all ready for some coffee. I'm sure everything will go much better and quicker with coffee at hand. Don't you find that to be true?"

His face was wrinkled and pink and grew pinker with her words He had a double chin and dewlaps that were also pink. He glared at his partner, but fell into step.

"Oh, this is nice," Barbara exclaimed when they reached the kitchen. It was large, with a big cooking island, a long table with six chairs, and what seemed to be endless counters and cabinets. Wide windowsills held many plants, some in bloom. Barbara felt she should know what they were, but no name followed. Just flowers. "See," she said cheerfully, pointing to the table, "we can all sit down, get comfortable, have coffee and ask and answer questions. Perfect."

She went to the head of the table and sat down, then rummaged in her briefcase and brought out a legal pad, two pens, and a tape recorder and set them down in front of her. She looked at Gina who had stopped moving and was watching her with a fixed gaze, as if awaiting instructions.

"Are you going to make coffee or do you want me to?" Barbara said. "I have to warn you that my coffee never turns out very good."

Hastily Gina went to the counter nearest the sink and began to open cabinets.

Hardesty took the chair at the other end of the table, and Jackson sat down and watched Gina measure coffee and water. Hardesty put a notebook and a tape recorder down on the table and scowled at Barbara.

"It's always good when we all stay on the same page," she murmured.

When the coffee maker started, Barbara rose and said, "Gina, why don't you sit down now. I'll keep an eye on the coffee and bring it when it's ready."

They began with Hardesty stating the date, time of day, and who was present. He got to the night of Robert Valducci's death without delay. "Tell us in detail exactly where you were from seven o'clock until you arrived at the house that night." His deep baritone tended to sound rumbling, and he was very matter-of-fact in tone.

Gina cleared her throat. "I was in the greenhouse until a few minutes after eight. I drove home to my apartment and stayed there until Jeff called me. I got here at about ten. I'm not sure about the exact time." Her voice was low, but steady as she answered.

Hardesty referred to his notes, then asked, "How do you know exactly when you left the greenhouse?"

"The grow lights always go off at eight, and I looked at the clock over the entrance when I left," she said. "It was three minutes after eight."

"Did you see anyone at your apartment?"

"No."

He asked what kind of car she drove, where she parked when she was in the greenhouse, if anyone had seen her at her apartment that night. Barbara poured coffee for them all and took her chair at the table, but she did not interfere and would not unless Hardesty got out of line. He was being methodical, referring to his notes before every question.

"Why did you stop out in front of the store?" Hardesty asked in the same neutral tone he had been using.

"I didn't," Gina said. "I drove straight to my apartment."

He asked about guns then.

"No one here had a gun, except for an old shotgun they found when they searched the house," Gina said. "It dates back to 1878 and hasn't been fired for sixty years or longer."

"Did your father carry a gun?"

She shook her head. "I don't know. He never mentioned a gun."

"Were you living with your grandmother prior to her death?" he asked in the same monotonous, rumbling voice.

Gina started at the question, then nodded. "I moved in with her when she had an accident that resulted in a broken leg and other injuries."

"Were you in residence here when your father came to visit last month?"

Gina looked at Barbara as if asking for help. Barbara nodded for her to answer the question. She said she had been living in the house then.

"On that first visit of his, did you two have a violent argument?"

"No!" Gina cried. "We had a disagreement, not a violent argument."

"Were you staying in this house during your father's visit?"

Gina hesitated before answering. "I returned to my apartment. My father said he planned to stay several days and he would prepare Grandmother's meals. I thought they wanted time together and I needed to see to a few things in my own apartment."

Hardesty turned a notebook page, read his notes, then asked, "Did you stay in this house a single night when your father was also staying here during the past two weeks?"

Gina's face had flushed during this sequence and her voice was almost inaudible when she said no.

Hardesty began to rephrase some of his earlier questions and Barbara tapped her pen on the table. “She already told you what time she left,” she said. “Do you have anything new to ask?”

He scowled at her, then asked Gina, “Is it possible that you remembered something you meant to take home, and you pulled in at the store that night?”

Quickly she said, “No.”

“Sometimes we put something down and forget to pick it up, go back to get it,” Hardesty said, sounding like a patient coach.

“She told you she drove straight to her apartment.” Barbara said in a chiding way. “Twice.”

The doorbell rang and they all glanced toward the hall door. Hardesty motioned to Jackson. “See who it is.”

Jackson left the door open when he walked from the kitchen, and after a few seconds a woman’s voice carried from the front door to them at the table.

“What the hell are you talking about? Of course, I can come in. This is my house. And I demand to see my daughter. Detective or no detective. Get out of the way.”

Gina suppressed a moan. Her mother had arrived.

Barbara watched the next several minutes with great interest. Gina stiffened unnaturally in her chair, and her hand on her coffee cup tightened enough to show fine tendons. Hardesty turned his glower onto Debra Valducci when she entered. He did not rise. Jackson, at Debra’s side, looked undecided, almost embarrassed.

Debra strode into the kitchen and stopped at the table, glancing at Hardesty, Barbara, and finally Gina with a frosty, brief look. Debra was wearing a long, rust-colored, leather coat, rust-colored high-heeled boots. Her hair was loose, wavy, ash blond, down over the collar of her coat, and she was heavily made up complete with eyeliner, shadow, mascara, and enough makeup to hide any possible blemish she might have had. Her perfume seemed to replace the air instantly with her arrival. It was a sharp, spicy fragrance. It made Barbara think of a candle shop where, if she entered at all, she usually got a severe headache.

“Mrs. Valducci, if you will please wait in the living room, we’ll be done here in a minute,” Hardesty said.

Debra began to unbutton her coat. “I will not wait in the living room. I repeat, this is my house, and Gina is my child. She has been through quite enough without being harassed by the law at this terrible time in her life. She needs her mother's support, and I intend to provide it." She pulled off her coat and draped it over a chair back, then pulled the chair out and sat down.

Only then did she turn her gaze to Barbara. "Who are you? Another police officer?"

"Not at all. Barbara Holloway, Ms. Valducci's attorney."

Debra's eyes narrowed. "Holloway?" She frowned as if trying to place the name, then nodded. "Oh. I see." She faced Hardesty again. "Well, are you going to ask questions or not? Have you heard enough?"

Hardesty picked up his tape recorder and spoke into it, terminating the interview. He rose, pocketed his notebook and the tape recorder, and motioned to Jackson. Both officers walked out the back door to the porch.

For a moment there was silence in the kitchen. "Mother," Gina said, breaking it, "there's coffee in the carafe."

Debra was studying Barbara intently and simply shook her head at the suggestion. "I want to tell you here and now," she said to Barbara, "my mother-in-law was delusional the last few weeks of her life. I want this settled without causing an irreparable rift between me and my child. We will take the offer from the Halsey group, and I'll give Gina more than enough to buy some acres of her own, put up her own greenhouse and do whatever it is she and her friends are planning. I will be quite generous."

Gina jumped up and pushed her chair back hard. "No we won't!" she cried. "That gang isn't going to touch this place. I'll fight it with everything I have!"

"Since you have virtually nothing, that can't be much of a fight," Debra said. "Gina, stop acting like a spoiled child. It's time for you to grow up and face the reality of life. This farm is a big operation, one you simply can't run. You'd have to hire managers, accountants, bookkeepers, everyone, and it will all erode and we'll end up with nothing in the end. It's been marginally profitable for years only because Magda worked hard at it until she couldn't any longer. You're not capable of running it all. You can't fill her shoes and don't fool yourself into believing otherwise."

"You don't have a clue about what I can do," Gina said coldly. She began to gather the coffee cups.

At that moment Frank entered the kitchen. "Mrs. Valducci," he said. "They told me you were here. I'm Frank Holloway. Good morning." He nodded at Barbara. “They finished in the greenhouse. Nothing. How did it go in here?”

“No problem,” she said.

Debra rose from her chair and raked Frank and then Barbara with a frigid glare. Dismissing them both she faced Gina. “I won’t stay. I think you must have things to discuss. Gina, what I really came by for was to warn you. I happened to see Donald Tilsen in the hotel last night. I didn’t know he had returned and I was surprised to see him. He said he began to remember some things after the shock of that terrible night faded. He came back to tell the police, seeing it as his civic duty.”

She turned to Frank to continue. “That night we arrived at the same time for a nine o’clock appointment with Robert. I didn’t know who Tilsen was then. He introduced himself. When no one came to the door, he suggested that he would go around the house to the kitchen door and see if it was unlocked. He said he and Robert had used that door several times. He entered and opened the front door for me and together we discovered Robert’s body in the den. But he said that later other memories began to surface. He says he heard someone running on the back porch when he approached, and that the front French doors to the living room were open. He also said that on that dreadful night, when he was driving on River Road and then turned on Green Briar Road, he saw a gray car parked outside the store. He thinks it was a Honda or an old Toyota.”

She regarded Gina again and said, “I didn’t see any car parked outside the store, and I didn’t hear anyone running. But I thought you should know what he’s telling the police.”

Standing at the end of the table with several coffee cups in her hands, Gina had turned deathly pale. One of the cups began to tilt, and in almost slow motion but before anyone could intervene, the cup fell to the table, where it splashed coffee. Gina stared at it and didn’t move until Barbara reached her side, took the other cups, put them down on the table, then eased Gina back down onto her chair.

Debra had not moved, but now she began to put on her coat. “Gina,” she said sharply, “if Jeff Cobbe killed Robert, it has nothing to do with you or me.”

While Gina continued to sit statue-still, Barbara began to clean up the coffee. Debra pulled on her coat and walked to the door, where she paused to gaze for a moment at her daughter. She turned to Frank.

"Gina's hardly more than a child," she said. "And she's been hit with one shock after another. She's in no condition to start a drawn-out fight she can't win and one that can only do her great damage psychologically. Consider the emotional toll on her before you proceed any farther." She looked at Gina again, started to say something more, then shook her head and walked out.

"Well," Frank said, casting a glance around at the big bright kitchen, "is there any coffee left in the carafe? Sit still, Gina. I'll see for myself." A minute later he was busily preparing a fresh pot of coffee.

From where he was at the counter, he said, "Let's stay in this nice kitchen and talk a bit. Are you up for that, Gina? And have you had anything to eat this morning? I didn't stop for breakfast and I know Barbara didn't. I also know she'll get as mean as a wet cat if she doesn't get some food pretty damn quick. I can put something together for all of us."

Gina was slowly coming back to the reality of having her attorney make coffee in her kitchen and offering to make breakfast. She looked helplessly at Barbara. "They think I killed my own father?" Her voice was no more than a whisper.

"That was a fishing expedition," Barbara said. "They do that just to see what they can snag. Now about breakfast. Let's have some. My old man likes to cook." She spread her hands in a way to suggest that it was incomprehensible to her that anyone liked to cook.

Minutes later with scrambled eggs and toast served up, they sat at the table and Barbara said, "Between bites, tell me something about your mother and father, your life here in your grandmother's house."

Frank heard little that was new until Gina said, "They were never well matched. He was so ambitious. Always looking for the next step upward. First as an associate professor, jockeying for tenure, then the offer from the Halsey group. I don't know that he was ever interested in GMO until they hired him and he became a fanatical convert. He thought I was following in his footsteps, horticulture, agronomy, botany, the same path he had taken. When I turned down his offer of a job in his research group, he blew up. He was furious, yelled about all that money wasted on my education. I was an ingrate, a know-nothing, a Luddite. Technology is the only way to save the world." Her voice faltered and she stopped and drank coffee. She had eaten little and now pushed her plate back. "Thanks, Mr. Holloway, it's really good, but I guess I just wasn't very hungry."

"What about your mother?" Barbara asked, pouring more coffee for Gina and herself.

Gina added cream and sugar to her cup and stirred it, keeping her gaze on the pattern the cream made, until Barbara touched her hand. "I'm trying to figure her out," Gina said in a low voice. "You know how some people say they're looking for themselves, their real selves? She's like that, searching for herself. I don't think she's found that inner self yet. She hated the academic scene. I remember how she hated the social affairs, academics, spouses, visiting lecturers, all of it. Dad liked to entertain important people—you know, people who might be useful. She never fit in and she seemed to think everyone looked down on her because she hadn't gone to college, didn't know this or that reference to poetry or art, architecture, whatever it happened to be."

This time when she stopped, Frank said, "You mentioned before that she took classes."

Gina shrugged. "Beading, watercolors, diet classes, exercise, belly dancing, real estate classes. I think the business she's in down in Los Angeles might be the best thing that ever happened to her. She loves beautiful clothes, the beautiful people, the beautiful houses, having drinks or lunch with rich and famous people. She can do that sort of thing pretty well. They don't talk about literature or world politics, science, anything like that. They talk about buying and selling beautiful houses. Property," she said. "They deal in beautiful properties."

"She has no interest in this property?" Barbara asked, waving generally at the door, beyond.

"She hates it here and always did. Corvallis was even worse because of the academics, so she stuck it out here. Dad was in Corvallis most of the time, commuted back and forth, and Mother and I lived here, but she never spent any more time than she had to in this house. I don't think she ever went into one of the greenhouses, and I know she wouldn't go out in the field."

She frowned and shook her head. "When Dad and I had it out over the job offer, she took my side. She told him to knock it off, then took me by the arm and said let's go somewhere and have a drink. And you saw her today, concerned that I not be hurt by a fight with her over the will. She meant that. That's why I can't figure her out," she added in a low voice. "She probably really believes what my father said, that Gramma was behaving irrationally. To turn down that much money meant that she was irrational, out of her head, suffering from a head injury. Basically, I think Mother wants what's right for me, just not at her expense. She thinks she knows best what's right for me. She always did. And I think she's afraid of a coming fight."

She looked distant then as if considering something she had never thought of before. "She's afraid," she repeated in a whisper. "What she said about me, having to hire bookkeepers, managers, all that, she knows it's a lie. That's what she would have to do, and she knows I can manage. I've been at my grandmother's side all my life learning the business, all of it." Abruptly she rose from the table. "I should straighten up in here and get out to the greenhouse. There's so much to do."

"Sit down, Gina," Frank said, not in the pleasant avuncular voice he had been using with her, but in the voice he used with uncooperative clients in a jam. She stared at him for a moment, then sank back down into her chair. "You retained me to represent your interests in the matter of the will," Frank said, "but this affair has expanded beyond that. You want to form a company with your friends and if any one of them or you yourself become a person of interest to the investigators, you will each want to have an attorney present when any questions are asked. That could involve a heap of attorneys and a heap of money. Because nothing was stolen the night your father was shot, the police will dismiss a burglary gone sour, and they will start to focus on personal motives. They'll be back with more questions for you and your friends. What I suggest is that you retain me to form a corporate entity for you and your friends and name me as the attorney for that entity. Probably an LLC, a limited liability corporation, with you four as officers. As the corporation attorney I can bring in an associate to protect you if investigators begin pressuring any of you, exactly as I did today by bringing Barbara with me."

Gina was shaking her head. "I don't have any money. I can't afford to do anything like that. You said it might be months before the probate is settled."

"Contesting a will means it probably will be months. But, Gina, I'm not really a corporate attorney, and it will take a long time for me to do the research, the necessary paperwork and such, and in the meantime we'll file for corporate status, with bylaws and other details to come later. As soon as that's done, we'll be set."

"You think they'll accuse me of murdering my father?" She had turned pale down to her lips again. "Mr. Holloway, I loved my father, and I love my mother. Dad and I fought terribly at times. We lost our temper with each other and yelled a lot when we fought. That night the detective asked about, before my grandmother died, we yelled at each other that night. He said a violent argument, I said a disagreement. I still say that, but we did yell at each other. I understood him. I knew he had to fight for what he thought was important, and I think he knew the same about me. I loved him, and he loved me. I never would have hurt him, really hurt him, killed him! And I believe with all my soul that he would have died himself before he would have let anyone hurt me. He saw selling the farm as being in my interest, not something that would be harmful for me. But if they accuse me, who would believe how it was between us?"

"I don't know what's on their mind," Frank said. "You never know what they have until they show their hand, and we don't know exactly what Tilsen might have told them. But we should be prepared for whatever they do."

Looking bewildered, Gina gazed first at him, then at Barbara. "I thought there was something like conflict of interest, more than one client, something like that."

"Barbara would be protecting the corporate interests," Frank said blandly. "No conflict at all." Barbara didn't shift in her chair or make any other overt sign, but Frank turned toward her with an innocent expression. "I think if I hustle I can have the preliminary corporate papers, a boiler plate to be amended later, ready for signatures by this afternoon, get it postmarked today, and we'll be all set. Don't you agree?"

"Absolutely," she said.

"Can you have your fellows here by three?' Frank asked Gina.

She appeared dazed and confused, but she nodded.

Barbara and Frank didn't linger much longer. Frank said they would be back in the afternoon, and they walked out, got in his car, and started for town.

"No conflict of interest, my ass!" Barbara said as soon as the car was on River Road. "Her mother practically accused Jeff Cobbe. You want me to be attorney for both of them? What else is goading you? Something is."

"Indeed there is," he said soberly. "I told you I had Bailey do a little poking, not much, but some. And I did some poking, especially into the Halsey Enterprises group. There's really big money behind them, and a lot of power, political power. If they've got their mouths set for this property, this valley, and they're determined to have it, Gina and the fellows are in for a lot of rough sledding. I don't like it that Tilsen suddenly had a memory jog that puts running footsteps on the back porch and an old gray car outside the store. You know Gina drives a thirteen-year-old Honda? Happens to be gray."

Barbara and Frank returned at three that afternoon and found Gina and her three partners together in the kitchen. After introductions, Frank suggested they stay there, where they could spread out papers.

"Mr. Holloway, there's something you should know first," Gina said. "You and Barbara, I mean. Detectives questioned Jeff for over an hour this morning. They made him go to the police station to be questioned. And they searched his apartment."

Barbara studied Jeff Cobbe as Gina said this. He was tall, six feet, muscular, as if he worked out regularly. With light brown hair, brown eyes, he looked like a college athlete just past his playing days at twenty-nine years old. And he was furious, tense, coiled, so tightly controlled he looked inhumanly robotic.

"Did they have a search warrant?" Barbara asked.

He shook his head. "I didn't even think to ask for one. I thought they were arresting me."

"What did they ask? What did you tell them?"

"They wanted to know if I knew Tilsen had made an offer for the farm, if Valducci was considering accepting it. Sure, I knew that. Everyone did. And they wanted a minute-by-minute account of my time the night Mr. Valducci was shot." His jaw clenched and he swallowed hard. "I told them I was in the greenhouse from about six until they came out to ask me questions and told me about the shooting. They let me call Gina."

"Okay," Barbara said. "Par for the course. Don't take it too hard. After today that won't happen again. Now, while you guys are talking about incorporating, mind if I have a look around, Gina?"

Gina shook her head, then motioned. "The dining room's through the swinging door over there."

Barbara went to the door and glanced in. Potted plants flanked high, wide windows overlooking the porch. There were cabinets with china, crystal, silver dishes, a long table with eight chairs, a side table, buffet table. When the door swung shut, she turned and left the kitchen through the hall door. This time, where one hallway was joined by another at a right angle, she made the turn toward the living room. She passed another closed door, to the dining room she now knew, and walked a few more feet to the living room. Here she paused to take in the French doors at both ends of the long room. Tilsen said the doors to the porch were open that night.

She walked to the doors and opened them, stepped outside for a moment, visualizing the scene Tilsen said he remembered. He had come around the end of the house, past the big terrace, turned at the corner, and heard running footsteps on the porch. It had a wooden floor; footsteps could have been audible. The porch stopped at the kitchen, a distance of about twenty-five feet from the French doors. The runner must have gone behind the kitchen then. Out to the road? On to the parking space at the store? She shrugged and went back inside.

All the rooms were big. Comfortable rooms with comfortable furnishings, old but still lovely carpets, good framed pictures on the walls. Not screaming of great wealth, but rather of family possessions accumulated over many years and cared for.

She left the living room by way of a door to the study, and here she came to a complete stop and studied the room carefully. Conspicuous by the absence of a carpet was a bare spot easily defined by a difference in coloration from the rest of the floor; the spot was shades lighter, six by eight feet. It was in front of a desk on the side wall, left of the windows. That's where he got killed, she thought. Of course, a blood-stained carpet would have been removed. The floor revealed nothing more than the absence of a carpet.

She moved into the room farther and stopped again, this time to survey the whole room: A sofa covered with deep-red leather and two easy chairs arranged for television viewing; a polished desk with a lamp, telephone, and a cup of pencils and pens; several other chairs near overflowing bookcases, with books horizontal on top of shelved books; table lamps and standing lamps by chairs. It was another good room, comfortable, inviting, and evidently well used.

She walked to the far side of the room with more wide windows like those in the dining room, and flanked by plants in ceramic pots. Drapes were pulled back and there were no curtains at the windows. Outside was the terrace, and beyond it a wide space with potted trees, shrubs, benches with plants, people moving among the benches; barely visible through the greenery, she could see the greenhouses. Had the drapes been open the night someone shot and killed Robert Valducci?

She turned to examine the room again from the vantage point of the windows, and nodded to herself. If anyone had been out there that night, if the drapes had been open, whatever happened in the den would have been visible. A border of shrubs edging the terrace had many gaps and low growing plants. A good screen, but not a complete screen. Also, she added to herself, if the drapes had been open and Tilsen had glanced inside, he could have seen the body of Robert Valducci. Walking past the undraped windows, looking for Valducci, who had called a meeting, wouldn't Tilsen have looked in?

She glanced inside the remaining downstairs rooms; a bathroom, and a room that evidently had been used by Magda Valducci. A wheelchair and a reclining chair were both in the bedroom that otherwise might have been in any good hotel, with few personal touches indicating permanency. She continued on her way, hesitated at the stairs, then went up, just to make her cursory inspection complete. It was easy to spot Magda Valducci's room. Here were the personal touches, hair brushes and combs with her monogram in gold, pictures of Gina from childhood to present on the walls and one of Gina, her father, and mother on an end table by a seating arrangement near a window. Many pictures, landscapes, more flowers, a beautiful wall mirror with what appeared to be an intricately carved ivory frame, pretty lamps with frilly shades, face creams on a dressing table. There were many books on tables in this room, and a half-size chair. She backed out of the room and closed the door gently.

Gina's room was easy to spot also. A carelessly made bed, some clothes strewn about on chairs, two books on the bedside table, a backpack near a closet door, several closed boxes all suggested someone moving in or moving out, and too busy to be a fussy housekeeper in a room few others would see. Barbara nodded approval of various posters and prints on the walls: an Escher print, Stonehenge poster, a brilliant Miro print, a Tardis poster…

Enough, Barbara told herself, leaving the room. She glanced inside two other bedrooms, then went to the head of the stairs, where she paused again. The staircase was about four feet wide with a bannister on one side, and carpeted with a runner in a pattern of blue and red. She tried to visualize a scene in which Magda Valducci would have started down, lost her balance, and tumbled all the way to the bottom. Would it have been harder going down than it had been going up? Ask Darren, she told herself. Her lover, Darren, a physical therapist, knew things like that.

Back on the first floor, she walked to the kitchen door, opened it a crack, and stood listening to Jeff Cobbe.

"…so with over a thousand acres, we could provide a hell of a lot of food for this part of the valley. And we'll be joining other groups already up and running with the same kind of co-ops throughout the country. Worldwide, in fact. We'll have to provide locally grown food. When the crunch time comes, it's going to be imperative that local food is available. Transportation costs, shortages, desperation… That's what's going to happen, Mr. Holloway. Already they're predicting Dust Bowl conditions for nearly two thirds of the country, and those genetically modified crops will fail. They aren't producing the root systems today that survive droughts. Water tables falling, polluted water where it's available, super weeds, super bugs, super diseases. Those GMO plants can't adapt to survive. Not when they're been genetically modified to exist in a carefully controlled environment, and only in that environment—"

He stopped speaking when Barbara pushed the door open and walked inside the kitchen. With dismay she thought that Jeff Cobbe was a fanatic. His voice was that of a fanatic predicting the end of the world.

"About wrapped up?" Barbara asked, walking to the table.

"Indeed we are," Frank said. "I told them that if anything comes up concerning the matter of the will, I'm the one to call. I think Sal Barrasso advised Mrs. Valducci that she should continue to act as personal representative to the estate, and let the business continue to operate until the matter of the second will is resolved."

"Right," Barbara said. "The will business, call Dad. Anything else, call me. If they want to ask questions, conduct searches, anything at all, just give me a call, and don't say another word until I'm there." She found her card case in her briefcase and passed out cards. "Day or night, don't hesitate to call. At this time, I don't think there's anything for you to worry about especially. The investigation is still in an exploratory stage and they'll be fishing for leads for a while. Just one question, Jeff. I heard you say a thousand acres, but I thought this property was about two hundred acres."

"There are seven different farms involved," he said. "We've been talking a lot at local granges, explaining what we're up to, getting others to come along with us. Some of them don't call themselves organic, but neither do they use sprays, and they don't want spray drift contaminating their berries or other crops."

Barbara nodded. "Okay, got it."

He looked skeptical. After glancing at Gina, he said, "If we could talk to you for an hour, explain… Or I could put together some reports, some data from reliable sources for you to read when you have time." He looked at Gina again and when she remained silent, he said in an almost desperate tone, "Barbara, no one who hasn't followed the science for the last decade has any idea of what's really going on. And unless you understand what it is we're opposing, we'll just be those quixotic kids tilting at windmills, the way Gina's father regarded us."

She looked from him to Gina, on to Greg and Daniel. They all looked desperate. Where Gina's father had seen windmills, they saw dragons.

"Send me the reports," she said. "I'll read whatever you think I should." She glanced at her watch. "Dad, it's getting late, but we'll have time to make it to the River Road Branch Post Office if we leave in half an hour. Do you have that envelope ready to mail?" He nodded, and she sat down at the table. "Gina, this is hard, but I want you to try to remember exactly what happened when you got to the house the night your father was shot. Can you do that?"

"I told that detective. You were here," Gina said in a tight voice.

"I want more than that. You drove here. Where did you park? Which door did you use to enter the house? See? I want details."

Gina moistened her lips. "I parked behind the greenhouses, on the access road."

"Why there?"

"There were police cars, flashing lights, other cars in the driveway, even on the road in front of the house. I just went on to the access road. That's where the workers all park, where I park when I'm living in my apartment."

"Okay. Was Jeff in the greenhouse? Did you see him?"

"He was outside, down where he could see the house windows. I went to him, but he didn't know anything except that my father had been shot. He said Mother looked ready to keel over, and he came to the house with me. Most of the way. They wouldn't let him in. I came in through the living room door, the one facing the greenhouses. An officer let me in and I ran to my mother. She was sitting on the sofa wrapped in an afghan. She was shivering, her eyes wide open, staring ahead. In shock, I think."

"Did she say anything to you?"

"Yes," Gina said in low voice. "She kept talking and talking, almost in a whisper, but talking. She was shivering so hard, her hands were like ice. She looked blanched. She said he didn't come to the door when she rang and she thought he was in the bathroom. She said Tilsen came up behind her when she was ringing the doorbell and he left her there to find an open door. He opened the front door from inside and they yelled up the stairs, and she went upstairs. Tilsen walked into the study. He yelled for her and she went in and saw him." Her voice became lower and lower as she talked, and finally it faded out altogether.

"You're doing fine," Barbara said. "Then what?

"I made tea for her," Gina said after a moment. "She was so cold. It only takes a minute to heat the water in the microwave. They said I could make tea. A detective went with me to the kitchen. Men and women were everywhere. I don't even know what they were all doing. I turned up the thermostat in the hall and took hot tea for her. To warm her hands even if she didn't want to drink it. She couldn't stop shaking, and I told one of the detectives I had to take her to her hotel room and put her to bed. Maybe she needed a doctor. They let me take her to her hotel. I gave her a sleeping pill. She had some in the bathroom. And I sat by her until she fell asleep. I lay down on a sofa but I didn't sleep. I think that's when it hit me that my father was dead, that someone had killed him." Her voice broke completely.

"Just a little more, Gina," Barbara said. "Did you see Tilsen that night?"

Gina shook her head. "Wait," she said, "once. In the hall when I turned up the thermostat and had the tea for Mother. There were so many men coming in, going out. I was afraid for my mother. I didn't give him a thought. I can't remember seeing him before or after that one time."

"Did you make any calls after you took your mother to the hotel?"

"No."

"One more," Barbara said. "Were you wearing those boots that night?" She pointed to them. Knee-high, leather, with leather soles and one-inch heels.

"Yes. Why?"

"Just checking." She turned to Jeff. "Can you see the interior of this house from the greenhouse at night when lights are on in here?"

"No. We use the last greenhouse. It's down a ways from here. You could tell that lights were on, but that's about all you could see."

"Gina found you where you could see the interior, didn't she? Were any of the drapes drawn? Could you see inside the den and the living room?"

"Yes. The drapes were all the way back. I could see them moving around, taking pictures, looking over the desk, stuff like that. I could see Mrs. Valducci looking like she was ready to faint or something. I couldn't see Mr. Valducci's body," he added as if anticipating her next question.

"Were you wearing those boots?" She pointed to them the way she had pointed to Gina's. They were ankle boots, waterproof, with rubber or synthetic soles. She had similar boots.

"Sure. What difference does that make?"

"I don't know," Barbara said. She looked at her watch again and stood. "We have to be on our way. But listen up, guys. If anyone asks questions, you call me or my father and don't say another word. No comment for the press if they come around, and they probably will. From what little I know at this time, they can't have anything like a case against any of you, but we don't know what Tilsen told them. Keep that in mind. Call me if anything comes up, if you recall anything you think I should know. And for now, we all just sit tight. The ball's in their court, the next move is theirs." She and Frank left the small group sitting at the kitchen table, each and every one of them looking frightened and desperate.

In the car, with Frank at the wheel, she said, “God, I hope they settle for a maniac out for revenge for a long-gone grudge.”

Frank nodded. “Every answer Gina gave was the wrong one. She didn’t see anyone at her apartment. Jeff called her and she went straight to him, not straight to the house. She kept her head enough to make tea and take care of her mother. Could be seen as brave, cool, or something else.”

“And her boots could have been heard on the porch. His not so much.”

After a lengthy silence Frank said, “Probate hearing will come up next week. You want to sit in?” He started to drive.

“You bet I do. Even that’s a bitch to add to this mess. Motive tied in a neat package of several million dollar bills.”

April had come in cold and wet with steady rain that had persisted for days, still persisted. Welcome to climate change, Barbara thought, leaving her car at the courthouse parking garage.

"Today's meeting is to reach a settlement, if that's possible," Frank had said about the first probate court procedure. "The judge goes back and forth between the two parties and passes on whatever offer is being made, looking for a settlement. Back and forth to nowhere," he had added cheerfully.

What did it do for Gina's insides to turn down her mother's million-dollar offer? Barbara wondered. Gina had stated her position at the beginning and she had stuck to it.

And now the trial was on the docket.

Frank and Gina were already in the courtroom when Barbara arrived. She hurried to join them, noticing that at the opposing table Debra Valducci was in place with a stranger. Blindfolded, she would have known Debra was there; her perfume announced her presence from a considerable distance.

"Where's Barrasso?" Barbara asked, seating herself behind Frank's chair.

"And good morning to you, too," Frank said in a low voice. "I expect that he told Debra that she couldn't win this case and that she fired him on the spot. She found someone willing to give it a go. Name's Carl Dunning."

Something Frank had said a long time ago, regarding one he called a shyster, ambulance chaser of an attorney, came to mind: Doctors and lawyers, win or lose, will get paid. Count on it.

Dunning was forty something, slender, with thinning black hair and black-framed glasses. He looked studious and a bit pompous. Barbara had no time to study him further as the judge entered the courtroom. And she was another newcomer. A black woman, heavy-set with steel-gray frizzy hair and a scowl on her face.

"Judith Twining," Frank whispered. "Dragon Lady."

Both sides had agreed to waive a jury trial, to let the judge make the determinate decision in this case.

Judge Twining made a hand motion for them all to be seated. "Sit," she said. "Mr. Dunning, let's get on with it."

"Thank you, your honor. It is our contention that the original will written and executed eleven years ago is the only valid will in this case. Because Magdalena Valducci suffered an incapacitating accident prior to her death, she was rendered helpless and vulnerable to pressure from her granddaughter, Gina Valducci, to write a bogus will. Heavily sedated and confused, she was pressured to allow said granddaughter to make use of the facilities of the farm for her own purposes at great expense. As the weeks passed she became more and more dependent and, fearful of being left alone, she was unable to resist whatever demand the granddaughter made of her…."

Gina gasped at his opening remarks. Frank patted her arm reassuringly, and she leaned back in her chair, pale and shaken, but quiet.

Dunning embellished his picture at length, brought up the idea that Gina and three male companions had plotted to seize the property. Eventually he called Debra to the stand.

Barbara noticed with amusement that the Dragon Lady judge drew back a little, when Debra took the stand. Her scowl deepened and her mouth seemed to close harder.

Dunning was soon finished with establishing Debra's identity, where she lived and worked as a successful real estate agent.

"Mrs. Valducci, please tell the court the reason you believe that your late mother-in-law was incompetent and irrational, possibly demented."

"It was apparent to us that she must have hit her head when she had the accident that broke her leg. She could not make rational decisions and dismissed all attempts to communicate to her the irrationality of her obsessive behavior. A respectable company made her a most generous offer, even above market value, to buy her farm, which she could no longer manage, I might add, and she turned it down without even considering what it meant. And she rejected it without a minute's hesitation. Simply said no, and no amount of reasoning could change her mind. She seemed not to understand that this was a once-in-a-lifetime offer, that it would never be repeated or met by another possible buyer. She was confused about it, and irrational in her response. And the way she relied on Gina was obsessive and childlike, as if Gina were the only one whose desires mattered, and she just a child herself really, with no idea of what it means to manage a huge farm like that. Magda's faith in a child managing the farm was irrational and obsessive. And then writing such a childish will instead of having a real lawyer draw up a will if she really wanted to change anything. That was irrational."

Debra paused as if to draw a breath, but before Dunning could ask a question, or encourage her to continue, she said, "Add to all that the way she treated her own son, my late husband, who was murdered, and charged with that murder is one of Gina's closest friends and more-than-friend."

Quietly Frank said, "Objection. Irrelevant to the matter of the will."

"Well, it's not irrelevant to me or to my dead husband!" Debra cried.

Even more quietly Frank said, "Objection. I ask the court to strike Mrs. Valducci's last remark."

"Sustained. Both objections. Mrs. Valducci, please restrict your testimony to the matter of the will."

"Mrs. Valducci," Dunning said, "you were testifying to how Mrs. Magdalena Valducci treated your late husband Robert Valducci."

"She treated him like an enemy, or else she made fun of him. It was mortifying to him to have her laugh at him and his company's offer,which was made in good faith and would have been in a cash deposit to her bank account. Not a laughing matter."

It went on for a few more minutes, but there was nothing new in her testimony. Dunning turned to Frank with a token bow and sat down.

"Mrs. Valducci," Frank said pleasantly, "what was the situation in the Valducci house eleven years ago when the first will was written?"

"What do you mean, situation?"

"I mean, who lived there at that time?"

"I did, and Gina did, and Magda, of course. Robert lived mostly in Corvallis where he was a professor. He was with us most weekends."

"So Gina was fifteen, and Robert was Magda's only child. Is that correct?"

"Yes, of course."

"How long at that time had Mrs. Valducci been a widow?"

"About six months."

"When did Robert Valducci accept an offer with the Halsey Enterprises corporation in Chicago?"

"About eight years ago."

"When did you move to California?"

"The same. Eight years ago."

"And Gina stayed in Eugene. Is that correct?"

Debra darted a glance at Gina, another at her attorney before answering. "She was in high school and wanted to finish the semester. And she wanted to go the U of O for her undergraduate degree, and on to OSU for her master's. It was convenient for her to remain with Magda."

"Mrs. Valducci, did Gina ever live anywhere other than with her grandmother before she finished her education?"

Debra paused again, then said, "She never wanted to move to California. Her grandmother spoiled her, denied her nothing, and she was content. Besides, she's only been out of college for a year. She could change her mind any day."

"When was the last time you saw Magda Valducci?" Frank asked then, no longer conversational and easygoing, as he had been up to that point. His voice was crisp, the question sharp.

Looking startled at the change, Debra said, "At Gina's graduation, a year ago."

"Did you fly into Eugene the day of the graduation?"

"Yes."

"Did a group of friends and relatives gather at the farm after the graduation ceremony?"

She said yes again and he shot the next question at her. "Did you go to a dinner with a group of friends and relatives that evening?" Barely waiting for her affirmative answer, he said, "Did you spend that night at the farm with your husband and your mother-in-law?"

"No. I had an early flight out the next day. I didn't want to bother anyone with taking me to the airport. I stayed at the Hilton."

"How do you know how changed Magda Valducci was from that occasion, that last time you saw her a year ago, in the midst of a large celebratory group, to the time you say she was confused and irrational?"

"Robert told me," she said.

Frank turned his gaze from her to the judge. "Your honor, I move that all of Mrs. Valducci's remarks concerning the state of Magda's mental health be stricken as hearsay. She had no direct knowledge of any of it."

"Objection!" Dunning cried out. "Mrs. Valducci and her husband's conversations are to be treated as equal spousal statements."

"Only insofar as each spouse is readily available to verify each statement," Frank said.

"Mrs. Valducci's testimony reflects exactly what her husband confided in her and must be treated as if coming from his lips directly," Dunning said, his voice growing more strident with each word.

"That's nonsense and you know it," Frank said. "Mr. Valducci's opinion was very likely highly prejudicial due to his financially vested interest in the outcome of the contentious offer to purchase the property. We can't judge how much his bias might have influenced his interpretation of Magda Valducci's behavior without being able to question him directly, which of course is impossible."

The judge was banging her gavel midway through Frank's last response, and now she said in a harsh voice, "Mr. Holloway, you are out of order. Mr. Dunning, sit down and be quiet. I shall take the motion under advisement and advise both of you of my decision in due time. Now, both of you stop this unseemly behavior and get on with the business at hand."

"No more questions for this witness," Frank said and he sat down.

Donald Tilsen took the stand and while Dunning was taking him through the preliminaries, Barbara studied his face, which was sharp featured, with a bony nose, deep set eyes that were open a bit too wide, giving him a startled look, but more than that, his eyes were too close together. Birdlike, she decided. A raptor, hawk maybe. Or an owl.

Frank passed her a note and she had to suppress a giggle and fake a cough. Frank had written: *His nose is too close together.*

Dunning finally began asking about the present case. "Exactly why were you and Mr. Valducci in the state at that time?"

"Our company was eager to purchase farmland that met certain criteria. Good soil, a temperate climate, and adequate rain. This section of the valley met our needs precisely, and Robert had every reason to believe his elderly mother would be happy to sell the property."

"What was Mr. Valducci's reaction when his mother refused the offer?"

"Oh, for a time he was angry, but then he expressed worry that his mother was delusional, her behavior erratic and irrational, and that she was generally confused. I had to agree with his assessment. He said he was considering an incompetency hearing because he believed she needed medical care and a legal guardian to protect her assets. He said he thought she must have hit her head, damaged her brain when she was involved in an accident. He thought that his daughter Gina was taking advantage of the impaired old woman, and he was outraged about that."

There wasn't much more and it was Frank's turn. He stood at his table and asked, "Mr. Tilsen, is the offer to purchase the farm still on the table with Mrs. Debra Valducci?"

"Yes, of course."

"Did you ever meet Magdalena Valducci?"

"No. I never had that pleasure."

"So everything you know about her is what you heard from Robert Valducci. Is that correct?"

His answer was a little slower this time. "That is correct."

"Have you had medical training, an education in medicine?"

"No, of course not."

"So, when you stated that you agreed with Robert Valducci's assessment of his mother's condition, that was in effect being a yes man, confirming what you knew he wanted to hear. Is that correct?"

Dunning was on his feet calling an objection instantly. "That is an improper question on the order of 'When did you stop beating your wife.'"

"Withdraw the question," Frank said when the judge upheld the objection. "Let me put it this way. Mr. Tilsen, did you know anything about Mrs. Magdalena Valducci other than what you heard from Robert Valducci?"

"No."

"Your honor," Frank said, turning his gaze to Judge Twining, "I move that the entirety of Mr. Tilsen's testimony regarding the mental health of Magdalena Valducci be stricken as hearsay."

Dunning was even louder and more strident when he objected, and Judge Twining was more emphatic with her gavel when she ordered him to desist.

"As I ruled earlier, I shall take this under advisement and decide later. Mr. Holloway, do you have more questions?"

Frank sat down. "No more questions."

Dunning said he had no additional witnesses. And that was his case, Barbara realized. A nothing case that he could not win. Gina turned to look at her, and she also realized that Gina was still frightened, that she didn't know how shallow Dunning's case really was. She had been stung again and again by testimony from her mother, and now Tilsen, which had denigrated her, made her look like a money- or power-hungry predator, a leech, a moocher. How it must hurt, Barbara thought with regret. She smiled encouragement. And she wanted to take Debra Valducci out into an alley and beat the shit out of her, she added to herself.

Frank called Mike Krusich, who testified that he had worked on the farm for twenty-two years, had known Gina that long, and had watched her grow up at Magda's side all those years absorbing everything that Magda was teaching her.

"Does she know the business end of running a large farm?" Frank asked.

"You bet she does. She knows how much it costs to grow a head of cabbage, exactly when to plant the seed and when to harvest the crop, how much to hold in reserve in case of an equipment breakdown, how far in advance to hire help to make sure they're on hand when needed, how much labor will cost. All of it. She knows it all."

"When was the last time you saw Magda Valducci?"

Mike's big face had a tragic expression when he said, "On the morning of the day she died. We had a business meeting every morning, Magda, Gina, and me. We'd talk things over, plan our day sort of, and if there was anything new happening, a new order or something like that, talk about it. We had our meeting that morning just like we did every morning."

"Was Magda Valducci her normal self the days before her fatal accident?"

"Yes, sir. She couldn't move around much, but she was sharp as a tack. She knew exactly what was going on and was keeping her hand in it all. She was still in charge, there wasn't any doubt about that."

Frank thanked him and sat down.

Dunning tried to shake his testimony; Mike didn't budge, but rather doubled down on some of his statements, and he was dismissed.

Frank called Sophia Mirano and her housekeeper Ethel Juarez next and their statements were that Magda had called them to come visit and share scones that Gina had made. Magda had brought out two sheets of handwritten lines and had them witness her signature and her initial on the first page. She had folded the papers and put them in an envelope that she put in the side pocket of a bag strapped on her wheelchair. Frank showed them the will and they both confirmed that those were the papers and identified their signatures.

"We ate scones with raspberry jam and we gossiped awhile, and then we left," Sophia Mirano said. "I thought it must have been a will, but I didn't ask questions. I thought Magda would tell me when she wanted me to know."

And: "Of course, she was herself. Normal as always. Impatient with being cooped up with a cast on her leg like that, but just the same as she was for the last thirty-four years that I knew her."

Dunning had no questions for these witnesses, and Frank called Mildred Barry, a receptionist in the office of the law firm of Barrasso, Treadmore, and Wyandot. She was a plump and pretty woman with an open face, who seemed genuinely interested and pleased to be there.

After eliciting her name and her present employment, Frank got to the point quickly.

"When was the last time you spoke with Magda Valducci?"

"February 24," she said promptly.

"Please, in your own words, tell the court about that incident."

"Yes, sir. She called at eight forty-five and asked to speak with Mr. Barrasso. I informed her that he was out of town and would not be back until late April or possibly early May. He was in Hawaii. She said something like, oh dear. I suggested that a different attorney might help her, and she laughed and said that wouldn't work. She had intended to ask Mr. Barrasso to drop by her house for a matter that needed an attorney. She said her leg was in a cast that didn't let her bend her knee and that her leg stuck out like the prow of a pirate ship." She smiled when she said this. "Mrs. Valducci was joking, laughing about her leg. She said she would need a medical van to transport her and it wasn't worth the trouble, she could wait and by the time Mr. Barrasso got back, her damn cast would be off. Those were her words. She asked for an appointment as soon as Mr. Barrasso returned. I made that appointment for her and she thanked me and we hung up."

Dunning didn't even try to make a dent in her testimony beyond having her admit that she didn't know what legal matter had prompted Magda's call.

Frank called Gina to the stand finally.

After the preliminaries, he had her recount how she had found the will.

For the first time her voice faltered as she talked about cradling her grandmother's head and hearing her last words: *Remember the Lorax.*

He asked her what she and her partners planned for the future of the farm if she gained control of it.

"We intend to have a self-sufficient and sustainable farm. We believe that climate change is real and presents a possibly existential threat to human life, that water shortages and growing desertification will force a mass migration from many states, and that the valley here must be prepared to provide food for a growing local population. We intend to add to the supply of food for the immediate surrounding population in the years to come. As the situation worsens, importation of food and of chemical fertilizers and pesticides will be problematic, and we plan to prepare for that contingency."

"Did your grandmother share these beliefs?" Frank asked.

"She did. She kept up with the literature about global climate change and was in complete sympathy with our plans."

"Objection," Dunning called out. "Young people's starry-eyed view of themselves saving the world is beyond the scope of this hearing."

Judge Twining hesitated a moment, then said, "Sustained. Move on, Mr. Holloway."

Frank nodded. "Gina, is it your intention to try to save the world?"

"No. Just to help keep this part of it in food when catastrophic change comes."

"Objection!"

"Sustained. Mr. Holloway, I advise you to move on."

"Yes, your honor. Just one more bit. Gina, is this the mission statement for your corporation, the Valducci Corporation?" He showed the document to the judge and Dunning, then held it up for Gina to see. She said it was.

"I want to enter this document as Exhibit A," Frank said equably. "I have already made a copy for Mr. Dunning."

There was no table for exhibits, and he looked around as if baffled what to do with the document. Judge Twining's mouth grew even tighter, and she pointed to her desk. "Just put it down here."

"Thank you, your honor," Frank said humbly.

He faced Gina again. "Gina, did you have a special bond with your grandmother?" Frank's voice was gentle as he asked, but it appeared that Gina had not been prepared for the question. She looked surprised, even apprehensive.

"Just tell the court about your relationship with your grandmother, when it started and how."

Still she hesitated. Then she ducked her head and said softly, so softly that Judge Twining leaned forward to hear her, "A long time ago when I was about six, I took off my shoes out in the cornfield and I was just standing there, feeling strange, tingly maybe. My grandmother came out and knelt beside me. She pressed one hand down on the earth, and took my hand in her other hand. She said, 'You feel it, don't you, child?' I said I felt something but I didn't know what it was. She said, 'It's life, Gina. The earth is so alive and you can feel it now and then, like this instant.' We never talked about it, but it was special and we both knew it was." Her head was still ducked, her voice low, when she added, "We never had to explain anything to each other. That was special."

Listening to those words, Barbara felt an intense rush of what felt almost like sexual desire, but different somehow, the way an electric current rushing through one might feel. It passed swiftly, but it left her unaccountably shaken.

For a moment or two Frank said nothing when Gina became silent. Then he smiled at her and said, "No more questions." A shot in the dark, he thought. A wild guess, a flash of intuition had led to that question with no answer in mind, except that he had known from the first time he met Gina that there was something beyond ordinary in the young woman and her bond with her grandmother, and her fierce determination to keep her farm.

Dunning appeared to be caught off guard by Frank's sudden end to his presentation. Debra leaned into him and caught his arm and they had a whispered conversation. When he started to rise, it appeared that she was restraining him, whispering vehemently.

"Mr. Dunning, do you have questions for the witness?" Judge Twining's voice was sharp and impatient.

"Yes, your honor." He got to his feet, but didn't move from his table. "Ms. Valducci, if you were offered millions of dollars for the farm, knowing that you could buy even more acreage with that amount if you chose to do so, would you consider such an offer?"

"No. Mr. Tilsen could buy other farms with so much money. Why this one?"

"Objection," Dunning said. "Strike everything after the negative response."

"Sustained," the judge said.

"Would you consider such a refusal irrational?"

"Absolutely not."

"If someone offered you double the price your car is worth, would you consider selling it?"

"Yes. A car is easily replaced, a four-generation farm isn't."

"Your honor, please instruct the witness to answer the questions without added comments."

"Just answer the question," the judge said.

Frank sat back in his chair without any intention of interfering with Dunning at this point. Gina was making her case just fine.

"Ms. Valducci, what is your relationship with Jeff Cobbe?"

Gina glanced at her mother before answering. "Jeff is the vice president of the Valducci Corporation. I am the president. He is my colleague and my friend."

"Is there a romantic relationship between the two of you?"

"Objection," Frank said. "Ms. Valducci's personal life has no relevance to this hearing."

"I agree," Judge Twining said. "Sustained."

Looking directly at her mother, Gina said, "No," and answered the question in spite of the sustained objection.

Dunning tried to get her to admit knowing about the will, to admit to helping her grandmother write it, to admit that she had subtly influenced her grandmother by threats of leaving her alone in the house, of not informing her grandmother of her plans for the farm. Gina remained firm and unshaken throughout.

"Why did she write such a childish will and then hide it in a children's book?"

Dunning demanded.

"I don't know. I can only guess."

"Wasn't that irrational on her part?"

"I don't think so, but I can only conjecture about her motive for doing that."

"We don't need any more guesses or conjectures," Dunning snapped. "No more questions."

Frank rose in a leisurely way. "Please do tell us what you believe the reason was for your grandmother to hide the will in a children's book."

"She had been hit by a car backing out of a parking space at the grocery story. In just an instant she was hit and seriously injured. The matter of the sale of the farm arose and that instant that her accident took must have been a worry. It could happen again. She wrote the will and put it in a place where it would be safe and remain indefinitely because she had an appointment with Mr. Barrasso to write a new will. At that time or afterward, it would have been simple for her to retrieve the handwritten will and destroy it. It no longer would be needed. But if she had another accident before her appointment, and if she was incapacitated or even killed, she knew I would move out, that I would pack up my belongings, including my books from childhood, and at that time I would come across the will. Knowing her, how her mind worked, I believe that was her reasoning."

Frank nodded. "Thank you, Ms. Valducci. I have no more questions. That concludes our case."

Judge Twining tapped her gavel. "I'm going to call a recess until one-thirty this afternoon. Court adjourned." She picked up the mission statement and walked away from her desk, out of the courtroom.

"What do we do now?" Gina asked. "Stay here and wait until she comes back?"

Frank laughed. "Nope. We go to lunch and during the next hour and a half I'll inform you about the legalities that we'll have to tend to in the next thirty days. Then we'll come back."

"Onward and out," Barbara said. She grinned at Frank. "Dad, you're still the greatest. Good show."

At one-thirty, the cast of characters was in place like well-rehearsed actors at curtain call, Barbara thought when the judge entered and seated herself at the bench.

Without preamble, Judge Twining said, "I agree with Mr. Holloway that the testimony from Mrs. Debra Valducci and from Mr. Donald Tilsen is hearsay and will be stricken from the record. Mr. Valducci was too heavily invested in the outcome of a possible sale to remain unbiased in his assessment of Mrs. Magdalena Valducci's mental health. I hereby decide that the hand-written, signed and witnessed will dated February 24 to be valid and binding, making Ms. Gina Valducci the legitimate heir to the property."

"Your honor," Dunning cried out, but he got no further than that. Judge Twining banged her gavel hard.

"Mr. Dunning, be advised that it was ill considered for you to bring to trial a case without credible evidence, rendering it a frivolous case that did a disservice to both you and your client. Be advised, sir, do not try the court's patience any further." She leaned forward, glaring at him. After a moment she nodded to Frank, and said, "You and your client will be sent a written decision in the coming days, with a copy going to Mr. Dunning. This court is adjourned."

As soon as the judge was out of sight Gina jumped up and down and threw her arms around Frank and cried, "I can't believe it! You did it! You really did it! I was so scared."

Barbara, grinning, turned to see Debra stalking from the courtroom with Dunning trailing behind her. Tilsen was already gone. Back to L.A. for her, back to Chicago for him? The perfect outcome.

At the courthouse door Frank stopped and said, "Gina, I want to send someone to change the locks on your doors, and to make sure your French doors are fitted with decent locks."

Gina regarded him soberly for a second or two, then said, "Mr. Holloway, I can't pay for any of this, not your work on the corporation, today, a locksmith, Barbara's advice and counsel. I mean, land rich, cash poor. Isn't that the phrase?"

"We'll work something out," Frank said. "In fact, I'll have papers for you and the gang to sign tomorrow or the next day. I'll give you a call to set up a time. Can you continue to use the greenhouse? Can you pay for it?"

"What choice do we have?" Gina said. "The days are getting warmer so we won't need much heat. We'll manage somehow." She pulled the hood of her jacket over her hair and left them.

"This is tough on her," Frank said. "And she's handling it like a trouper. Good for her. Do you want some coffee, on me?"

Barbara laughed. "Sorry. I have work to do. My day at Martin's. I think that Darren and I might go to the coast tomorrow right after lunch, back Sunday afternoon. Short trip, but a storm's coming in and we want to watch it. They say this rain will ease up after it blows out, and we might even get some sun next week." She motioned toward the doors and the rain beyond. "Want me to bring you fish, clams, anything?"

"Nope. Dinner when you get home. Give me a call about the time, if you remember while you're braving gale winds. Don't get washed out to sea."

Laughing, she took him by the arm and they went out into the April rain together.

Saturday night, dark, howling wind, rain turning the wide windows of the cabin opaque in sheets of water that reflected the interior light provided by blazing logs in the fireplace. It was perfect, Barbara thought in contentment. "Lovely storm," she murmured, snug in the crook of Darren's arm.

He grunted agreement. "It will blow itself out overnight. I'm glad we did this."

"Me too. When I was a kid and we'd come out when a storm was brewing, Dad held my hand so tightly when we went down to the beach. He said he was keeping me from blowing away and I thought he was kidding. He wasn't kidding."

"We have a bushel of wet clothes to haul back and dry out. Your face is wind burned, and we ate a peck of clams. Good mini-vacation." He tightened his arm around her and she snuggled deeper against him.

At the Valducci house Gina pulled off her wet poncho on the porch, removed her boots, and entered the kitchen. Dead tired, she thought. Now she knew the real meaning of the phrase. Everything about her was tired, down to her teeth and hair. She should have a snack, she knew, remembering her promise to herself when she ate a TV dinner hours and hours ago, but she was too tired and too dirty. She walked through the house, checked doors, turned off lights, and saw that the greenhouse light was off. Good. Jeff needed to knock off as much as she did. Now, a hot bath, then food, if she didn't fall asleep first. She trudged upstairs and stripped off her messy, muddy clothes while the tub was filling.

She soaked until the water cooled, added more hot water and soaked longer, toweled briskly, and was fastening the tie of her robe when she heard the doorbell. At that time of night, she wondered, ten o'clock? No one visited at ten o'clock. She hurried downstairs and to the front door. When she opened it, her mother practically crashed into her in her rush to get inside. Tony Mirano was with her.

"Mother! What happened? What's wrong?" Gina cried, holding Debra, who was shaking hard.

"He tried to kill me!" Debra said. "Jeff Cobbe tried to kill me!"

"Mother! What happened? What are you talking about?"

"Maybe she should sit down," Tony said.

Gina looked from her mother to him, her neighbor, one she had known her entire life, and for a moment his face was that of a stranger, lined, angular, with opaque black eyes, and a hard, rigid line about his jaw.

She guided her mother to the living room, to the sofa, where they both sat down, Gina's arm about Debra's shoulders. She was shaking hard, so pale that her makeup looked garish on a white background.

"Mother, for God's sake, tell me what happened!"

"He called me and said you both wanted to make a deal, you wanted to talk, I should come out and we'd settle things." Her voice was shrill, quivering, with many pauses between the words, then her words sped together, making it hard to grasp what she was saying. "I turned off River Road and he must have been behind the trees up there and he began shooting at me, a lot of shots. I swerved off the road and ducked down. He must have thought he hit me. There was glass everywhere. He stopped shooting and I tried to find my phone and call 911. I don't know where it was. I just stayed down, out of sight, and prayed he wouldn't come closer and shoot me. Then Tony came."

Gina looked at Tony. He nodded. "I saw her car mostly off the road and stopped. When I saw she was still inside, maybe hurt, I opened the door and she started screaming. Then she saw who it was and said she was all right. I got her out and into my truck and came here." He had been standing near them, and now nodded toward the hallway. "Gina, I'm going to call the police and they'll be here pretty soon probably, seeing that there's been trouble here already. Maybe I'd better make some coffee or something. I guess no one's going to get any sleep for a long time." The stranger was gone, he was again the elderly neighbor, friend of her grandparents for a lifetime, friend of Gina's all her life. "I don't think they'd like it if I left before they get here. Might as well try to be useful."

"Wait! Close the drapes!" Debra cried in a piercing voice. "He might still be out there!"

Tony crossed the room to close the drapes at the terrace doors, then at the porch doors. Done with that, he went to the hall doorway. "I'll just put on a pot of coffee."

"Mother, please listen to me. Jeff wouldn't do that. There's no reason, no earthly reason for him to want to hurt you. We didn't talk about a deal or anything else. Someone else must have called you. Not Jeff."

"No reason?" Debra jerked away from Gina. "Stop protecting him! Stop being a fool!" Her voice grew shriller and she drew her arms about herself, pulling even farther away from Gina. "He has every reason. He killed Robert and now he wants to kill me so you'll have everything, and he'll have you! Isn't that how it works? He gets the girl, the farm, the Halsey deal, everything!"

Barbara smelled coffee, smiled and drew the covers up farther, burrowed deeper into a great down pillow. Dreaming, half awake, guiding her dreams into a fairyland of love, comfort, warmth, of Darren's arms around her, murmuring into her ear, reciting— Abruptly the dream world vanished and she realized the fairybells she had been hearing were coming from her cellphone. She groped for it, saw that it was Frank calling and bolted upright.

"Dad? What's up? Are you—" She saw Darren in the doorway, as alarmed as she was by an unexpected call from Frank at an unusual hour. She couldn't help it. Ever since Frank's mild heart attack a few years earlier, she could not prevent the flash of fear that accompanied unusual calls. A warning attack, his doctor had called it.

"I'm fine," Frank snapped. "Wake up and listen. The police are holding Jeff Cobbe for questioning in the murder of Robert Valducci and the attempted murder of Debra. Get your act together and get back here as soon as you can."

"Shit!" She watched the expression of concern pass from Darren's face before he retreated to the kitchen. "Tell me more," she said.

"I told you what I know. Jeff called me a few minutes ago. I told him to button his lips until you get here. Call when you get in the valley. Maybe I'll know more by then. I already sicced Bailey on it."

She was pulling on her robe when she rushed into the kitchen where Darren was breaking eggs into a bowl.

"We have to go," she said. "The minute I turn my back all hell breaks loose. Jeff—"

Darren put his finger on her lips. "What you have to do is take a shower and get dressed. Then we'll eat the spinach omelet I'm making, and after that we'll drive out. Twenty minutes won't make any difference unless they've pointed a gun at his head, and even if they've done that, you couldn't get there in time to stop the bullet. Now, beat it."

She knew he was right, but still… But still nothing, she told herself under the shower. He was right. She was spoiling his little mini vacation again and it couldn't be helped. Angrily she turned off the water and grabbed a towel. Then she was thinking about the drive through the Coast Range where they would have no signal. No more information until they reached the valley.

Half an hour later, as they wound through the mountains, she kept trying her cellphone for a signal. Finally she got it and instantly pressed the speed dial for Frank.

"Tell me," she said by way of greeting.

He was equally terse. "Story is that Debra got a call from Jeff saying he and Gina wanted to deal. It was after nine, that's as close as anyone's come to the time. Debra turned off River Road, drove about twenty or thirty feet on Green Briar Road when someone began taking pot shots. She ran off the road, got stuck, and ducked down. Tony Mirano, next-door neighbor, drove up, got her out of the car, and hauled her to Gina's house. Debra stuck to her story when the police arrived. The usual, cops running around, car impounded, statements taken, and apparently a bunch sent to look around Jeff's place waiting for a search warrant. Before they got it, they found a revolver in some bushes outside his place and decided it probably was the gun that killed Robert. At five-thirty this morning, they got the warrant, moved in to search the apartment and to haul in Jeff. He's cooling his heels in the county jail waiting for you."

"Good God!" she said. "Where are you?"

"Holding Gina's hand more or less."

"Right. I'll talk to Jeff, sit in on questioning, and as soon as that's done, I'll join you. What about Debra? Is she still hanging around?"

"Nope. Bailey says she was escorted to the airport and put aboard her flight to L.A."

At home, Barbara dashed into the house and snatched up her briefcase. When she turned, Darren was right behind her. "I'll call just as soon as I know what's up, when I'll be free."

He kissed her lightly on the lips, took her by the shoulders and turned her around. "I know the drill," he said. "Scat."

He did understand, she knew. At one time, not too many years earlier, he had been the one to upset her routine. He had been her client, the defendant in a murder case. He really did know the drill. She hurried out and drove to the jail.

Jeff was brought to her in a small interrogation room. He looked angry, almost wild-eyed, when he came in and sat opposite her. "Just tell me what the fuck is going on," he said. "Why did they haul me in, put me in a cell? What's going on?"

"They haven't told you anything?"

"Nothing. They started asking questions and I said I wanted a lawyer. Since then not a word."

"Okay. I don't have much yet. It appears that someone took shots at Debra Valducci last night and they seem to think it was you. They found a gun near your apartment. It could match the gun that was used to shoot Robert Valducci. That's all I know."

He stared at her in disbelief. "That's crazy!"

"Maybe it is, but that's why you're sitting there and I'm sitting here. Tell me exactly what you did last night from about six on."

He continued to stare hard at her, and leaned back in his chair shaking his head. "Crazy," he said again, this time in a near whisper. He shook his head hard. "Okay. Last night. We were all working late, our group as well as a few others. Potting up plants that should have been sold and set out by customers. No customers in this ongoing rain, so we had to repot stuff. Most of the workers left a little after six. Seven, seven-thirty maybe, Greg and Daniel both left. At least another hour. Nine, nine-thirty. I don't know what time it was. Just pretty late. We—Gina and I—were both muddy, wet, cold, tired. I just wanted to get home, have a beer, a hot shower, eat something. I drove to my apartment and had a beer, had a shower, a sandwich, and I went to bed. At five-something this morning the cops came."

"Did you see anyone at your apartment? Did anyone see you?"

"I didn't see anyone. Rain, you know. I hurried inside. How the hell do I know if anyone saw me?"

"Do you own a gun? Have a permit?"

"No, to both."

"Have you ever spoken to Debra Valducci?"

"I've never even seen her except through the glass door the night Valducci was shot. Never said a word to her."

"Do you have her cell phone number?"

"No. Why would I? And by the way the cops have my cell phone."

"Did you and Gina talk about making a deal with Debra Valducci?"

"Of course not! No deal. That's settled once and for all. What are you getting at?"

"Debra Valducci said you called her, that you and Gina wanted to make a deal, and that's why she drove to the house last night. I don't know if she used the word ambush, but that's what it sounds like."

"Jesus Christ!" he said in a hoarse voice. "She's a crazy bitch! It's a lie! All of it. A lie." He had turned pale with her words, then red flared on his cheeks as his anger deepened. "Her word against mine, and she's the one with clout. It's a setup!"

"Sounds like it," Barbara said. "Now listen carefully, Jeff. In a minute I'll have to let them question you. Keep your answers as brief as possible. Yes and no work fine. Don't volunteer anything. Just tell them what you've told me. And for God's sake don't lose your temper. No name calling. Okay?"

After a moment he nodded. "Yeah," he said. "I know this scenario. But it's a setup."

"Right, but don't say that. I'll let them know they can go at it now."

It didn't take very long. Barbara sat by Jeff and he answered the same questions she had put to him. Two detectives, one she had already met at the Valducci residence, Detective Hardesty, who kept notes and referred to them before asking a question, and a second one she had never seen before and who didn't say a word during the interrogation. Jeff did exactly what she had ordered, answered each question as briefly as possible and did not raise his voice, but his body language, his expression, his tone all suggested a deep contempt and deeper anger.

When it was clear that nothing more was going to be gained by repeating questions, rephrasing questions, casting doubt on answers, Hardesty rose and turned off the tape recorder. "Mr. Cobbe, be advised to remain in the area until further notice. You're free to go now."

"I request a receipt for anything that might have been removed from Mr. Cobbe's apartment this morning," Barbara said. "His cell phone, for example."

Hardesty gave her a look of disapproval. "We removed nothing. We examined his cell phone, but we are not retaining custody of it." He nodded to his companion. "Go get it." The other one left and quickly returned with the cell phone. He handed it to Jeff without a word. Both detectives walked out at that point, leaving the door open behind them.

"You thought they'd keep the phone?" Jeff asked, rising.

"They would have if they'd found anything relating to Debra Valducci," she said. "I suppose they were also looking for a prepaid cell phone and didn't find one?"

He shook his head. "Don't have one."

"Good. Let's get out of here."

Minutes later, in her car, Jeff wiped his face and hair with a tissue. He was very wet, as was Barbara, but she had on a raincoat with a hood and that made a difference. Jeff said, "What do we call that, Act One of a surreal Kafkaesque parody?"

She gave him a pitying look, started the engine, and said, "Not Act One. Simply a prelude." Waiting for the windshield to clear, looking at Jeff, she said, "If ballistics proves that the gun they found is the same one used to kill Robert Valducci, and the same one used to shoot at Debra Valducci, and if she sticks to her statement that you called her and set up a meeting last night, no doubt they will charge you with murder and attempted murder."

He laughed a short, bitter, mirthless sound. "Barbara, if I had shot at her, she'd be dead."

"Why did you call my father and not me this morning?"

He looked startled, glanced at her, then straight ahead. "I found his card in my pocket. I must have left yours in my jacket or something."

"Jeff, do you want me to be your defense attorney? If you are uncomfortable with that, this is the time to say so."

"Sure, I do. We looked you up. No problem." His answers were fast, the words clipped. Another glance at her was swift, then back to the windshield.

It was clearing now. "Let's get me to my apartment and let me change to dry clothes. Then what? Out to the farm?"

"Absolutely out to the farm. I want to hear from Gina exactly what happened last night."

"I'll drive my own car out," he said. "And yeah, I want to hear what Gina has to say about her mother." He was facing straight ahead, but to Barbara's eye he looked as unnaturally stiff as a wooden cutout.

She put the car in drive, and headed for his apartment on Jefferson, deeply disturbed by his poorly concealed contempt for the detectives, his attitude about Debra—a woman with clout—his acknowledgment that he knew this scenario, why he stiffened up like that when he spoke about Gina, his defensiveness about calling Frank and too-quick denial about being uncomfortable with her, and, perhaps most of all, his remark that if he had wanted to shoot Debra, she would be dead.

Gina must have heard the car, Barbara thought, because the door opened before she even touched the doorbell. Datum point, she told herself.

"Where's Jeff? Is he all right? Have they arrested him?" Gina's gaze darted this way and that beyond Barbara. She was pale and looked as if she had not slept for a long time.

"He's fine," Barbara said, entering the house. "He stopped at his apartment for a shower and change of clothes. He'll be along soon." Barbara spotted Frank down the hallway and waved. "Gina, I think Jeff will be hungry and he'll definitely want coffee. Think you can manage something like that while I have a word with Dad?"

"Yes. Of course. God knows, I want to do something besides pace." She turned and walked down the hall toward the kitchen as Frank approached.

"Let's duck into the study," Barbara said, nodding toward the closed door. They entered together. She closed the door and tossed her briefcase down on the sofa and went to the wide windows, turned there and scowled at Frank, who had seated himself in one of the comfortable chairs.

"It's a goddam mess," she muttered. "They'll come after him, maybe wait for one more piece to fall into place, maybe not. But they want him. What about the gun?"

"It's the one," he said. "Ballistics came through. They had guys out with metal detectors all over that pumpkin patch this morning. They picked up some bullets, don't know yet how many. One shot went through the rear driver-side window, hit the opposite window frame, and fell to the floor, no other hits."

"I want a big watch dog out here," Barbara said. "Like the one Shelley has. This place is too big and open. And I don't want Gina alone in this house. I think all the guys should move in with her. There's plenty of room. Safety in numbers, or something."

"Good idea," Frank said. "They'll save some money if nothing else. Anything worth mentioning about Jeff?"

"No. Nothing. He went home, had a sandwich and a beer, showered, and went to bed. They woke him up and hauled him in for questioning, and he called you. Period. They had a search warrant, looking for cell phones, ammunition. Nothing found. They returned the phone."

Watching Frank's face, she added, "He called you instead of me because he had misplaced my card."

"Ah," Frank said, frowning. "Time to step aside?"

"I don't know yet. I'll talk to him at length after we both get an accounting of what happened here last night. I just can't make him out yet. Let's go see how Gina's coming. I want coffee."

"All right," Barbara said at the kitchen table where she, Frank, Jeff, and Gina had just finished off a giant frittata loaded with spinach, peas, shallots, and chopped olives. "That was wonderful, Gina. Thank you. And now, down to business. Gina, you've given a pretty good picture of how things were here last night, your mother hysterical, cops in and out, general chaos. Now, try something a little different. Try to recall exactly what your mother was saying when she gave her statement to the police. Can you do that?"

"I told you already. Things like Jeff called and wanted her to come out—"

"I know you told us that. I want to know exactly, as exact as you can recall, what she actually said to the police. I want to know what they know."

Gina flashed a glance at Jeff, then shut her eyes. "It was after Tony gave her more coffee," she said. "I think he laced it with brandy or something, the way she calmed down after drinking it." She was silent a second or two, then said, "Her words, as much as I can remember, were: 'Jeff Cobbe called me in my hotel room. He said he was Jeff Cobbe and he told me that he and Gina had come to an agreement about a settlement and wanted to talk. He asked me to come out before Gina had a chance to change her mind.'" She opened her eyes, frowning. "There was that, but there was a little more, something about the caller saying he was sorry it was so late but, because she was leaving tomorrow, it couldn't be helped."

She looked at Barbara, holding up her hands as if asking for something. "I can't remember exactly that part. I was too furious with what she was saying, what she had already said. I'm sorry."

"That's fine," Barbara said. "So it wasn't just a two- or three-word statement. It went on at some length. That's what I wanted to know. Was Mr. Mirano still here when she made her statement?"

"Yes. He stayed until the police left."

"Did he say where he had been, why he was driving at that hour?"

"A grange meeting. He drove Tom Gurley home and was on his way home himself."

"Okay. Now, what I'd like to do is talk with Jeff before you both get busy in the farm business again. Are you okay with that?" she asked, turning to Jeff, who had not spoken a single time after reassuring Gina that he was good, and telling very briefly about his questioning. Now he simply nodded.

"You could use the study," Gina said. "I'll clean up in here and then go out to the greenhouse," she added. It was not at all clear if she was saying this to Barbara or to Jeff.

"I'll help Gina and fill her in on those other matters we were discussing," Frank said.

The watchdog and having her three partners move into the house, Barbara knew. Gina might be hesitant, but Frank could be persuasive.

They all rose, and she and Jeff walked together down the wide hall to the study where Robert Valducci had been shot to death.

Despite the rain, the room was bright and even cheerful with its red sofa and chairs and lush green plants in lovely urns. Barbara nodded to the seating arrangement in front of the television, two matching easy chairs with an end table between them. She sat and drew her legal pad and her tape recorder from her briefcase. She placed the tape recorder on the table, then regarded Jeff soberly. He was standing near the other chair.

"I sense an uneasiness in you," she said, "and I need to know if it's the situation you're in causing it, or if it's me. If I'm the cause, you have to make a decision. You either want me to represent you or you don't. If you don't, now's the time to say so, before this goes any further."

He sat in the other chair, returning her gaze evenly. "You're fine," he said. "We looked you up, of course. But tell me this, Barbara, does it really matter who represents me? I have a great big target on my back. I know how they treated me both times now, how they looked at me, what they tried to get me to say."

"It matters," she said. "But we have to be perfectly clear with each other. If I am your attorney through this, you have to agree to cooperate with me, to be honest with me, and above all to tell me the truth. No suspicions, no dodging questions, obfuscation of any kind. You're right in that you are their prime suspect as of this moment. That could change, or not. They will be poring over your past, neighbors, instructors, friends, finances, whatever is readily available, and no doubt they'll be searching for something more concrete than they have now. It's pretty circumstantial at the moment, and that could change, also. They will run your name through their database for any past interactions with the law, anything on record. If the district attorney doesn't think they have enough to go to trial, they'll look for more and look deeper. I have to know what they're going to find. And I will record whatever you tell me for future reference."

His expression did not change as she spoke. "Nothing. They'll find nothing. And I understand that it's going to get personal. Tape away."

"Okay, but first there's a client-attorney agreement to sign. It spells out my duties and yours." She drew out two copies from her briefcase and handed them to him. "Read it over first, then sign it if you agree with the terms."

He shrugged and read the document. He was a fast reader, nodding now and again, frowning at something, moving on. Finished, he said, "Pen? I don't have one on me."

She handed him a pen and he signed both copies. She signed them and returned one to her briefcase. Done with that, she said, "So tell me about you."

He leaned back in his chair, his gaze on some indefinite point in the room. "Bio stuff. I'm twenty-nine. Never married. Two brothers, one thirteen years older than me, one eleven years older. Curtis, the oldest, killed in Afghanistan. Eric wounded in Iraq. Captain, resigned, PTSD, seriously damaged. My mother died when I was eleven. Lost my father when I was eighteen. He was army, too. One-star general. No other living family. Community college two years in Lancaster, PA. Penn State year and a half, bachelor of science degree. OSU the last five years. Master's degree in horticulture, working on my doctorate, a dissertation to write, done with course work. No previous run-in with the law, no tickets or warnings."

"Good," Barbara said. "That doesn't sound like a Pennsylvania accent. Have you spent time in the south?" His accent was slight, made harder to detect by the crisp way he had snapped out his brief biographical information, but it was there.

"First four years in Virginia. My mother and her parents were from Virginia. I lived with her and them in Pennsylvania from about four until Mother died. Formative years," he added with what appeared to be a touch of bitter humor.

"Finances," she said. "Debts. That kind of thing. How have you paid for your education?"

"My mother left me some money for my education. Not to be touched until I was ready for college. It was invested, grew a bit. That, part-time work, loans, scholarships, grants. I'm in debt, fifty thousand worth, and I'll have to add your fee to that."

He was openly appraising her for a reaction to his last bit. She waved it aside. "Why Oregon, OSU?"

"I wanted to work with Dr. Aaron Tideman. He's a leading expert in plant genetics. World famous. He's introduced dozens of new varieties over the years."

"GM plants? I thought you guys were against that."

"No GMO stuff. Breeding the old-fashioned way, selection of the fittest kind of thing."

Mocking her, her ignorance of the world of horticulture? It was hard to tell. There was a sardonic edge in his voice that had not been there earlier, and his gaze continued on her face, as if he was examining her closely, trying to read her as much as she was trying to read him.

"And you made the cut with this world-renowned scientist. That was quite an achievement."

"Yes, it was."

"What is your relationship with Gina?"

For the first time she seemed to have startled him, to have shaken him slightly. He hesitated for the first time, then said slowly and with deliberation, "Gina and I are colleagues, business associates, partners in the Valducci Corporation, friends. Nothing else."

"Okay. That's enough for now. The ball's in their court. Nothing for us to do except wait and see what develops. One more thing, though. Your family is military, father, two older brothers. Why not you?"

He rose from his chair. "My mother protected me. She said he couldn't have her last son..."

He crossed the room and had his hand on the doorknob when she asked, "Jeff, what did you mean, back there at the police station, when you said you know this scenario?"

Facing her from across the room, he said, "You give little people a title, a uniform, badge, gun, whatever symbol of power is at hand, and you give them the legal right to exact punishment, anything from a slap on the hand to the ultimate punishment of death, to anyone who doesn't yield to that power and authority, and you create a system of tyranny. It's not an unfamiliar scenario. We see it played out over and over. I really should go to work now." Without waiting for a response, he turned, opened the door, and walked away swiftly.

"How it was," Tony Mirano was saying in the kitchen, "my grandparents, or maybe great-grandparents, came over about 1890, along with Luigi Valducci and his wife Anna. He took this parcel and we got the one next to it. My grandmother brought dried apples with her. Italians always make sure there's going to be something to eat wherever they go. Apples, cheese, wine, makings of pasta, garlic, olive oil."

They were sitting at the kitchen table. Gina had gone back out to the greenhouse, and no one else was present. Frank had suggested that Tony Mirano might want to talk to Barbara, if he had time, and they had settled down where they were most comfortable, in the kitchen.

"Anyways, there were half a dozen seeds in those dried apples and they planted them, and what we now call Tuscan Gold flourished. It's the world's best apple. We think so. They expanded, put in an orchard, a dozen varieties now, but Tuscan Gold is still the best. Limited supplies, though. Locals buy all we can produce, but other people, they want named varieties they recognize. Red Delicious, the biggest waste of ground space there ever was. Fuji. Granny Smith." He stopped speaking as Barbara walked into the kitchen, and both men rose.

"Hi, Dad," she said. "I thought you had left."

"Nope. Talking with Tony here. Barbara, Tony Mirano, next-door neighbor who was here after the shooting last night. Tony, my daughter, Barbara. She represents Jeff. Tony came to make sure Gina was all right."

They shook hands and sat down again as Barbara pulled out a chair to join them. Mirano was a slightly built man, wiry, gray haired, with deeply tanned, almost leathery skin. His eyes were dark, his eyebrows thick, flecked with gray. He was dressed in jeans, boots, a plaid shirt, all well-worn, the jeans almost to the point of threadbare. His probing gaze was shrewd as he studied Barbara.

"You'll want to know about last night," he said. "Frank said I should wait and tell you both at the same time. Good thinking. You tell the same story over and over and it begins to sound like something you memorized out of a book."

Barbara agreed. "You've got that right. And of course, I want to hear your story."

There was nothing she had not already learned. He had driven a friend home from a grange meeting, saw Debra's car off the road, assisted her and got her inside the house. Ten, he said, by the time they were both inside. She had not stopped screaming yet, he had added, not until the police came, and he had given her a good shot of bourbon in coffee.

"Did you see a car, anyone on foot?" Barbara asked.

"No one. No car. Just her off the road."

"Did you hear what she reported to the police?"

"Sure, it was all she said from the time I got her parked on the couch until they took her to her hotel. She kept saying Jeff called her and said to come on out for a talk, that they wanted to settle things. But that was a lie. Jeff didn't want to settle with her, and neither did Gina. Not last night. Not ever."

"You approve of their plans for this acreage?"

"One hundred percent," he said without hesitation. "Look, Ms. Holloway, my orchard's right next door to this farm. We share the boundary line. Last fall we started planting what's going to be nice hedge row, all native plants, twenty feet wide, the length of our borders. Me, my son Johnny, Gina and her boys, all of us dug and planted. We got about three hundred feet planted, and we put in trees every hundred feet. Oregon plants, natives. Ten feet on my side, ten feet on this side. Our hedge row. It means year-round shelter and food for God's creatures, birds, bugs, and animals, big and small.

"Right now my trees are safe from poison sprays, both foliage sprays and poisons in the earth itself, safe from strange modified organisms, super bugs, and super weeds, and I want to keep them that way. I have colonies of mason bees that pollinate my trees and I want to keep them thriving and multiplying the way nature intends for them. Bees don't recognize property lines. If there's nectar, pollen, they'll find it, poisoned or not. Others around here feel the same. Sure, a lot of us approve, and I personally know for a fact that Jeff would not make any deal with any company into all that genetic modification business. Neither would Gina. I've known her from the time she was a barefoot toddler with pigtails, out there picking peas and eating them from the vine. She's Magda made over, and Magda would have taken on an army to defend her land."

His speech was long and fervent from start to finish. Now he rose and said, "If you want a sworn statement or anything from me or my wife, my son, any of us, you just have to ask." He looked at Frank and nodded. "I know you got a statement from Sophia about that will business. If you want more, we'll be here."

"Well," Barbara said after Tony Mirano had left, "he looks as if he would take up arms to defend his property, too. I think I'll have Bailey find out when that grange meeting ended, when he dropped off his friend, how far away that was."

Frank nodded. He would have suggested exactly that if she had not spoken first.

"And that's it," Barbara told Shelley that afternoon in her office. "It could get big and ugly, or it could dry up on the vine and be nothing. Waiting time."

"I can see about a dog. I'll call Philip, the trainer who brought out ours."

"Maybe you could meet him there," Barbara suggested. "Get to know our client, get to know Gina. I imagine she'd talk to you. There's something going on with her and Jeff, and I'd like to know what it is. Or was, if that's the case. Debra thinks he's behind everything, that he'll get the girl, the farm, the whole shebang if he isn't found guilty of murdering her husband."

Shelley dimpled, the way she did, making her look like a coddled and brainless beautiful blonde from an exclusive and pricey college. That image was a lie, but a useful lie, Barbara often acknowledged. Shelley was a hell of a fine attorney. If anyone could get Gina to loosen up and talk about her personal life, it would be Shelley. With Barbara, Gina was still on guard, still aware of running up attorney fees she could not afford, and still generally afraid because she was so uncertain of what each day was going to bring. She was too close to shock caused by the deaths of her grandmother and her murdered father, having her mother targeted. Shelley could get past those mind-numbing concerns with a quick smile. She could play the part and lead the talk, just two sorority sisters utterly failing the Bechdel test, which was designed to demonstrate that in movies and television dramas, whenever two named women shared a scene they talked about something other than men. Barbara wanted Gina to talk about a man.

Gina sank down into the full tub of just hot enough water, leaving only her head above the water line. It was late, after eleven, but she had waited until there was enough hot water for a long soak. Crazy days, crazy nights so dream laden that she sometimes felt as if she had not slept at all. She and the boys were working hard, such long hours, making up for the handful of employees who had left since they had to be paid on time or give up eating. And there wasn't enough money coming in to pay them. Not enough to pay Jeff, Greg, or Daniel, or her. Money would come in later; invoices would be sent out, bills paid, but slowly. Too slowly. The money she had inherited from her grandmother would come eventually, but it wasn't there yet.

She shook her head. She had promised herself not to think of the bad things, to condition herself to be relaxed and ready for bed and deep sleep by the time the water cooled. Greg, she said under her breath. He had held out when she proposed having them all move into the house, each with a private bedroom, the run of the house, share expenses, cooking, cleaning… He had looked at the floor, looked at his hands, looked anywhere except at her and mumbled something about his mother. At twenty-two, secretly gay, which was not a secret to anyone who knew him except his father, he lived at home where his mother was determined to keep him. Maybe she knew, maybe not, Gina had no idea, but she held on to him and he let her. Then Rusty happened.

Shelley had come at the same time a large Irish man had arrived, Philip Halloran. And Philip had a big dog on a leash. "He's a mutt," he had said cheerfully. "Not quite two-years old, part lab, part border collie maybe, part alligator, all heart, and plenty smart. Name's Rusty." The dog was buff, black, and white, with a plume of a tricolored tail.

Philip had suggested that he and the dog, along with Gina and Shelley, make a tour of the property, get an idea of how much of it Rusty would be asked to guard. "Not all of it," Philip had said with good humor. "Too big.

Let's take a walk. If you ladies will give us a little space, I'll explain things to Rusty as we go."

It was a long walk around the periphery of the farm. Gina and Shelley hung back, unable to hear more than a soft word now and then as Philip kept up a steady conversation with Rusty. Now and then the dog stopped to pee. "Just marking the boundary," Philip said the first time it happened. "A cautionary note to visitors, coons, other dogs, deer, rabbits, possums. Just a friendly message that there's a dog around."

"Is he okay with you?" Shelley asked Gina as they walked. "I don't think he'd win a beauty prize."

"He's just right," Gina said. "A comic-book dog is just what we need, if he's as good as Philip says he is."

"The dog he provided us is tops," Shelley said. "We absolutely rely on him, and we're sort of out in the middle of nowhere even more than you are here." They watched Rusty mark another spot. "Tell me about the guys," Shelley said. "Did they agree to move on out here?"

"Jeff and Daniel both jumped at the chance. Daniel has a girlfriend who seems to be pushing him for a commitment he isn't ready to make, but he doesn't have enough money to move into a separate apartment. He was feeling pretty guilty about the situation, I think. And Jeff really needs to cut expenses to the bone. This gives him that opportunity. Greg?" She laughed softly and shook her head. "I don't know who he's more afraid of, his father, his mother, generally men in suits. If his mother nixes the idea, it's a no-go for him. His father is a million-a-year ophthalmologist and they give him a school boy's allowance and treat him like a kid. He's really quite brilliant as long as it's computers he's dealing with." She paused and drew in a long breath. She cast a sidelong glance at Shelley, then away.

"I was in love with Greg for a few months when I first met him. His face is so beautiful. Don't you think so?"

"Absolutely. He could pose for artists. But then?"

"I got to know him," Gina said. "Now, just friends. He never had a clue about my crush on him."

"What about Jeff?" Shelley asked then. "Those three are so different one from another, aren't they? Does Jeff have a girlfriend?"

Gina had stiffened slightly but she shrugged and tried to keep the same light tone she had assumed when talking about the other two members of her group. "I don't think he has time for a girlfriend," she said.

Shelley nodded. "My husband was like that, all work, and serious stuff, no time for anything frivolous. I threw myself at him over and over before he even noticed me. It worked out," she added, holding up her left hand with her simple wedding ring. She never wore her dazzling engagement ring at work.

"You? How could he not notice you?" Gina said in disbelief.

"Self-discipline," Shelley said promptly. "I think some men give themselves orders not to be distracted, and they have enough discipline to follow those orders for a long time."

In the bathtub, Gina felt her face grow hot as she thought how those words from Shelley had opened a gate she had thought firmly locked. How she had talked about Jeff. She had thrown herself at him, waving her midterm paper with a big red A on it. Gushing about how she had won over Aaron Tideman with the paper. Not a red mark on it, except the A. She would have her master's degree in three months! She wanted to go out and celebrate. Jeff had taken her by the shoulders and pushed her away.

"Congratulations," he had said and walked away, leaving her hurt, disappointed, confused, furious. All the above, she had told herself then, and repeated now in the bathtub. She doubted that she had been close enough to touch him since then. Always keeping a safe distance, polite to the point of being ridiculous with each other, yet bound together by a shared vision that neither could put aside.

She shook her head hard, let out some water, and turned on the hot water again to replace it. Greg, she told herself. Remember how Greg had greeted the comic-book dog.

Philip had asked for them all to gather to hear his instructions regarding the guard dog's duties, what commands they needed to know, what area was to be guarded. Jeff and Daniel were already in the house when Greg arrived, dirty and tired as usual. He saw Rusty and stopped just inside the kitchen door.

"Hey!" he said. "You're a funny looking mutt!"

"Friend," Philip said softly, and Rusty advanced to Greg with his plume of a tail wagging.

Greg dropped to his knees to greet the dog. He wrapped his arms around the animal and whispered something inaudible. After a moment he released Rusty and stood up. His eyes were moist.

"You've had a dog before?" Philip asked.

"Yeah. When I was a little kid, four, five, something like that. I haven't thought of him in years. He got fleas and vanished. I never learned what happened to him. No one would talk about it." His boyish face hardened, then relaxed. He knew damn well what happened, it was clear. His mother had gotten rid of a flea-ridden nuisance. No one spoke then, but he looked at Gina and said, "By the way, I'm in. I'll move my gear tomorrow."

Rusty was already his best friend, Gina knew, as she reluctantly opened the drain of the bath tub, as little ready to fall asleep as she had been when she stepped into it.

"It's been ten days since someone tried to kill Mother," she whispered to herself, toweling her back vigorously. "If they planned to arrest Jeff, they would have done it by now."

It was not a prayer, she had told herself on day one, the first time she had reassured herself that all was well. Day by day she repeated it, encouraged by the advancing number, now up to ten.

On day eleven Jeff was arrested, charged with the murder of Robert Valducci, and the attempted murder of Debra Valducci.

The assistant district attorney, Sheila Weinburg, was forty-something, a compact, sturdily built woman who looked comfortable in her severely tailored gray suit, with a gray blouse a shade lighter and no jewelry except a heavy gold watch. Barbara wondered how she could look so comfortable since the blouse appeared to be heavily starched and ironed, as did her blonde hair. Starched and ironed, straight, shoulder length, it looked like a pale helmet. She had two children, Barbara knew, a son and a daughter, one eight, one ten. They would be good children, obedient, polite, respectful. They would not dare be anything else.

A twelve-year veteran in the DA's office, Sheila Weinburg did not engage in discursive monologs. In the courtroom that morning she came to the point succinctly and decisively. "We believe that Mr. Cobbe is at risk of fleeing. He has no connections here, no family here, no real reason for being in the state, other than his educational experience. Now that is concluded, except for a dissertation. There is nothing here to keep him. We argue that he should be held in the county jail awaiting trial." She sat down and busied herself with papers before her, as if the matter were settled.

Barbara rose. "Your Honor, Mr. Cobbe's record is without blemish, spotless. He has never been charged or even suspected of any criminal or civil crime or misbehavior. At the age of seventeen Mr. Cobbe started his long educational journey, with one vision guiding him all the way to the present, a doctorate in horticulture. He worked part-time, made high grades that rewarded him with scholarships and grants along the way, and he won a coveted spot with a world-class horticulturist at Oregon State University... His vision as a freshman at a community college and now as a graduate student was to create a process, a method, if you will, that results in a self-reliant and sustainable farm that will provide seeds, plants, and produce for a local community.

"Without arguing about the cause of global warming, it is generally acknowledged that it is happening and it is imperative that we strive to ameliorate its effects. Today two-thirds of California is under a catastrophic drought, and California produces forty percent of the produce grown in this country. As the drought worsens and temperatures continue to rise, more and more farmers are being forced to abandon their fields, let them lie fallow. Mr. Cobbe and his colleagues are positioning themselves to make up for the loss of the imported produce that California will no longer be able to provide. This is not a quick fix, done in a single season; it is a long-term investment of time, talent, and grueling hard work. It is not a vision to be embarked on lightly. Mr. Cobbe is the guiding force in seeing that vision realized, today, tomorrow, and into the future...."

She glanced at Sheila Weinburg, who looked as if she could barely contain her impatience with this long discourse. Her lips were pursed and a frown deeply creased her forehead. She was glaring at the judge and at Barbara, back and forth, back and forth.

Maybe she had a luncheon engagement, Barbara thought, and her stomach was growling, aching. Maybe a hunger headache was pounding. Keeping her words reasonable, speaking almost conversationally, she continued. "It would serve no purpose to keep Mr. Cobbe incarcerated at this time. He is needed at the farm, working with and guiding others to fulfill his mission. I propose house arrest and an electronic monitor with a range of mobility that includes his greenhouse and residence, the surrender of his driver's license and his automobile. Mr. Cobbe is virtually penniless, with no one to call upon for financial assistance for flight. He is not a flight risk. He is a dedicated scientist and farmer who wants to do only what is right."

Sheila Weinburg objected. "Snow packs, climate change, farms are not what this hearing is about, Your Honor. It is about whether or not Mr. Cobbe is a flight risk. My office believes absolutely that he is."

Judge Poynter disagreed.

‡

"It helped that Dad knows Judge Poynter is as avid a backyard gardener as he himself is," Barbara commented outside the courtroom when Gina threw her arms about her and thanked her profusely. She extricated herself from Gina's arms. "They'll take him to the farm, determine what is more or less a central point, pace off the distance to the greenhouse and residence, put the anklet on him and that will be that. They'll warn him that if he steps outside his boundary for thirty seconds they'll be on him like a swarm of ants, and off to jail he'll go. But it's better than being in a cell for the next five months."

"My God, yes! You were wonderful!" Gina said again. "Without him we'd be floundering around thinking big things could happen, but not knowing how to make them happen. You knew that, didn't you?"

Barbara was not certain that she had known that. She was not even certain that it was true. But what she was sure of now was that the barrier Gina had erected earlier had been demolished, and that was a good thing.

"Go on out to the farm," she said. "Keep out of the way when they bring Jeff home, and make damn sure that Rusty doesn't attack the cops. I'll come around later and we'll talk. Now, scoot. Later, after lunch."

"Good job," Frank said after Gina left. "She's demonstrative, isn't she?"

"Emotional, demonstrative, probably hot tempered, and smart," Barbara said as they walked from the courthouse to the parking garage. "I can imagine how it was when she threw herself at Jeff and he backed off, alarmed and stiff as a post. Well," she continued, "I'm going to take a long walk and try to think of what my next move will be. I have Bailey digging into neighbors and grange people, but for me, nothing. I might take up knitting." She ignored Frank's laughter. "Until I get discovery I don't have a clue about what they came up with to make it seem enough of a case to go to trial. Bailey hasn't been able to find out yet. Apparently Weinburg runs a tight ship, no leaks. Wanna bet she keeps a whip on display in her office?" Frank laughed harder. "And all I have going for the defense," she added, "is Jeff's statement: 'I didn't do it.'"

"About the shape you're usually in at this stage," Frank said. They had reached the parking garage, and he turned toward downtown. "You walk by the river. I'll walk to the office. See you later."

He had kept a light tone with Barbara, but as he walked toward his office, Frank's thoughts were bleak and heavy. He had considered one of the grange fellows as a possible killer, had considered Tony Mirano, and he had dismissed them all. A man or a woman might fight like a tiger to hold onto his or her land, but kill to keep someone else's land from the grabbers? That was a hard sell. Tony Mirano might have remained in the suspect basket, Frank mused, in order to protect his apples, except he appeared to have a solid alibi for the night of Robert Valducci's murder. Tony had been home with his wife, his son, his daughter-in-law, and a twelve-year-old grandchild. A damned good, persuasive alibi.

Weinburg would fight to keep out of the trial all attempts to introduce the kids' vision of a sustainable farm, feeding the local community, global climate change, the coming disaster. She could mock those ideas as the idealistic dreams of youth, abstractions, distractions. Don Quixote's dragons. It wouldn't be too hard since the reality of the kids' vision touched on fears few people wanted to think about, much less do anything about. She would help the jury dismiss that reality. She would concentrate on motive and opportunity. He could write the script himself: By the time of the trial, Gina would have the farm that was worth millions, and Jeff would get Gina. Or Gina would get Jeff, however that worked out, same thing. Case closed.

Barbara had forgotten to pick up something for lunch, and she had walked until her thighs were afire. And absolutely nothing was the result of starvation and cruel and unusual punishment, she told herself as she pulled into the drive of the Valducci house. The dog Rusty greeted her with his ridiculous, tricolored tail pumping furiously, his tongue hanging out almost obscenely, and a big dog smile on his face.

Gina opened the door before Barbara had a chance to ring the bell. "I told the boys that I'd call them in the minute you showed up," she said by way of greeting. She had already hit a speed-dial button. "She's here," she said. "Greg and Daniel are out in the field, Jeff's in the greenhouse. They'll get him on their way in. Do you want coffee?"

"Yes indeed. Were you watching for my car, or did you hear it?"

"I heard it on the cobblestones. I have pretty good hearing, I guess. Cars make a certain noise when they hit the stones, different from the concrete drive." She was leading the way to the kitchen as she spoke. "I thought we'd meet in here," she said, pointing to the table as they entered. "The boys will be dirty. Lots of mud out there from all the recent rain, but a kitchen can take a lot of mud and dirt. God knows I've hauled in more than my share over the years."

Barbara touched her arm. "Gina, relax. Take it easy. Okay?"

"I'm so scared," Gina said. "That woman this morning. The way she looked at Jeff, as if he were vermin. The way the police treated him when they came. They put the anklet on too tight, and he didn't say a word. I told them it was too tight, that I'd call you if they didn't loosen it. I was afraid of what he might say if he let go. He was like a carved man, but ready to explode. And I can't blame him. I'm ready to explode."

"Not on my watch," Barbara said. "Neither of you will explode on my watch. Now, was that offer of coffee real, or a tease? Did they loosen the anklet?"

Gina nodded. "He said it was okay. Do you use sugar or cream? I have half and half if you want it."

"Just black," Barbara said. She sat at the table and pulled out her legal pad where she had written notes to refer to that afternoon. Soon after Gina brought her coffee, the three other corporate members arrived. As Gina had said, Greg and Daniel were both dirty, and they both took off their boots on the back porch and left them there. Jeff was unmuddied. His monitor didn't stretch as far as the fields. After they were all seated, they sat looking at Barbara as children might look at a teacher, waiting for instructions.

"Jeff," she said, "first things first. Do you still have things in your downtown apartment? Have you notified your landlord that you won't be back, anything like that?"

"Sure," he said. "Books, papers, clothes. A desk and chair. A blanket."

She held up her hand, stopping him. "Right. Someone has to clear out everything, leave it spotless. Did you pay first and last month, a damage deposit?"

He nodded. "May would be the last month, already paid for. There's no damage."

Greg spoke up then. "Daniel and I can go clean it all out. Use a truck?" he said, turning to Gina.

"Of course."

"Give me a call when you're done," Barbara said. "I'll go by and take pictures and get the landlord to refund the damage deposit and last month. If possible," she added. "Sometimes they cooperate, sometimes they don't. We'll see. I'll need a name and number for that."

She glanced at her scant notes. "Next, I want to spend some time with each of you tomorrow and into the following day if it takes that long. I need to know exactly what each of you has already told the police."

"But the trial won't be for months," Daniel said. "Why now, not later?"

"Now it's fresh in your minds. Look, some of the officers are pretty good at interrogating amateurs. They can make statements and sort of get you to agree, all friendly, palsy-walsy, buddy-buddy stuff. Months from now the DA will have your agreements to refer to. Mr. Smith, did you not tell Officer Jones that the defendant has a terrible temper? Mr. Smith denies it and the DA reads from the officer's notes that indeed Mr. Smith agreed with something or other that led to that conclusion."

Daniel blushed and looked down at the table. Barbara stifled a sigh, wishing he had not done that. "What I will need," she said, "is for each of you to think back through every time you were asked anything, try to remember exactly what you said, what was asked."

She looked at Gina then. "Same for you, but more. From the first time your father came here, everything he said and did. Everything that he and Tilsen said to each other, to you, to anyone. You have acute hearing, there may be something that you simply have forgotten, or thought unimportant."

Finally, she turned to Jeff. "Same for you, and again, more. I'll want a list of schools, locations, instructors, your transcriptions, jobs. What kind, where, with whom? A complete fill-in of your past."

Jeff's expression appeared frozen in a distant, disapproving way. Although he was gazing at her, Barbara thought it was as if he were seeing something alien, unknowable, and possibly repellent.

Impatiently she said, "Jeff, that's the kind of material they will gather. I have to have it, too. I don't want to be blindsided midway through a trial. You have to accept that as soon as anyone becomes a defendant in a murder trial, all secrets are up for grabs."

His expression changed subtly. She realized that although his gaze had been directed her way, he had been seeing something else, not her. He blinked and now he was seeing her, and he was nodding. There was a hint of sarcasm in his voice when he said, "Whatever you say, Barbara. I can teach you how to garden, you can teach me how to be a defendant in a murder trial."

"That's it for today," Barbara said, rising. "Tomorrow? Around ten?"

The others were getting up, moving chairs, nodding. Jeff walked to the kitchen door where he paused and looked back at Barbara. "I know you're a gambler, but are you also a betting person? Doesn't matter. I'd bet you a ten spot that Sheila Weinburg is a veteran and that she made sergeant."

"What's all that?" Darren asked that night, pointing to a box that Barbara had just opened.

He was seated in an easy chair across the coffee table from her, positioned in the center of the sofa. In the kitchen the dishwasher was making its getting-the-job-done sounds.

"Paperwork," she said. "Articles, books, pamphlets, printouts, journals, magazines. God knows what all. Two categories," she continued, "GMO modifications and climate change. First thing is to divide it. Two piles." She patted the sofa on her left and right. "Jeff was putting it all together and when the kids went to clean out his apartment, they found this and dropped it off at the office. Busywork."

"Enough for you and a couple of others," Darren said. He picked up a book he had dog-eared and opened it.

That he didn't offer to help was a blessing, Barbara knew, and she was grateful for the fact that he knew it also. He really could not help without having been with it from the start. When she first moved in with him, he had made it clear that he would never interfere with her work, never complain about her hours or her sometimes obsessive preoccupation with a case. Or complain about her cooking, she added to herself. She knew he would never offer to help but would be there if she asked for help. Sometimes she wondered how it was that she had found a man with his patience, his understanding, his love. He knew where the boundary lines were and respected them. She felt certain at times that nothing in her life, nothing she had ever done, let her deserve him. At those times she hastily closed that door.

She was startled later when Darren asked softly, "That bad?"

She looked up from an open journal that she had not been seeing. Darren was regarding her with a slight frown.

"You've been staring at that page for minutes," he said.

"It's bad," she said in a low voice. "You know, we see a mention in the news, a short article in the newspaper or online, and we pay so little attention. There's too much to do, jobs, shopping, what to make for dinner, when's the next dentist appointment. We move on. We might change lightbulbs, buy an energy efficient this or that, and pat ourselves on the back because we're doing something. We worry about smokestacks when it's a true global crisis looming. It's too big to think about, to worry about, so we don't, except we really do. We just don't talk about it. Existential fear seems to be driving the world, all of us, crazy. It's too big, too much, we're too little. It's like trying to kill an elephant with a peashooter."

"It's worse than you know," Todd said from the doorway.

Barbara and Darren both jerked around to see him. He had a sandwich in one hand, a glass of milk in the other. A child, a boy-man on his way to becoming a climatologist, he would graduate high school in a few weeks with many college credits already earned. Then an internship for the summer with a NASA group studying climate change. On to Stanford in the fall.

"There's a new model coming out," Todd said. "It says that we're in for a megadrought that will last for thirty-five to fifty years, and it will stretch from California to the Mississippi River and up into the Plains states, the Great Basin and the east front of the Rockies. It will be like the one that wiped out the Pueblo people in about 1300 or so. They had a great civilization, a thousand years old, with aqueducts, orchards, farms, livestock, plenty of food, and they occupied parts of California, Utah, Arizona, New Mexico, then they vanished. Megadrought wiped them out." He took a step away from the door. "Where will people go when the full effect of a new megadrought hits? Great Lakes region, New England, up the west coast into Canada, on to Alaska. Millions might be forced to move. Good night."

He left, on his way to the basement den he had claimed as his bedroom, study, play room. Neither Barbara nor Darren moved or spoke for an extended time. Finally, she closed the journal and placed it on her side with several others. She stood and now looked at Darren. "Will they despise us, hate us for what we've done? What we'll leave for them to endure?"

Darren's big open face that could never hide anything looked stricken. He rose and held out his hand for her. "They'd have a right," he said.

She had known sleep would be elusive, Barbara thought much later. Nearly three o'clock and she was wide awake. Beside her, Darren snored softly, lying on his back. When she moved, he shifted to his side and the snoring stopped. She got out of bed carefully, picked up her robe, groped with her feet for slippers and gave them up as unfindable in the dark, and she walked from the bedroom, down the hall to the stairs, down to the kitchen. A hallway night-light was enough, she decided, and sat at the table in the dim, cool kitchen with a glass of water.

Darren's words echoed and reechoed in her head. "They'd have a right." Agreed, she told that voice. For Todd, a trip with Darren to observe melting glaciers had been the tipping point to turn him into a believer, to make him declare his future, to become a climatologist.

What had happened to Jeff to turn him into a nascent farmer with a goal to save as many people from starvation as he possibly could? That was his real goal, she told herself. He had seen what was coming, what it meant, and he had determined what he could do about it personally. She had seen it as zealotry, and maybe it was, but his cause was undeniably real.

Mitigation, meaningful mitigation of the coming crisis, had to be governmental, globally governmental, and around the world the politicians failed to take action, while too many denied the reality of climate change itself, or its cause. Some even rejoiced, seeing it as the beginning of the end of days with the second coming sure to follow.

Petrochemical farming was not the answer, Jeff had stated. It was part of the problem. Making farmers dependent on giant corporations to supply seeds, fertilizers, weed killers, disease control would be catastrophic in itself if transportation failed, if martial law had to be declared when masses of people began to run out of water in the States and worldwide. Coming water wars, a joke in the past, now assumed a reality of its own. That would happen, Barbara thought, sipping her own water. Megadrought, she thought, pronouncing it in her head.

So, Jeff was right, she told herself. It was right to be in touch with similar groups spread throughout the globe, sharing information, practical advice, warning of mistakes, making the most of the social media available.

And Jeff was the driving force behind the Valducci Corporation, whose mission statement included that its intent was to provide food for the immediate valley community. Whatever else, Jeff had to be cleared of the murder charge lodged against him. She had no other suspects to investigate. Robert had not lived in the area for nearly eight years, and neither had Debra. Who could have held a grudge that long? More important, the killer had to have known about Jeff, about the deal being offered, and that excluded anyone from a distant past or anyone who might have followed Robert from Chicago. She knew she was making the prosecution's case, but it couldn't be helped. That's where the case was.

At three-thirty that night she admitted that she didn't know if Jeff had shot and killed Robert Valducci, or if he had shot at Debra Valducci. "If he did," she whispered, "he was justified."

She stood abruptly, caught the half-filled glass before it tumbled to the floor, and held onto the back of her chair, momentarily off-balance from her sudden rise. She thought about where her musings had taken her, and she nodded.

"See, I didn't think he was interrogating me or anything."

Gregory looked at Barbara with a despairing expression. He seemed almost ready to cry. They were in the red chairs in the Valducci study, and he was as awkward and shy as a middle-school kid alone with his first real girlfriend. Or maybe boyfriend, she thought. "I know how it goes," she said. "Just tell me what you said, what he said."

"After you told us, you know, like they'll pretend to be pals or something, and I didn't think he was really asking questions or anything. I didn't realize…"

"Greg, I know their tricks. What did you say to him?"

He swallowed hard and looked at his hands. "Right. I was repotting some transplants, broccoli. He was watching me. Not in uniform. The other guys were in the house questioning Jeff, or waiting for you to get here, or something. Anyway, he began to talk about Gina, said she was really hot, a knockout, and he bet all the guys were after her. It was after Valentine's Day and I'd made a card that everybody signed. It said 'Everybody loves Gina' and we all signed it because everybody does love her, you know. Ten, fifteen of us signed it. Maybe more. I said something like that, everybody loves Gina. And he says something like, even Jeff Cobbe? Does he love her, too? And I said sure he does, everybody does."

He glanced up from his hands to her face, and he looked guilty as hell, anguished, contrite, and she had to fight the urge to pat him. "Anything else?" she asked.

"No. I didn't say anything else. I was real busy and I just wanted him to go away."

"Good. No harm done. That's what I wanted to know." She almost said, you can run along now, but she caught it before it was vocalized. Instead, she rose and held out her hand for an adult-to-adult handshake. "Thanks, Greg. That's helpful. If you see Jeff, will you ask him to come on in?"

He left hurriedly and she walked to the desk and pondered the difference in it since Greg had moved into the Valducci house. Big, almost bare and polished to a high shine before, the desk now was covered with computer components. Apparently his parents had denied him nothing in the way of computers, speakers, and other equipment that she didn't recognize. The desk held three monitors, four keyboards, a mouse plugged in to one of the computers, headsets; snake nests of cords and wires were on the floor on one side. This was Gregory's domain.

"Pretty incredible, isn't it?" Jeff said from the open door. He was carrying a tray that contained a pitcher of water with ice, two glasses, a thermos, and a mug. "Gina sent it," he said, coming into the room. He put the tray down on the table between the two red chairs. "She said you take your coffee black."

"Everybody loves Gina," Barbara murmured, going to the tray. She poured steaming coffee.

"He confessed to us last night," Jeff said. "Did you pat him on the head?"

She laughed. "I wanted to, but I resisted." She took her place in one of the chairs.

"He's really a genius with all that stuff," Jeff said, indicating the desk. "But now, to business." He drew a folded paper from his pocket and sat down. "I thought it would save time if I made a list of schools, addresses, dates, whatever I could remember. Some names of teachers, not many, because I wasn't paying a lot of attention back in the day, more as I made my way through academia. All yours."

She took the paper he held out, and she thought that, although seemingly friendly and even cooperative, he couldn't have been more distant if he were standing out in the middle of the farthest field. She examined the lines of events. From birth until four he had lived in Fairfax. Four to eleven, Lancaster, elementary school there. Eleven to twelve, again in Fairfax. Twelve to sixteen, a boarding school, Ridge Academy, New York state, near Rochester. Sixteen to eighteen, Lancaster, community college. Penn State…

There were names under some of the locations, not many. How many names of teachers could she recall from years ago, she asked herself. She came up with a single word: few. Some of the names listed had check marks, others had crosses. Warning: Don't go there?

"Okay," she said. "Now let's fill in some holes. Did your parents divorce when you were four or five?"

"She left him, no divorce. She took me to live with her parents in Lancaster. It had been a farm, but they sold off most of it in lots, and were down to an acre. We had a big garden and chickens."

"Was your father abusive to her? To you? Your brothers?"

"Not to my mother, not that I knew. Just words. Arguments. He was a disciplinarian, not a wife beater, if that's what you mean. I don't know how he was with my brothers. They were in school when I was little, and then we left."

"That's exactly what I mean. Disciplined how?"

Jeff seemed even more distant as he regarded her without any readable expression whatsoever. "He had a thin wand that he called his switch. He would order me to go get his switch and he'd whip my bare butt with it. When Mother found out, we left. Period."

"What does that mean, when she found out? Didn't she know what he was doing?"

"Usually she'd be out shopping or something. He said if I told her, he'd punish me again, harder. Then she came home one day and saw it." His expression didn't change as he said this, and from the tone of his voice he could have been talking about watching birds at a feeder.

Filling some holes, he said his mother had died of pancreatic cancer and the day after her funeral his father had come for him.

"At that time when you were eleven you lived with your father for something like seven months," Barbara said. "Tell me about that. You were in the sixth grade."

He shook his head. "I have little memory of that year," he said after a moment. "I guess I acted out a lot. Was disciplined a lot. Ran away once and was hauled back. Then he took me to Ridge Academy. It was named after a Civil War general, by the way."

"A military academy? At twelve?" A name with a cross was listed under it. Major Rudebacher.

He nodded. "I think my father ordered them to make a man of me." His gaze shifted from somewhere over her shoulder to her face briefly, then away again. "You really don't want to know a lot about those years. Let's let it go at this. Academically I was an A student. I failed in everything else."

"Okay. One question. Were you expelled or did you run away?"

"I left at sixteen. It wasn't running away. I'd learned that didn't work. I wasn't expelled. I just left. I packed my things and told them I was leaving and that was that. I think they were relieved to see the end of me. I believe the major was on the phone to my father as I walked out the door. It didn't matter since I didn't leave a forwarding address." A hint of a smile softened his face for a brief moment. "I had enough credits for high school graduation and I didn't see any need to stay for more than that."

Right, she thought. One day they would come back to his years in a military academy for children, but not this day, she decided. She asked more questions and he filled in more blanks. He drank water and she drank hot black coffee. When he had lived with his mother and grandparents, he had become friends with a yard man, a landscaper, and when he left the academy he had turned to that old friend. His grandparents, devastated by the death of their daughter and the loss of their grandson, had sold their property and moved to Tucson where they both had died within a year of each other. He had offered his services to the landscaper, and told him that he intended to go to the community college in the fall, but he needed a summer job and a place to sleep. He had worked for him until he finished his two years at the college.

Here the name Jake Munro had a check mark by it.

She asked about his brothers then. "Were you in touch with them at all?"

He shook his head and poured another glass of water, keeping his gaze on this small task. "I read that Curtis had been killed and I went to the funeral. I was seventeen. Remember, Barbara, he was thirteen years older than me. Eric is eleven years older than I am. I never really knew either of them. But I went to the funeral at Arlington and Eric caught up with me. He was in uniform, of course. My father in uniform, a raft of uniforms there, and I was wearing a windbreaker and jeans. I didn't own a suit." He took a long drink. "I was staying way back, not in the group at the grave, but I saw my father and Eric, and they saw me. My father's face turned stroke-red, and as soon as Eric could get away, he hurried to me and grabbed my arm. He said we should get out of there and we did. He took me to a diner and told me about the money my mother had left for my education, the name of the law firm handling it. He begged me to keep in touch even if only a card now and then. He was due to return to Iraq in a week."

That was the last time he had seen his father, he said. He had gone to the law firm in Lancaster and they had handled a lot of paperwork for him, opened a bank account, and the day he turned eighteen, they had deposited the money, thirty-four thousand dollars. It meant, he said, that he could go to Penn State, pay in-state tuition with the money he had already saved up, and this money plus a part-time job would be enough to get him through a year at OSU to work on his master's degree.

"Did you and Eric keep in touch?" Barbara asked.

"Christmas cards," he said. "Five years ago the army notified me that he had been wounded. He had given them my name. I flew back east to see him at Walter Reed. He's totally fucked. Head wound, lots of shrapnel in his legs, some in his head. PTSD. Shrapnel," he said bitterly. "Small, very sharp nails. IED. They're good at improvising. We still do Christmas cards. I do. Sometimes he sends one. He's back in Fairfax."

There was little more to ask, little more he would tell her until he narrowed the distance he maintained. He said again that he had never spoken to Debra or Robert, and he had not killed Robert or shot at Debra.

She turned off the tape recorder and poured the last of the coffee. He had gone to Penn State at eighteen, the year he said he lost his father, the year after his brother died in Afghanistan. He didn't mention going to his father's funeral and she didn't ask.

She made a note on her legal pad: How did his father die?

Jeff put the thermos and mug on the tray with the pitcher and glass. "I'll take it back to the kitchen," he said. "Want me to send Gina in?"

"No. I need to walk a little. I'll find her later."

He was on the way to the door when she asked, "Jeff, when the officer put on the ankle monitor, why didn't you tell him it was too tight?'

He stopped moving. Slowly he turned until he was facing her again. "He knew it was too tight. It was deliberately too tight. He wanted me to ask, to beg maybe, and he would have tightened it a little more. I don't play their games." He didn't wait for any response, but turned and continued to and out the door.

Barbara felt that that moment was probably the most telling of all the time she had spent with him. Hubris? Too much pride to ask for help? Arrogance? Contempt for any and all authority? A lesson learned from his father?

Complain and be punished even more. She always debated whether or not it would benefit her client by testifying, and now she shook her head slightly. Jeff Cobbe couldn't be anywhere near the stand when his trial came up.

When Barbara walked out of the house, the dog Rusty came bounding around the corner with his ridiculous tail wagging furiously. "You're the silliest looking watch dog I ever saw," she told him. He bumped into her leg and she couldn't decide if it was his way of greeting her or because he was an oaf. He walked at her side to a point invisible to her, but a boundary for him, and he sat down. She walked on to the sales yard, crowded now with many benches of potted plants, tubs of shrubs and trees, a few bare root bushes in moist sawdust, and a lot of people loading carts. After many rainy days, the sun had come out, the temperature was up to seventy, and gardeners were catching up with spring planting.

She kept walking to the store where many people were in search of the season's early vegetables: snap peas, other peas, lettuces, asparagus, artichokes…

Passing the bin of snap peas, she picked up one and ate it, and realized how hungry she was. It was a quarter to two, another surprise. She had spent more time with Jeff than she had anticipated and it had been a long time since a hurried breakfast.

Put Gina off for another day? It might be her best move, she decided. Her stomach growled as if the single snap pea had awakened it and now it would protest until she added something more filling. She saw Mike Krusich, the general manager, coming her way and stopped.

"Ms. Holloway, Gina said if I saw you to tell you she'd be in the kitchen. Just go on around the house to the kitchen door. That's where she'll be."

She thanked him and headed to the far exit, avoiding the sales yard this time. At the invisible boundary Rusty came to greet her again and walked with her to the kitchen door. Barbara blinked in surprise at the door itself. Grass green, with a big dog door. It hadn't been there before. She pushed it open and entered. Rusty stayed on the porch.

"Hi," Gina said from the sink. "Come on in. Isn't that the ugliest door you ever saw? Greg and Rusty bonded on sight, love at first sight, something like that, and Greg couldn't stand the thought of keeping Rusty outside all the time so he and Daniel went to Bring, the recycle place, and bought that door and cut out the bottom to make a door for Rusty. They didn't want to deface the property, you see. Solution, a ten-dollar door that can be cut apart."

She was grinning broadly, holding a wicked-looking knife. Pointing it toward the table, she said, "Sit down. I have a sandwich for you. I made one for myself and thought you must be getting hungry, so I made two. I already ate mine." She put down the knife and went to the refrigerator to bring out a sandwich wrapped in waxed paper. "It's ham and cheese on whole wheat. Is that okay? I baked the ham last Sunday so we'd have sandwich makings all this week."

"More than okay," Barbara said. "I'm starving."

"I thought you might be. Our budget doesn't allow anything as frivolous as wine or beer. We take turns cooking and we're all nearly broke, so we're making our pennies stretch as far as possible." She was pouring water into a glass, setting it down, pouring coffee and putting it on the table, adding a napkin, talking all the while.

"I'm today's cook, making chicken, so I'll keep doing this while we talk. I want to get it in the oven by two-thirty." She went back to the counter by the sink, picked up the knife, and began to cut red onions in thick slices.

Barbara saw a large chicken on an oven rack and nearby a large shallow roasting pan. As she ate her sandwich, watching Gina, listening, she marveled that the young woman could talk so easily and so much while her hands were doing incredible things with a dangerous knife. She cut an onion into even slices, poured some olive oil into the roasting pan, and used an onion slice to spread it around. She put down a layer of the slices, then minced garlic she had already peeled. She sprinkled the garlic over the onions, and began to slice another onion, and she never stopped talking.

"Dad came on the nineteenth of February," she said. "I didn't know he was here until I came in to start dinner. I invited him, but he said he had an engagement. He had aired out his old bedroom and planned to stay a few days."

Barbara stopped her. "Did he say who the engagement was with? Anything at all about it?"

"No. I didn't ask and neither did my grandmother."

She had added another layer of onions in the roasting pan and several slices of lemon, salt, and pepper, and she topped it all with sprigs of rosemary. She placed the chicken on the rosemary, but didn't put it in the oven yet. She began to peel more garlic.

"Then a day or two later Dad came out to the greenhouse and looked around. He didn't really come in far, just a few feet. I introduced the guys and he barely nodded to them. I was invited to dinner."

She stopped speaking and looked at the peeled garlic on the counter, which she began to smash with the flat blade of the knife. Silently she put the garlic inside the chicken cavity, added more rosemary sprigs, and the rest of the sliced lemon.

In a vague sort of voice she said, "You want it to reach room temperature before you start roasting it. It cooks more evenly all the way through."

Gina shook herself and looked at the chicken, then at the clock. She turned on the oven. "Good timing," she said. It was twenty minutes after two. "So, back to that night. That was when he brought up the offer to buy the farm. Grandmother said no, and Dad and I got into our argument."

"Did he mention Tilsen at all?"

Gina shook her head. "But I began to think about his stay here. My grandmother told me, and Sophia said the same thing, Dad was gone for hours every day that he was here. I think he and Tilsen were out looking at other properties, scouting other farms, in case my grandmother really wouldn't sell." She put the chicken in the oven as she said all this, and then washed her hands thoroughly, sprayed the counter top and scrubbed it. Barbara could smell bleach. After that Gina picked up the carafe and poured more coffee for Barbara. When and how she had noticed the empty mug was a mystery to Barbara.

"So Dad left and I was back in my room, and Grandmother told me about how Dad had kept at her about selling, making a real nuisance of himself, is how she put it. I think Dad must have told Tilsen about our argument. How else could the police had found out? I certainly didn't mention it, and no one else was here. Dad told him, and he told the cops." She nodded emphatically and Barbara had to agree that it was probably how that happened.

"Gina, do you know if your grandmother ever talked to Tilsen? If she even met him?"

Gina shook her head. "I'm sure she didn't. She would have mentioned it. When Dad left, he said he'd be back on Friday, so I was here from Monday on. She would have told me. Your father asked that, too. He said Tilsen claimed that my grandmother was confused and irrational, and that's a damn lie in every way. He never was with her and she was not a bit confused or irrational."

She took down a mug and poured coffee, added half and half and sugar, then sat opposite Barbara. "The night my grandmother fell, I called Dad's cell phone from the hospital and he got there in about two hours. He must have been staying in Portland to get here that soon. I'd taken it for granted that he was going back to Chicago, but he didn't." She looked down at her coffee, swirled it round and round with a spoon, and kept her gaze on it when she continued. "There were really bad days after that and I don't have many memories of most of them. A lot of people in and out, they brought piles of food. The funeral, and half of the county must have been there. But then the appraiser showed up. Somehow Dad had found time to get in touch with her, arrange for her to be here and for Tilsen to be here."

Her anguish was unmistakable as she talked about the hours spent with the appraiser, heard snatches of conversation between her father and Tilsen, or the appraiser's remarks and questions. "Tilsen said there would be a farm auction for all the greenhouses and tractors, trucks, all of it. He would arrange that. And the appraiser said she could arrange for dealers in fine furniture to come in and bid on furniture, to be followed by an estate sale by invitation, then an open estate sale, and whatever was left after that donated to St. Vinnie's. None of the family had to be here. She would take care of it all. With the appraisal, it would be easy to place a value on everything, for tax purposes.

"Do you have a copy of the appraisal?" Barbara asked when Gina paused.

"No. It never came. She was here on a Wednesday, I think it was Wednesday, and Dad was shot on Sunday. I never gave the appraisal another thought until your father asked about it. I never saw it, and I would have. I bring in the mail every day. There wouldn't have been time for her to do her research, write up a report, and get it in the mail. I guess she saw a notice in the newspapers about the murder and decided it was no longer an issue, or something."

"What is her name? Do you remember?"

"Chadwick. Something Chadwick."

Barbara made a note. Then she asked, "Can you talk about the night your father was shot?"

Gina rose from the table and started to do kitchen things again as she kept talking. "Yes, of course. I was in my apartment when Jeff called..." She told it the way she had told it before until Barbara stopped her.

"Please try to recall details. You said Tilsen was there. What was he doing, for example?"

"I don't know. When I made tea for Mother, he was in the hall and he told me they had found Dad's body. And he had gotten the blanket to put around Mother. He was sorry, something like that. I didn't want to talk to him. I don't think I said a word to him. It was so cold in the house, Mother was wearing her coat and had a blanket around her, but she was shivering hard. Before, I said an Afghan, but it was a blanket and it wasn't enough to warm her. I was really concerned, and Tilsen just seemed like an unwelcome intruder. I pretty much ignored him. I turned up the thermostat, and I don't remember seeing Tilsen again after I took in the tea." She frowned, then said, "I don't think Mother knew a thing about the company offer, or that she had known Tilsen before that night. She ignored him as much as I did. Later they got to be buddies."

Barbara let it go at that, and Gina talked about moving out her belongings, finding the new will, and consulting Frank.

Gina had even less to say about the night shots that were fired at Debra. She had not heard shots. She had been in the bathtub; music playing, windows closed, and enough distance had pretty much sound-proofed her room and bathroom.

"So the only time Jeff and your father were even in the same space was when he met the guys in the greenhouse the day he invited you to dinner?"

For the first time Gina appeared hesitant, even reluctant to talk. She began to scrub sweet potatoes. "One other time," she said, not looking up from her task. "Dad came out and told us we had to clear out in thirty days. We were all there."

Gina left the sweet potatoes on the counter by the sink, crossed the kitchen, and looked for something in the cabinet. She brought out a package. "Penne," she said, returning and placing it on the counter. "Heavy carbs for dinner, but we all get so hungry."

"What happened when you were told to clear out in thirty days?"

"We were pretty stunned. Jeff sort of lost his temper. He smashed a pot, threw it on the floor, and left fast."

She opened the refrigerator and this time brought out lettuce and a big bowl of snap peas. "See, the onions, peas, and pan drippings top the penne, and the snap peas don't get cooked at all, plus a green salad and chicken. I thought since we wanted to talk, it would be good not to waste too much time away from the greenhouse, or out in the field. Two birds, one stone."

"Did you tell the police Jeff threw a pot?"

"No, of course not."

"Did anyone?"

"I don't know," Gina said in a despairing voice. "Greg might have, but I don't know. I didn't want to ask. Maybe he forgot or didn't think anything of it. I just don't know. I didn't want to remind him."

Barbara thought about this for a few moments. How bad would it look to a jury? A reasonable reaction, anger at being kicked out. Some might see it that way. She watched Gina wash the snap peas and put them in a colander, then start to wash the lettuce.

"Does Jeff have a bad temper?" she asked then.

"Absolutely not," Gina said. "That was the first and only time I've even seen him lose his temper."

Over the possible loss of his dream, his mission in life, Barbara thought. This thing he had struggled for from the time of his childhood, gone, lost to those he considered to be his worst enemies. She opened her briefcase and put her legal pad inside, turned off the tape recorder, and stood.

"Enough for one day," she said. "I know this has been difficult for you, and I'm grateful you took time off to talk to me. Thanks for the sandwich and coffee. And your chicken is starting to smell heavenly."

Gina looked at her with an agonized expression. "None of us has to mention that, do we?"

"It depends on what the prosecutor asks," Barbara said carefully. "And that might depend on what the investigators have already told her. She has the right to ask about Jeff's reaction to a sale and the loss of everything he had been working for. I certainly won't bring it up."

Gina turned off the running water and picked up a dish towel. Wiping her hands, not looking at Barbara, she started to say something. Very much afraid it would be to ask permission to perjure herself, or to declare that was her intention, Barbara said briskly, "I have to be on my way. Much to do these days."

The image Barbara took away with her that day was of Gina at the sink looking at lettuce with an expression of total despair and fear.

Maria and Shelley were in the outer office chatting that Monday morning when Barbara arrived. "'Morning," she said. "Lovely day, sun shining, and you're both early or I'm late. I opt for you're early."

"We're all a little late," Shelley said, grinning. "And this came exactly one minute ago." She pointed to a box on Maria's desk. "Discovery," Shelley added. "Looks like about a thousand pages, give or take a few."

Barbara groaned. "Great. Come on in. And, Maria, Bailey's due any second. Just send him on in when he gets here." She looked at the sputtering coffee machine, nodded, and said, "When it's done, give me a buzz, will you?"

She picked up the box and headed for her office, with Shelly a step in front of her in order to open the door. Inside her office Barbara put the box down on her desk, then went to the seating arrangement around her big ornate coffee table. She sat on the sofa and put her feet on the table, motioned for Shelley to be seated, then said, "Looks like I'll be busy a couple of days with that." She pointed to the box. "What's on your plate at Martin's, here in the office?"

For the next few minutes they talked about the ongoing cases, and one new case that Shelley had. A few letters, a plea bargain, not much more to any of it, Shelley said. "If there's anything for the Cobbe case that I can do, don't hesitate."

"There may be," Barbara said, but then a light tap on the door sounded, followed almost instantly by its opening to admit Bailey. Even that early in the morning, he looked rumpled, as if he had been hustling for hours, or had slept in his clothes. Barbara well knew that Bailey's wife would never let him sleep in his clothes, and she knew that he had not been out and about and busy for hours. It was a knack of his to never look well pressed, or wear anything other than what he had pulled off a rack at Goodwill twenty minutes ago. He was carrying his old duffel bag that he called his junior detective kit.

Maria followed him in bearing the coffee carafe, mugs, sugar and cream on a tray. Barbara thanked her as she set it down on the table and left again without a word.

"Give," Barbara said to Bailey as she poured coffee.

"Nothing," Bailey said. "Nada. I couldn't find a single guy, or woman either, who gave a damn about Robert Valducci. Not that they didn't like him or anything, just didn't care one way or the other. No good word, no bad word. Nothing. I believe indifferent is the word for it." He took a mug of coffee from her, added far too much sugar, and a splash of cream. "Barbara, most of them had to stop and try to remember ever talking to him even." He shrugged. "I can still dig a little in the backgrounds of the grange people if you want, but I don't think it will go anywhere. Valducci was an outsider to them all, out of state for years, never really part of the farming community to start with."

"What about Debra Valducci?"

"Blank stares." He drank coffee, put his mug down, and opened his duffel bag to withdraw a notebook. "I got something from my pal at the DA's office. Two names, man and woman, who they claim saw Cobbe dump a gun in the shrubbery the night someone took shots at Debra Valducci."

Barbara glanced at the box on her desk. It would be in there, in discovery, whatever they had stated. "The whole kit and caboodle on them both, back to the day of their birth," she told Bailey. "And there's something else I want you to dig out for me. Gina thinks that Tilsen was staying somewhere in Portland, maybe scouting other possible locations for his company. It could be that they've set up an office, or rented space for land scouts or something. I'd like to know if he's been hanging around, how long, and why, if possible."

"Want to let me in on why?" Bailey asked.

That was one of the things, she thought irritably, that pissed her off about him. He would never question any order from Frank, no matter how outrageous it sounded. If he weren't the best in the business, she sometimes wondered, would she even use his services? The answer always came back yes; he had been priceless too many times, but that didn't keep her from asking. She shrugged, then said, "If he thinks that Jeff will be convicted, that the fledgling corporation will be left without a head, Gina might be more approachable about a sale. I don't really have a good reason to want to know, but I do."

"Sounds like you have a pretty good reason," Bailey commented and helped himself to more coffee. "Okey dokey, Tilsen and company."

Turning to Shelley, Barbara said, "What I started to say before was that if you can find the time, keep track of land sales, farm sales, just to find out if they've bought another parcel or two, or if they're still salivating over the Valducci property. Can do?"

"You know it," Shelley said. "Remember, I spent a year in California tracking land sales and deeds, before I came up to work with you."

Barbara remembered that quite well. She also remembered how earnest Shelley had been when she declared that she'd work for nothing, just to be able to work with Barbara. She smiled and spread her hands. "At the moment, that's all I have. After I go through discovery I may have a lead."

"Barbara," Bailey said, "from where I sit it looks like you need more than a lead. You need a miracle. Your boy's got nothing more than a denial going for him. If those eyewitnesses hold up, that denial looks about as shaky as a frayed-rope bridge over a canyon."

"Well, give me a lead to a miracle. Now I've got reading to do. Beat it."

He closed his bag, drained his mug, and stood. "Righto," he said. "Be seeing you."

Barbara jerked in startlement when her buzzer sounded, followed by Maria's voice, "I'm going out to lunch now. Do you want me to bring you anything?"

Lunch? She looked at her watch: ten after one! She shook her head hard, remembered Maria was waiting for answer, and said, "Thanks, but no. I'll be leaving in a few minutes."

She was still holding a sheet of paper that now seemed strange, even alien, with words that made no sense. Slowly she put it down and rose from her chair. Asleep at her desk? Had she dozed off into a deep dreamless sleep? She crossed the office to a small bar with running water and poured a glassful, then drank most of it. It helped. Back at her desk, she lifted the paper she had held and this time recognized it as part of discovery, but the contents were new to her. She had not yet read it. She picked up a sheet that was face down, and it was as unfamiliar as the first had been. The next, next after that, unfamiliar but face down as if she had read them. Her hands were shaking when she returned all the papers to their folder and closed it.

Moving with deliberate care, she put the discovery box in her big drawer with a lock, turned the key in the lock, and left her desk. She had to walk, to think. At least she couldn't fall asleep if she was upright and walking.

A few minutes later, after parking at Alton Baker Park, she started her favorite walk along the river. It was a fine, sunny day, warm and breezy; the river flashed whitewater over rocks, ran deep blue and satin smooth over deep spots, as it raced and danced on its way to the sea with its message from the mountains.

What happened back there? Barbara asked herself. Her mind had rejected reading the discovery, but why? She had to read every word of it and the sooner the better, but she had gone blank instead. Indifference came to mind, the word Bailey had used to describe the reaction of those he had questioned about their attitudes concerning Robert and Debra Valducci.

"Indifference can't be a motive for murder," she said under her breath. If she were the prosecution, that was what she would stress, she thought. The total indifference of neighbors, other farmers, grange members, everyone in the valley with the exception of Gina and her colleagues, especially Jeff Cobbe. Barbara knew she did not have to point a finger of suspicion at another person or persons; that was above and beyond the duties of a defense attorney. All she had to do was introduce enough doubt about Jeff's guilt to make a not-guilty plea acceptable.

As prosecutor she would make it clear that no one else had a motive. She would call Tilsen to state that his company had loved Robert Valducci, who had had a great future there. No one with evil intentions from Chicago could have known of Jeff Cobbe, his relationship to Gina, his plans for the farm, his knowledge of Debra's whereabouts and her phone number. A possible would-be Chicago murderer would have had no reason to follow Valducci to Oregon to do him in. Tilsen and Robert Valducci were colleagues, friends, in negotiations for the sale of the farm to their company, a deal of great benefit for their company and both of them, and a fatal blow to Jeff Cobbe.

Debra would testify that Cobbe planned to gain the farm through Gina, that Cobbe had called her, setting up an ambush that had failed in order for Gina to inherit the property without a legal hassle.

As prosecutor, she thought bleakly, she could make a case. If her two eyewitnesses held up in their testimony that they had seen Jeff hiding a gun in the shrubbery outside his apartment, a plea bargain would be the best that Barbara could hope for because as defense attorney all she had was Jeff's denial.

Reluctantly she took the next step in her reasoning: She didn't know whether he was guilty or not. What she did know was that he did not trust her enough to tell her the truth.

"All right!" she told herself irritably. "I've been through this before. Why did I black out instead of reading the discovery material?"

Answers flooded in: It was boring, it was same old same old, it was repetitive, officers A, B, C…all saying the same thing, it was irrelevant, reports were ungrammatical, wrong questions asked, other questions not answered coherently…

Then: The prosecution doesn't have a clue about what really happened. It's not in discovery.

Barbara came to a dead stop to the annoyance of two strollers walking behind her. Ignoring them as they walked around her, she whispered, "Back to the starting gate."

She did a fast about-face and headed toward her car, thinking about her first real conversation with Gina, two to three hours of taped conversation, starting with the evening that Robert Valducci had appeared on the scene. She had to listen to all of it again. Then she was recalling her last conversation with Gina, watching her prepare dinner as she talked. How deftly she had moved about with a sharp knife, accomplishing what to Barbara's eyes had been minor miracles, and never faltering in her speech, keeping up a constant flow of words.

Chicken, she thought, onions, sweet potatoes. Her pace quickened and now she knew what she was going to do. First a supermarket, shop, follow Gina's unspoken cooking instructions, and make dinner.

At four-thirty a chicken was on a rack coming to room temperature. Rosemary sprigs were on the counter, as was a chicken neck on a plate. She was bewildered about the chicken neck, an incredibly ugly, repulsive object to her eyes. She didn't have a clue about what to do with it. Bake it with the chicken? Cook it separately? Throw it away? She had put it out of mind until later, when she would take the time to decide.

One layer of red onion slices, topped with a scattering of minced garlic, was in the baking pan, and Barbara was slicing another red onion. She was concentrating on the next slice, not too wide, not too narrow, even all the way through…

"What are you doing?"

Todd's voice broke her concentration and she looked up to see him standing in the doorway with an incredulous expression, his eyes wide with disbelief or astonishment.

"I'm clearing my mind," she said.

Barbara and Frank were on his back porch watching Todd baste a chicken on a spit at the grill. Tandoori chicken, Frank had said. He had done all the preliminaries, whatever that consisted of, but on their arrival—hers, Darren's and Todd's—Frank had retired to a chair, pointed to the chicken on the spit and told Todd it was all his from here on out. Darren was at Todd's elbow, talking with him. Todd was an inch taller than his father, Barbara thought, surprised at not knowing that before. They sneaked up on you, she thought, grew when your back was turned.

"He's going to miss the boy," Frank commented.

"More than he knows yet," Barbara said. "It's as if he can't waste a minute now, almost smothering in his attention. Todd's being very patient."

The next morning Darren was to drive Todd to Stanford, to meet a group gathering to go on a summer mission to measure the extent of permafrost melting in the Arctic Circle. Todd had been accepted as an intern. In the fall he would attend Stanford. This was the last time a day like this could happen, Barbara suspected. A bittersweet, happy kind of day, celebrating a new phase in Todd's life, a loss in Darren's, and hers, she had to add. New beginnings, endings, a mixed-up kind of day. She took another sip of her wine.

"What's new at the farm?" she asked then.

"The kids have installed a giant tank on a suspension system that lets them turn it every day, mixing garden waste, animal waste, dirt, worms, you name it. If it will decompose, in it goes. That's their mantra. Couldn't be happier, or dirtier. She has the money from her grandmother's estate finally and they are buying stuff right and left, the tank, irrigation system supplies, I don't know what all. A few days after the probate hearing Tilsen showed up to make an offer to Gina. She gave him the heave-ho. He tried to follow her to the house and when she crossed the line that determines what Rusty guards, he tried to keep up with her. Rusty growled and showed his teeth, and Gina warned Tilsen that he bites. He took off after that. Maybe that's the end of him." He gave her a shrewd look. "And what about your case? How's it coming?"

"It isn't," she said. "Nothing. I'm exactly where I was a month ago, two months ago. Their side: Robert shot at fairly close range, three, four feet, no fingerprints, no witnesses; same gun used to shoot at Debra; same gun hidden in shrubbery outside Jeff's apartment; two irreproachable eyewitnesses who saw him or someone toss the gun. He's the only one with both motive and opportunity. My side: his denial. Period."

She drained her glass and set it down too hard. "I've listened to every word everyone uttered from the start, and read every word of discovery, and still nothing. Not even a direction to follow. The one thing that makes sense is the fact that several people saw Gina the night Valducci was shot. They saw her carrying stuff to her apartment. That explains why they never asked her anything more about when she left that night. But it leaves hanging whose car that was parked at the store. Not a word about it."

Frank knew it was bad and he had nothing to say to hide that. He stood. "I'll go toss the salad. That chicken's nearly ready."

How could he know that from where he was? she wondered, then shook her head. He knew things. She could envy them all, she thought then. Todd knew what he wanted to do and was on his path. Darren had the clinic and the wonderful things he could do for and with patients. Gina and her boys knew exactly what they wanted to do and how to go about it. Even Frank—she added him to her list—had a new book contract and was whistling and humming all day long. And she was in a quagmire, stuck, with no one to throw her a saving rope or line of any sort. She poured herself more wine.

Now that the will business was settled and accounts unfrozen, Gina had come to love long Sunday evenings with her guys. They had come to an agreement: They no longer had to work twelve to fourteen hours a day, seven days a week. On Sunday, the store closed at five, quiet settled over the farm, and they could relax for a few hours. She leaned back in her sling chair, and listened to Greg playing his guitar. They had grilled hamburgers and roasted potatoes, Daniel's doing, his day to cook, followed by strawberry shortcake. Daniel had apologized for the store-bought cake. And now they were on the terrace enjoying the music and the rest after another week of hard work.

Gina was content. It was working exactly the way they had hoped, planned, and prayed for. She had hired a few more workers, and that was the biggest relief. It made evenings like this one possible. They couldn't do all of the big things they had listed months and months ago; that would take a lot more money than she had inherited, but they had started, and it would go on into the indefinite future.

There had been little talk that evening, but they didn't need to talk a lot, and that was good, too. No one ever mentioned the monitor on Jeff's ankle, or the trial coming up in a few months. Sometimes Gina wondered if Jeff thought about it much, but she didn't dare ask him. Afraid of his answer? she mockingly asked herself now and then, and always answered, yes.

A low growl from Rusty roused her from her state of reverie. She sat upright in time to see the dog leave Greg's side and trot up the walk toward the driveway. He began to bark, and now Greg rose and hurried after him. "I'll see who it is," he called back over his shoulder.

Gina felt as if every muscle in her body had gone rigid, and both Jeff and Daniel had risen and were listening intently, not moving.

Greg came back with Rusty and a stranger. Rusty was still bristling, listening, watching for a signal that the stranger was to be accepted as friend or as a possible target.

"Jeff," Greg said, "he says he's Eric Ballantine, and he's your brother."

Eric Ballantine took another step or two forward. Rusty growled, louder this time; he bared his teeth and the hair on his neck stuck out, his ears slicked back. He didn't take his eyes off the man.

"What the fuck are you doing here?" Jeff demanded.

"Maybe you can call off the dog," Eric Ballantine said. "I wanted to see for myself. Dad said you killed a man."

Still no one moved until Jeff shook himself, motioned to Greg, and said, "Tell Rusty to relax." He hesitated, then added, "*Friend.* Eric, stand still until Rusty gets acquainted."

On the signal, Rusty sniffed Eric over thoroughly, then trotted to the group by the chairs and lay down.

"Can we talk?" Eric asked. He remained where he was.

"We'd better," Jeff said. "Come on inside."

The light on the terrace was dim, furnished by the living room lamps, giving Gina no way to see much more of Eric than that he was tall and appeared thin, that he was wearing jeans and a windbreaker, and then he and Jeff passed into the house. A few seconds later the light from the study brightened another section of the terrace.

Only then did Greg and Daniel move. "Wow," Daniel said softly. "That's a surprise. I didn't even know he had a brother."

"I thought the brother was in a hospital or something," Greg said.

Gina stood. "Let's clear up this stuff. I'll move some things from my room into my grandmother's room, let Eric have my room for tonight. I guess he'll be staying at least overnight."

Half an hour later Gina stood in her grandmother's room, gazing about through tear-blurred eyes. She had planned to move into this room, she reminded herself, but not so soon, not now. Sophia Mirano had offered to come with her housekeeper to clear out everything, to pack up and donate clothes, and to throw away a lot. Open powder, face creams, lotions, whatever was in the medicine cabinet in the bathroom. Gina had thanked her gratefully, but had not named a time. Now she would have to. It was time.

She regarded her clothes piled on a chair, shrugged, and turned to go downstairs. She would deal with her stuff later. She went to the study door, straightened her shoulders, and knocked lightly. She didn't wait for an invitation to enter, just opened the door and stepped inside. Jeff was standing by the window overlooking the terrace, and Eric was sprawled in one of the red chairs. Eric rose when she entered.

"Jeff, when Eric wants to go to bed, show him my old room. I've moved some stuff, and there are clean sheets and towels. Eric, I'm Gina, and you're welcome to stay as long as you'd like. Good night."

She was shocked now that she had a chance to really see Eric. He was pale, not merely thin, but gaunt, drawn, with sunken eyes. Looking at him she said, "Please help yourself to whatever you want in the kitchen. There's some beer, eggs, cheese. And even strawberry shortcake. Make yourself at home."

Not waiting for a response, she stepped back and closed the door. She went upstairs quickly and straight to her old room, where she stripped the bed and put on the clean sheets. Eric looked too sick to have to do that. Then, in Magda's room again, her own new room, she thought clearly, she sat on the side of the bed and Googled Eric Ballantine. It might be a good idea to know something about the man she had invited to share her house, she told herself. When Eric said Dad told him that Jeff had killed a man, did he mean his father, or their father? Hadn't Jeff mentioned he was an orphan? If he had lied about that, what else had he lied about? If *their* father, why was Jeff's name Cobbe, his brother's name Ballantine? And more importantly, why would he have lied to her about his parents?

Gina lay awake a long time that night. She heard Eric come upstairs and go into her old room, close the door. She heard both Daniel and Greg go to their rooms, and then silence settled deeper than ever over the house. She was thinking of what she had learned on the Internet. Jeff's mother's maiden name had been Cobbe, and she really had died when he was eleven. His father, alive, was a general, now retired. There had been three sons. Curtis the eldest had died in Afghanistan; Eric had been grievously wounded in Iraq; and there was not a single mention of Jeff beyond the fact that he had been born a Ballantine.

She tossed and turned, knotted the blanket hopelessly and had to get up to straighten out her bed. Facts, she muttered to herself, damn facts, what good were they? Meaningless facts, facts be damned. What did any of it mean? What was the truth behind the damned facts?

When she finally drifted into sleep, she dreamed she was pursuing Jeff, that she came close enough to catch him a time or two, but when she grasped his arm, it was like trying to hold Jell-O. The tighter she held on, the less she had in her hand, until he was gone again and she in pursuit again.

Barbara was thinking of Juan Juarez that Monday afternoon. He was seventeen, a senior in high school, and saving for community college in another year. He had sat opposite her at Martin's and explained very carefully how he knew that Mrs. Waterson really owed him seventy-five dollars. "See, I keep a record on my calendar," he had said, showing her a gaudy, oversized calendar with a picture of a scantily clad woman standing in a field of cacti. Incongruous was the only word she had for the calendar illustration, but Juan's notes of when he cut grass for this person or that was quite clear. He had cut Mrs. Waterson's grass four times, a total of ten hours, at seven dollars and fifty cents an hour. She owed him seventy-five dollars. She had owed him for six weeks now and stalled when he asked for payment.

Barbara finished the letter she had written to Mrs. Waterson and leaned back in her chair, thinking of Juan, thinking of Todd on his way to Stanford and an adventurous summer ahead. It wasn't fair, she had to admit, for one to have so much, the other so little. But, by God, she thought then, Juan would get his seventy-five dollars plus the twenty-five she had added, for processing and handling.

Her phone rang, and Maria said Gina was on the line. Barbara took the call.

Gina's voice was low and sounded conspiratorial. Background noise suggested that she was in the store. "I think there's something you should know, but no one else is going to tell you."

"So tell me now," Barbara said.

"Jeff's brother is here, and you should talk to him," Gina said, her voice dropping even lower. "I remember what you said about knowing everything the prosecutors know, so you won't get blinded or something."

"Blindsided," Barbara said. "You're right, of course. Is the brother there now?"

"Yes."

"On my way," Barbara said. Brother? She dredged up what little she knew about him: older than Jeff, a basket case? PTSD? Severely wounded in Iraq. What the hell was he doing in Eugene? She glanced at her watch. Nearly five, but that made little difference. She would have dinner sometime and, with no one at home, what time that turned out to be didn't make any difference.

She waved to Maria on her way out, and twenty minutes later she pulled into the parking area at Valducci's store. There were many shoppers that late afternoon, more than she had expected. Strawberry season, cherries, blueberries, abundant vegetables to be had, sunny weather, all added up to shoppers. Gina came to meet her as she entered the store.

"I'm glad you could come," she said. "I didn't know what to do, if I should call you or not, make Jeff mad, make Eric uncomfortable. He's in bad shape. Recovering from surgery, and he drove out here from the East Coast. He said he doesn't fly. Actually he can't fly or stand to be in terminals with too many people and too much noise." She talked fast, her hands moving fast as she talked, hands as expressive as her face, which concealed little or nothing of what she was feeling.

"He's in the house, maybe watching television. He worked in the field for about half an hour this morning and it was too much. I think he wants to work, to do something, but he can't. Not yet anyway. That was too much for him, driving here from the East Coast. He's still too weak." She was leading the way through the store as she talked, nodding to people, touching a woman lightly on the arm as they moved past her, murmuring something to her.

"I know why I never got that appraisal," Gina said as they left the store and headed toward the house. "Just before I called you I got rid of my insurance agent. He came to talk about homeowner's insurance. He said I should make a video of furniture, computers, everything, and put it in a safe deposit box, just in case I ever need to prove something. That reminded me of Mrs. Chadwick, and I called her office. I mean, even if she can't arrange the sales she talked about, at least she must have the camcorder stuff, but no luck. She's dead. Oh, here's Rusty to greet us."

The dog came bounding up to them with his tail wagging furiously, and a big happy-dog expression complete with a tongue hanging out of his mouth. Barbara had to laugh at him. He greeted her like family.

They walked around the house to enter by the kitchen door where, inside, they saw Eric Ballantine at the long table with a book. He stood, and looked as if he might dash out.

"Eric," Gina said quickly. "This is Barbara Holloway, Jeff's lawyer. Eric Ballantine," she added, obviously an afterthought.

He looked Barbara over, up and down deliberately, then said, "You don't look like an attorney."

She glanced down at her jeans and sneakers. Her T-shirt had a dragon on it. She nodded and said, "I have a dress, but I save it for court."

For a moment she thought he might simply stalk out, or even bolt and run, but the moment passed and a fleeting grin softened his bony face. "Sorry," he said.

"Will you talk to me?"

"Yes. I'd better do that. Not here. Greg said he'll be making dinner tonight. And he's in and out of the study working on the computer. Out under a tree?"

"I have a better idea," Barbara said. "Take a ride with me."

He hesitated, then nodded. Barbara turned to Gina. "What time is dinner usually?"

"Seven-ish, depending on who's cooking. With Greg it might be a little later. We'll save plenty for Eric if he's not back yet."

The ride had been silent, and now walking in the Rose Garden, they were still silent. Barbara led the way, taking the shortest possible route, to a bench with a view of the magnificent cherry tree that was as old as the city itself. Massive, structural supports held up mighty limbs and the tree was covered with cherries, not yet ripe, but promising a bacchanalia for the birds in a week or two.

The scent of roses filled the air, and behind them, the rushing river hummed a soft, murmurous, ever-changing song.

"Nice," Eric said after a few minutes of continued silence. "One of your favorite spots?"

"Yes. When I'm really frustrated, bewildered, upset, anxious, down in the dumps, you name it, this is the place to be."

He laughed softly. "The tree that endures all."

"Exactly."

After another drawn-out silence, he said, "What do you want to know?"

"Whatever you can tell me about Jeff. I have some facts, but facts mean little or nothing without context. I need the context."

He nodded and, keeping his gaze on the tree, he said, "First though, you should know that I came out here to offer Jeff some money. I thought he must have a public defender and I was going to help pay for a full-time attorney. I looked you up. He already has one. And Jeff exploded when I made the offer, but it's on the table."

She said okay and nothing else, and after a minute or two of more silence he said, "You know I'm nearly twelve years older than Jeff?" At her nod, he continued. "He was just a few months old when I went off to Ridge Academy, and I saw very little of him after that. That's a lot of years to span. Boys twelve and older don't have much use for babies."

His accent was stronger than Jeff's, Barbara thought, listening to him. She did not interrupt him as he talked, but she did reach into her purse and turn on her tape recorder.

"The first time I really noticed him, really paid attention, I mean, was when he was about three or maybe even four. Mother had taken me shopping for shoes and when we walked into the house, we saw Jeff with his shorts around his feet, and Dad switching his butt. Jeff was crying, not making a sound, but with tears running down his face."

Eric became silent again, drew in a breath, and leaned forward with his hands cupping his face, elbows on his knees. "He hated him, Barbara. Curtis and I talked about it, not then, later. Dad hated Jeff from the day he was born. Curtis told me that Dad raped our mother and Jeff was the result. He wasn't an alcoholic, but sometimes he drank too much and he got ugly. I was too young to pay a lot of attention, but Curtis told me our mother had a lock on her door for years to keep Dad out. Curtis was older than me and he was thinking about girls and sex way before I had an inkling. Anyway, he knew what was going on, and for all that I saw and gave a single thought about, I might just as well have been blind. That day, the day of the whipping, might have been the first time Mother ever left Jeff with Dad. It was the last time. I know that much. Dad hated him, still hates him, because he reminds him of the night he raped Mother. Guilty conscience? I don't know. Maybe. Maybe he believes Jeff came between him and Mother. He didn't, the locked door did, but Dad was never quite sane as far as Jeff was concerned. Anyway, after that day, Mother didn't even pretend to be his wife. She packed up and took Jeff to our grandparents' farm in Pennsylvania. For a few years Curtis and I spent part of our vacation time with her and Jeff out on the farm and part with him in Fairfax. They never got divorced. He begged her not to go through with one. He said it would destroy his career."

He straightened up and stretched his legs out, and now his gaze was again on the mighty tree. "For a long time I thought it was her fault, our divided family, I mean. Curtis and I were okay with Dad most of the time, he took us hunting and camping, fishing. Played ball with us. You know, father-and-sons kind of stuff and we liked it. He gave me my first gun when I was ten, a twenty-two-caliber rifle. When I found out it wasn't Mother's fault, it was too late. She was dead by then. Jeff wasn't quite twelve when she died. And at twelve, Dad shipped him off to Ridge Academy."

"You and Curtis went there, too, didn't you?" Barbara asked when Eric stopped again, this time longer.

"Yeah, but it was different with us. We got time out, vacations, Christmas breaks, spring breaks, even weekends now and then. Taking orders, facing discipline if you got out of line, all of that was old hat to us, what we were used to at home. Jeff was different, and he was there 24/7 for years, until he was sixteen. School for us, prison for him."

He drew in another long breath, and she was wondering if he was strong enough to continue this talk that obviously was painful for him. A tic in his jaw had started to show, and he clenched and unclenched his hands several times, seemed to notice what he was doing, and folded them in a tight grip that made tendons stand out.

"At the academy, I know a guy, an instructor. He was there when I went, and he was there when Jeff was there. I saw him after Jeff took off and no one knew where he was. He told me that Jeff was a difficult student, obdurate, stubborn, rebellious, non-cooperative, and greatly admired by the other boys and some of the staff. Jeff, it seems, excelled academically from the start in every subject, and he excelled in every sports activity they required, up to a point. For example, the twelves, what they call them, have to take swimming as P.E. Jeff swam like a fish, mastered every stroke they required, and was as fast as a dolphin in the timed events. They enrolled him on the swim team, and he refused to participate. He showed up, fully dressed, and simply stood there when ordered to put on his swimsuit. They punished him, of course. Not corporal punishment, they don't do that, but shame and humiliation. They made him take off his clothes at one end of the corridor in the bunk room wing and walk the gauntlet of every kid watching him walk naked to the isolation room. He did that every night for a month, and still refused to be part of the swim team." Eric glanced swiftly at her, then turned his gaze back to the tree.

Softly he said, "It was like that with every sport, every non-academic activity they put the kids through. He could outrun a deer, and refused to be on the track team. Baseball, basketball, even target practice. He took up everything they demanded, got to be the best, and then dropped out. He could qualify for super sniper, but no. He refused. And he got punished for every refusal."

Barbara remembered what Jeff had said, if he had wanted to shoot Debra, she'd be dead.

Eric's voice dropped a little when he continued. "I think Dad tried to crush his spirit when he was a little kid, and he thought the academy would break him, and God only knows what the few months were like for Jeff after Mother died and Dad took him home. He wouldn't talk about those months. I didn't insist. But when he showed up for Curtis's funeral, I thought that if Dad had had a gun available, he might have shot him on sight. I grabbed Jeff and got him out of there and we talked; for the first time in our lives, we talked."

"Did he tell you he planned to change his name?"

"No. Not then. He didn't know anything about the money Mother left him, or who the lawyers were that handled her estate. Dad never told him anything about that. Jeff wrote to me and told me after the fact about the name change. He said he no longer was Dad's son, that Dad was dead to him. He kept me informed of his whereabouts from then on. Neither of us is a good correspondent, but we kept in touch. Then, when I was sent home, not in a box, but in a basket, they thought I might not make it through the first surgery, and I told Dad where Jeff was and his name change. My mistake. I thought Jeff would want to know if I kicked, that Dad would have the decency to tell him."

"What are you afraid of, Eric?" Barbara asked after he fell silent again, this time for what she decided was too long.

"Barbara, I said that Dad hated him as a baby, as a kid, and now he hates him as an adult. Maybe more than ever. It's hard to say. It's irrational, without cause, but there it is. And he said that Jeff killed a man in cold blood and he was afraid he'd get away with it, and that would be a sin."

"What are you suggesting?"

"He could take it on himself to prevent a miscarriage of justice," Eric said flatly. "He said that he doubts that Jeff is even his son, that he was born evil, that he killed his mother, devil spawn, Satan's child…" He laughed, a bitter, mirthless sound. "He said that Jeff killed a man who was a father figure, and he would do it again and again until he got the right father. I thought you should know." He started to say something else, then clamped his lips hard and stood. "Maybe we can start back now?"

She rose and caught his arm and was shocked by how thin it was. His shirt had concealed that. "Eric, what else? There is something else, isn't there?"

Deliberately he took her hand in his and removed it from his arm. "Maybe," he said. "Just maybe. He won't go to prison, Barbara. He'll never go to prison." He started to walk. "I need to get back and lie down. Now, Barbara."

Beads of sweat were on his forehead, and his pallor seemed to worsen even as she gazed at him. Silently she started to walk, and after a moment she took his arm again. This time he didn't pull away.

On Wednesday Barbara read an email message from Frank: Gazpacho, followed by ratatouille. Want some? 7ish. She laughed and answered: YES! Sly old fox, he knew very well that the leftovers he had sent home with her on Sunday night would be plenty for Monday and Tuesday, and here it was Wednesday, and she might be in danger of starving. She laughed again.

That morning she finished two cases, wrote a letter or two, and from all appearances no one could have guessed that she also had a pending murder case. After lunch a Mr. and Mrs. Blackston arrived with their own problem.

In their sixties, they had been married so long that they finished each other's sentences. "See," Mr. Blackston said, "we sold our place out near Veneta, and are looking for a house in town here. So we had to move out before we could move in, so to speak."

"We had our eye on a house," Mrs. Blackston said, "but it wasn't going to be empty for a few months, so..."

"We rented an apartment, just for temporary, but we have a lot of furniture..."

"We moved some of it to the apartment, some to storage, and now that man claims we stole his furniture."

"Like a love seat we bought twenty-two years ago. Who keeps receipts for anything that long?"

"And the clock my mother gave us for a wedding gift! And her in her grave."

They went on for several more minutes before Barbara held up her hand.

"Okay, I get the picture," she said. "I'll send someone to your house to take photographs of all the items in dispute, and you give him a list of people who can attest to the fact that you had them in your previous house in Veneta..."

They were effusive in their gratitude, and as soon as she managed to usher them out of the office, she closed their file folder but left it on the desk. It was nearly five-thirty, too late to call Bailey, she decided, time enough to dump it in his lap in the morning.

"Wonderful, Dad, as it always is," she said on his back porch where they had just eaten. In his garden the two coon cats, Thing One and Thing Two, were chasing something invisible to her. The late sun made their gold coats look mythical—cat gods, shining in sunlight, fading to shadows in deep shade.

"What do you hear from Darren and Todd? Has the muckety-muck big shot made it out of Antarctica yet?"

"Nope. Darren and Todd are acting like tourists. Trying to have fun in Palo Alto and trying not to think about Todd's frustration." A big-name Russian scientist, whose name she could not remember, or pronounce if she could, was stuck in Antarctica due to stormy weather making flying impossible, and he was one of the leading scientists for the project.

"I went out to the farm today," Frank said. "Got those tomatoes we just finished eating." He was gazing at his own tomato plants as he spoke. His tomatoes were like little green marbles. "Three, four weeks earlier than usual," he commented. "That's the sort of thing those kids will be doing, making seasonal vegetables available more months of the year. They're all working their butts off. And I met Eric Ballantine."

Frank chuckled. "Eric said Gina's treating him like a fledgling on a three-hour feeding schedule. Regular as clockwork she appears with some goodie loaded with butter, heavy cream, or something else equally high caloric. Her newest mission in life is to fatten him up a mite."

"What do you think of him?"

"He's a very ill young man," Frank said soberly. "A haunted man. He may never recover."

Barbara nodded. "I know. I talked to him on Monday." She recounted the conversation. "If he's right about their father, if he really does show up to shovel coals on the fire, that could be the final straw."

"Still nothing?"

She nodded.

"I know how much you hate it, but you might have to plea bargain."

"And if Eric is right about Jeff never going to prison, that's the last thing I want to bring up with him."

"No rush," Frank said. "Not until it's closer to the trial. Right now Jeff is working like a man possessed. Planning, ordering items for the fall, like a mile or two of drip irrigation tubing, lining up solar-panel specialists." He paused, thinking about Jeff, Gina, the other two corporate members. "Jeff's the driving force behind the corporation," he said. "He's pushing that train as far along on the right track as humanly possible."

"He's got a few months to make sure it's secure enough not to derail if he has to step out of the picture," Barbara said in a low voice. She felt as if she had solved one of the puzzles that Jeff Cobbe had presented to her.

"And that's it," Barbara told Bailey the next morning. "Get pictures, a list of people who know something about the items, then statements. Can do?"

"I'll sic Alan on it," Bailey said.

"Why? Busy these days?"

"Not that. See, I work cheaper than you do, and Alan works cheaper than me, and he can get a photographer who'll work for a baloney sandwich. Everyone saves a penny or two. And besides, Hannah has a wild hare about putting in a little water feature in our backyard and she wants me to oversee it."

"A water feature? You mean a pond or something like that, with fish? Why? You have a lovely backyard and garden already."

"Barbara, when's the last time I could explain why Hannah's doing anything? And come to think of it, why are you messing around with stolen furniture? Nothing for me on the Cobbe case?"

"Nothing for you, for me, for anyone." She had given him the name and address of the Blackston couple, and now went back to her desk. "So put Alan to work. I don't care who does it, just so it gets done."

"Okey dokey," he said, gathering himself up from the easy chair by the sofa. "I'll give you a call when it's done."

She eyed the folder, opened it to include a note about Bailey, then stared at the yellow sheet she had made her own notes on. The name Chadwick stood out, circled and underlined.

She leaned back in her chair frowning. Gina had mentioned an insurance agent telling her to make a video of furnishings, then Gina called Chadwick, only to learn that she was dead. Something about a video and appraisal of possessions in her house that never arrived. Then Blackstons and their tale of woe, trying to prove ownership of their possessions without a video. Coincidence? Absolutely, she told herself.

She closed her eyes and summoned the memory of the tapes she had made of Gina talking about everything and narrowed it down to what she had said about Chadwick and the day she had spent with her camcorder in the Valducci house at Robert Valducci's request.

After a few minutes she opened her laptop and researched Chadwick Appraisals. It was Chadwick and Harris, and their website had a black-bordered announcement of the savage death of Mildred Chadwick, who had been bludgeoned to death during a robbery at her shop on Saturday night, March 7.

Barbara stared at the announcement. Robert had been shot to death on March 8. Another coincidence?

She remembered what Gina had said at the probate hearing: Why did Tilsen want this particular farm?

She knew this piece of geography did not contain oil or diamonds; no gold mine had ever been uncovered in the valley as far as she was aware. Not the land, not the farm, something in the house? A valuable piece of furniture, a rare something or other worth a fortune? That beautiful mirror with the ivory frame? Something Mrs. Chadwick might have discovered in her research? If so, that something might still be on her camcorder or on file in her computer.

Stop it! she ordered herself. Looking for any straw to cling to because she was sinking? Chadwick and Harris, she thought then, followed almost instantly with the idea to go to Portland and talk to Harris. Maybe buy the laptop, camcorder, whatever device the information was on regarding what Chadwick might have found. Even if the woman had not finished the appraisal and this was another dead end, at least Gina might have the video of furniture and other items.

Without debating herself further, she looked in on Shelley and told her and Maria that she was off to Portland and wouldn't be back that day.

Chadwick and Harris had a sign in a front window of a nice old house on Burnside, a neighborhood of residences turned commercial for the most part, with shops, businesses of various kinds, eateries. She parked and walked to the front door and entered a small room that must have been a foyer of the old house when it had been a residence only. A bell announced the opening of the door, and before it closed all the way a woman came in from the rear of the room.

"Can I help you?"

"Ms. Harris?"

"Yes. I'm Lucy Harris." She was a plump little woman with a mass of fading red curls streaked with gray. Her skin was flawless, pink and unlined, like that of a China doll. She had bright blue eyes and dimples in both cheeks. "Did you want to have something appraised?"

"I'm afraid not," Barbara said. "But I do want to discuss an appraisal Mildred Chadwick made a few months ago."

"Oh, dear," Lucy Harris said. Her smile vanished and worry lines creased her forehead, making her look older and tired. "Well, you'd better come on back where we can sit down and maybe I can explain things." The small room, or foyer, had no space for chairs. There was a counter, and many shelves on the walls, filled with books, brochures, folders. A silver candelabra was on a shelf.

Lucy motioned for Barbara to follow and she led the way past the open door into a living room with handsome print-covered easy chairs, a sofa covered with gold leather, tables, straight chairs against the wall, and a long coffee table with a blooming plant on it. The flowers were fuchsia and white.

"Please," Lucy Harris said, motioning toward the sofa. "I just put on coffee, not a minute before the bell sounded. Would you like some?"

"I'd like that very much," Barbara said.

"It won't take a minute," Lucy said and left the room.

She needed time to gather herself, decide what to say, prepare herself for recriminations or something, Barbara thought. The poor woman probably had been traumatized by the death of her partner; the passing weeks had lessened her shock to a degree, and now an inquiry brought it back to the forefront.

Lucy returned with a tray, handed Barbara a cup of coffee, and sat down. Then, with coffee in hand, she said, "Are you inquiring about an appraisal Mildred was to do, something like that?"

"Something like that," Barbara said. "I'm an attorney. My client expected an appraisal to arrive nearly two months ago and when it didn't she asked me to look into it. We didn't know that Ms. Chadwick had been so brutally murdered. Can you tell me something about that?"

"Of course," Lucy said. "I was out of town, up in Bellingham. My daughter was having a baby and I went up to be with her. I was there five weeks when it happened and I cut my visit short and came home. The police told me what they knew, I guess, and it isn't much. It seems like someone came into the shop to rob it and Mildred interrupted them. We could hear the bell back here, you see. She would have gone out to see who it was, what they wanted, the way I did when you came in."

She stopped and shook her head. "They should have known we don't keep any money in the office out front, or in the back either, as far as that goes. We don't buy and sell anything. The same person shouldn't ever do the appraisal and buy the items they appraised. Keep that in mind. Why'd they have to kill her?"

"Did they take much?"

Lucy shook herself and sat up straighter. "She was hit in the head out in the office, out front, and then the robbers must have gone through the house. They took her laptop and camcorder, her cell phone and watch, notebook, everything electronic. Thankfully I had my computer with me. They missed a little cash in her purse, forty-four dollars. Nothing else was taken as far as I could tell."

Barbara suppressed a groan at the words about the camcorder and laptop. "They left the candelabra out front?" She said this simply for something to say. What she had come for obviously was not available.

"Not worth stealing. No one could get more than a couple of dollars for it. It looks like it was picked up at a thrift store and maybe someone brought it in thinking she had found a bargain. People do that now and then, bring something to the shop for a quick appraisal, family silver, something found in a yard sale. We don't want them to leave things, but now and then they do. That candelabra had a tag on it, brought in on the day of the murder. The police believe that whoever brought it in is afraid to come forward and claim it. Might be charged with murder or something."

"Ms. Harris," Barbara said when Lucy became silent, "is it possible that there's a record somewhere of the appraisal Ms. Chadwick made just days before her death?"

She shook her head. "It would have been on her computer and it's gone."

"Did she talk to you about the business, appraisals, estate sales while you were in Washington?"

"For the first couple of weeks, but not after that. She could tell my mind wasn't on business, not with a newborn grandson, and two other little ones to keep me occupied. She would tell me she had an estate sale in the works, but nothing in particular about it. She had one or two not finished yet the last time we talked, the Saturday she was killed. She was pleased, happy about one of them, excited. I didn't ask anything and she said it could wait until I got home the coming weekend. She was really busy, Ms. Holloway, doing it all herself when we were used to working together. We were together for seven years, after our husbands died and left us widows, not even a year apart, my Joseph and her Stan. Both gone. Now I don't know what I'll do." She looked around the room with a vague expression.

Barbara didn't stay much longer. No point in it, she told herself, taking her leave with a half-hearted promise to let her client know that Lucy Harris would be happy to do the appraisal again.

"Dead end," Barbara muttered in her car, and now Portland traffic to navigate with rush hour at hand and no doubt bumper-to-bumper traffic until well out of town. She gritted her teeth and started.

It was a hot, sticky July day, unusual in Oregon, but happening more and more often. Reluctantly Barbara had turned on the air conditioning, and now she was finishing reviewing a case with Shelley. They agreed that Shelley's client should go for a plea bargain. Guilty as hell, was how Barbara put it, but not worth ten to fifteen years. He had stolen a carton of cigarettes and a couple of candy bars from a car, and he had two juvenile larcenies of dime store stuff in his past. Dumb, poor, ignorant, and happy-go-lucky, he couldn't believe anyone would really hold it against him if he needed stuff. As dangerous as a mayfly, he had just turned eighteen.

"Come on out to the house," Shelley said, closing her folder. "Swim in our lake, cool down, and let the world spin by itself."

"Can't. Tilsen is paying a call on Dad this afternoon, and I'm invited to sit in."

She thought a second or two, stood, and said, "Who do you know who can spot antiques at a glance?"

Without hesitation Shelley said, "Melanie Worther."

"Does she owe you anything?"

Shelley dimpled and nodded, but gave no details, nor did Barbara ask for any. They both had people who owed them something, and she had found that the less said, the better in most cases.

"One of these days, will you ask her to join you in a tour of the Valducci house, just a casual walk through and see if there's anything of great value.

You know, a Louis something or other chair worth fifty thousand, something of that nature."

Shelley nodded. "Consider it done. You think it's something like that?"

"I don't know what to think. But why in God's name is Tilsen hanging around? Gina told him in no uncertain words that the answer is no, was no yesterday, and will be no tomorrow. What's not to understand about N.O.? Yet here he is with an appointment with Dad. Give Gina a call first. She'll have to introduce you and your friend to the dog."

She arrived early at Frank's office, and found him in the law library. She didn't intrude. When it was appointment time Patsy would collect him and meanwhile he was doing what he loved, research for his new book. Books were stacked up next to an open book by his laptop.

She waited in his spacious office that he used to say he was keeping warm for her someday. He hadn't said anything like that for a long time. But as a senior partner of the firm that he and Sam Bixby had established many years before, no one could wrest him away from his office even if he did a minuscule amount of the firm's work. He had carried it for years with his criminal law cases, but in time the firm had shifted to corporate clients, wealthy clients, trusts, and matters of genteel white-collar—possibly criminal—activity that he scorned. And he wrote books and used the law library and his own lovely office as he chose.

It was pleasantly cool there, and Barbara sat with her feet on his coffee table, her hands behind her head, and relaxed as much as she could. But the problem was, she knew, that her inability to get a handle on Jeff Cobbe's case was eating from within. She was even getting irritable with Darren, and he certainly didn't deserve that.

Frank arrived, waved to her, and put his laptop on his desk. "I'll just wash my hands," he said, going into the bathroom he shared with Sam Bixby. He emerged soon afterward and went to his desk. "Those books are dusty. I don't think anyone else even uses them anymore. They look up everything on the Internet these days. A pity. Another layer of obfuscation between the truth of what happened, what laws were passed and their meaning, and anyone looking for the facts. Another layer of MBA editors messing with text that only the best-educated attorneys can comprehend."

Barbara laughed. "Not an egomaniac, no sir, not my old man."

His buzzer sounded, and Patsy said Mr. Tilsen had arrived.

"Give me two minutes," Frank said, "then show him in." He walked around his desk and moved one of the client's chairs to the corner of it, faced in such a way that both he and the client could be observed. "Your chair," he said to Barbara. "An interested party, but not directly involved. I think that will do nicely."

He returned to his own chair, but before sitting down, he removed his coat, very nice gray silk, light-weight, summer wear, and draped it carefully on the back of his chair. He rolled up his sleeves a turn or two, opened a drawer, and took out a file folder and placed it and a pen on his desk. At last he sat down. Patsy tapped on the door and opened it to admit Tilsen.

Barbara compared the two men: Frank, unruffled, cool, courtly, oozing self-confidence, and Tilsen, uncomfortable, too stiff, not at all cool, and, at the sight of her, assuming a somewhat sour expression. He looked like a petulant owl.

Frank rose as Tilsen walked across the office. "Mr. Tilsen, I believe you have met my associate, Ms. Holloway. Please have a seat. What can I do for you?" He did not offer to shake hands.

Tilsen gave Barbara a quick duck of his head, a semi-bow, she thought, not smiling. She ducked her own head in way of acknowledgment. Both men sat down.

"Mr. Holloway, I would like to discuss the issue of the Valducci property."

"What is there to discuss? You made an offer, Ms. Valducci rejected it."

"Mr. Holloway, the night Robert was shot dead I arrived with a memorandum of agreement in my briefcase. That was the purpose of my visit, to sign the MOA, to start the procedure to transfer ownership of the property to our company. That MOA would have been a binding legal agreement, as you are aware. Then, with such clear-cut evidence of her father's wishes, Ms. Valducci chose to nullify them, dishonoring herself and her father's memory. That is regrettable. However, she is very young, quite inexperienced in such matters. Actually, what she and her friends want is exactly the same thing her father wanted, and what my company wants, that is to provide food for a hungry world. We would agree on so many things, if we could have a dialogue. She has refused to talk with me or take my phone calls.

"She asked at the probate hearing why my company wants that particular farm, and the question deserves a more complete answer. This valley and its deep soils and excellent drainage are important to us. The size of the farm is important. Also important is the nearby city of Eugene with its cultural attractions, the coast and the mountains, water sports, winter sports, all outdoor sports, restaurants, a highly rated university here and another one a few miles away, easily accessed air service, rail line, and the interstate highway, plentiful water, though that may change. All of those things make this a desirable location for our company, our personnel, and for visiting guests. Amenities are a very important consideration for keeping employees content and productive."

When Frank nodded without speaking, he continued. "We agree that climate change is here and doing great damage every day, and it will only become worse in the next decade or two. We must be prepared to meet the need for food for the multitudes. Unfortunately, the way she and her young friends have chosen will not accomplish this. Agriculture, like transportation, communications, medicine, all of modern society, cannot turn to the past for the needs of the future. Agriculture is big business today and will only become bigger business tomorrow and on into the future. Ms. Valducci will use her inheritance to bring about changes to her farm that will take it back into yesterday, last century even, and in the end she will run out of money and be in serious debt. I have seen it before, Mr. Holloway, and that is the inevitable fate of her enterprise. Failure, debt, and bankruptcy."

Frank glanced at his watch and then picked up the pen on his desk. "I'll certainly pass on your concerns to my client," he said in a tone clearly meant to dismiss Tilsen.

Tilsen leaned forward, and his mouth looked even tighter, his eyes narrower. "Mr. Holloway, I have outlined the conclusion of Ms. Valducci's enterprise absent any outside influence. But there is outside influence: the upcoming trial of her vice president, Mr. Cobbe. I have sources, Mr. Holloway, who have confided in me the certainty of his conviction. There is compelling evidence that his past will play a part in his trial, a very detrimental part. There is no doubt that he will be convicted, and when that happens, Ms. Valducci and her remaining corporate members will be devastated. Two boys and a girl, they cannot proceed without him. The corporation will collapse and so will the dream of a fantasy farm. That collapse won't be in a matter of years, but of months. What I am here to do is to renew our offer. It will be on the table for the next few months, time enough for the farm to fulfill its contracts for this season, with an admonition not to sign contracts for the future. Time enough for Ms. Valducci to accept the reality that she cannot continue her plans as she had hoped, that it is a doomed enterprise, and her best option is to accept our offer, to buy a smaller piece of ground to try her experimental farm on where the risk of failure will still be present, but when it comes it need not ruin her financially."

Frank stood now and nodded at Tilsen. "As I said, I shall inform Ms. Valducci of your remarks."

Tilsen rose, stiff and angry, and without a glance at Barbara, he nodded curtly to Frank, walked to the door and out.

"Well," Barbara said after the door closed, "what do you think?"

"I think Mr. Tilsen is constipated," Frank said judiciously. "But I also think he made excellent points about why they want the farm. I've heard many other people make the same points when they explained their reasons for choosing to bring business or to settle themselves here in the valley."

Barbara jumped up and shoved the chair back to its usual place. "Bull shit! Maybe he made promises to his superiors that he can't keep and he wants to hold onto his job. Or simply to save face. In any event, I don't give a damn about his reason. What does he know that I don't know? I'm going to go have a talk with Jeff. If I have to shake some truth out of him, I'll shake until his teeth rattle. And if that doesn't work I'm just about ready to wash my hands of his goddamn case." She snatched up her briefcase and purse, glanced around, and started to walk to the door.

"Hold on a second," Frank said, restoring his sleeves to their own usual place. He put on his coat. "If you don't mind I'll drive you out to the farm. Cherries and raspberries. No point in taking two cars. And I need to report to Gina."

She glared at him and he smiled his most innocent smile and they both knew that he did not want her to drive anywhere as angry as she was. They both pretended not to know that. She shrugged. "Suit yourself."

At the farm, everyone was busy: cashiers checking out customers, workers replenishing bins of vegetables and tables with tubs of blueberries, small containers of raspberries, pints of cherries. There was a large bin of corn, first of the season, and many people around it filling bags. Frank asked a worker unloading corn about Gina and was directed in a vague way toward the grounds beyond the rear of the store. The same worker told Barbara that Jeff was in the house. Frank headed out one way and Barbara the other.

Frank spotted Gina at the wide space between two of the greenhouses where a truck had backed in partway. Two young men were unloading blooming chrysanthemums from a long garden wagon onto rows of shelves built inside the truck. Gina stood with a clipboard and papers, checking out the plants. She picked one up and gave it to one of the men loading the truck, said something to him, and looked over the rest of the plants. She rejected a second one, then waved him away. He left in a hurry and she spoke to the one standing by the driver's side. Frank nodded and walked back to the store without interrupting her. Cherries, blueberries, raspberries, he was thinking, visualizing how much free space his freezer had.

Barbara hurried to the house, walked around it to the porch in order to enter by the kitchen, with Rusty keeping her company. As she passed the dining room windows, she could see Jeff, along with Greg and Eric, standing at the table, talking, pointing to a large white sheet of paper or poster board that appeared to cover the entire tabletop.

She entered the kitchen, went to the swinging dining room door, opened it, and said, "Jeff, we have to talk. Now." She made no attempt to soften her tone or to make it anything less than a command.

All three men looked up, startled. Greg looked terrified for a moment, then relaxed. Jeff looked angry, and Eric grinned and said, "Me too? Can I come to the party?"

"It's up to him," Barbara said, nodding toward Jeff.

"Why not?" Jeff muttered. "This is as good a place as any."

"No," Barbara said. "Living room, away from all that." She indicated the poster board that had been drawn on, and had small buildings and driveways, open spaces with lettering, heavy black outlining of a perimeter. It was a layout of the farm, she realized, and knew that if they talked with it in sight, Jeff would not be able to resist looking at it, thinking about it, maybe even adding to it.

"Come on, bro," Eric said. "Living room. You two go get started and I'll bring in some iced tea or iced coffee, whichever you prefer."

He looked to Barbara for her choice and she said coffee. He was not so desperately ill, she thought, watching him walk past her to the kitchen. Still alarmingly thin, he had more color and had lost the dead-man-walking appearance he'd had before. Sleep, rest, Gina's get-fat food, maybe peace and quiet… whatever it was, it was working.

Jeff left through the door to the hall and the living room, and she followed him.

Inside the room Jeff turned toward her and said in an angry tone, "Just what is so important that we have to talk about it right now? What more do you want from me?"

"A hell of a lot more than you've given me," she said, as angry as he was. "Today I learned that the DA has something I don't have, something his office thinks is enough to smash you like a bug. I told you not to hold out on me at the start, and, by God, if you are holding out now, this late in the game, you just might deserve to be smashed like a bug. What does he have that I don't have? What have you left out?"

"What difference does it make?" he said in a grating voice. "I know how this game goes, where I stand. It's been a done deal from day one. I know it, and you damn well know it, too. You're the one playing games, pretending I have a chance when you know I don't. Jesus! Stop dicking me around. Level with me. Just once, level with me. I told you all you need to know. It's not enough? Well, shit! Make up something!"

"I told you on day one that you can bow out with me at any time, tell me to take off, pack my bags and darken your doorstep no more. Well, kiddo, that's a two-way street. I can bow out at any time, too. You tell me the truth, or I'm out of here. I can't defend anyone who lets a load of shit fall on my head in the middle of a trial. You've told me a lot, but not everything. What happened during those months you lived with your father after your mother died?"

"Nothing," he yelled. "There's nothing to tell!"

From behind Barbara's back Eric spoke. "You have to tell her," he said. She and Jeff both spun around to see him standing in the doorway. He came on into the room.

"There's nothing to tell," Jeff muttered. He sank down onto the sofa.

"There's something," Eric said. He sat in a chair opposite his brother and motioned for Barbara to be seated in another chair. "When I went to the academy after you vanished," he said in a low voice, leaning forward, addressing Jeff, "I talked to Major Farleigh. Remember him, Jeff? Major Avery Farleigh. He said he befriended you from the start. I believed him. He was my friend when I attended. He said when Dad dumped you on them, you were bruised and a black eye had not yet healed. He said you had a cut or two on your back that should have had stitches, and that it was too late for that. He said that Dad told them you were violent, with a dangerous temper. Dad told them you tried to kill him."

No one spoke when he became silent. After a moment Jeff rose and walked to the French doors overlooking the terrace and the farm beyond. "How could anyone know anything about that?" he said in a distant voice. "The attorney who handled my name change and Mother's estate said my juvenile record was sealed."

"Money, influence can break seals," Barbara said. "Tell us what happened to you, Jeff."

He turned to face his brother and Barbara, and he remained a silhouette against the bright outside light. "The night he took me home, the day after Mother's funeral," he said in that distant voice, "he shoved me into a bedroom and said that was my room and he left me there. Later, he came back. I was crying. Lying on the bed, crying my eyes out. He yanked me up and slapped me, called me a pussy, a whiny little girl, with little girl tears. He'd been drinking. He slapped me a couple of times and said no supper for a sniveling little girl, and he left again."

Barbara hadn't known she had been holding her breath until she exhaled. She felt frozen in place. Eric had not moved.

"There was a pattern," Jeff said from the doors. "For a few days I was invisible to him almost. There was a man there, he called him sergeant. I think he had been under Dad's command in the past. I never found out. His name was Sergeant Leemer. He was okay, but he never got between Dad and me. I think he was afraid. I had to wash dishes, take out the trash, normal things like that, and for almost a week, it was okay. I avoided Dad when he was around if I could. He had time off for the first month. After that he was gone four days a week, home for weekends. One day he came in while I was watching television and he yelled at me to stand up when he entered the room, and to stand until he gave me permission to sit. He told me to call him Sir, the way Sergeant Leemer did."

Jeff moved away from the doors and resumed his place on the sofa. He buried his face in his hands for a few seconds, then leaned back with his eyes closed. "I'll cut it short," he said tiredly. "Sometimes I didn't stand up when he came in and he slapped me. One time I stood for such a long time, I got dizzy and fell down, and he kicked me. One time when he yelled at me to call him Sir, I said it, and he slapped me and yelled that he hated my little girl voice. I tried to speak in a deeper voice, but I wasn't very good at it, and that got more slaps. Then, one day he took off his belt and I remembered how he had switched my legs and butt when I was small. I ran out into the backyard and he caught me and hit me with the belt and he punched me in the face and chest, on my arm. I don't know where all. I was rolling around on the ground and I closed my hand on a flower pot and swung it at him. Dirt covered us both, the plant, broken pot. Sergeant came running out and dragged me inside, then went back out to help Dad. He wasn't hurt. The pot caught him on his shoulder." He became silent. "That night I ran away. He called the police and they found me and dragged me back. I don't know what he said, what they have in their report. The next week he took me to the academy, and I never saw him again until Curtis's funeral."

He straightened up on the sofa and looked first at his brother, then at Barbara, and he said in a low voice. "I wanted him to stop hitting me. And I wanted to kill him. He was right about that. I tried to kill him. And he's the only one who knows about it. He didn't tell them at the academy, I'm sure. Not the details. But it's in their books that I was violent, with a dangerous temper, that I attacked him."

"I'll go get that iced coffee," Eric said. "Right back." He left them.

Barbara brought out her legal pad and wrote the two names: Sergeant Leemer and Major Avery Farleigh. Jeff watched her without expression. He shook his head, and he sounded very sad when he said, "Barbara, give it up. What's the use?"

On Saturday evening, it was pleasantly cool in the shadow of the Coast Range mountains, and Barbara was pleasantly cool after a long swim in the lake on Shelley and Alex's large plantation. She called it that, although neither Shelley nor Alex did. They called it a house and yard. Now they were all on the terrace where a grill was still smoking and candles in perforated-iron lamps were sending dance patterns of flickering light on their faces. Shelley and Alex were holding hands, as were Barbara and Darren. Dr. Minnick was resting in a chaise lounge.

Alex had grilled salmon, and Dr. Minnick had made a salad that only he could make. His secret, he had confided, was to toss in almost anything edible, steamed crisp and tender if it needed that touch, otherwise raw: potatoes, green beans, snap peas, slivers of carrots, red onions, avocados, olives, hearts of artichokes, radishes, asparagus. Barbara called it an uncooked stew. What made it so special in her opinion was his aioli dressing.

"No vampires tonight," Alex said.

"See? It works," Dr. Minnick said.

Barbara sipped her espresso. "Dr. Minnick, let me describe some behavior and you tell me what it means. Okay with that?"

He was a widely respected psychiatrist, who had specialized in adolescent behavior. Alex had been born with a hideously disfigured face and at fourteen had been suicidal. Dr. Minnick had pulled him away from the edge of the cliff, and now in retirement continued to make his home with Alex and Shelley.

"Shoot," Dr. Minnick said. "Warning you, though. I'm out of practice."

"Right," she said. "Here goes. He's a little kid, twelve, not yet into the adolescent growth spurt, still quite childish. He's smart. So, he's put in a school geared toward military training, along with all the academic stuff. He excels academically, straight As, and he excels in all the required physical exercise classes. Best swimmer, runner, shooter, all of it. But when they try to pressure him into joining a team, any team, swim, baseball, track, marksmanship, anything, he balks. He's better than his peers, but he won't join a team of any sort. He is warned that he'll be punished, and he silently accepts his punishment. Not physical abuse, but humiliation and shame, like parading him naked in front of the school body. Keeping him isolated. He endures this for four years, never a complaint from him, and never compliance with the school authorities."

After a brief silence when she stopped speaking, Dr. Minnick said, "I rather imagine that at first he was mocked, ridiculed, and that changed to admiration. Is that correct?"

"Pretty much so. Not admired by the head of the school, but by several instructors and most of his classmates."

"Peaceful protest," Dr. Minnick said. "Gandhi-like resistance. For him it could imply distrust, even contempt for authority, withdrawal in the face of adversity. Other effects that would have to be evaluated in dialogues with him, behavior observations. But for the authority in question, that's passive-aggressive in its most insidious form, if you are the one who administers the orders and the punishment. If he escaped seemingly unscathed, those responsible for his insubordination and his punishment feel threatened; they know they lost this battle, and they quite often hate and fear the winner. Authoritarianism with the power to punish dares not lose the battle with those they would control. There could be a ripple effect, manifested by admiration of the victor. Your lad defeated them, and they know it. They can be dangerous under the right circumstances. How far does their power to punish extend? Is your friend safe from retaliation?"

"I don't know," Barbara said. "I just don't know." She changed the subject then. "Is there any more coffee? I know it's late and I probably shouldn't, but it's too good to stop yet."

The conversation drifted around the way it does with old friends, and then it was time for Barbara and Darren to leave. Darren drove, in no hurry on the winding country road without a mark on it. "You were talking about Jeff Cobbe, weren't you?" he asked.

She had told him little about her case, she rarely did, but now she said yes. "That was his situation for four years, from twelve to sixteen when he escaped or, as he puts it, simply left."

"That poor kid," Darren said. "He deserves a medal or something. Does he know how heroic he was?"

Surprised, Barbara looked at him, his profile, and said, "I doubt it has ever occurred to him to think of it as heroic."

"Maybe he needs to hear that. Something happened to change you," he said, keeping his gaze on the road ahead. "You've been down, maybe not out, but not flying high, either. What happened? Can you talk about it?"

She could and did. She told him about her last talk with Jeff and Eric. "And yes, something changed. Jeff has been an enigma. I don't know how many times I've had to deal with anyone I so little understood. He didn't escape unscathed. From the time his mother died until he was sixteen, he endured, and now he's keeping himself so far back sometimes I think it's hard even to see him. There's that. But more than that, until now I haven't had anything to push against. Just a squishy circumstantial case. Dr. Minnick really helped me straighten out some things. Now there is something and the wind is strong. I can push back against a strong wind, but not dead air."

Darren laughed softly. "God, don't I know that."

Barbara was smiling as she entered the office on Monday. She had been considering her perfect weekend, and how just a couple of days made the sun shine again. Dinner with friends, most of Sunday in bed with Darren while a fan blew cool air on them, taking turns murmuring something about getting up and doing something or other that needed doing. Then dinner with Frank who had told funny stories about the cases he was researching, something about a defense attorney turning a pig loose in court at a crucial time in the prosecutor's closing statement, when the jury panel had been ready to hang the defendant. "Hung jury," Frank had said, concluding the story. "Never got around to trying him again." She smiled broader at the memory, then waved airily to Maria, who was uncovering her computer.

"Send in Shelley and Bailey when they get here," Barbara said and entered her own office. Maria had turned on the air conditioner, already making the office cool, a blessing. Few people had them in their homes, but offices were different, she told herself, the way she always did when it was on. A legitimate business expense, she also always told herself, to still the pang of guilt that insisted on disturbing her.

Shelley entered minutes later. She looked as radiant as Barbara felt, but Shelley managed to look radiant most of the time. Bailey slouched in seconds later, followed by Maria with a tray that held the coffee carafe, mugs, cream, and sugar. Maria knew the Monday morning drill.

"Okay," Barbara said, seated on the sofa, with Shelley to her left, Bailey to her right in easy chairs. She poured, but let them help themselves to the sugar, much too much for Bailey, none for Shelley, and the cream, too much again for Bailey, enough to discolor Shelley's coffee. Her own coffee was black and sugarless. "You first," she said to Bailey.

"Blackstons' sewed up. Six people, six statements about who owns what. Cup of cake, done."

She blinked at "cup of cake." He handed her a folder, and she put it down unopened. She had forgotten about the Blackstons. They could wait.

She gave Shelley and Bailey a summary of her talk with Jeff and Eric, and Dr. Minnick's assessment. "We had a long conversation after Jeff came clean about his stay at the academy. I have some addresses, and names of possible character witnesses, people who either befriended him or at least knew what was going on. I'll call some of them."

"I have a couple of them for you," she told Bailey. "First, a Major Avery Farleigh. He was an instructor at Ridge Academy when Jeff was there. Twelve years ago, more or less. I need to find him and talk to him. The academy is somewhere in upstate New York, near Rochester. Then, a Sergeant Leemer. No one knows exactly how it's spelled. That's how it sounds. He was under the command of General Ballantine sometime in the past, and his man servant, aide de camp, or something when Jeff was eleven. That's eighteen years ago and he might be hard to track down. The general gave up his house about five years ago and lives in a residential hotel in Fairfax. Leemer isn't with him. I have some addresses for you to start with."

Bailey was looking at her with disbelief writ large on his homely face. "Give me a break, Barbara. Twelve years ago, eighteen years ago! They might both be six feet under."

"If so, dig up the info for me. I want to talk to both of them, or their ghosts." She ignored his indignation and said, "Also, find out if Tilsen still has an apartment or house or whatever headquarters he was using in Portland. And if any associates are still with him, and what they were all doing in the state. Why he's still here may be too much to ask of you." She handed him the addresses.

"Oh, it could be a bit much," Bailey said. "Just a little bit much." He was making notes in a small notebook. He stopped to drink his coffee and refill his cup.

"You eat too much sugar," Barbara said.

He grunted and added more, then went back to making notes.

"Shelley, any land transfers to Tilsen and his company?"

"Not a thing. They don't want just any piece of ground, they want that particular piece, apparently. Also, I took my antique guru out to the farm Saturday. Gina gave us a walk through the house, talking all the time about various items: the Murano glass pieces, local artists' pictures, that sort of thing. Melanie told her she really should get an appraisal or at least a video of the furnishings and tuck it away in a safe deposit box, because it would cost a fortune to replace such nice furniture, if it can even be found these days. She would get used-furniture prices if she sold, and pay a fortune to replace. That's how Melanie put it. She really regretted that the ivory-framed mirror didn't have an artist's name on it or even initials. As it is, it's a beautiful item that could bring a thousand dollars, or five, depending on who attended a sale that included it. If it had provenance that put it on the wall of Marie Antoinette's boudoir, or the Borgias', it would be considered priceless." She dimpled and added, "I'd pay a thousand for it if it turned up at a yard sale." She spread her hands in a helpless gesture. "And no, nothing like a priceless antique chair or credenza."

"Way it goes," Barbara said. "Anything else?"

"Maybe, maybe not," Shelley said. "Gina, in her rambling, mentioned that Tilsen had sent a goon out to take pictures, and she ran him and his assistant off with a threat to call the police and charge them with trespassing. The problem is the guy with the camera happens to be Geraldo Reyes, a legitimate photojournalist. He's had stuff in most major magazines. *National Geographic*, *Sunset*, *Vanity Fair*, and so on. Awards coming out his gazoo, including a Pulitzer. He's really well known and respected. Hard to think he's playing ball with Tilsen's group. Why would he?"

Bailey made a rude noise. "Money can buy a shitload of respectability."

Barbara silenced him with a glare. "Did Gina say what excuse Reyes had for taking pictures?"

"He told her he was doing a story about small farmers, the hardships they face, the competition, why they are hanging in there, things like that. It sounds like the sort of thing he might do, actually. She didn't believe a word of it."

Barbara shook her head. "Leave it alone, I guess. Gina said nothing doing, private property, her right to refuse to cooperate, and that's that. So that's a wrap for today, I think. Now and then, Shelley, take a look at land purchases. I don't think anything's going to show up, but let's cover the bases, just in case. And, Bailey, finding those two guys is a priority right now." She stood. Bailey closed his notebook and drained his coffee cup. He rose, ambled to the door, saluted, and left.

Shelley lingered only a minute. "Gina's really something else, isn't she? People keep saying Jeff's the one running the show. I'm beginning to wonder. Gina can be pretty assertive, and she sure does know what she's doing out there. Amelia and I walked around a couple of minutes and saw her running a couple of teenaged boys out of a greenhouse with a No Admittance sign. She didn't mince words."

After Shelley went out to her own office and her own work, Barbara sat down again and poured the last of the coffee into her mug. Again, she was thinking, again the suggestion that Gina should get a video of the furnishings. And again, an expert stopping at the ivory-framed mirror. That was the key, Barbara decided. Something about the mirror was important, and she didn't know what it was. It was beautiful, but apparently not collectible, not priceless without an artist's name attached. "Mirror, mirror, on the wall" she said under her breath. "What's the secret you alone know?

"So it doesn't rhyme," she said crossly. She drained her cup, rose, and decided to have another talk with Gina in the near future.

She had not yet reached her desk when Maria buzzed to say a Mr. Simon Alterman was in the reception room, wanting to see her about Geraldo Reyes.

"Tell him to make an appointment," Barbara said, almost reflexively. Immediately after saying this she said, "Hang on a second. Geraldo Reyes?" The photojournalist Gina had kicked off her property? At Maria's affirmative, she said, "Give me a minute, then show him in." She started toward the table with the coffee service and mugs, but Maria beat her to it.

"I'll take these thing out, and put him on hold for a minute," she said, gathering up the things on the table.

"Thanks," Barbara said. She retrieved her notebook from the table and went to her desk where she closed a file folder, brought out her tape recorder to check the battery light, put it in her top desk drawer, which she did not close all the way, then waited for Simon Alterman.

He was tall and very good looking, too good looking to be a lackey whose job it was to carry water for a boss. Forty-something. Dark brown wavy hair, dark blue eyes, good tan, well built, he could have been a male model. His smile on approaching her desk revealed teeth that could have starred in a toothpaste commercial. He was carrying several magazines.

"Ms. Holloway," he said, "so good of you to see me, not on short notice, but on no notice whatsoever. Thank you."

She nodded toward a chair, thinking it was too much. Motion picture handsome, and with an accent. Too damn much! Irish? British? A mix? "You're welcome," she said. "What can I do for you?"

"Not me. My employer, Geraldo Reyes. I have brought you these, to demonstrate more or less that he's on the up and up. I think that's the expression I want. Legitimate, that is." He put the magazines on her desk. "It was an idle impulse, you see, to stop at that country store, never suspecting the story behind it. Geraldo isn't interested in greengrocers, only small farmers. But a few questions, a little observation revealed that he had arrived at his dream farm and dream farmer. Now the intrigue is overwhelming for Geraldo. He's a romantic, you know. He believes fate led him to that country store, that it is his duty to tell its story. I suppose I have to agree. Fate, damsel in distress, a lover possibly condemned to die... A lovely young woman, her travails in obtaining what is rightfully hers, struggling against great odds, only to find herself working like a peon, but with a smile that could light the world." He paused, smiling, then added, "You must admit that it is a stirring story, heartwarming, operatic. We spent most of yesterday digging it out from the Internet."

"Interesting," Barbara said. "What are you doing here now in my office?"

He laughed. "I am here on orders to seduce you into interceding for Geraldo. Spanish, you know, too proud to ask for anything in person. Send the hired help to do it. That's me. All he wants is permission to take a multitude of photographs, obtain releases from people who will appear in them, do a few interviews, and write the story of the Valducci Corporation and its little farm tucked away in this lovely valley."

"I believe Ms. Valducci already responded by inviting Mr. Reyes and you to leave her property or face legal consequences," Barbara said.

He leaned forward and said in low voice, "And that's exactly why Geraldo is so intrigued. The forcefulness of her response, her quick dismissal, contempt, and dislike so expressively communicated, her every gesture bespoke hostility, possibly even hatred. That's the intrigue, Ms. Holloway. Her response. Why? We had done no harm, presented no possible danger to her or her property. Geraldo was especially deferential to her, treated her with the utmost respect, and was treated like a mortal enemy. We both were. His pride is wounded, his work devalued; he feels misjudged, mistreated, and he wants to know why, and to make amends if that is possible. But above all he wants to add her farm to his story."

Barbara laughed then and rose from her chair. "You're very good, Mr. Alterman. If you had ten more minutes you might have done what you admittedly came to do, that is seduce me into joining you and Mr. Reyes. However, you don't have ten more minutes. Let's cut to the chase, another good old American saying. Mr. Reyes wants something that only Ms. Valducci can give him, and she refused. My advice is for you to convey to your employer that he find a different small farm and get on with his project. Now I'm afraid, I have to ask you to leave, as I too am quite busy."

He rose unhurriedly. "It's been a pleasure, Ms. Holloway. Finding a worthy opponent is always a pleasure, albeit a rare one."

"Jesus!" she whispered, when he left and the door closed behind him. He was good, too good. If he was Reyes's water boy, he was miscast. His accent with that charming lilt added, his handsome face, steady unblinking gaze that suggested intimacy, it was all too perfect. Even what he hadn't done added to the effect. Not offering to shake hands, not trying to get closer physically, not plying her with compliments that would have rung false. All too perfect, as if he were an actor so well rehearsed that not a single nuance had gone unpracticed until it was inherent in everything he did and said.

Another thought followed swiftly: Gina had to be protected from him.

A few seconds later she was rummaging in her desk drawers when there was a tap on the door, followed immediately by opening to admit Shelley.

"Barbara, if you don't want him, can I have him?" She had her hand over her heart, tapping furiously.

Barbara laughed. "You just happened to be hanging out in the reception room when he appeared out of the blue?"

“Not at all,” Shelley said. “Maria gave me a heads up that I shouldn’t miss the prettiest man to lighten our doorstep in maybe forever. What are you looking for?”

“Ah, here it is,” Barbara said picking up a small black case. “Magnifying glass. That hunk who just walked out is Simon Alterman, Geraldo Reyes’ right-hand guy, case carrier, water boy, driver, something.” She slipped the magnifying glass case into her purse. “And now I’m off to the farm. Someone has to fight off the dragon that would attack Gina’s virtue. I’m not sure that at her age I would have been able to resist Mr. Alterman.”

“I wouldn’t even try to resist,” Shelley said with a wicked grin. She waved and retreated to return to her own office.

When Barbara arrived at Valducci's, she passed through the store after a quick scan of customers loading carts with produce and fruit, and hurried out back. Still nothing, she thought, and started toward greenhouse number six when she spotted Simon Alterman. She walked toward him and now could see Gina, clutching magazines to her chest, face to face with Alterman. Gina took a step backward and he took one forward, a little too close, but not touching her. He was backing her up toward the house, Barbara realized. She quickened her own pace.

They were just eight or ten feet from the invisible fence that kept Rusty on one side and the world on the other. Rusty was there, his tail wagging, tongue out, apparently happy to see Gina coming. Barbara strode up to Gina and touched her arm.

"Gina, I'm glad I found you." Gina jerked at the touch. She looked startled and confused. Barbara smiled at her. "There's something we have to talk about. Hello, Mr. Alterman. You certainly do get around, don't you?"

"As do you," he said smoothly. "I was explaining to Miss Gina how devastated Geraldo was by her rejection."

"I'm sure you were," Barbara said. "Gina, would you mind waiting in the house a couple of minutes? I'll help Mr. Alterman find his car."

Hurriedly Gina turned and took the few steps that had her across the invisible fence. Alterman started to follow and Barbara said, "Rusty, guard."

Instantly Rusty changed into a guard dog. His tail was between his legs, ears slicked back, teeth bared, and his eyes trained on Alterman. He uttered a low growl.

"I'd advise you to stop moving forward," Barbara said. "He's only seventy-five pounds, but he's very swift. We think he has alligator genes, the way he opens his mouth. There's a signal for him to stop an attack, but I'm not a family member and I never can quite remember it. And Gina's hands are so full I doubt that she could give the signal in time to prevent some damage."

Alterman took one more step forward and Rusty crouched and showed even more teeth. His growl was louder, more prolonged. Alterman backed up.

"Gina," Barbara said, "I'll be only a minute or two. Mr. Alterman, shall we try to locate your car now?"

Gina took a quick look over her shoulder at them, then walked fast toward the house; Rusty didn't move, his eyes narrowed, remaining in a fixed gaze on Alterman, who made a gesture of surrender, throwing both hands up. He wheeled about and started to walk. Barbara walked with him.

"Perhaps," Alterman said, smiling at Barbara, "in the next few days Miss Gina will have the opportunity to look through the magazines, as I trust you will also do, Ms. Holloway. I wrote the name and telephone number of his editor on the cover of the *National Geographic*. Geraldo really does have a contract to do the story. But for now he wants to see the fabled Oregon coast, and possibly the equally fabled Crater Lake. We'll be back in about a week to beseech Miss Gina one more time for permission to use her charming farm and more charming self in the story."

When Barbara didn't comment, he laughed. His laugh, like his smile, was too familiar, suggested intimacy, and it was mocking. "Ah, the extended silence that speaks more eloquently than words can convey one's complete and sufficient disapprobation of the proposal. That's Jane Austen language, by the way. Lovely word, disapprobation. And here is my automobile." He opened the car door and slid in behind the steering wheel, smiled broadly at her, and said, "I think we shall meet again, my dear Ms. Holloway. But for now, it's adieu."

She watched until he backed out of the parking space, turned, and drove to River Road, and was gone. Then she hurried to the house. Gina was in the kitchen holding a glass of ice water.

"My God," she said when Barbara came in. "Dear God, he was impossible. I felt almost as if he was hypnotizing me or something. Svengali, alive and breathing. Incredible, and I fell for it, hook, line, sinker, all the way. I couldn't seem to make him stop, to go away…"

"Well, he's gone now. Just don't let yourself be alone with him if and when he comes back, probably not for a week, but eventually. Anyway, what I really came for was to examine that mirror. It keeps coming up as possibly very valuable, but unfortunately not without proper papers, provenance. Did your grandmother buy it in Italy when she bought those Murano glass pieces?"

"No. It was already here when she married my grandfather in the sixties. Her mother-in-law, my great grandmother, had it in her bedroom, and when she died, my grandmother took it. Now I have it."

"Do you know where or when it was first bought? Who bought it? Did the first Valducci bring it when he came?"

"No to all the above," Gina said. "My grandmother found me doing the 'Mirror, mirror on the wall, Who's the fairest…' You know, Snow White. I was pretending it was that mirror. What they told my grandmother and she told me was that a letter came from a distant relative who said he was sending a trunk with his belongings and that he would explain when he got here. Well, he never got here but the trunk did. They kept it in the hall for a few months, then moved it to the basement, and that's when they broke the lock and opened it. They were hoping to find the relative's address, telephone number, anything to identify him and return his possessions or at least to get in touch with him. I think there was no return address on the envelope, and nothing but the shipping label on the trunk. Anyway, they didn't find any identification, but they found the mirror. Everything else is junk. A man's clothing, crockery, pillows, horse pictures, boots, a moth-eaten blanket. It's all junk, except the mirror. I think he tied the pillows around the mirror, to keep it intact. There was heavy twine in the trunk when my grandmother looked through it, but I guess no one told her if the mirror was between the pillows when they first found it. At least, she didn't tell me that. But what else were the twine for, and pillows? Of course, when I was a kid I had to open the trunk and see for myself, and that's it, junk."

Barbara stifled her sigh of frustration. "Gina, may I have a crack at the mirror? No pun intended. I brought a magnifying glass. Maybe there's a signature in micro-writing, or initials, something."

Gina looked at the wall clock. "I don't care if you want to look, Barbara, but I really have to get back to the greenhouse. We're expecting some people to come talk to us about going solar, how much it might cost, how effective it would be. I really want to be there. If that's what you came to do, sure. Do whatever you want in the house, as long as I don't have to stay and watch you. Is that okay?"

"More than okay. Scat, and I'll do my Sherlockian impression without an audience."

Gina drank deeply of her ice water, then hurried out the kitchen door, and Barbara walked through the hallway to the stairs, up to Magda's old room that was now Gina's bedroom. From one generation to the next, she was thinking, passing on the house, the furnishings, the farm, even the mirror.

It was so beautiful, she thought then, regarding it. Intricately carved in a recursive, repeating pattern, like a fractal. Old ivory, creamy gold in color, lovely beveling at the glass edges, two fine gold wires holding the pieces together, deep, clear mirror surface, it could well have been *that* mirror. She repeated the refrain under her breath as she removed the mirror from the wall and placed it on a chair near a wide window where the light was good.

Kneeling, she started to examine it with the magnifying glass. Moving slowly, taking her time, she peered at it around one side, up and over the top. Her knees began to hurt and she shifted her position, then shifted again. Down the other side, and then she found something not right. A mistake, she thought, holding the magnifier closer, comparing one side to the other. The pattern was broken, she realized. The mirror was flawed. Too small a mistake to be noticed at a glance, or even a fairly close examination, it was revealed under the magnifying glass, a missed fluting part of the design, less than a quarter of an inch in length, but there.

She shifted her position again, this time to sit on the floor in front of the mirror. "He knew he made a mistake," she said under her breath. "The artist saw an imperfection and knew he couldn't fix it. He wouldn't add his name to a flawed work."

After a few minutes she continued her examination, then turned the mirror over to scrutinize the other side, but she did not expect to find anything to identify the artist. Nor could she unsee the flaw now that she knew it was there. It would have leaped out at him, she thought. That's what he must have seen whenever he looked at it, a flawed masterpiece. She found nothing else. After hanging the mirror back on the wall where it belonged, she patted the carved ivory gently. "You're still very beautiful," she murmured. "I won't tell."

Slowly she went down the stairs to the kitchen where she poured herself a glass of ice water. It was very hot again, ninety plus, and she was sweating and sticky. This summer was breaking heat records, setting new records. She started toward the door, then stopped. Why would anyone pay the freight for a trunk full of trash when he could have carried the mirror in a big attaché case with sufficient padding to protect the glass? Why hadn't he followed up, arrived to claim his belongings? What if the trunk itself was the solution to the puzzle he presented? A secret compartment, something glued to the bottom or under the lid, papers of some importance, even money could be concealed in it. No one would have looked for anything like that in all likelihood. The mirror might have been enough of a treasure to still other questions.

She looked at the basement door, and even cursed under her breath, but she went to the door and down to the basement to look over the trunk. Cover all bases, she told herself, and wiped sweat off her forehead with the back of her hand. A consolation prize, she told herself in the basement when she descended: It was several degrees cooler.

The trunk was against the wall with several boxes stacked on it. They contained Christmas tree ornaments. She removed them and opened the trunk, and then carefully emptied it. Two pillows, boots, crockery bowls and a platter, cheap, heavy, ugly, and chipped, loosely wrapped in newspapers. A man's suit, cheap, badly worn, frayed at the cuffs, at the sleeves. She felt in the pockets, nothing. When she removed the blanket, she unfolded it, looked at both sides then folded it again. Nothing. Next she removed the horse pictures, also loosely wrapped in newspapers. She put them on the blanket and now with the trunk empty, she examined it thoroughly. No secret compartment, nothing glued to the sides, under the top or bottom. Nothing, period.

She began to reload the trunk, returning everything more or less to where it had been before. When she got to the horse pictures, the newspaper came off the first one she picked up, revealing a Clydesdale horse in a meadow, the kind of picture that a kid might buy in Target, or Freddie's, any big box store. A wooden frame looked amateurishly done, with black paint flaked off in several places. She picked up the newspaper to rewrap the picture and saw that the back of it, covered with brown paper, had come loose, tape had become brittle and crumbled when she touched it. She tried to replace the brown paper, and it came off in her hand.

She caught her breath, and stared. Another picture was under the horse picture.

She turned the second picture over carefully and gasped. "Oh, my God!" she said hoarsely. She was looking at a Picasso portrait of a woman.

She had been hot and sweaty, but now a chill seized her, and her hands shook as she carefully laid the Picasso down and lifted the newspaper covering the next horse picture. The tape was as brittle as the first one, and she tried to keep it in place while lifting one corner of the paper. Carefully she put this picture next to the first one when she saw another picture face down behind the horse picture. She didn't touch the other two pictures yet, nor did she remove the newly revealed face-down painting. Moving almost as if entranced she finally lifted the corners of the remaining two horse pictures; two more paintings face down. She did not examine them, but stood transfixed by her discovery, her gaze repeatedly returning to the Picasso portrait. Then she shook herself and hastily turned the painting over. Now what?

She couldn't just put them back in the trunk, and she couldn't tell Gina, not yet. But she had to get them to a safe place and consider what to do next. Frank's safe, she decided. Get them to a safe. Lock them up. Call Bailey. Her thoughts were coming fast, overriding one another.

First, she had to get them out of the house safely. She looked at the pillows, in discolored pillowcases that smelled musty. Without hesitation she pulled off the pillowcases, and moving gingerly she replaced the Picasso behind the Clydesdale horse, wrapped it in several layers of newspaper, and slid it into the pillow case. She repeated this with the other three, using all the newspaper available, slipped the filled pillow case into the other one and folded it down over the bundle. She set it aside long enough to finish reloading the trunk, close it, and replace the boxes of Christmas ornaments on top.

Then, listening for anyone in the kitchen above, she carried the bundle up the stairs, hesitated at the kitchen door, listening, and finally opened the door to see that the kitchen was empty. Hurrying now, she carried her bundle through the hall to the closet near the front door, where she deposited her pillow cases with priceless paintings. She was breathing heavily when she closed the closet door and stood for a minute leaning against it, thinking.

Bailey. She needed Bailey. She punched in the speed dial for him and listened to the ring. "Pick it up! Pick it up!" she whispered with her eyes closed. He hated the cell phone and used it for emergencies only whenever possible. Sometimes he waited until he had a landline available to return her calls, to her annoyance. "Bailey, pick up the damn phone!" she snapped. "This is an emergency."

He came on the line. "Yeah. What?"

"I'm at Valducci's and you have to come out here with your SUV. Don't park at the store, take the road to the driveway and stop at the front door so that you block anyone's sight. Don't get out of the car or the dog will bark. I'll explain when you get here. How soon can you make it?"

"Barbara, for crying out loud! Give me a break. Are you okay?"

"How soon, damn it? Get on your horse and get out here as fast as you can. I'm okay for now. Don't be followed."

"Geez," he said. "Half an hour." He disconnected.

She called Frank, and he had the good sense to answer when he saw that it was her calling. "Dad," she said, "Bailey's going to bring a package to your office and I'll be on his heels. Are you at the office?"

"Yep. Nice and cool here in the library, hot as blazes at the house. A package?"

"I'll explain when I get there. Guard it with your life, Dad. Lock the door, don't open it until I arrive. Okay?"

Half an hour to kill, she thought when she disconnected, and to stay out of sight of Gina and her gang. Maybe fate would be kind and they would be tied up with solar consultants for the afternoon. She went to the kitchen for more ice water, and then to the terrace to sit in shade and fret about Bailey and his half-hour prediction. She closed her eyes and forced herself not to think of half an hour as an eternity.

It took Bailey twenty-five minutes, and she felt as if she had walked miles from the terrace to the front door, back, again and again and again. Rusty growled when the SUV drove in and stopped at the front door.

"Rusty, friend," Barbara said rushing to the side of the van. Bailey rolled down the window. "Open the side door," she said. "I'll get a package and put it inside, and you deliver it to Dad. Be sure no one follows you. I'll be right behind you, as soon as I can."

"That's it?" Bailey said in disgust.

She was already hurrying to the front door. Inside, she made sure no one was in the hall or in the kitchen where they might see her if they happened to look her way. Still moving as swiftly as possible she retrieved the pillowcase-wrapped pictures and rushed to the van to shove them into the back. Bailey closed the door.

"Go!" she said. "Just go!"

He waved and began to back up, and she drew in a long breath of relief. As soon as the SUV was on Green Briar Road, on its way to River Road, she patted Rusty on the head and walked fast to the store, through it, and to her own car parked out front. Only then did her breathing return to normal and her heart stop pounding hard.

Barbara didn't bother with the receptionist, or with Patsy with her open door and questioning gaze. She went straight to Frank's office, banged on the door, and entered. Bailey, sprawled in an easy chair, already had a drink in his hand, and Frank was pouring wine into a glass. On the handsome coffee table the bulging pillowcase, dirty, discolored, musty, looked incongruous. She locked the door behind her.

"Hi, Dad. A little something to brighten the day," she said, going to the table. She was surprised at how dry her mouth was. She dropped her purse and briefcase on the sofa and then carefully removed the outer pillowcase. Then, again moving with great care, she drew out the pictures wrapped in newspaper. Frank had put down the bottle of wine and the glass and moved closer, and Bailey was leaning forward watching.

When she uncovered the Picasso, Frank whispered, "Christ on a mountain!" and Bailey muttered something indecipherable. Without a word Barbara pulled out the next horse picture and pulled off the brown paper, turned the concealed painting over: Rembrandt. One of his burghers, that could have been out of his Night Watch. "Good God!" she also whispered. No one else made a sound. The next one was a sheet of drawings, Leonardo drawings. "Sketch notes for 'The Last Supper,'" Barbara said in a hoarse voice. The last one was a Raphael Virgin and Child.

As she removed the masterpieces, Barbara discarded all the newspapers, and put the horse pictures on the floor. Now she spread out the priceless paintings across the coffee table, sat on the sofa, and regarded them in wonder. Frank sat in one of the easy chairs, also speechless. Bailey emptied his glass and silently went to the bar Frank had opened and mixed himself another drink without asking permission, the first time he had ever done such a thing in this office.

Now what? Now what? Now what? The words were on a loop in Barbara's head. She stared at the works of art and was only vaguely aware of Frank's movement until he pressed a glass of wine into her hand.

"Who do we tell?" Bailey asked in a hushed voice. "Cops? FBI? Interpol?"

"No one!"

"We don't!"

Barbara and Frank spoke simultaneously, and she was roused from her trance-like state with the sound. She gulped wine and closed her eyes for a moment. "No one," she repeated. "We'd have the world press down on us in a flash. No one until after the trial. Especially not Gina."

"Where did they come from?" Bailey asked, pointing to the paintings. "Where did you get them? You rob a museum or something?"

"Something," she said. "We have to get them put away in the safe, out of sight before someone comes in." She stood and started to gather the discarded newspapers.

"Hold on," Frank said. "Not that way. Back in a second." He took another drink of his wine and went to the door and out.

"Help me clean up this mess," Barbara said to Bailey. "At least get the papers off the floor."

Bailey drained his glass and rose to help her. "Chicago newspapers," he said after a moment. "Back from 1957."

"*The New York Times*, 1956," she said.

"No way. *Chicago Tribune*, January 1957."

She looked again at the newspaper she was holding. "December 1956. Let's put them in two heaps. Could be the packing started in December, finished in January. Two newspapers, maybe two cities."

They had most of them picked up and sorted when Bailey said, "This is interesting." He passed her a torn page from a telephone directory. There was a brief ad for Valducci's Produce with a circle around it.

Frank reentered the office carrying oversized envelopes, both padded and unpadded. "Let's package them up," he said, going to his desk. Using a letter opener, he slit one side of each of the unpadded envelopes; then at the coffee table again he slipped the Picasso, still backed by the Clydesdale horse, into the cut envelope. It was only partly covered. He used another envelope to cover the rest of it, turned in the self-seal flaps and closed them. He put the snugly packaged painting into a padded envelope and sealed it. Barbara began to fold the newspapers into two manageable stacks and stuff them into her briefcase.

When Frank finished packaging the paintings, he opened his safe and put them on a shelf, tossed the pillowcases inside, closed the door and locked it, and then went straight to the bar with his glass and refilled it.

"Now," he said, resuming his seat on the easy chair. "Tell us."

Barbara finished her wine and went for a refill. She told them how she had found the paintings. "They were shipped from Chicago, no name, no return address, just a cryptic note that Gina never saw. It may be somewhere in the house, maybe not. No one in that house ever suspected what they had. All those years, locked away in the trunk, secure, clean and dry, and not a single suspicion."

"They belong to Gina, if they can be said to belong to anyone," Frank said.

"I know. But she can't be told. You know her, how she talks, how her expression changes with each change of moods. Not a secret keeper. It would cause a sensation, a world-class circus! God, anything but that! Not until after the trial. What a motive that would give Jeff if it came out before the trial. But who else knows? That's the question." She bit her lip. "Does Tilsen? How could he have found out? Mrs. Chadwick? That con man Simon Alterman? Why did he suddenly show up with his snow job? Geraldo Reyes? A world-class thief?"

"Barbara, slow down," Frank said. "You're right, mum's the word for now." He thought a moment. "I know a fellow who might know how to proceed. William Tate, retired museum director or something like that. I'll give him a call, have a drink with him, and pick his brain. And we all need to think."

"Bailey, a couple of things to get on right now, as soon as you can," Barbara said in a rush. "We need the telephone record from Mildred Chadwick's calls in March, whom she called and when. Did the mirror tip her off? Did she tip someone else off about what else could be in the house? How could she have known about the trunk? Did she know about it? I knew that mirror was the key. I just knew it. And there's a candelabra in the shop she and Lucy Harris ran together. Someone brought it in and left it and that's not what they do."

"Bobby!" Frank said. "Knock it off for now. We need to think this through. Why bring Chadwick into it and a candelabra?"

"She was murdered the day before Robert was," Barbara said. "All her computer stuff, her cell phone, camcorder, her tablet, all her records were taken. And the candelabra turned up. They don't buy and sell, don't hold onto items to be appraised. But someone left it and never came back for it. I don't know why. I just need to know. I want the fingerprints on that candle holder. And Harris might close shop and leave any day to be close to her daughter and grandchildren in Bellingham. It can't wait."

Frank stood. "I'm going to call William Tate. Barbara, go take a walk, think what this means. Let's get together in the morning, nine, your office."

"Bailey, do you know anyone in the Portland homicide unit?" Barbara said, rising. "I'll dig out *The Oregonian*, but that will be a truncated account of Chadwick's murder. Get a police account if you can."

Frank shook his head and went to his desk. "Beat it, both of you. Do what you can, Bailey, but be there in the morning. Maybe we'll be a little more coherent by then."

Barbara's thoughts kept up the mad race as she walked, and she realized she was walking faster and faster, as if trying to keep up with a whirlwind of thoughts, ideas, doubts, suspicions... She was wet with sweat and came to a complete stop all at once and was nearly run over by a cyclist, who swerved, waved, and kept going.

"No good," she told herself. "This is a goddamn waste of energy." She turned and headed back to her car, only then realizing how low the sun was, how many fewer people were in the park, on the trail than when she had started. Darren would be home, might even wonder where she was, although that was doubtful, she told herself. He knew how it was when she was working. Still, she hurried a little faster, reached her car, got in, and drove home, without much more of an idea of her next step than she'd had at the start of her marathon walk.

Darren met her at the door. When he put his arms around her, kissed her lightly, she drew back. "Icky sticky," she said. "That's me. Probably stinky, too."

He laughed. "Go shower and I'll dish you up some dinner. I already ate."

Minutes later she joined him in the kitchen. She had put on a thin summer robe and sandals and for the first time that day felt comfortable. They sat in the kitchen and he served her spaghetti with brie melted through it, topped with a pungent pesto sauce. A tomato avocado salad with Bibb lettuce was on the side, as was a glass of wine.

"Not room temperature," he said, "properly cooled to a drinkable state of about sixty-five to seventy degrees. Martin taught me to do that. Room temp would be close to boiling."

She took a bite of the spaghetti and only then realized that she was starving. Darren laughed again as she ate ravenously. "No lunch today?"

"I didn't have time, or forgot," she admitted. "I have to tell you something," she said, with her mouth full.

"I was hoping that was the case. After you eat. Then out on the patio. It will be cooling down out there."

She cleaned her plate, drank her wine, nodded when he lifted the bottle to refill her glass, and breathed a sigh of contentment. They left the table and she pretended she didn't see Todd's cat Nappy waiting for them to clear out in order to leap on the table to see if she had left anything for him. She hadn't.

She sank down into one of the sling chairs; he drew another one close and she told him about her day. When she got to the part about the paintings, he swung his legs off the chair and sat up. She finished the story and drank the rest of her wine. "This changes everything," she said then, putting her glass down on the table at her side.

Darren took both her hands, surprising her by the tightness of his grip. "Barbara, you can't sit on this. It does change everything. Someone might know what's at stake suddenly, millions of dollars, tens of millions of dollars. That someone might have killed Valducci and Chadwick already. Those paintings should be in the hands of the authorities, locked up in a vault somewhere, and straighten it all out afterward."

His voice had dropped into a low musical, rhythmic mode, the way it did when he was anxious, afraid, or, sometimes, angry, and his grasp of her hands had tightened until he was hurting her. She tried to pull loose and he relaxed his grip a little. He drew her closer. "Don't put yourself in danger with them, Barbara. It's not worth it. Nothing is."

She twisted her body around, swung her legs off the chair and then, sitting face to face with him, his face dim in the light from the kitchen, she said, "I can't let anyone know until after the trial. No one knows now and no one will know or can know. It could seal Jeff's case if it came out now. An international sensation, the area would swarm with journalists, thrill seekers, and the prosecution would jump on it as the real reason Jeff Cobbe killed Robert Valducci. I can't let that happen."

Darren groaned, pulled her to him, and held her hard pressed against his body. "You're shivering," he said.

"I know. It did cool off out here. Let's clean up the kitchen."

He held her tighter.

They had cleaned the kitchen, had watched the news, had sat with little or nothing to say. She had brought out the newspapers from New York and Chicago and started to go through them page by page looking for something she couldn't even name, but then had given up when Darren kept going to the doors to make sure they were locked, and hovered until she'd felt like screaming. They had gone to bed and made love, and after he was sleeping, she had slipped out of bed and now was again scanning one page of newsprint after another.

She found an ad from the sports section of the Chicago newspaper about a guided fishing trip on the Rogue River for the prized steelhead, celebrated by none other than Zane Gray in a bygone era. The reference numbers were in Medford and Eugene. She put that aside.

Later, she became aware of Darren's presence in the doorway. He looked tired and sleepy. "It's three o'clock," he said.

She jumped up. "God, I'm sorry," she said. "Did I wake you?"

"Yes and no. Come back to bed. That can wait until tomorrow."

She went back to bed with him and fell asleep in his arms.

‡

Barbara and Shelley were already in the office when Bailey and Frank arrived at the same time; Barbara had been there for more than an hour, and she had briefed Shelley, who still looked a bit dazed by the new twist.

Frank put a box of pastries and a stack of napkins on the table next to the coffee carafe and cups. With a soft grunt he seated himself in one of the easy chairs. Bailey helped himself to coffee and a Danish, and Barbara refilled her own cup. As soon as they were all seated and served, she leaned back on the sofa and looked at Frank.

"You first. Did you learn anything from your curator buddy?"

"A bit. Problem was he wanted to talk about his glory days when he was curator at MoMA. Museum of Modern Art," he added when Bailey looked puzzled. "I had to tack him back to art theft several times, but eventually he told me a few things. Paraphrasing, of course. No one wants publicity, not the insurance industry, or the museums, or the top one-percenters who have been robbed. So that's good. There's a pricey database that lists stolen valuables, silverware, crystal, art in all forms. You can find the best price, last price it sold for, things of that sort. It lists still-missing items along with recovered things, and there will be a flag on them. If several things were stolen together, they're all flagged so that inquiries about one might lead to the others still missing. That sets in motion insurance investigators, FBI, local police, Interpol, museum investigators, and so on. And we have to include various nefarious characters who also like to track down valuable artwork and lay claim to it, or at least lay their hands on it. So whoever notices the flagged item alerts those who try to track down where the inquiry came from, auction, yard sale, art dealer, whatever, and go on from there. Problem is this theft happened more than half a century ago. It could be days, weeks, months before a flag gets real attention. Lesson learned: Don't ask questions about any of those pieces, or the mirror. Don't bring down a flood of investigators, at least not yet."

"Great," Barbara said. "No publicity. That's a real plus. Dad, did your pal say whether anyone could trace back and learn anything about when or why the individual item was flagged in the first place?"

"What he said was that anyone willing to put in enough time, and with the know-how could do exactly that."

"Not so great. Well, it's something. We don't know and probably can't find out whom Chadwick might have told or even what she might have learned. But what we can do is eliminate people who didn't know about the paintings. None of the Valducci family, for instance."

"Why not?" Bailey asked.

"The day Chadwick did the appraisal she was telling them what her company did. Bring in high-end dealers, down the line to a yard sale, on to a thrift store, and anything left after that to the landfill. Strip the house to the wallpaper. Robert was okay with it. And Tilsen was talking about a farm equipment auction. No one from the family would be involved in any of it. She said it was best if they stayed away, let her crew handle everything. Debra couldn't have known; she was willing to walk away from everything with a big check in her hot hand. And obviously Gina knows nothing about them, or the whole world would also know. So, no family."

"So it comes back to who Chadwick told," Bailey muttered. "And her telephone calls."

"That's pretty much it," Barbara said. "Now we have two new players, the photographer and his assistant. A full rundown on both of them, Bailey. Geraldo Reyes and Simon Alterman. And there could be others lurking out of sight that we know nothing about yet."

"And Jeff's brother," Bailey said. "He suddenly shows up."

Barbara felt a shockwave ripple through her, along with a quick denial. She didn't voice the denial. Eric *had* suddenly showed up.

After a moment of silence, Shelley said, "This could be too big for just us. There are too many unknown factors."

"I know," Barbara said. "Let's look at what might have happened. Chadwick does the appraisal and the mirror catches her eye. She makes inquiries about it and learns about the paintings. She tells someone, but she can't say where they are. No one knows where they are or even if they're in the house, but it's a possibility. The day of the appraisal they didn't go down to the basement. Robert probably didn't give it a thought. A few days later Chadwick is murdered and all records vanish. Then Robert is shot dead. The house is crawling with people and no outsider can get in to search. Then Debra is shot at and frightened away. That leaves Gina, but instead of running away, she brings in her three partners and a guard dog. And that's where it stands today. Valuable paintings could be hidden in the house, and the problem is how to get inside and make a search."

"Does Eric have the run of the house?" Bailey asked.

Barbara nodded. "And Simon Alterman very nearly got inside when he charmed Gina. He'll try again. And, no doubt, if Geraldo Reyes gets inside with his cameras, he'll get photographs of every picture hanging in that house, and a lot more."

She emptied the carafe into her cup, stood, and took the carafe to the door. "I have one more tidbit to pass on. First, more coffee." She opened the door, waved the carafe in Maria's direction, and was not at all surprised when Maria took it and refilled it from a freshly brewed pot of coffee.

"I went through all those newspapers we found in the trunk," she said, resuming her place at the table. "I think this is what happened. The guy who sent the trunk was an imposter. There's an ad for a fishing adventure on the Rogue River, a guided trip, with a telephone number in Eugene, and another in Medford. I think that gave the guy an idea. Maybe he had traveled from New York to Chicago, most likely in my opinion, but unproved. Anyway, in Chicago he saw that ad and circled it. And he got hold of a Eugene telephone book. He came across a small ad for Valducci's Produce and that gave him a name and address. So he sent the trunk, claiming to be a long-lost relative who would be along any day now. The shipping tag is rail freight out of Chicago, no sender's name. Of course, he never showed up.

Why Valducci's? Who knows? Maybe he's really Italian and the name appealed to him. Maybe it's his real name. Maybe a flip of a coin. Anyway, that could explain the trunk. Why he never showed up, another mystery. If he had stolen art and was cashing in on it, it could be that he was attracting attention, that he just wanted those paintings to be somewhere relatively safe until he could pick them up again, and Eugene must have seemed like a faraway place that possible enemies would never think of." She shrugged. "Who outside of Oregon, even today, has ever heard of Eugene?"

There was another prolonged silence until Shelley said, "Something that hasn't come up is the fact that Gina might be in danger. If she won't run away, or be frightened enough to sell out and leave, whoever killed her father and shot at her mother might get impatient."

"It's damned if you do, damned if you don't," Frank said. "Rock and hard place. Tell all and have the media circus, and probably increase the odds against Jeff by some unimaginable number. Stay quiet and put Gina at risk."

"No bodyguard," Barbara said. "What good would that do? She's all over that farm, in and out of the store, overseeing everything, and swarms of people coming and going."

"Tilsen's counting on a conviction," Frank said after a moment. "He's sure that when Jeff is found guilty, sentenced, out of the business of running the corporation, Gina and the other two will fold. Then she'll sell to him. If the paintings are made public, that will take him out of the picture, at least. Gina won't sell now when she might be tempted by big money, but with millions possible, she'd have no reason to sell ever. Maybe publicizing it would make the killer hightail it out, too, but maybe not. He might be vindictive. Robbed of millions of dollars could annoy him."

"Dad, did Gina turn any of the property over to the corporation?"

"Not yet. We talked about it, but when we drew up the papers, it was boiler plate. Remember, she hadn't been named the heir at that time. It might be an idea worth pursuing now."

Barbara thought a second or two, then shook her head. "She will hold onto the house even if she turns everything else over. She will want to pass it on to her children in some future that sees her married with a family."

Sounding resigned and reluctant, Bailey said, "I could send Alan out to keep an eye on things. Get him some kind of job at the farm. Not picking beans," he added. "I don't think Alan would go for that."

Alan Macagno was his most valuable operative. Bailey was offering a sacrifice, Barbara realized. And she also thought what he really meant was that Alan could keep an eye on Eric Ballantine, Jeff's brother.

"We could say it's to ward off Geraldo Reyes and Simon Alterman," she said. "What do you think?" she asked Frank.

He nodded. "Still rock and hard place," he said. "But it's something."

They talked of the other things that needed attention. Shelley would start calling some of the people who would be good character witnesses. Barbara and Frank had long since agreed that character witnesses were almost worthless. Even the devil could gather them together. But juries seemed to pay attention to those who could be counted on to say something like, 'He's a good man, good to his family, friendly, helpful. Never a cross word.' She voiced none of this.

"You might have to go for depositions," Barbara warned Shelley. "Places like upstate New York, Fairfax. Maybe elsewhere."

"No problem," Shelley said.

"And I have to go back to the beginning of discovery, see if anything stands out now that was invisible before the paintings came to light," Barbara said. "Six weeks, guys. We have six weeks."

Then, minutes later in her office alone, she went to her desk, and tried not to think of rock and hard place and, having to choose, knowing her choice had put Gina at risk.

Barbara drove to the farm three days later and found Gina and Jeff in the dining room with Eric and Daniel. They were leaning over the table with an aerial view of the farm displayed. Eric was talking, pointing. "If you divide it into six growing plans—Plan A through Plan F—you can rotate crops without any repeat planting in a section for six years without contiguous sections posing a problem. Say, plant Plan A in section 1 the first year, in section 3 the next year, and in 5 the third year, then on to 2, 4, and finally 6. All the other Plans, B through F, would follow the same course. Isn't that better than the four you've been counting on?"

"It is," Jeff said. "Get one section up and running, start the next one, until all six are playing musical chairs. Great idea, Eric. You'll be a farmer yet."

Eric laughed and shook his head. "I plan. You plant."

"The perennials would be anchor crops," Gina said. "We'd have to keep—"

"Excuse me," Barbara said from the kitchen doorway. "Sorry to interrupt, but I have a couple of questions for Gina and Jeff. Okay?"

All four were startled and twisted around to look at her. For a second or two Eric looked almost panic-stricken. He had been animated a moment before; there had been humor in his voice and words, now the light dimmed and he looked haunted again. At least physically he was looking better each time she saw him.

"More questions. Why not?" Jeff said in a resigned voice, his previous enthusiasm gone. "Shoot."

"Here?"

"Why not?"

"Okay." She brought out her tape recorder. "It's either this or I have to make notes, and that's always distracting. Do you mind?' He shook his head. "Good. On the night Robert Valducci was shot, who came to the greenhouse and told you?"

"Don't know," he said. "A detective, sheriff's deputy, that's all I know."

"Right. Exactly how did that go? You were working on the plants, then what?"

He gave her a look of disgust. "I was working and he came in and said Robert Valducci had been shot and who was I and what was I doing there at that hour."

"Not that way," Barbara said. "Exactly how it went. You were working, your back to the door?"

"Yes. My back was to the door. I didn't hear him come in, didn't know he had come in until he touched my arm. Scared the hell out of me."

"Why didn't you hear him until then?"

"I was listening to a series of lectures, a colloquium, earbuds. He touched me before I knew he was there."

"Okay. Then what?"

"He took my name and address, noted what I was doing, like I said. I answered his questions, and he told me there had been a shooting, that Robert Valducci had been shot. He asked if I had heard the shot. If I had seen anyone about. I said no to both questions, and he went away."

Barbara nodded. "Think, Jeff. Had you been out at all during the past hour or so before he came in?"

"No. For God's sake, Barbara, what are you getting at?"

"It started to rain at a quarter after eight," she said. "Not hard, but enough to get you wet if you'd been out. You said you went out after he left, that you went far enough down to see into the house. What did you wear when you went out?"

His eyes narrowed and he thought a moment, then nodded. "I get it," he said slowly. "Right. It was pretty cool in the greenhouse; I had my jacket on that I wore to work that morning, and I had a poncho with a hood hanging up. I put on the poncho. It was dry. My jacket was dry."

"Exactly," she said. "See? Not meaningless at all. Now, Gina, can you tear yourself away a few minutes? I want a play-by-play from you, too, if you're up to it."

"Not here, the way Jeff did?"

"Afraid not. More complicated than that for you. Game?"

"Sure. Where?"

"Living room."

"Can we watch?" Eric said.

Barbara looked at Gina, who nodded. "But only if you don't make a sound," Barbara said, and she led the way to the living room with the others trailing after her.

"What we'll do," Barbara said, "is start when you reached the French doors with Jeff. Who opened the door?"

"I… I think I did," Gina said. "Or a detective inside opened it. I don't know. I saw Mother on the sofa and I ran—"

Barbara stopped her. "Close your eyes, Gina. Imagine yourself at the door. Jeff is by your side. Who opened it?"

"I think it was the sheriff," Gina said after a moment. "He stopped me and said, 'Who the fuck are you?' and I said, 'That's my mother.' Then I jerked away from him and ran to her."

"Good," Barbara said. "Now, you run to the sofa where your mother is sitting. You said she was wrapped up in a blanket. Sit down where you sat that night, Gina. You are wearing your raincoat. Did you take it off?"

Gina sat on the sofa in an unnaturally stiff position. She shook her head.

"Okay. Close your eyes for this part, Gina. Why didn't you take off your coat? Was it wet?"

She nodded. "Wet, dripping even, but it was so cold I kept it on."

"And what was your mother wrapped up in?"

"It was a blanket. A maroon blanket."

"Where did that blanket come from?"

That stopped her for a moment. Then she said, "The upstairs linen closet, at the top of the stairs."

"Who got it for her?"

"Tilsen. I remember he said he tried to warm her up with the blanket."

Step by step Barbara took her through her movements that night. She went to the kitchen to make a cup of tea. Heated the water in the microwave, added a tea bag, and was taking it back when she almost spilled it after Tilsen appeared. "One of the detectives told him to get back to the living room and stay there. He said he'd been to the bathroom."

"Where did you run into Tilsen?"

Again Gina had to stop and think. "Just a few steps outside the kitchen, in the hall before the turn to the living room. Near the bottom of the stairs, not far from the downstairs bathroom."

"When did you turn up the thermostat?"

"After seeing Tilsen. On my way back with the tea. It was so cold in the house, and it was turned all the way down."

"So you took the tea to your mother. Were the French doors still open?"

Gina's eyes opened wide. "I forgot all about that," she said. "I asked the officer who went to the kitchen with me if I could close the doors, because it was so cold, and he said not until forensics got there. He's the one who told Tilsen to get back to the living room. The doors were still open."

"So you sat down by your mother again and she drank tea. What else was going on?"

"Nothing. I don't remember anything. I had to hold the cup for Mother. Her hands were shaking too hard to hold it."

"How much longer were you there before they let you take your mother to her hotel?"

"Another half hour maybe. Oh, they were questioning Tilsen and after that they wanted to ask Mother questions, but she couldn't even speak. She just stared straight ahead and shivered. Her teeth were chattering, she was so cold. I told them she was in shock and I had to take her out of there, and they let me. A deputy drove us to the Hilton. More men had come, and some had gone into the study, and some of them were dusting the doors." Her eyes widened. "They were looking for fingerprints, weren't they? That's why they left them open. And Dad's body… he was still in the study, wasn't he? They needed forensics to do whatever they do. Mother knew he was still in there. She kept staring at the study door, like someone in a trance."

"And they also had to wait for the medical examiner," Barbara said. "The sheriff's deputies are scattered around the countryside. It takes a while to assemble the team. Do you know what time it was when you took your mother to her hotel room?"

Gina shook her head. "Eleven? Later? I don't know."

"A quarter to eleven," Jeff said. "I was outside watching. They let Tilsen leave at the same time. They had to move cars in the driveway to clear the way for Gina and Tilsen to get out. All that took another few minutes, five or ten probably, before they actually drove out. The coroner came five minutes later. That's when I left."

"Thanks," Barbara said. "That's really helpful."

"What's this all about?" Jeff asked. "I thought you had all the police reports."

"Tying up loose ends," Barbara said. "The official reports sometimes are a little muddled."

"Muddied," he said. "Isn't that the word you want?"

She nodded. "Sometimes that's the right word. I won't keep you any longer." She hesitated a moment, then said, "Jeff, I'll need to have a couple, three hours alone with you in the next week or two. There are things we have to go over in detail before the trial. Will you set aside that kind of time?"

"Sure. I'll be on hand."

Driving back to town a few minutes later, Barbara mulled over things she had learned that day. Jeff had hung around keeping an eye on Gina until she was safely away from a murder scene. Simple curiosity? Concern about her? But perhaps more important for the time being, she told herself, was the fact that apparently she herself had passed some kind of test, or crossed a line and was no longer regarded as a semi-adversary, but maybe even an ally in Jeff's mind. Maybe, she told herself, there was a crack in his fatalistic wall of self-defense. Such fatalism was translated by jurors as guilt, and it was so clearly perceived that the one exhibiting it might just as well have worn a placard saying, "Hang me."

She glanced at her watch and sped up a little. There were other interviews to get to.

At twenty minutes after four Barbara sat behind the wheel of her car and debated going back to the office, or driving straight home. She drew out her cell phone and checked for missed messages. She'd had it muted for the last two interviews, and now saw that Bailey had left a message ten minutes ago.

"I'm on I-5, heading in. Should be at your office by four-thirty." That was it, and it was longer than his messages usually were.

Her self-directed debate had been settled for her. She drove to the office. Bailey was already there when she arrived. He was showing Maria a card trick.

"Now you see it, now you don't," he said, opening his empty hand. "And now you do." He picked the missing card up from the desk and handed it to her. She laughed.

"How do you do that? Do you ever gamble with real gamblers? They might skin you alive if you try something like that."

He grinned, waved at her, and followed Barbara into her office.

"The works," he said, dropping his duffel bag on her round table. "Happy hour yet?"

She nodded and went to the small bar to open the lower cabinet doors to take out a bottle of Jack Daniels. "Good enough stuff to warrant good stuff?"

"You betcha. No water, just ice."

She fixed his drink, poured wine for herself, and sat on the sofa. "So, let's have it."

"First, Chadwick. I have the telephone numbers she called. Haven't checked them out yet. Will do it tomorrow. It's a long list. All of March. I'll skip the days before her visit to Valducci's." He took a long drink, then opened his duffel bag and brought out several file folders. "It's in there. I kept a copy. Next, the candelabra." He brought out a plastic bag containing the candelabra and set it on the table. "Some prints, some smudges. I haven't lifted them yet. Tomorrow. On Saturday, the seventh of March a lampshade dealer saw a man go into Chadwick's with a shopping bag, and that in his other hand." He pointed to the plastic bag. "It was nearly five-thirty, as close as he could come to the time. He was helping a customer load lampshades into her car. Finished with that, he went back inside his shop. He closed at six and noticed that Chadwick's lights in the front were off. That's it for him. No one paid any attention that night or the next day to the fact that the closed sign stayed in place and no lights came on. Sunday, dead time on that stretch. Couple days later a friend stopped by to go to lunch with Chadwick. She saw her car in the parking space and saw the closed sign and when she couldn't get an answer to her phone call, she called the cops. Chadwick died sometime after five-thirty and before midnight on March 7. The guy with the candlestick could have done it, or someone could have entered later. And it came to a dead end right there. No fingerprints in the office, or anywhere else to give them a lead. All computer-related items missing, nothing else, including forty-four bucks in her purse."

He rose and ambled to the bar to refill his glass. Once he was admitted to the bar, he reckoned it fair to help himself at will in Barbara's office. This time he added a little water. "They'll be checking pawnshops against the registration numbers, and cell records to see if anyone tries to use the cellphone. Sell stuff like that on the street, pennies on the dollar, but what the hell, it's free stuff." He resumed his seat, put his drink down, and rummaged again in his duffel bag. "I think he left the candlestick holder because his shopping bag was full."

"Why didn't the police keep the candelabra as evidence?"

"They didn't know about it," he said smugly. "I talked to the lampshade guy, and he said he forgot to tell them about it, and besides people did that now and then. He had taken a lamp to be appraised once—"

"He didn't want to get involved," Barbara said sourly. "I get it. Any description of the guy who delivered it?"

"Man, medium everything, dark raincoat, dark hat. Didn't see his face, didn't see a car."

"How did you get the telephone numbers and the candelabra?"

"Told Harris we're still investigating Chadwick's murder. They could be helpful. She was helpful. It's the telephone bill from March."

He had taken out another file folder and now tapped it. "Geraldo Reyes and Simon Alterman," he said. "Reyes is legit, or I should hang up my shingle. He's got an international reputation for his photos and articles, never tied to any government entity or criminal organization. He gets everyone on film, right, left, dictator, saint, and he goes everywhere. Just nothing to find. You could find out exactly where he was any day you want to name. He's popular, four published books, two of them best sellers, got a following, fans who keep an eye on him, paparazzo. Open like a book. Alterman, on the other hand, is an amateur art guru or something. Never married. Not much about him available, not a social media guy apparently, no Twitter, no Facebook. Good family, money, land holdings, like that. Sounds like a playboy who's managed to keep his nose clean. Surface stuff. I'll go deeper." He spread his hands, shrugged, and brought out yet another folder.

"Tilsen and company," he said. "They rented an apartment, four guys, a lease for three months, and they split up with Tilsen and Valducci coming down here, the other two keeping in the northern part of the state, covering the valley, top to bottom."

She frowned. "It appears that in the beginning they really were looking for other farms to buy. Scouting them out. Tilsen had not seen the Valducci farm yet, apparently. But he knew it was exactly what they wanted. I imagine both of them would have earned bonus points, bonus cash, stocks, something in payment for finding the right place. And there must have been a kickback scam, or why the overpriced sales figure?" She drank her wine, then asked, "Are the other two still around?"

"Nope. They all came together in the first place on a corporate jet that detoured to Portland, then flew down to L.A. A week or so after Valducci's killing, the other two took off on commercial flights back to Chicago. Tilsen uses the apartment now and then. In this area he stays at the Valley River Inn. He's been back and forth to Chicago a couple of times, commercial flights."

"That's interesting," she said a moment later. "Tilsen had a memorandum of agreement for the sale with Valducci, voided by murder. Then he had a deal going with Debra Valducci, voided by the court naming Gina as the heir. He seems to think that Jeff will be convicted and Gina will sell out at that time. He must be pretty sure of that or they would still be looking at other farms. Maybe he really does know something I don't know."

"Or they're looking for gold and he found a nugget on the farm and is convinced that the mother lode is there, too." He drained his glass. "I told Hannah I'd be home for dinner, and she told me she's making chicken and dumplings. No one else on earth can make chicken and dumplings like hers. I'm out of here. I'll track down telephone numbers tomorrow and lift prints from this."

He picked up the candelabra and put it back in his duffel bag, glanced around and heaved himself upright. "I'll be in touch." He ambled to the door, saluted, and left.

Barbara took the folders to her desk, where she sat gazing at them. Inside, there would be a complete police record of the murder of Mildred Chadwick; everyone they had interviewed, every bit of evidence they had collected would be documented. Bailey always gave her the gist of what he had uncovered, and it was always a fraction of what she found in his full reports. The Tilsen and company information would be equally dense, most of it inconsequential, but she had to read it all, examine every detail. And finally, if Bailey had not been able to find out anything interesting about Simon Alterman, it could be that there was little or nothing to find, or it could be because someone had made an effort to hide anything interesting. And then the question was why? Who was he?

A tap on her door sounded and the door opened enough to see Maria, with Shelley close behind her. Shelley spoke first. "If you don't have anything for me tonight, I'll take off. It's five-thirty."

"Nothing. See you tomorrow."

It wasn't as if either of them made any appreciable noise when they were in the other office, or the reception room, but without them the silence always seemed deeper, more profound. Barbara looked at the file folders on her desk, opened the large lockable drawer, but then opened the folder marked Reyes/Alterman.

Bailey was meticulous in his reports; he detailed his failures as well as his successes. What had he found about Alterman, or not found?

There was another tap on her door, and this time when it opened, Darren's broad face was there. "Time to put it all away," he said. "We have a reservation for seven-thirty at Martin's. I ordered whatever the special of the day is, and it will be ready to serve when we get there. Martin said he has a special wine for you to try."

"Oh, God!" Barbara said. Again, she thought. She had done it again. She closed the file folder, put them all in the big drawer, turned off her desk lamp, and went to the door, where Darren took her hand and kissed it.

She didn't look back, but as they walked out, she had the sobering thought that there wasn't a thing she could have suggested for Bailey to try to find out more about Simon Alterman. He was still the mystery he had been from day one.

Barbara sat on her sofa and regarded the many piles of papers spread out on the round table before her. Bailey reports, discovery, her own transcripts of various interviews, newspaper clippings… She sighed and picked up another folder. So much to amount to so little. Treading water, she thought, that's all she was doing, treading water, waiting for Bailey.

He sauntered in, came to a stop when he saw the disarray, her desk and the table all covered with papers, folders on the floor, and an easel with a map of the farm. "Fire hazard," he commented. "Don't drop a match."

"Don't even sneeze," she snapped. "I'm not through sorting and I don't want a draft to send them flying around. What do you have?"

He eyed the bar and she snapped even sharper. "No way. It's not even lunch time yet. Help yourself to coffee if you want it."

His motto was never to refuse anything to drink. Accordingly, he helped himself to coffee and sat in one of the easy chairs. "I have a couple of prints from the candlestick, two good ones and a partial, and smudges. Give me prints to compare them to and we're in business."

She scowled at him. He shrugged, then drew out a sheet of paper from his duffel bag. "And a list of the people Chadwick called after she left the farm until the night when she got it. Mostly friends, a couple of clients, who all check out, and what do you know, a call to Valducci's."

Barbara had been slumping on the sofa. She straightened with a jerk. "She called Valducci?"

"A landline in the name of Magda Valducci. They talked for two minutes."

"Goddamn it! Are you sure?"

"Come on, Barbara. Give me a break. Eleven in the morning on March 7, for two minutes she was on the line to Magda Valducci's landline phone."

"Jesus, this changes everything," Barbara muttered. "But Robert Valducci couldn't have known. He must have known the story of the trunk, where the mirror came from. Why didn't he go find the paintings? Damn it, why?"

"For what it's worth," Bailey said, "she must have done her research online. No calls to suggest she got in touch with anyone involved in art theft, no authority, insurance company, anything like that. Online research, ain't it grand?"

Barbara jumped up from the sofa and walked to the window, back to the sofa and round table, to the door, back to the window.

"She must have figured there would be a hefty reward, finder's fee, something like that up for grabs," Bailey said. "Consult with the client, make sure to get it in writing that she deserved her share, and only then get in touch with the proper party. That might make sense—"

"Bailey, shut up. I have to think and you're not helping. Is there anything else you have to make it a more complete screw-up of my day?"

"One more. Simon Alterman's been Geraldo Reyes' water boy only since late April. His regular guy is Hernando Betancort, assistant, water boy, driver, significant other for eighteen years, and now absent. No reason that I could find for the switch without going to one or the other and asking. Maybe Alterman's just prettier and Reyes wanted a change."

She ignored that. "Alterman said he'd be in touch after they do some sightseeing. I'll try to get his prints. If I can't, maybe you can. If they turn up again, find out where they are staying, what they're driving. You know, just keep tabs. But for now I have to talk to Gina. Could her father have known about the art without giving even a hint of something big? Did she see enough of him to be aware of it if he was excited about anything?"

Bailey cleared his throat and she stopped pacing to glance at him. "Unless you have another little hand grenade in your magic sack, go. I'll call if and when I think of something for you to do."

He rose and made his way to the door in his slouching manner, waved, and was gone. She paced a few more minutes, then she too left. Locking her office door in the reception room, she told Maria not to let anyone go in there, she would be back. "I have papers everywhere and I don't want a hurricane to disturb anything. Out to the farm."

This time she found Gina in the greenhouse talking to Jeff. They were on opposite sides of one of the benches filled with immature tomato plants. A few men were building something on one side of the greenhouse. Barbara beckoned Gina, who seemed reluctant to leave the conversation she was having with Jeff, but the hammering and several other people present made it impossible to talk there.

"I'm terribly sorry," Barbara said, "but I have to talk to you. On the terrace by the house?"

"That's okay," Gina said when she joined Barbara. She turned and waved to Jeff, and they walked through the busy sales yard and on to the invisible fence that kept Rusty on the other side. He greeted them joyously.

"What is it this time?" Gina asked as soon as they were out of hearing distance from customers or workers. "I thought we covered everything and then some."

"There's almost always more," Barbara said. "This might seem insignificant, but it's something else I really need to know. First, the day Mrs. Chadwick did the appraisal, you, your father, and Tilsen were with her. Did you stay with them the whole time, right up until she left?"

Gina spread her hands in a helpless gesture. "I told you. I did. Dad said he and Tilsen would have a drink. They were bored. He asked me if I wanted one and I said no. Then I left."

"Think back to that instance, Gina. Did your father tell Mrs. Chadwick to call him, or to send him the appraisal?"

Gina's thoughts seemed more on what was going on in the sales yard, or perhaps in the greenhouse, than on Barbara. She kept looking out at the distant greenhouse, all but invisible through the greenery. "He just gave her a Valducci card and told her to send her report and he'd get back to her."

"What card? His personal card, company card?"

"No. The Valducci card, about the farm, produce, and stuff. Do you want one? What for? Wait a minute and I'll get you one. I want a drink."

She darted off to get a card and water. When she came back with a glass of water, she held out a card to Barbara. It had line drawings of various vegetables and potted plants, the Valducci sign and address, and a telephone number.

"Dad went to the study to get the card," Gina said. "There's a bunch of them in the desk drawer. He handed it to her, for the address, he said. Send the report to that address and he'd get in touch." She drank most of the water after saying this.

Knowing she had to be careful and that her questions made no sense to Gina, Barbara asked, "Did you see much of your father after that day, after the appraisal?"

"As little as possible," Gina said, sounding impatient. "For a couple of days he and Tilsen were all over the farm, making notes about machinery, tractors, trucks, everything. Probably putting price tags on everything but the dirt. On Saturday night, oh, about six or a little later, he stopped me in the hall. I was taking some of my personal things out day by day, clothes mostly, and he heard me and came out from the study to stop me. He said I couldn't take any of the items I said I wanted until after we had the appraisal report. I told him those were my clothes and I wouldn't take anything else." She stopped trying to see through leaves and flowers and looked at Barbara, suddenly more subdued than impatient. "I think he was all at once very sad. He said that now that Tilsen was gone he would be going through my grandmother's things. He said he had come across letters and cards I had written to her, that she had saved everything, and he would gather them up for me to keep."

"Tilsen had been hanging around that long?"

"Like a bad smell," Gina said. "Greg said he left before lunch that Saturday. Greg was scared to death of him, of what he represented, men of power and authority, men who hated gays, lesbians, 'perverts' of all stripes. He's sensitive to bad vibes and Tilsen gave off bad vibes, so Greg kept an eye on him in order to keep out of his path. And after he left, that's when it must have hit Dad, how cold and calculating he had been, the reality that he had lost his mother, all that it meant. Before, with Tilsen around, it had all been about the coming sales, the value of everything, new world order being established on the old world's ashes."

She stopped abruptly and lowered her gaze to her hands that had been moving rapidly and now lay quiet on the table. She picked up her glass and finished drinking the water. "I think in his own way he was trying to reach out to me," she said in soft voice. "There was so much sadness in his voice, and in his expression, and I was too angry to see it then. I was brusque and even rude in how I responded. I said I wouldn't dream of taking another thing from that house until he gave permission. I said something like that, really sarcastic, and I ran out, too angry to see how down he was."

"Did you see him again?" Barbara asked gently.

"On Sunday. I saw him sitting on Gramma's bed, a couple of boxes open, stuff on the bed. My grandmother kept putting things in boxes and drawers in no particular order, just to get them out of the way until she found time to deal with them. Invitations, cards, receipts, old pictures, snapshots... She never got around to it, so the drawers were stuffed pretty full and she began using boxes. I think he was looking at some snapshots, going through them, one after another, turning them over to see what was on the back, dates, names of people maybe. I watched for a minute or two and then went to the greenhouse without speaking to him. He looked old, sitting there like that. I had never thought of him as old before, but for a few seconds that's what I thought, how old he looked. And I walked away."

Barbara put her hand on Gina's and held it for a moment. "I'm sorry to bring back such pain. Thank you very much. Just one more thing to clear up. This card. What's the number here?"

"The landline," Gina said. "Grandmother changed our ad in the telephone book, but she never changed the cards. She kept the landline. Some old friends and customers used it. She preferred talking on what she called a real telephone."

"So does my father," Barbara said. She stood. "Go on back to work, Gina. I'll take the glass to the kitchen. I do want a drink of water, after all." If Gina even tried to hide her relief, it didn't show. Barbara watched her hasty departure and her fast walk that quickly became a jog. Slowly she went into the house with the empty glass. She put it in the sink, took down a glass for herself and filled it with water, and then stood regarding the wall telephone that she had dismissed so easily on all of her previous visits. A black wall phone near the back door, with a shelf under it that held a notepad and a few pencils and pens in a cup.

What had they talked about? If Chadwick had told him that beautiful mirror had led her to a stolen art site, that there might be a large fortune in stolen art to be claimed, could he have been depressed, even sad, going through old photographs? He had been evaluating everything in sight. He had known the mirror was connected to that old trunk; wouldn't he have gone straight to that trunk? But what else would she have called about? Maybe Bailey was right, Chadwick had made up a story just to get back inside the house, to stake a claim early.

Barbara knew that speculating was without meaning since there was no way to find an answer with both of them dead. But if Chadwick had called no one else, and according to Bailey none of her other calls could be considered relevant, was her murder just a coincidence, after all? Jumping to conclusions, connecting dots that were not linked, making unwarranted assumptions, trusting intuition instead of hard evidence, chasing shadows, trying to make a case out of fairy dust— She bit her lip considering how much time she had wasted. She remembered the glass in her hand and took a long drink, poured out the rest and put the glass on the counter. She was exactly where she had been months earlier. Nowhere.

Back in her office, she surveyed the piles of papers with resignation. It couldn't be helped, she told herself; it had to be done and she alone could do it. There were patterns, rhythms, connections that she could make without being able to explain her methods to anyone else. When the right order was achieved, she would make timelines for the major players, putting each one in place for every hour of any significance when their whereabouts had been established, and when the gaps showed up, as she knew they would, then try to find someone who could plug the holes. She thought of how Greg had been keeping tabs on Tilsen, something she had not known until that morning. Greg, reputedly afraid of men of authority, men in suits, when what he was really afraid of was his father and how he would react when he learned that his only son was gay. His father, the wealthy ophthalmologist, pillar of society, member of several boards, chairman of some, philanthropist, cursed with a gay son. She felt certain that was how Greg saw it, his father would feel cursed. And Greg would live in fear until that terrible moment of his outing was faced, over and done with.

But Greg had kept tabs on Tilsen, and she knew that was how it worked. People saw things, noticed things without attaching any importance to them, exactly the way she had seen the wall telephone in the Valducci house and had put it out of mind as unimportant. Once she had the gaps to work with, she could start to fill them, but first came the sorting. She started again.

Some time later there was a tap on her door, followed by its opening and

Maria stepping inside the office. Barbara was sitting on the floor at the low coffee table. "It's better this way," she said. "My back was killing me leaning over so long. What's up?"

"Mr. Reyes is on the line. He almost begged me to tell you about his call. What should I tell him?"

"I'll take it," Barbara said, pulling herself up. She was stiff. She went to her desk as Maria withdrew and closed the door.

"Mr. Reyes," Barbara said. "What can I do for you?"

"Ms. Holloway, please join me for a drink this afternoon. I must talk with you. In public, at the restaurant they call Sweet Waters at Valley River Inn. Will you please be so kind as to accept my invitation? I promise I shall not keep you an inordinate amount of time, but I really feel that I must talk with you."

Barbara looked at her watch and was surprised to see that it was three-thirty. "I am very busy, as you probably surmise," she said. "But I would be happy to join you for a brief time. Shall we say four-thirty? I'm afraid I can't make it earlier than that."

"Splendid! Excellent. Four-thirty is exactly right. I look forward to meeting you, Ms. Holloway."

As soon as they disconnected, Barbara hit the speed dial for Bailey. She didn't expect him to answer, and he didn't. She left a message: "Having drinks with Reyes, four-thirty, Sweet Waters." It was enough. Then she left a message for Darren: "I'm having drinks and appetizers with Geraldo Reyes at four-thirty. I won't want dinner, so go ahead and eat. And I have to come back to the office after I meet with him. It looks like a tornado hit here today. Love you." That was enough too.

She had time to go home, she decided, wash her grubby hands and face, change her clothes for something not wrinkled and dirty, and suitable for drinks with an internationally famous photojournalist. Her tone as she told herself her plan was mocking.

When she entered the restaurant she spotted Reyes and Alterman instantly at a table by the window wall overlooking the verdant garden and flashing river. And she also spotted Alan and a pretty young woman at another table. A chair at their table held two motor cycle helmets. She did not acknowledge Alan any more than he gave her a glance. The restaurant was half filled, the buzz of conversation like white noise, and soft music behind that.

Reyes and Alterman rose as she approached their table. Alterman bowed slightly. She nodded to them and a waiter appeared, to hold her chair. They all sat.

"Ms. Holloway, thank you very much for agreeing to this meeting," Reyes said. He was a stocky man, middle aged, with graying hair and a graying mustache, and bright dark eyes that seemed to have a light of their own. His eyebrows were heavy, thick and surprisingly black without a touch of gray.

A waiter came to the table with menus. At almost the same moment, the woman with Alan walked past the table toward the restrooms.

"If you will permit me, I would like to order wine," Reyes said, putting his menu down and picking up the wine list. He was still studying it when the young woman returned, and this time it was obvious that she was interested in Reyes. She slowed at the table, then came to a stop.

"It is you," she said in a hushed voice. "I thought it was, but Danny said I shouldn't bother you. We studied your article and photographs last year, the one about the Amazon, and an opera house in the middle of the jungle. Manaus, I think it was. I'm a journalism major, you see. You put me in the jungle, Mr. Reyes. It was like magic how you did it. We studied every single word of that article."

Alan came to her side and said something in her ear, tugging at her arm. He looked embarrassed and very young. But he always looked young. That day he was wearing a U of O T-shirt.

"Mr. Reyes, could I have your autograph? Please. I would treasure it, and the other kids in my class would be so jealous. They'll never believe I actually saw you and talked to you."

"Stacy," Alan said, pleading. "Let's go. You shouldn't embarrass him like this."

"Nonsense," Reyes said, waving Alan away. "A fan is always welcome. Or course, I shall be delighted to give you an autograph."

Stacy looked down at herself, nice pants, T-shirt, no purse. She looked at Reyes almost helplessly, then picked up the menu Alterman had held a minute earlier and handed it across the table to Reyes. "Would you sign this? I don't have a book or anything with me."

He smiled at her and signed his name: bold letters, flourishes, a notable autograph to value for a lifetime. Or until Bailey got his hands on it, Barbara thought, sitting back, watching the playlet.

Alan pulled on Stacy's arm again, and this time she let him lead her from the table, smiling at Reyes, clutching the menu to her chest with both hands. They returned to their own table and seconds later, carrying their helmets, they left the restaurant. Mission accomplished, Barbara thought.

"Does that happen often?" she asked Reyes. "I should think it might be a nuisance if it did."

"No, no," he said with a broad smile. "I am not a celebrity like your film stars or sports figures. Only journalism students would take any notice of me, and they are rare." He held his hand up and snapped his fingers with an impressive pop. The waiter hurried to the table. Reyes ordered wine and then said, "And bring us one of each of the appetizers, but only two at a time, and when the little plate is empty, then bring another. If we like any one in particular, we shall order it again." He turned to Barbara and asked, "Is that satisfactory to you?"

"Absolutely," she said. Through all this Simon Alterman had sat back in his chair without a word. Reyes didn't ask him if that was satisfactory and he didn't volunteer anything. He looked amused.

"Now, a little story," Reyes said when the waiter hurried away. "Many years ago, when I was young, fresh from university, I secured a position on the local newspaper in Barcelona. Car crashes, visiting dignitaries, various civic affairs, all tedious but necessary in order to keep my position. Then one day my editor gave me a special assignment, to provide photographs of Barcelona for a special to be published in the spring at the start of tourist season. I was elated, as you can imagine. Ah, my photographs, so beautiful: magnificent parks, plazas with statuary and blooming flowers, tiled walls, gardens, the waterfront with sailboats and yachts, flags waving, so bright, so gaudy, museums and cathedrals and monuments. All perfect, all stunning. The editor picked the ones to be included in the special, and when it came out, I strutted like a cock that's had its way with every hen in the county. My parents, my friends, my peers, everyone congratulated me, praised me. And I thought how well deserved their praise was."

The waiter brought the bottle of wine and they performed the wine ritual with a taste, a sniff, acceptance, and a pour. Alterman had changed his attitude, Barbara observed. As Reyes told his story, Alterman had sat up a bit straighter and had listened attentively, as if he never had heard any of this before. Now he tasted his wine and nodded approval.

Barbara took a sip of hers and said, "It's excellent." Reyes looked pleased.

"Well, back to Barcelona," he said after taking a drink. "A week or two after my triumph I was with friends at a café, and my old instructor at university happened by. I ran to him and asked if he had seen the article, my photographs. He nodded, but did not comment. I asked him if he did not think the photographs were good, and again he nodded. 'Very good pictures,' he said. Then he said, 'The camera does not lie, but the photographer often does.' I demanded to know what that meant and he told me I had shown only part of the story, and omission can be construed as a misstatement, even as a lie. He walked away and I was crushed. He had accused me of lying!"

He became silent as the waiter approached with the first of the appetizers: shrimp cocktail and a dip with crisp flat bread triangles. Reyes took a shrimp and dipped it in the sauce, tasted it, and nodded approvingly.

"What I learned during the week that followed that encounter, Ms. Holloway, was that I was a phony, a fake, a dilettante. I began to explore the other side of Barcelona, the side I had been willfully ignorant about. We do that, we humans, we become ignorant, not by happenstance, but by choice. We don't want to see many truths in sight and not seen. Seven years after that rude shock, I did another long piece about Barcelona, and this time the newspaper rejected it. A magazine published my piece with my photographs, and it won an award. It was truthful, Ms. Holloway. Harsh in many ways, unsparing of the city I love, brutally honest. My old instructor sent me a card after it was published and he had written: 'Now I can point to you and say I had a small part in your education. That makes me proud.'"

They finished the shrimp and the gamoush, and quietly and efficiently the waiter removed the dishes and brought out two more delicacies. Reyes poured more wine.

"Thank you for telling your story," Barbara said, "but I still don't know why you invited me here today."

"Yes, of course, an explanation. You see, Ms. Holloway, when I first entertained the idea of my current project, it was simply to tell the story of the vanishing small farmer, the extinction of an unsung hero who has been with us since the dawn of civilization. I was uneasy, even edgy about it, but I set out. Then I came across an article in a Portland newspaper, a small filler-type article, mind you, but it reported that a young woman in the valley had fought her mother over her inheritance of a small farm. The daughter won and one of the giants in the agricultural/chemical industry had suffered a defeat. On the verge of acquiring the farm, they found themselves confronted by a lovely young woman who said no. And that's the story, I realized. Small farms are disappearing around the world, but here and there someone has the courage to say no to the giant and his gold. David and Goliath, except David is Gina Valducci, and she is winning. That's the story."

"Mr. Reyes," Barbara said, "Mr. Alterman made the case to Ms. Valducci and she rejected it. She is not—"

"Please," Reyes said somewhat sharply, "permit me to finish. In the weeks since I first entertained this idea, this concept, I have done a great deal of reading. It is not the case of one small insignificant farm, it is the case of many, many people, of cities, of megalopolises, of humanity itself. Not tomorrow, not that swiftly, but in a decade or so, incrementally, as water shortages increase, deserts grow, unforeseen and outrageous weather events occur, crop failures will drive many to desperate actions. Precision farming, reliance on satellites and drones, on computer technology and the highest of high technology will be needed. Large cities, your New York, Chicago, Los Angeles, a few others will compete for dwindling supplies controlled by those high-tech companies and their precision farms. And they will take second place to the military in most countries. It will be the same throughout the world, and throughout the world the poor people, people without means, will eat nothing or accept the most egregious food-like substances available to them by means of factory farms. There will be famines. Your villages, towns, small cities like Eugene will basically be on their own. Up and down your beautiful coast, people who cannot afford the ever-rising cost of imported food stuffs will be forced inland. Rising sea levels will most certainly be a driving force, but hunger will be the decisive one. Who will feed these pockets of hungry people, Ms. Holloway? Satellite farms may be the only possible answer. Farms that encircle pockets of struggling civilization, farmers who don't look to export food to foreign countries, or even neighboring states must be the answer. Farms not reliant on imported fertilizers and chemical pest controls, because if the infrastructure fails due to insufficiency of maintenance and to ever-increasing costs of transport, no imports will be affordable or possibly even available. Ms. Valducci and her small crew of believers may or may not have carried the philosophy of their enterprise out to its logical conclusion, but that is the future I foresee, and that I believe they are preparing for, consciously or unconsciously. That is the story I want to write, that I will write."

Barbara was taken aback and silenced by his fervor, the intensity of his brilliant dark eyes as he held her gaze with his own. A flush had darkened his olive complexion to swarthy and he was breathing fast. Abruptly he leaned back and drew in a long breath, and his motion caused her to shake herself a little, to break what had seemed an almost trance state. She lifted her glass and sipped wine.

"Forgive me," Reyes said. "Poor host that I am." He added wine to her glass and his. Alterman put his hand over his own, smiling.

"Mr. Reyes," Barbara said, "surely you know from your research that Gina Valducci is not the first to manage a farm to provide organically grown food, not the first to encourage locavores."

"Of course," he said. "But none of them that I'm aware of have the added romance, in the old sense of the word, of a young woman's battle with her own mother, the murder of her father, and her defiance of a giant adversary. That is what makes her story compelling." He smiled. "And perhaps a romantic interest, in the other sense of the word."

Barbara took another sip of wine, refused a tidbit from the last appetizer, and prepared to stand. "I'll certainly consult with Ms. Valducci," she said. "I cannot make a commitment on her behalf until I do so."

"That is all that I ask at this time. Ms. Holloway, please advise her that it is her duty to allow me to proceed. I understand that she is to report on the activities that she and her young associates are engaged in at a local grange. I shall be there to listen to her talk. I shall not photograph her without her permission. All I ask for now is permission to photograph the bounty of her farm, the abundance being produced there. I would not interfere in any way with Mr. Cobbe or with Ms. Valducci. I understand completely that his upcoming trial must take precedence and demands their full attention. But after the trial I would ask for her cooperation in a meaningful manner."

He paused, shrugged, and said, "My last two books were best sellers, worldwide, I might add, and this one will be also. Gorgeous photographs, museum-worthy art, plus truths that too many people do not want to acknowledge. Willful ignorance is running out of time, Ms. Holloway. Your young Gina Valducci has a message for the world, and I am to deliver it. Please convey that to her, as well."

"Dad," Barbara said on Sunday evening, "I promise no talk about my case. Not even thinking about it. Just a nice family evening. Darren has the latest from Todd, a dozen or more pictures of frozen wilderness to amuse you with, and that's as heavy as it's going to get tonight." She tried to keep her tone light, carefree, and failed.

"So be it," Frank said. "Back porch, nice and breezy, and I'll be using the grill in a little while."

Darren and Frank exchanged glances to her annoyance, knowing well that they were both aware of her frustration, and that they had just made a silent agreement to keep the evening exactly as she had stated: a nice family evening.

But it really was nice on his back porch, watching the two golden cats mosey now and then to the grill table where Frank was marinating steaks, watching them calculate their chances of snagging a piece of cheese from the larger table near where Barbara was seated, watching Darren and Frank go through the pictures on Darren's cell phone. Todd was having the time of his life; the grinning selfie he had included couldn't have revealed a happier kid. When the sun lowered a little bit more, Frank put potatoes on the grill. He had said it was a simple summer supper, steak, corn on the cob, grilled potatoes, a salad, tomatoes with garlic and basil... She knew he had made a peach cobbler; she had smelled it. Good food, good wine, and all Barbara could do was watch two big scheming cats and twitch restlessly again and again.

Bailey had called to say no match with Simon Alterman on the candlestick. Nothing more than that, as was his style. She shifted again and again and drank her wine, filled her glass once more, and watched Thing One and Thing Two circle the grill and the table. Darren and Frank were talking politics. She had nothing to say.

She had a busy week coming. The district attorney's office promised to send her their witness list, and depending on what the list included, she had prepared two different lists of her own to hand over. If General Ballantine, Jeff's father, was on their list, her list would include Eric and three depositions: two from instructors at the academy that had been a prison for Jeff for four years, and one deposition from the sergeant who had been the general's orderly when Jeff was in Fairfax for several months at age eleven. If no general, one deposition and, subject to change, her list shrank down to that one and character witnesses from Oregon State University, to a couple of local farmers, Jeff's landlady, another of his neighbors, and Gina. She knew it was pitiful, but there was little she could do about that. The state had to prove its case; she had to cast doubt on its conclusions.

She also had an appointment with the prosecutor and the judge scheduled for a pretrial meeting. That was a bummer, she had admitted to herself. No one knew much about Judge Harvey McNulty. He had been a prosecutor for six years in Multnomah County, tough and thorough from all accounts, and somewhat of a bully, with a lot of wins and few losses on his record. He had been a judge for less than a year, providing not much of a record to inform her about past decisions or biases, or to gauge how he conducted trials—maintaining a rigid order at all times, or allowing a looser, more flexible approach?

There was the lengthy session with Jeff that had to happen; she had delayed it until she got the witness list. If his father was on it, he had to be prepared. She was dreading the session if the general's name appeared on that list.

"Barbara!"

She blinked and saw one of the cats dragging a piece of cheese off the table. He ran with it in his mouth and his brother following.

"Some cheese guard you are," Darren said with a grin.

"A case of entrapment, pure and simple," she said.

After that she tried hard to keep in mind that it was a nice family dinner, but on the way home later she couldn't remember a thing she had eaten, except peach cobbler. Frank had added blueberries and it had been scrumptious.

Monday morning at nine a low-level assistant from the district attorney's office delivered the witness list. After a brief scan she gave him the one she had prepared, the one with depositions and Eric included. Unhappily she tapped on Shelley's door as soon as the courier was gone.

"I'm afraid we'll need those depositions," she said. "That bastard, General Ballantine, is going to testify against his son. God, maybe he'll be struck by lightning before the trial!"

"I'll be out of here before night," Shelley said as she reached for her telephone. "Reservations," she added.

Barbara nodded and withdrew. Shelley would get her reservations. And she would fly first class, then bill the office for the cheapest flight available. She would stay in four-star hotels and bill the office at Motel 6 prices. It was the way she operated as the very wealthy daughter of an even more wealthy man who built yachts. Shelley had once offered to work for nothing, even to pay for the opportunity to work with Barbara, and Barbara had rebuked her quite sharply, so now she simply did it her way.

Barbara spent some time gathering her materials for the meeting with the judge at one, and she called Jeff. "Can you find time tomorrow?"

"Sure," he said. "I told you I would. Nothing's changed. About ten? Is that okay?"

"Great," she said. "Jeff, something else. Is it true that Gina's going to give some kind of presentation tonight at a grange?"

"Yes. Why do you want to know?"

"I hope someone will go with her," Barbara said.

"For God's sake, Barbara, she's a big girl." His impatience came through loud and clear.

"I know. But I also know that Geraldo Reyes and Simon Alterman plan to attend that meeting. Maybe she shouldn't face them alone."

"Jesus! You know I can't go. I'll get Greg or Daniel to go with her. Anything else?"

"No. See you tomorrow."

Not Greg, she hoped. Reyes would eat him alive and Alterman would stand by and grin. Then she was thinking again of Alterman's behavior at that curious tea-time get-together. Reyes had virtually ignored him, and he had been distant, cool in a way that suggested he didn't like Reyes very much. Why was he traveling with him at all, she wondered. That day he had been bored, except when Reyes had told his story about his comeuppance at the hands of his former instructor. Then Alterman had been interested, but not in anything else Reyes had talked about. And to her dismay, the more she thought about Reyes and his impassioned explanation of why he wanted Gina's story, the more she felt inclined to believe him. He had not been faking it, she was convinced. He really did want to do a book of little Gina pitted against the giant and its implications. She would decide what to tell Gina by the next day, she reminded herself. She regretted that Reyes and Alterman had not been swept out to sea by a rogue wave. She did not need them complicating her pitiful case at this particular time. They presented too much of a mystery with one seemingly as transparent as water and the other like a white shroud in a dense fog.

She met Gil Weymouth in the judge's outer office where he was chatting with the judge's clerk. She had been surprised that Sheila Weinburg had not been assigned the try the case, that Weymouth had been brought in. Rumor had it that Sheila had wanted out, that she was in something of a pickle herself with her husband under indictment for embezzlement.

"Ah, Barbara, right on time, one minute behind me," Weymouth said amiably. Outside of court when they met socially or casually, she was Barbara, and he was Gil. Once the curtain lifted in court, it would be Ms. Holloway and Mr. Weymouth. "Do you know him?" he asked, nodding toward the door to the judge's chambers.

She shook her head. "First time for me."

"Me too." Gil Weymouth was a slender man with a paunch, and he favored flamboyant neckties that featured tropical birds, flowers, wild animals of various kinds. That day it was tigers. It was said of him that he had a remarkable memory, that he never forgot a thing, and possibly was telling the truth once when he said he remembered his birth. His features were regular, his hair dark brown, reasonably thick and straight, and there was nothing about his appearance, except for his neckties, that was memorable. Normally his voice was pleasantly modulated, a little high pitched, but when he became angry or excited, or when he feigned such a state, he became flushed, his voice became high pitched, and his words tended to flow faster and faster.

At the clerk's nod to them, and his motion toward the door to the judge's chambers, they approached it together. Weymouth opened the door and stood aside for Barbara to precede him in a most gentlemanly manner, and they went in to meet Judge McNulty.

He was massive, over six feet tall, more than two hundred pounds, with mammoth hands that held a Kindle reader when they entered. He put it down and steepled his fingers, regarding them over the top of his hands. "Good afternoon," he said. "Be seated and let's get this over with as quickly as possible. Miss Holloway, that chair is quite comfortable, I believe. Mr. Weymouth, that one will do." The chairs were identical, positioned a few feet from his desk. His voice was deep, somewhere between baritone and bass. He looked like a man who might sing in the Ring Cycle operas. Big through the shoulders, with a large face, big nose, wide full lips, heavy black eyebrows, and keen blue eyes, he would need little makeup to play the part of a Norse god.

He must have been intimidating to fearful witnesses, overwhelming to juries, Barbara thought, studying him. And he had called her Miss Holloway. She was glad that she had decided to wear a real dress for that meeting, and that the dress, although sleeveless, had a little shoulder jacket. She murmured good afternoon and took the chair he had indicated.

It was a short meeting, without contention until it came to several maps that Barbara wanted entered by stipulation. "There's no need to bring in experts to explain when the photographs were taken and by whom, since they are official street maps and/or Google maps," she said.

"That's just to impress a jury," Weymouth said. "And it's time consuming to consult a map when a verbal statement will do."

Judge McNulty allowed the stipulation regarding the maps.

"I demand that the defendant spend the trial days and nights in custody," Weymouth said a few minutes later. "As the trial proceeds, it will be increasingly clear to him that he should have accepted our initial plea bargain. He is a flight risk even now and will be far more of a risk as he realizes how hopeless his defense is."

Barbara objected, and argued vigorously that the present condition be maintained, but in the end the judge ruled that Jeff would be housed in the country jail during the trial.

"He is working ten- to twelve-hour days, and working on his doctoral thesis at night," Barbara said, looking at the judge. She turned to Weymouth. "Both are extremely important to him. If he must be housed in the county jail, can you guarantee that his laptop and his books will be guarded and kept safe?"

He shrugged. "He'll be treated exactly the same way others are treated."

"Mr. Weymouth, answer Miss Holloway's question," Judge McNulty said in his deep voice.

Both Weymouth and Barbara looked at him quickly. He had sounded menacing and sharp. Barbara remembered the summary she had read of him: He could be bullying, and she believed it. He was a man who would demand obedience without question, was her next thought. If questions were asked, he wanted answers.

"I'll guarantee the safety of his belongings," Weymouth said after a brief hesitation.

There was little more to go over, and soon she and Weymouth left together. Outside, walking toward the exit, Weymouth said, "Caligula is the word I've heard used about him."

She nodded. But she had a different concern. The judge had called her Miss Holloway throughout the meeting. And she had remembered another detail from his biography: His wife had been a practicing child psychologist before marrying him and was now a stay-at-home mother of twin boys aged eight and two younger children. Barbara imagined that Mrs. McNulty wore dresses, and possibly even aprons, and possibly signed her name as Mrs. Harvey McNulty.

Gina checked the materials for the grange meeting one more time that evening. She had not done any of the presentations yet, leaving that particular task up to Jeff, who was so good at it. It couldn't be helped, she told herself again, and put on a smile for the guys who were hanging around her. "All set," she said. "I'll want a cuppa when I get home. Maybe a glassa. And leave me some of that pie." She had made a blackberry pie earlier and had not wanted it at dinner. She had wanted very little at dinner and had denied that she was nervous about her presentation.

"Gina," Jeff said then. "Let Daniel or Greg go with you. Barbara said that Reyes and Alterman plan to be there and you shouldn't have to face them alone."

She gave him an incredulous look. "For heaven's sake! So will a dozen or more local farmers. I'll sick Mac Hanrahan on them if they get frisky."

They all laughed. Mac was a giant of a man and he had a temper.

Gina drove her little Honda, her mind filled with details of the presentation she planned to make, detailing what they had already achieved, and the near-future plans they had made. An hour, hour and a half at the most, she thought, then punch, coffee, tea or something, and someone would have brought cookies, another half hour with various people asking questions while they refreshed themselves. Two hours tops. Out by ten, home by ten-thirty. Her hands were sweaty on the steering wheel.

There were already many people in the grange hall when she arrived, to be met with hugs and handshakes and many enquiries about how Jeff was holding up, and if there was anything they could do… There were seventeen or eighteen people there, most of them familiar and even friends, a few strangers, and, staying in the background, Reyes and Alterman. She ignored them and was annoyed that others were chatting easily with them, even posing for photographs. Promptly at eight Hank Munro called the assemblage to order, and she mounted the single step to the stage to begin.

"This is a map of the entire acreage," she said, pointing to the large map Greg had prepared. "We divided the acres into six parts, and this is the central location, the hub, where we'll have the permanent buildings, such as this rotating compost drum, already installed. Everything drawn in black is what we've done so far. The red outlines are for what's to come…."

Every building had red blocks outlined—coming solar panels, she explained—and the hedgerows, one small section in black, most still in red, would be extended greatly in the fall. They were growing their own plants, of course, so the expense would be for labor. "Four of us work pretty cheaply," she added, and there was general laughter. They all knew that Gina and her guys, as they were called, were working on a tight budget. For the most part they all worked on tight budgets. They understood that.

When Gina paused and looked at her watch, she was surprised to see that it was twenty minutes after nine. She hurried to get through a few more details, and then there were questions. Finally, Hank Munro took the stage and said it was time for refreshments, with questions between bites if any questions were still hanging. It was getting late, time to move on.

He turned to Gina as the assembled people stood, stretched, and headed for a table spread with food and drink. "You did good, Gina," he said. "That was a very good explanation of what you and the guys are actually doing.

Some had doubts, you know. I think you erased most of those doubts tonight. Come on, have some lemonade or something."

Several of the farmers had questions: How did they decide what to do first? Solar or drip irrigation, for instance. She explained again how they did a cost/benefit analysis for everything. It might take five years to be fully solar, and the irrigation would take two years and even be a little cheaper; yet, going fully solar would be such a cost saving in their electricity bills, it would take precedence. On and on, she explained the reasons for their choices, and the grange was gradually emptying until there were only three other people there with her. The table had been cleared, her various maps and notes packed, ready to be taken to the car, and Hank Munro was standing by the light switch, prepared to close up.

She didn't know when Reyes and Alterman had left, and she had not met the two or three strangers who had come that night, although she had meant to make it a point to introduce herself to them. She walked out to the parking lot with Munro, waved goodbye to the Sholti brothers as they drove out, and got into her car. Munro followed her to the road where he turned left and she turned right.

Gina was both elated, buoyed by her successful presentation, the way it had been received, and she was also weak with relief that it was over. Adrenalin had fueled her, and now drained back to wherever it hung out when not needed and fatigue hit her hard. The road was narrow and black, with many curves, flanked on both sides by peach orchards, with a ditch on her side. She wanted to be home and relax, but the road needed attention and allowed for no speeding. Headlights came up behind her, high beams, to her irritation. She flicked her mirror to dim the lights, but they were coming closer fast. She pulled as far to the side as the road permitted and she slowed to let the impatient driver have plenty of time and space to go around and be on his way.

The lights were approaching too fast, she realized, and the driver was not making any attempt to pass, but was coming straight on. She accelerated a little, knowing her old Honda couldn't outrun a bicycle on this winding road. The car was near enough to touch, and it bumped her car, jolting her. She swerved wildly on the curve, struggled to regain control, and righted the Honda. She tried to speed a little more, then had to slow again on another curve. The car attacking her had dropped back when she swerved; now it was coming up fast again. On the curve she was on, she saw a second car's lights, and felt great relief. Nothing would happen with another driver witnessing it. The second car came up fast, and the car that had bumped her slowed and pulled over, exactly as she had done. This time the one given the opportunity to pass took it. She cursed under her breath; she wanted it to stay there, where the driver could deter the maniac who had hit her car. Instead, it passed the attacking car, but then pulled in behind Gina.

She bit her lip, shaking now, with two cars behind her and one of them apparently intent on forcing her off the road, and the other one with unknown intentions. They could even be working together, she thought. She saw a sign ahead for Sonderman's Peaches and, in the distance, lights from the house. When she drew near enough, she jammed on her brakes and, skidding, turned into the driveway and kept driving almost to the house itself, where she stopped and turned off her headlights, shaking hard. She twisted in her seat to watch the road she had just left.

The car that had been immediately behind her slowed, hesitated, she thought, then picked up speed and kept going. A few seconds later a second car also passed the driveway and kept going. She couldn't stop shaking, now with a mixture of relief and fear.

She didn't move for five more minutes. No other car passed the driveway. Finally, with much maneuvering, she made a U-turn and headed out to the road. There were no car lights in sight in either direction.

She drove as fast as she dared, started in alarm when headlights came from a driveway and fell in behind her. The driver did not get close, did not try to pass her Honda. She kept it in sight until she came to a more traveled road, and then continued to watch it when she reached Prairie Road and at last River Road. It was still behind her when she turned into Green Briar Road, and it kept going.

The house door opened before she got out of her car, and she ran to it and inside.

"How did it go? What's wrong? Are you all right?" Jeff took one look at her and then grabbed her and held her hard against him. "You're shaking. What happened?"

Greg and Daniel appeared, Jeff released her, but kept his hand on her arm, and they were all heading for the kitchen before she could speak, before she could tell them that someone had tried to kill her.

Barbara was surprised to be met by Jeff with both Greg and Daniel nearby when she arrived at the Valducci house promptly at ten. They all looked serious. "What's up?" she asked, entering.

"In the living room," Jeff said. He stood aside for her to precede him down the hall, through the other hall and into the living room where Gina was seated on the sofa with Eric standing behind her.

Gina looked as if she had not slept, and Eric was twitchier than usual was Barbara's first thought as she walked closer to them and sat in a chair facing Gina. "What happened?" she asked.

"Tell her," Jeff said curtly when Gina hesitated.

"I think someone tried to run me off the road last night," Gina said in a faint voice. "It could have been a couple of drunk kids having fun," she added hastily.

Barbara exhaled a long breath. "No one went with you?" She turned an accusing look at Jeff. He shrugged and sat down. Greg and Daniel seated themselves and no one spoke for a moment. "Tell me about it," Barbara said.

Gina told it succinctly with her hands folded tightly in her lap, and Barbara knew that was not a good sign. "Did you report it to the police?"

Gina shook her head, and Jeff said harshly, "What good would that have done?"

"Right," Barbara said. It would not have made any difference. Young woman, kids out having some fun, no witnesses, woman gets hysterical... She brought out a legal pad from her briefcase and handed it and a pen to

Gina. "Write down as many names as you can remember from last night. I'm going to call my investigator and he can ask them about the strangers, maybe even identify them. You get started while I call him."

"Tell him to look into Reyes and Alterman," Jeff said. "What are they up to, hanging around?"

"Good question," she said. "We'll get to them." Ignoring Jeff's look of disgust, she took her phone out to the veranda and called Bailey. "Get Alan out here," she said after telling him the brief facts. "We were wrong not to get him on the job before. I want him now."

They had talked about it and, to her regret, had decided it would be almost impossible to protect Gina when she had so much ground to cover every day, and so many people coming and going, unless they told her the bigger story, the one that involved millions of dollars' worth of stolen art. And they couldn't do that until after the trial. Catch 22 and a half, she had thought then. Now, following an overt attack, it was no longer an option, and no questions asked, no explanation required. She didn't believe in drunk kids having fun anymore than Gina did, or Jeff, or any of them.

Back inside, she resumed her chair and watched Gina who was still writing, stopping to think, then writing another name. She waited until she said that was all she could remember.

"Okay. That's enough for Bailey to start with. Now, about the strangers. What do you recall about them? Anything you recall might be helpful."

Gina shook her head. "I wasn't paying any attention to them. I knew a lot of the people there, of course, and they kept coming over to speak to me, and I was trying to avoid even looking at Reyes and Alterman." She shook her head again. "I was nervous about the presentation… Oh, one of them had big ears, you know, the kind that sort of stick out." Her hands were in motion now, and Barbara asked more questions.

Gina gave more details about the incidents on the road, being bumped, out of control, skidding as she turned in at the driveway. Her hands were eloquent. No one else moved or spoke as she described it all. She had not been able to see the driver, anyone else, only headlights. She could not describe either of the two cars, again the headlights had made it impossible. "Dark," she said. "I had the impression that they were both dark, maybe black."

"That was pretty damn smart, turning in at the driveway," Eric said when she finally stopped. "You were pretty damn lucky that you didn't go off the road altogether with that turn, and it might have saved your life." He was staring at her fixedly, a tic in his jaw jumping. He was very pale.

Looking at him, Barbara thought that this life or death occurrence had triggered something that had been quiescent. She hadn't seen that tic for weeks. Abruptly, he turned and walked from the room, saying as he went that he would put on some coffee. Jeff watched him with an intent, worried gaze.

"Gina," Jeff said then, turning to her, "while Barbara and I have our long talk, why don't you get a nap. You didn't sleep at all last night, up and down all hours."

"So were you," she said. "And so was Eric."

He spread his hands. "Eric never sleeps through the night."

Rusty started to bark then and Greg went to admit Bailey, closely followed by Alan MacCagno.

After introductions, Barbara filled them in on the incidents of the previous night. "Gina provided ten names," she said, handing the list to Bailey. "Some of them might have known the newcomers, or at least can provide the rest of the locals. Tony Mirano is on the list and he's the next-door neighbor, a good place to start."

"Okey dokey," Bailey said taking the list. He looked at Gina and said, "This isn't going to work unless you agree to take orders from Alan here. We'll walk around a little to give him an idea of what's involved, and after that he'll be the one to decide where you go and so on. You okay with that?"

Gina simply nodded. Trying as hard as possible, she had not been able to convince herself that kids had been out to have fun with her, and the other explanation filled her with fear. She looked at Alan and nodded again, but a bit more doubtfully. He looked too young to be an experienced detective and or body-guard.

"Show her your gun," Bailey said in a grumpy but resigned way.

Grinning, Alan lifted his shirt to reveal a holster with a handgun.

"And he's a top-notch shooter," Bailey said, still grumpy. He sometimes said that Alan could shoot fleas off a dog, but he didn't go that far this time. He nodded to Alan. "Let's take a walk. One of you guys want to show us around?" Both Daniel and Greg stood.

Eric returned to say coffee was ready and asked where Barbara and Jeff planned to talk. He was asking to be invited, Barbara suspected, but she did not acknowledge that. "Not the kitchen," she said. "People will be in and out. Here?" she asked Jeff, indicating the living room.

He shrugged. "Why not? Gina, really, try to get some rest now."

Gina rose, but hesitated. "Should I wait to see what Alan wants?"

"Take a nap," Barbara said. "He'll be here when you come down."

Gina walked slowly from the room, down the hall to the stairs, thinking about her terror the night before, how the headlights had blinded her, how the car had swerved when she was hit. But even more she was thinking about how Jeff had grabbed her, how he had held her pressed against him so hard that she had felt his heart beating almost as much as her own racing heart.

"I'll bring the coffee," Eric said in the living room.

"Three cups and the pot," Jeff told him. "You might as well sit in, see how the legal system works."

Eric looked at Barbara, who nodded. She made her decision at that moment to bring up the general early. Since Eric would be present, they might as well get the hardest part over with and go on from there.

She sat by an end table with room for her notebook and a cup of coffee and waited for Eric's return. When he came back he poured for them all and took a seat a little to the side, as if to signify that he understood he was the audience without a playing part in what was to come.

Barbara talked first about jury selection, and the fact that she had a consulting psychologist to help assess the possible members, but then warned them both that it made little difference. Juries were always unpredictable. If Jeff felt a concern about any of them, he was to tell her immediately. "That is one case where your gut feeling, your intuition can be important. Just a feeling of uneasiness might be a signal to reject someone without cause." Jeff nodded silently.

"All right," she said then. "Next will be all the investigatory business, we'll get to it soon, but first you have to know that General Ballantine's name is on the prosecutor's witness list."

Eric started up from a slumping position, paler than he had been moments earlier, and Jeff carefully put his cup down on the coffee table and rose. He walked to the doors overlooking the nursery and stood there without speaking.

"I don't know what he'll testify to," Barbara said. Before she could continue, Jeff spoke.

"I do." He didn't turn to look at her. "He'll tell them I was a violent kid, that I killed my mother and tried to kill him. Disobedient, willful, hateful, uncontrollable temper. I know, because that's what he told them at the academy when he dumped me there."

"I have three depositions that will say otherwise," Barbara said.

"And so will I," Eric said.

Jeff turned then. He looked tired. "It won't matter," he said. "What the jury will see is the general, decades of loyal service, decorations from Vietnam, advisor to presidents. His sacrifices, a widower, one son sacrificed in Afghanistan, a second gravely wounded in Iraq, and the youngest a misfit, a coward, a murderer. You know him, how masterful he is, how direct and honest, plain spoken; he'll be saddened to have to tell such truths about his youngest son. He'll struggle to contain a tear or two and they'll believe him. He always made people believe him, no matter what he said. He speaks with such conviction."

"Not this time," Eric said. The tic in his jaw was working hard, and he looked so tightly wound that a touch might make him explode.

Jeff looked at him, then away. "You never did stand up to him," he said. "Mother was the only one who could stand up to him and she did it by putting a lock on her door and then leaving. That's just how it was, how he was."

"Not this time," Eric repeated.

"Jeff," Barbara said, "sit down. It's my job to expose the truth, and that's what I intend to do. We'll take it one step at a time and bring out the truth. He hasn't even really seen you for nearly twenty years, and that counts for a lot."

Jeff shrugged, but he returned to the sofa and sat. He picked up his coffee and took a long drink. "Next item," he said, sounding defeated.

Barbara was talking a few minutes later when the kitchen phone rang. It was very loud in the quiet house. It rang again and again. Jeff pressed his hands over his temples and closed his eyes.

"I'll get it," Eric said. He rose and hurried from the room. A minute later the phone stopped ringing.

Before Barbara could resume, Jeff leaned forward and said in an intense, hard voice, "I don't want him to testify. He can't do that, not in the state he's in."

"Isn't it his choice?"

"No, goddamn it! It's mine! I'll confess before I'll let a tough prosecutor break him in public."

"Let's put it all on hold for the moment," she said. Not just the moment, she thought, the whole day; Jeff was too tense, too upset to keep at it much longer. The news about his father testifying against him had been too wrenching. Now this, this need to protect his brother. The attack on Gina, all too much. And it didn't matter, she also thought. He wasn't going to testify on his own behalf. He would be a passive observer at his own trial, and that was just the way it was. If she had to tell him more, it could wait a day or two.

"One other thing for now. The prosecutor will try to get Gina to admit to a love interest with you, a relationship. Have you ever been in a relationship with her?"

He looked away from her and shook his head. "No. I don't have a goddamn thing to offer except a lot of debt, and she's the princess on the hill. Nothing's between us or has ever been. Let him try to prove otherwise."

"You're a fucking idiot," Eric said reentering the room.

Jeff started up from the sofa, but halfway to his feet, he sank down into it again. "Who was on the phone?" he said in a strangled voice.

"No one, about starts of something. I told her someone would call back."

Barbara closed her notebook and began to put her things in the briefcase. "That's enough for now. I'll want a little time with you tomorrow. And I'll need to speak with Gina. Will you pass the message for me?"

"We're done?" Jeff asked in disbelief.

"Done. There are a couple of things, but they'll keep for when I come back. Get some rest, Jeff. And you, too, Eric. It looks to me as if the lot of you need a good dose of sleeping gas."

One of the things she had not brought up, and did not intend to, considering all that Jeff had to absorb first, was the fact that he would have to spend time in the county jail. Tomorrow, she told herself. He needed to sleep and let rest dull the sharp edges of a very hard day before he was hit with another hammer.

Barbara always used the outside stairs to the second floor of her office building. There was an elevator in the building lobby, but she couldn't even remember the last time she had used it, or if she had ever used it. That day, midway up, she heard footsteps behind her and glanced back over her shoulder. Simon Alterman. She kept going, and at the landing, as she used her key, he joined her.

"I have something for you," he said, smiling his charming smile.

"I'm too busy," she said sharply. "Make an appointment." She opened the door and he pushed it farther and followed her in to the corridor that led to her offices, just a few feet away.

"It can't wait, and it concerns the attempt on Gina Valducci's life last night. I think you can make time." His tone was light, bantering, a kind of dare-you tone.

"What do you know about that?"

"In your office," he said, stepping past her to open the office door.

She entered and was relieved to see Maria at her desk. With a nod to her, Barbara walked on to her own office with Alterman behind her. "Hold the calls," Barbara said and entered her office. Alterman stepped inside and closed the door.

One time, long ago, Frank had said that whoever sat behind the desk was in charge, while at the informal seating arrangement at the coffee table it was a free-for-all. She went around her desk and sat down.

"What do you want? What do you have for me?" She kept her voice brisk, her tone neutral.

"A license plate number, for openers," he said. He took an envelope from his coat pocket and extracted a notepaper with a number on it and handed it to her. "We were driving along and saw Ms. Gina driving erratically and decided to escort her home, for fear she might run off the road and hurt herself."

"Did you see the other car try to force her off the road?"

"Afraid not," he said with a slight shrug of his shoulders.

"Right. So you just happened to take down the license plate number of a random car."

"You've got it," he said happily. "And at the meeting at the grange, Geraldo took a lot of pictures. His business, you remember, is taking pictures. He said he would not photograph Gina without her permission, and he kept his word. But he did get a lot of other pictures, including shots of three people who appeared to be strangers to most of the locals at the meeting. We thought you might find them interesting." He brought out several sheets of paper with photographs. "Copies, I'm afraid, but very good photocopies."

Two of the pictures showed two men together, two different shots of them. The third picture was of a single man. All three men were dressed in jeans, windbreakers or sport coats, no ties.

"Did he get any names?" Barbara asked.

"This one is Joseph DeLoren, he grows grapes. He didn't bother trying to get names of the other two, since they aren't farmers."

"How do you know that?"

"Nice soft hands, good fingernails, no dirt under them."

Barbara put the pictures down on her desk and studied Alterman for a second or two. "Why are you and Reyes doing this? Going out of your way to see Gina home safely, providing help to track down her attackers?"

"Not me," he said hastily with a big smile. "I'm just the messenger. It's Geraldo's doing. He's decided that Gina is a modern Joan of Arc or something, that she must be protected, at least until he gets his story, and that the big bad corporation sent spies to see if she really can rally the troops to her cause. After seeing her in action last night, he thinks she can, and that means she's in danger."

"Do you share his opinion?"

He laughed. "Messengers aren't allowed to have opinions. They have duties. And part of my present duty is to learn if you have spoken with Gina about Geraldo's proposal to start photographing the farm while it's at its lush best."

"No. She was in no condition today to bring it up. And she might believe that you and Reyes were behind the attack."

He nodded. "That's a reasonable attitude for her to take, knowing only what she knows. Geraldo's high opinion of her probably will increase. And now that I've done my duty, I'm out of here." He turned and walked to the door.

"Mr. Alterman, where were you and Reyes on the weekend of March 7 and March 8?"

He had his hand on the doorknob when she asked. She could see that he was shaking and realized that it was with laughter. He didn't answer and didn't turn to face her again, but, laughing, opened the door and walked out, closing it quietly behind him.

Barbara sat at her desk gazing at the two men who were not farmers. Reyes would have noticed their hands. One of the men had ears that flared out, as Gina had noted. She recalled a boy in her elementary classes who had ears like that; the kids had called him Dumbo and he had fought a lot. Teasing, bullying, hazing was not new, she thought, and pushed the pictures aside. Then she called Bailey.

"I may have a shortcut to those two guys," she told him when he finally picked up after her second call. "I'm getting a sandwich sent in. Do you want one?" It was a formality. She knew he would say yes. After that call, she ordered two sandwiches.

While waiting for her lunch, and probably a second lunch for Bailey, she examined the three men in the photographs more carefully. A grape grower, probably okay. A man with stand-out ears, and another man with a thin face, beakish nose, thin lips. But there was something else, she thought. Something not quite right. She opened her desk drawer and brought out her magnifying glass and reexamined the three photocopies. The grape grower's picture had distinct, clear edges, a good sharp image, good focus, good lighting. Reyes was a professional, he would always get good photographs. But the other two? A little fuzzy and not very good lighting. They looked like the kind of photographs she usually got with her cell phone, good enough, but not professional. Two different cameras?

She shook her head and leaned back in her chair. Not merely different cameras, different photographers, and one of them as amateurish as she was. Alterman, she thought then. He had taken the two pictures of the strangers. Reyes would never allow such pictures to be attached to his name.

Who the hell was Simon Alterman? What was he after? It had to be the art, but how had he even known about it? The questions raced through her mind, more and more questions without answers. But most importantly, was he dangerous? Was Reyes part of whatever it was that Alterman was doing? She suddenly wished the trial was over, the incalculably valuable stolen art was gone, and the world settled back down to its often-boring, mundane daily rituals.

Sandwiches and Bailey arrived at nearly the same moment and Barbara moved to the sofa. When Bailey looked inquiringly at the bar, she nodded with resignation. It was three in the afternoon.

To her annoyance, when she showed him the photocopies, he said the two guys in the two pictures had been caught by a cellphone camera. The license plate number would be traceable in a matter of minutes, but he would have to get access to a face recognition data file to match the guys. That would take longer. All this she had known.

"Double down on Alterman," she said. "Get one of your people to get a picture or two of him and try for face recognition. I want to know what his game is. Con man? Art thief? Dealer?"

"Tried that," Bailey said. "When the prints didn't work out, I sent a guy with a camera and Alterman was on to him before he got the thing out of his pocket. He's slick."

"That's why I'm concerned," she said irritably. "Send a couple of thirteen-year-old girls who giggle a lot."

"Don't tell me how to do my job," he said, but in an agreeable tone this time, almost as if he was humoring her. She hated that. He finished his drink and rose. "I'll give you a call soon as I have anything to say."

She was too restless to stay in the office, pacing back and forth, trying to see a clear pattern that kept swirling into chaos, trying to separate the various narratives, keep them apart long enough for one story to dominate. Finally, she cleared her desk, picked up her briefcase and purse, and told Maria to go home at five, that she didn't know when she would be back, she had to walk.

Her frustration mounted when she reached the parking area at the riverside park. She drove slowly with an eye on the too many people already there, setting up picnics, playing with Frisbees, on bicycles, and no doubt all of them talking, talking, talking, laughing, listening to music that they shared with anyone who came too close. There was no place for her to park.

The rose garden, she decided, and left the park to drive the few blocks, where she did find a parking place, although here, too, it seemed too many people had come up with the same idea. It didn't matter; at least they couldn't ride bicycles or spread out picnics in the gardens. She walked, zigzagging, past the pink tea roses all gathered together, in full bloom, fragrant; past the whites, the reds, the ramblers, and the shrubs, all separated by type, by color, with fragrances mingling, overwhelming at times. Other people were walking, but she could ignore them and no one spoke to her.

She came at last to her favorite spot, a weathered bench set back from the path, with a view of the ancient, magnificent cherry tree, the spot she had brought Eric to weeks earlier. She sat down wearily.

She was thinking of what Jeff had said about the general, his father, and she was trying to reconcile his words with what Shelley had gotten in her deposition with Sergeant LeMuir. Even the name, Barbara reflected, said something about the general. Both kids had heard Leemer; the general had diminished the man by mispronouncing his name. LeMuir had been assigned as orderly to the general, and the day he finished his twenty-five years, assured of a lifetime pension, he had left him. And LeMuir had said that in his opinion the general would have killed Jeff if he hadn't intervened.

It was going to be a dirty trial. Gina and her mother, Jeff and his father, ugly and dirty. Barbara hated that, but saw no way to avoid airing it. Too many people were going to be wounded, and if she lost Jeff, the wounds might never heal.

She heard the words in her head: if she lost Jeff. She closed her eyes hard. Relax, she told herself with her eyes closed. Just relax. Listen to the river music. She could hear it, soothing and calming, a rhythm ever the same, ever changing, carrying news of the mountains, of the broad valley on its long journey out to sea.

Suddenly the river song was overwhelmed, obliterated by the strains of Bolero. It was loud, demanding, hypnotic. Barbara's eyes snapped open, she straightened and sat up stiffly, and she saw a teen-aged girl walking along the path, her cell phone in her hand, head tilted, listening to her ring music.

"Answer the damn phone," Barbara wanted to yell at her. Oblivious, the girl drew closer, her expression dreamy. "Answer it, or I will," Barbara muttered under her breath. She felt as if she could do that—rush the girl, grab the phone and stop the music, restore quiet. The girl saw her then and, with a guilty look, took her call and hurried along the path and out of sight.

Still sitting unnaturally upright, facing the giant tree, Barbara felt a surge of electricity race through her. The leaves of the cherry tree were moving under a breeze, a dancing movement that rippled through the boughs, again and again recharging the late-summer-tired green with bright silvery highlights.

"Oh, my god!" Barbara said in an exhalation of breath she had not realized she had been holding. "Oh, my god."

Barbara had opened folders; pulled out reports; her own notes; opened more folders; and had done it again, then again. She had set up the white board and had jotted a tentative timetable and a list of activities according to date and time of day. She was not through yet, but enough to know that she was right, that she had to keep digging, have Bailey do some digging. She was looking through yet another folder when she was startled to hear Frank's voice. She had not heard him come in, had not heard the key in her locked door, or the door opening.

"What are you doing here?" she demanded, sitting back on her heels on the floor by the round table.

"Had to do it myself," Frank said. "Darren told me the last time he brought you some food you nearly took off his head. Reckon you wouldn't be that violent with your old man. Food." He raised a shopping bag he was carrying, glanced around, and finding no place clear of papers and folders, put it down on one of the chairs. "Greek salad," he added.

"Good god!" She looked at her watch. Ten minutes after ten. But she had called Darren this time, she reminded herself.

"I hope it's good," Frank said, indicating the mess of papers. "Can we clear off just a smidgeon of space?"

"It's good," she said. "I'm finished with a lot of these." She began to gather folders and put them in a pile. "You made potato salad this late?" She knew his Greek salad started with a layer of Bibb lettuce, then a thick layer of his special potato salad with several varieties of potatoes, topped with shredded lettuce leaves or spinach leaves, avocado slices, cherry tomatoes, olives, scallions, whatever else he felt like adding, and finally shrimp, sometimes salmon, and his own vinaigrette.

"I made potato salad early today," Frank said. "Enough for several days. It gets better and better. The rest is what I had on hand." He brought out a covered blue glass bowl from the shopping bag and put it on the table, then added a napkin, silverware, and, last, he withdrew a bottle of wine. "Soave," he said. "I asked Martin to get me several bottles the next time he ordered it. Since he knows it's for you, I got a bargain price on the deal."

Barbara uncovered the blue bowl, and suddenly at the sight and the aroma of the food, she was ravenous. She had not thought about food all evening, had not felt any hunger pangs, and now she felt she couldn't wait to start, to dig in with both hands and cram the food into her mouth. "I'll tell you about it in a minute," she said and picked up a plump shrimp.

He laughed and poured the wine, then sat back nursing his half-filled glass, watching her. He liked to feed her, to prepare special dishes for her, to watch her enjoy his food. The only thing lacking from his salad was cucumbers, and, unbidden, the memory of her at age six or seven rose in his mind. She had come in hot and sweating hard from rough play with several friends. In the kitchen she had found a bowl of icy cucumber slices in a vinaigrette, and she had eaten them all. Then she got sick, sick as a dog. That was the phrase he had used then. Now she could not bear to smell them, and he never used them in anything when he was cooking for her.

Barbara did not say a word until she had eaten enough to still the rumblings of her stomach, and at that time she slowed down and said between bites, "It was the call from Chadwick that did it for me. We assumed that Robert Valducci must have talked to her, but that didn't make sense. He didn't take the call, Tilsen did. Once I came to that conclusion, everything fell into place." She picked up the last shrimp and ate it.

Frank leaned back in his chair. "And that doesn't make any sense either."

"But it really does. Let me go through the timetable with you." She told it slowly because she kept eating as she did. "Start when Valducci first came with Tilsen. Robert visited with Magda, then left and he and Tilsen spent several days looking over farms in the southern part of the valley. Robert made his proposal to Magda and she said no. He and Tilsen kept looking at other properties, not yet committed to the Valducci farm. Magda dies,

Robert is the owner, and now the talk gets serious, a deal is struck, but it will take a month or six weeks, maybe longer to settle Magda's estate, settle her affairs. Enter Chadwick and her appraisal. That was on Wednesday, and on Saturday she calls the number on the Valducci farm business card, the landline. Robert is busy or just doesn't want to take the call, and Tilsen answers the phone."

Barbara knew that Frank was skeptical if not outright disbelieving, but that couldn't be helped. She ate another cherry tomato and drank some more wine, then continued her narrative.

"Chadwick probably was excited and said enough that Tilsen knew he had to learn more, and he acted accordingly. Greg was keeping watch on him and saw him leave before lunch on Saturday, soon after that call. Saturday evening sometime he went to the Chadwick office, and whatever she told him, or if she walked him through the stolen art site, or just what happened we don't know. But we do know that she was killed and everything to do with her visit to Valducci's farm was taken away, even the business card with the Valducci number, leaving not a single clue to link her to the farm.

"I doubt it ever crossed his mind to share the windfall with Robert or anyone else. Millions on millions of dollars at stake, and Robert planned to sell off everything in the house and on the farm. Chadwick was gone, but there are a lot of appraisers out there, a lot of estate sales. There was no way Tilsen could find and take the art as long as Robert lived, so Robert had to die.

"Robert's death was planned to the *n*th degree," she said slowly. "That memorandum of agreement is nonsense; they were together for days when he could have had one signed. But he needed a reason to go back that evening. It probably was after dark, after the workers were gone, all but Gina and Jeff in the greenhouse. And they couldn't see in the house from there. He probably killed Robert soon after arriving, and then made a quick search for the art, and of course he didn't find it. He didn't know about the trunk. Chadwick didn't go down to the basement when she made her camcorder inventory. Tilsen opened the doors and turned down the thermostat to chill the house and fuzz the time of death, and when he returned to discover the body, he moved it, to make it even more difficult to determine the time of death. He left, checked in at the Valley River Inn, to establish where he was, when he arrived from Portland, set up his alibi."

For a time neither spoke until Frank said, "Shooting at Debra. Where does that fit in?'

She pushed the bowl back a little and finished drinking her wine. "When his deal with Debra fell through after Gina was named heir, he must have been feeling desperate. I think it was his attempt to frame Jeff, to make it necessary for his arrest and conviction. If he'd wanted to kill her, once she was off the road, it would have been easy to approach the car and shoot her in the head. No, he wanted to frame Jeff by putting the gun in the bushes at his apartment house. The attack on Gina was an act of desperation, I think. Alterman said that Reyes was impressed by Gina's presentation, that he had not known if she could carry on with their plans without Jeff. He decided she could, after seeing her in action. I think Tilsen had two guys sit in to make the same assessment, could she carry on without Jeff? Remember, he told you he thought she'd fold if Jeff went down. His guys said she wouldn't. So get rid of her, let the property go back to Debra, and she wanted nothing to do with it, just a big check in her hand and adios. After that, all the time in the world to find the stolen paintings."

Frank poured more wine for her. He still had most of his in his glass. After a moment he said, "It's all pure speculation. Not a single bit of proof."

"I know," she said. "That's why I need Bailey to hustle for me and find some proof."

Frank picked up the blue bowl and re-covered it, put it in his shopping bag. He added the silverware and napkin, finished drinking his wine and added that glass. "Bobby," he said then, "I don't see how this is going to help Jeff. You have a narrative that sounds good, but you don't have a single shred of proof. Even if you did, you can't get such speculation past Judge McNulty. He'll slap you down hard if you try to introduce it. And Gil Weymouth will yell objections that will be heard in Salem if you even try. They'll be sustained."

"I know all of that," she said as quietly as he had spoken. "That's why I'm going through this stuff." She made a sweeping gesture over the mess of papers and folders on the table. "I'm pulling out every single time anyone mentions Tilsen's name, and anytime he's present when Gina or one of the boys is around. There's something in here to find, and I intend to find it."

Frank stood. "Why don't we huddle in the morning. Get Bailey in, and Shelley, do a little spit balling. Nine?"

She rose from the sofa and nodded. "Thanks for dinner, Dad. I really needed it and didn't have enough sense to realize that."

Frank kissed her forehead and left, saying he'd lock doors behind him on his way out, and she sat down again and regarded the remaining folders she had not yet examined. He didn't really believe it, she thought, but was willing to give her the benefit of the doubt. Or he believed, and knew she would never be able to tell her good story in court, or produce convincing proof. If there was any proof, she would find it, she told herself. She made a pot of extra strong coffee.

When she got home, after two in the morning, she tried to crawl into bed without waking Darren. He moved and she heard his voice in her ear, "Turn over."

She rolled onto her stomach and moaned when she felt his hands on her neck, her upper shoulders, and he said in a low voice, "Like steel. Just what I thought."

His magical hands, she thought, as he massaged her shoulders, her back... She plummeted into a deep dreamless sleep.

Shelley, Bailey, Frank, and Barbara arranged themselves around the coffee table with coffee at hand, and croissants supplied by Frank.

"You first," Barbara said to Bailey. He was smearing strawberry jam on a croissant.

"The car, SUV, stolen in Portland," he said. "Not located yet."

It was what they had expected. She did not ask about the face recognition he would get for her as soon as his contact found the time to do it without attracting attention. A little money would change hands, his guy would come up with something or not, and Bailey's final bill would include some miscellaneous charges that she would never question.

"Okay," she said. "Here's what I have." She outlined the scenario she had related to Frank and added a little that she had omitted the previous night. "Tilsen left the group in the living room to find a blanket for Debra Valducci. Probably had a look around while he was at it."

"Looking in closets?" Bailey said in an I-don't-believe-it voice.

"Looking at the backs of pictures," Barbara said. "And again in the downstairs hall and who knows where else? Gina said he was in the hall when she was taking tea to her mother. No one seemed to have kept him under watch. Again, how long? There are a lot of framed pictures in that house."

Bailey nodded. "Okay, gotcha. What else?"

"I need his fingerprints. For now, back burner for Alterman, Tilsen's the one I want a lot of dope on. When he was in the apartment in Portland, how he came and went, if neighbors got curious enough to notice. When he flew in and out of Portland. The works. See if anyone at or near the apartment saw those two goons who tried to run Gina off the road. When the police locate the stolen SUV see if you can get their report, where it was ditched, and see if there were witnesses to anything or anyone."

Bailey's hangdog expression became even more morose. "And you want it all by this afternoon, seeing the trial's coming up in a week."

"Exactly," she said. She looked at Frank. "Anything?"

"Maybe," he said. "Next week Gina's going to be at the trial every second, that's a given. The boys probably will be with her. And that leaves Alan alone in the house. I want a couple of other fellows to be there with him. No one's to go in and start tearing things up searching for those pictures. Alan and one dog might not be enough to prevent an invasion."

Bailey nodded without comment. He never questioned anything Frank suggested or ordered. Sometimes that irritated Barbara, but not this time.

"Anything for me?" Shelley asked.

"We'll need extra copies of the depositions," Barbara said. "Yours, one for Dad, and one for McNulty. I bet he'll follow word for word, and with one single deviation, rule it out of order." Prosecutors hated depositions and McNulty had worked as a prosecutor for enough years to lean toward them even if unconsciously. At depositions, leading questions could be asked and answered. Answers were not always to the point or succinct, and there was no cross-examination most of the time. Especially when the depositions were all the way across the country, the state did not want to spend its scarce dollars on cross-country travel, or to hire out-of-state attorneys to take their own depositions. Shelley would read the questions she had asked, and Frank would take the part of the men deposed. It made for pretty good theater, she knew, but she also knew that it might not make a lot of difference. What Jeff had suffered as a child might not seem at all relevant to a jury panel.

"One other little matter," Frank said. "It might be time to find out the procedure for disclosing found art. It might take authentication, a flock of experts, armed guards... God alone knows what all."

Barbara nodded. "But we don't admit we have them in a safe place yet."

"Absolutely not. Just getting some ducks in line for when the time comes."

"Well," she said a few minutes later, "that's it for now. I have to talk to the guys out at the farm, prep Gina, see if Eric and Jeff have had a blowup, and inform Jeff that he'll spend time in the county jail. Just the usual pre-trial tribulations." She looked at Bailey. "Give me a call as soon as you have anything."

"If I get prints, and they don't match up to the candlestick, what then?"

"Then I'm up shit creek without a paddle," she said. "Get those prints."

Frank drove home and put his car in the garage. He planned to walk to his office, the way he did every day. One mile there, one mile home again, exercise taken care of. He was whistling when he entered his house and the two gold Maine coon cats came to sniff him suspiciously. They knew he had another cat somewhere and they didn't like it. He told them it was all right, it was Todd's cat and Barbara lived with it, and he had little or no use for it. The coons were appeased.

His phone rang as he was on his way to the kitchen. He intended to pick tomatoes to take to Patsy, and maybe some of the Bibb lettuce that was outdoing itself that year. When he saw that it was Darren calling, he answered.

"Frank," Darren said, "I need to talk to you. When will you have a few free minutes?"

Direct, to the point, yet not demanding in any way, that was Darren, Frank thought. "Whenever you like. I'm home now, will be in the office later, or lunch, whenever."

"Now? I can leave now if that's okay."

"It's fine. Come on over."

Darren was the best thing that ever happened to Barbara. He knew that the way he knew the sun would rise tomorrow. And he had seen no sign of discord. He remembered how fiercely Barbara had resisted commitment until it was no longer possible to do so, and how patient Darren had been, and how insistent he had been. Both simultaneously, a rare combination.

He picked the tomatoes, added a head of Bibb lettuce, and tossed in some green beans just because. He had too many, he told himself, and Patsy would appreciate them.

He was washing his hands when Darren arrived, coming around the house to the backdoor, the way he usually did.

Frank waved him in. "Iced coffee?" he asked, lifting a glass he had already prepared.

Darren nodded and Frank handed him the filled glass and fixed another. "Let's sit on the porch and watch the fool cats click their teeth at the chickadees at the bird bath. They're too lazy to do more than that, and it seems to give them satisfaction."

They sat on the porch and Frank waited for Darren to begin.

"I got a call from Todd yesterday," Darren said after a hesitation. "He's in Siberia somewhere, not really sure where. Some Russian scientists have joined the team. There are forest fires and lot of smoke, and it snowed recently. It was like that, disjointed, the call broken again and again by a bad connection. Anyway, the long and short of it is that they'll head to the nearest town that has an airport and isn't closed in by snow, smoke, fire, or God knows what else." He took a long drink of his coffee and set the glass down on the table.

"He said they might get away by midweek, next week. Maybe Wednesday or Thursday. Maybe not until Friday. He's tired. They're all tired." Darren looked miserable, his big mobile face revealed a lot of worry, a lot of indecision. "I haven't told Barbara. She got in so late last night and was so tired. And this morning, I didn't say a word. I didn't know what to say."

"What's the problem, Darren?"

"I don't know what to do. I feel like I shouldn't run out on Barbara in the middle of the trial. She'll forget to eat, maybe she won't even sleep. You know how she'll be, and I have to be there for her. But Todd will be so tired, so jet lagged, maybe hungry. I don't want to tell him to catch the first flight home..."

Frank nodded. "You tell him you'll be at the terminal waiting for him, and you'll take him to a good hotel, see that he has an hour-long hot shower, food waiting, and a good bed. He'll sleep around the clock more than likely."

Darren looked at the garden, at his hands, at the coffee he had abandoned. He picked it up and took another drink. Without looking at Frank, he said huskily, "I can't lose her, Frank."

Bluntly Frank said, "The best thing you can do for her is to get lost during the trial. Do you have any idea of the kind of guilt she battles when she thinks she's disappointed you, not come home for dinner, at the office until dawn, putting her work first? I know, because I've been there. It's worst when you really care about the person you think you're mistreating, and you can't help doing it. Right now, she's out at the farm talking to those kids. That's not how it's done. The client comes to you, the witnesses come to you, you don't go to them. But she's trying to save Jeff a little more grief, because she knows it would grieve her to be in his place, see Gina shower and dress in clean clothes to go trotting off to the attorney's office, to see the other fellows have to do the same, while she's chained to a stump. That's what she does, fills the shoes of the other and suffers with and for them. She sees herself slighting you to help someone else, and she can't help it, that's how it is, how it has to be. Then a flood of guilt. Guilt is corrosive, it's hard to live with, and that's her problem, not yours."

"I've never hinted—"

"I know you haven't. You don't have to. My wife never hinted either, but I came to know what I was doing to her. When Barbara was a kid, twelve, thirteen, she lit into me about it, and she had a tongue on her as a kid, believe me. Her mother was aghast, and I was stunned by her accusations. True enough, but false also, because we had a good marriage for thirty years. Women suffer this more than men do. I was barely aware of it until Barbara raked me over the coals. We, society, teach girls from infancy on to take care of others, and most of them assimilate the lessons so deeply they're not even aware of having been taught. Maybe that nurturing gene is already in place and we simply stroke it and strengthen it until the need to nurture is powerful. And when they feel that they're failing, some of them suffer terrible guilt. Some run away from it, some deny it, some simply acknowledge it and live with it."

"Barbara?"

"I don't know," Frank said. "I just don't know. This is a tough trial; she'll be working hard and keeping late hours, and she may lose. If she feels she's failing Jeff, and failing you at the same time, it could be too much. So go early and stay late, and when you bring your son home, I'll have celebration dinner for him. Don't worry about her. I'll see that she eats, and I'll suggest sleep now and again. It's all a fellow can do."

‡

Barbara had walked Gina through her part of the trial and now leaned back in the easy chair in the living room, which seemed to have become the conference room for all trial-related matters. "Any questions?" she asked.

Gina shook her head. "I'm just as nervous as I was at the presentation, maybe more so. More is at stake."

"You'll do fine," Barbara said. "You have nothing to hide, no need to dodge questions or hope some questions don't come up. Tell the truth and keep it simple and straightforward. Keep in mind that Gil Weymouth, the prosecutor, is clever and has a lot of trial experience under his belt. He's going to do his damnedest to get you to admit to a romantic relationship with Jeff. That's what the prosecution is based on, Jeff's expectation to get you and the farm. You can handle that. If you don't understand a convoluted question—and he can do that, too—ask him to clarify it. Tell him you don't understand the question. Throw the ball back to him, but not in an aggressive way. The judge, I'm afraid, is old-fashioned enough to call me Miss, and I expect he thinks a woman's place is in the home. Not proven, understand, but a guess. Be respectful and polite, but firm in your answers. You'll sail right through it."

They both stood and Barbara said, "Maybe something cold to drink while I'm talking to Jeff. What does he like?"

"Iced tea, lemonade, beer, any juice..."

"Whatever you think he'd like best. And I think I'll move the action out to the terrace." She wanted to move, but not out among the throngs of shoppers, not among the workers bringing in produce from the fields. The terrace had to do. She walked out to it and paced to the end of the walkway to the side of the house, back, several times. By then Jeff had appeared and taken a seat at the table and Gina came out a second later with two glasses of lemonade.

"Thanks," Barbara said, seating herself opposite Jeff. He was facing the farm, as she had known he would. Gina hesitated only a second or two before leaving. No one else of their group was in sight.

"There isn't much more to tell you about the trial itself," Barbara began. She tasted her lemonade. It was exactly right, tart and ice cold. "You'll have a notebook and pen to jot down anything that occurs to you as witnesses testify. If you want me to ask something in particular, or take issue with anything, a quick note, a nudge, and if it's possible, I'll address it. I'll be forced to stay within the limits of direct testimony in my cross-examination, however, and sometimes the next obvious question can't be asked or, if asked, is overruled and tossed out. Just so you understand the rules we have to follow."

He nodded. So far he had not said a word beyond greeting her. She looked down at her hand on the sweating glass, wiped her hand on her jeans, and leaned forward. "Jeff, this is difficult and I hate it, but you will be required to stay in the county jail for the duration of the trial. We argued it out in a pretrial meeting with the judge and that's how he ruled."

"Jesus! This isn't enough?" He held up his leg with the electronic monitor.

"The prosecutor argued that you're a flight risk and the judge agreed. I couldn't change their minds."

"They're right. Flight risk. Spread my wings and take off. They have my car, my driver's license, my passport. Fly away, fly away with the seagulls. You know why, don't you? You know they have to do it to prove I'm a desperate killer who can't be trusted in society. Humiliate me, make me realize how powerless I really am, make me bow before the powers that be. I know the game. The game they invented and take pleasure in."

"I did get the prosecutor to guarantee the safety of your belongings. Books, notebooks, your laptop, anything you'll want like that."

He gave her an incredulous look. "You think I'd take anything I valued with me? Library books, that's all. Let them steal library books. Who gives a fuck."

He looked at his lemonade and for a moment she thought he was going to sweep it off the table, sweep everything off the table, but he simply looked, then got to his feet, and walked away.

"I'll come by on Sunday," Barbara said to his back. He did not respond. Barbara took another drink of the excellent lemonade, then picked up his glass and took both glasses into the house and on to the kitchen. Gina was there.

"So fast," Gina said in a tentative manner; then, with a worried expression, "What's wrong? What happened?"

Barbara told her and Gina sank down into a chair and burst into tears.

Frank walked to the office, rode the elevator up to the second floor; having met his exercise requirement for now, he saw no need to climb stairs, and in the offices, he stopped by Patsy's own office to deliver his care package. Patsy, with her jet black hair that never showed a trace of white roots, her sensible shoes, and her round body that he had to remind himself now and then not to say or think was stuffed like a sausage, was delighted.

"Brandywines," she exclaimed. "Are you sure? They're so scarce."

"I'm sure," he said. "Enjoy. I'll be in the office a few minutes, then the library. Unless it's urgent, no calls, except the usual suspects." They both grinned, knowing well that he would never refuse a call from Barbara or Bailey.

Then, at his desk, he began to look at insurance sites, especially art insurance, and the FBI site, The National Stolen Art File. He had spent some time on it before and had hesitated to call up the file of stolen art. He still hesitated. He backed out of it again and returned to the next site on his list to do some more research on. This was one that his art curator friend had recommended, being the largest art insurance company in the world, he had said, and in business since time began, or thereabouts. The actual date was 1821, but that was a good long time. Frank clicked on various links: assessment of art; insurability; process of acquiring insurance; provenance... The present CEO, George Croft-Acton, smiled at him and invited his comments or questions. He had a title, Sir George, and his smile was benign. A form was available to be filled out describing the item of interest, its cost basis, present location… An item had to be worth two thousand dollars or more to be considered for insurance by the company.

There were offices throughout the world, the nearest one in San Francisco. Frank clicked on it and was greeted by a similar page to the home office page. Sir George was not smiling at him on this site, but a Raymond Hammond was. He was nearly bald and not as nice looking as Sir George, who would never be taken for an insurance salesman, but Raymond Hammond could be.

Frank copied the telephone number of the San Francisco office. He didn't want to fill out a form, give his email address, or any other information. He called the number.

A pleasant female voice came on and asked with whom he wished to speak.

"I just have a quick question," Frank said. "If I happened to come across a work of art that might have been stolen, do I go to the police or FBI, or your company?"

"Just a moment, sir. I'll connect you with our stolen property department."

Frank hung up. Neither did he want to have a tracer put on his telephone line, if that was what the procedure was, and he suspected that he was getting a touch paranoid about the damned pictures. He closed his laptop and tossed the telephone number in the trash. "Later," he muttered. "I'll tend to it later." He stood and walked out of his office and on to the law library, where he knew what he was doing.

Barbara had worked through lunchtime, had eaten a sandwich that Maria placed on her desk without a word, and now she was starting on the depositions Shelley had collected.

She had skimmed them, but she had to read them carefully, word for word, and know exactly what each man had said, try to read between the lines, get a hint of demeanor as well as words. Shelley was extremely good, but that wasn't enough. Barbara had to know them by heart. Her concentration was shattered at four when Bailey called to ask if she was going to be around.

"You have something?"

"Yeah, something. Half an hour. See you."

"Damn the man," she muttered. Not even a hint about what it was. She looked at the open papers on her desk, tried to get back into the one she had been reading. LeMuir's deposition was bleak, and hard to take. He had been observant and, she thought angrily, complicit in the general's mistreatment of Jeff as a small child, then as a prepubescent boy. Would his hatred of the general, clear to her, also be clear to jurors listening to Frank repeat his damning words? She couldn't tell. She would have to hear Frank say the words and decide then if she could use the deposition. LeMuir, Leemer to the boys, had been assigned to the general and had had no way to escape his orders, which mitigated his complicity somewhat. But not enough by a damn sight, she thought, and she closed the folder with the three depositions. Later, she told it. She would read them at home that night.

By the time Bailey arrived she was furious with herself for not being able to concentrate, furious with Bailey for tantalizing her with hints of discovery, furious with LeMuir, who had stood by while Jeff was being mistreated and even beaten, right up until intervention prevented a possible murder.

Bailey ambled in finally and headed straight for the bar. "Tough day," he said. She wanted to throw something at him. He poured Jack Daniels, added a drop of water, and slumped down into an easy chair. "Weasel Face first," he said after taking a long drink. "Long rap sheet, served time for assault and battery, charged with murder twice, had an alibi each time. Like that. He'll have an alibi this time, too. That's how he rolls."

He took another long drink. "Jug Ears. PhD psychology, prof at Northwestern for six years, booted out fifteen years ago. Some kind of scandal, but the papers are sealed, judge's order. After that, he was a consultant for the DoD, advised in the enhanced interrogation program. Torture," he added gloomily.

"I know that," she snapped. "What was he doing here?"

"Getting to it," Bailey said. "Seems his present gig is to be an expert witness for Tilsen's company, Halsey Enterprises. See, somebody sues, claims the company poisoned his crop with their spray, something like that. Jug Ears goes in and says the guy is paranoid, has shown hatred for the company in different ways, is holding a grudge, the favorite word is disgruntled, is psychopathic, is trying to extort the company, that his crop failure was due to his own incompetence, or was a deliberate action to bring suit and be paid off. Whatever it takes. He has the credentials to back up his expertise. An invaluable employee."

"Good God!" she said. "He was here to judge Gina, to pass a death sentence. Where are they now?"

"The apartment manager said Jug Ears came in about midnight the night of the attack. He has his own key. Someone dropped him off and left. He stayed overnight and left by taxi the next morning. I think Weasel Face got a red-eye back to New York, his home base. And Jug Ears flew back to Chicago, his base." He finished his drink, rose, and went to the bar to refill his glass.

"I got inside the apartment," he said. "Got fingerprints, but no match. I don't even know if I got Tilsen's, but I probably got Jug Ear's. They have a cleaning service and Tilsen hasn't been there for a week." He brought out a folder from his duffel bag and tossed it down on the table. "It's all in there, names, addresses, rap sheet."

"Thanks, Bailey," Barbara said. "Good job. Tilsen will be here for the trial. He stays at Valley River Inn. Maybe you'll have a chance to lift prints..."

Bailey nodded and he left soon after that. She sat at her desk again, drumming her fingers, and finally began to put papers away, straighten things generally. For once, she thought glumly, she might be home before Darren. She was in no mood for anything more serious than giving the cat fresh water and watching dust motes dance.

She got home almost simultaneously with Darren. She had not even cleaned Nappy's water bowl when she heard Darren's car. He came in carrying a bag from Fisherman's Market.

"Salmon and coleslaw," he said, taking out a package which he put in the refrigerator. He put another plastic container in the refrigerator and closed the door, then came to her and kissed her. "Hi," he said when they separated. "Gin and bitter lemon for me. What do you want?"

"The usual. Just wine."

He got the drinks and they went to the back patio with them. Darren talked about a new patient and she half-listened and sipped her wine. Then he began to talk about something else, and suddenly she sat upright and studied him intently.

"What's wrong?" she asked.

"Why? What have I done?"

"You've been talking ever since you entered the house. What's up?"

He took another long drink and set his glass down. "Okay, you've got me." His voice dropped into a lower register, became almost musical when he continued, the way it did when he was upset or angry. And he wasn't angry, that she knew.

"I got a phone call from Todd," he said in that other voice. "It was scrambled, broken up a lot with a bad connection. They've had bad weather, a forest fire with a lot of smoke, and snow, but they intend to fly out if they can get to an airport by Wednesday. Possibly not until Friday, but sometime after Wednesday next week."

"Darren, that's wonderful!" she cried. "Why didn't you tell me? I'm so relieved that they'll be getting out of wherever the hell they are. I've been so worried about him!"

"You've been worried?"

"God, yes! Thin ice, breaking through and freezing in the water. Avalanches. Blizzards. Polar bears. Overcome by methane gas. Running out of food and water, turning on each other." She paused for breath. "Maybe not the last one, but all the others. Haven't you been worried for him?"

He nodded. "Too much to talk about. I didn't want to seem like a hothouse parent who can't stand it when his kid is out of sight."

"So what's your problem? He's coming home! Next Wednesday? He can't simply hang out waiting to take another plane to Eugene. They might take a couple of days, delays with connecting flights, a cargo plane, metal seats. His trip might be hellish. You have to meet him and see that he gets some rest, good food, a real bed—"

"That's just it," Darren said. "I can't leave you alone in the middle of a hard trial. You'll need someone to bring you coffee, to rub your back, to be there. I may be able to be of some help in some way. I can't just go off and leave you when things get difficult. I'd feel like shit, guilt would eat me alive—"

Barbara put her hand firmly over his lips. "Don't be a jackass," she said. "You'll go get your kid and bring him home after he's had a little time to rest and eat. I won't have it any other way. For God's sake, I endured trials long before you came on the scene, remember. I think I'll survive. Now, let's make a plan. You say he might arrive Wednesday at the earliest. That means you'll have to leave here on Monday, take two days to drive down, get a room, a suite with a separate sleeping area for him. He'll be so tired..."

Gently Darren removed her hand from his mouth and kissed her palm. "Think you can wait an hour or so for dinner? We can make plans over salmon, and meanwhile, maybe we can relax a little. Upstairs. In the bedroom."

"I thought you'd never ask," she murmured, casting her eyes down demurely. "Beat you up stairs." She jumped up and ran into the house with him at her heels. She wanted to shout, "Thank you, God!" But that would require an explanation and it was not a time for more words.

All morning Frank and Shelley had been rehearsing the dialogues from the depositions she had taken. Barbara had sat listening and making notes. She had saved Sergeant LeMuir's deposition for last and now that it was done, she leaned back and shook her head.

"That's almost too damning to use," she said.

Frank nodded. "Great job, Shelley. Really fine. How far did you have to tamp him down to get that much?"

"It was pretty bad," Shelley said. "He would say things like the general was crazy, then back off and say crazy like a fox. The general really loved his wife, just didn't know how to treat a woman. In the next breath he'd say he hated her. Apparently there was no real marriage for a quite a few years, just a pretense, enough to keep face in public. She didn't want to leave her sons, and he would have fought for them, and he didn't want the disgrace of a failed marriage, possibly a blot on his career. She had two rooms for herself, a bedroom and a smaller room she called her sewing room, and when he was home that's where she spent her evenings after the boys were in bed. Then one night he got roaring drunk and forced himself on her. The next day she put the lock on the door, and nine months later Jeff was born. Eric was eleven and Curtis thirteen."

Shelley drew in a breath and then said, "He, the general, would tell LeMuir things, especially when he'd been drinking. He did that three, four times a year, binge drinking, falling down drunk, and talkative. He said it was her duty to pleasure him, that it was God's will, and for her to refuse him was a sin. He said Jeff was to blame for their being apart, that if not for him, they would be a happy couple like in the old days.

"When it really ended was the day the general walked in unexpectedly to find Curtis reading, babysitting, and Jeff playing with Legos on the floor. Curtis jumped to his feet, and stood at attention, the way the general demanded, but Jeff kept playing. The general grabbed Jeff's arm, hauled him to his feet and dragged him across the room to a closet where he kept a switch. He yanked the kid's pants down and whacked him, yelling that he was being punished for not showing respect. That's when Jeff's mother returned home with Eric. Within the hour she had packed some things for them and she was gone."

Shelley gave Barbara a woeful look. "I couldn't let him get into that very much because the more he talked about it all, the more obvious it became that he had loved her. Any prosecutor would recognize it and make it the issue." She spread her hands helplessly. "I tried to get him to tone it down, and he tried, but it kept coming through loud and clear."

"You got more than enough," Barbara said. "I just don't know if I can use any of his testimony. He sounds so bitter and angry."

Frank nodded. "I agree. I tried to soften the tone a bit, but the words are still there."

"Back burner for now," Barbara said. "Let's find out how much the general reveals, how much the jurors seem to like him, how much Judge McNulty appears to agree with his assessment of the wife's role in a marriage. If I have to use it, I will."

"Good enough," Frank said, rising. "Now I'm going home to make a BLT, and then on to the office. Barbara, Shelley, join me?" To his annoyance his phone rang and he saw that it was Patsy calling. "She knows better," he muttered and answered.

He listened, then said, "Hold on a minute." Holding his hand over the mouthpiece, he looked at Barbara. "It seems that a Mr. Stephen Worthington wants to talk to me about a mirror."

"Good heavens! When? Late today, four-thirty, or in the morning." She glanced at her watch. It was ten minutes before one.

Frank passed the times on to Patsy. "I'll wait," he told her. It didn't take long. "Sounds fine," he said and disconnected. "Four-thirty today."

"Shelley," Barbara said, "I need a subpoena for Stephen Worthington. Make it two while you're at it. One for Simon Alterman. Judge Wallis."

Judge Cynthia Wallis was not quite retired, as she put it, and she had worked swiftly with subpoenas in the past.

Shelley was already heading for the door. "I'll be at Dad's office," Barbara said. "Give me a call if and when you get them and we'll go on from there." She grinned at Frank. "Now I'm ready for one of your BLT creations. And we'll talk while we eat."

Promptly at four-thirty Patsy tapped on Frank's door, opened it, and Simon Alterman walked in. He took two steps, then came to a stop when he saw Barbara. His smile vanished momentarily, came back bigger than before, and he bowed his head fractionally. "Ms. Holloway, how pleasant a surprise to find you here." He continued to cross the office to Frank's desk.

"Dad," Barbara said, "meet Simon Alterman, aka Stephen Worthington. My advice for you is to refuse to buy the bridge he's selling until he shows you ironclad proof of who he is. Meanwhile, I'm out of here." She grinned at Alterman/Worthington and walked to the coffee table to pick up her briefcase.

Alterman said to Frank, "I can explain my name confusion, but I agree that identification is always a good starting point." He reached into his pocket and brought out a passport, opened it, and held it up before Frank's eyes.

Barbara laughed. She started toward the office door, saying, "How many people do you know, Dad, who produce a passport for ID? Mr. Alterman, how many do you have, in how many names?"

"Mr. Holloway, if you will be so kind as to go to the company site," Worthington said, still smiling, but the smile appeared forced now, "World Wide Art and Antiquities Insurance, I assure you we can clear up the matter of identification."

Frank shrugged and returned to the site he had investigated before. Again Sir George smiled at him and asked for a comment.

"In the comment section," Alterman said, "type in 'mirror, mirror.' That's all you need do." Frank did this and leaned back. Worthington walked around the desk and stood where he could see the screen. A message was displayed: *Please wait.*

Barbara had her phone out and called Shelley, who picked up instantly. "Shelley," she said. "I'm still at Dad's office. I'm afraid I'm going to be delayed and I'll go on home from here. Do me a favor, please. On my desk there are several folders. Find one labeled Number 2 and send it over here by courier. I'll take care of it at home tonight."

Alterman was glancing at the computer and her alternately. Then his attention focused on the screen. The image had changed. Now Sir George was there, not smiling, and apparently in a different location, possibly a living room. "May I?" Alterman said to Frank, placing his hands on the keyboard. Frank moved away enough to give him room, and he typed in: "Sir George, I apologize for this late message. I'm in the office of Mr. Frank Holloway, and I should like to verify my identity for him and his daughter."

Barbara walked to the end of Frank's desk where she could see the screen.

A reply came: *One moment*. The screen changed again and now showed a picture of Sir George and Alterman together, with a caption: *Stephen Worthington receiving his ten-year Excellence Plaque.*

"Enough?" Alterman asked. He directed the question to Barbara.

She nodded and he typed "Thank you. I'll call after we conclude our meeting."

"Why the charade?" she demanded. She went back to the coffee table and put her briefcase down hard. "Why so much mumbo jumbo?"

"Mr. Worthington," Frank said in a much quieter tone, almost a soothing tone, "why are you here now? What can I do for you? Please, both of you, sit down." He indicated the two chairs across from his desk and he sat in his own chair and waited for Barbara to be seated. Worthington moved around the desk and sat down after she did.

"I'm an insurance investigator, art theft is my specialty," Worthington said. "Some years ago a valuable painting went missing, a Rubens. In it there is a seated woman, and behind her on the wall there is a mirror of a unique design, a border of intricately carved ivory. We recovered the painting, but the mirror was not found at the time. Alone it has little value, but as a companion piece to the painting it is quite valuable. I was tasked with finding the mirror, and simple detective work brought me here." He smiled his beautiful smile and shrugged.

"Knock it off," Barbara said. She stood and paced to the door, back to the sofa, speaking sharply as she moved. "How did you link my father to that ridiculous story? Your company sent you half way around the world to find a mirror? You could get a mirror made for less than you've spent chasing this one. How is Reyes involved? Why the alias?"

"I always work undercover," he said easily. "You can understand the reason. I couldn't very well simply knock on doors and ask if anyone present happened to have a stolen mirror, now could I?"

She gave him a scornful look and started to snap a retort when there was a light knock on the door. "My courier," she muttered and strode to the door, jerked it open.

A middle-aged man in shirt sleeves pushed in past her, walked across the office quickly and said, "Mr. Worthington? Mr. Stephen Worthington?"

Worthington nodded and the man handed him a folded paper, turned, and walked out as quickly as he had walked in. Barbara closed the door.

"What the bloody hell?" Worthington asked, opening the paper.

"It's a subpoena," Barbara said. "You are required to make yourself available to testify at the trial of Jeff Cobbe."

"You can't make me testify!"

"Yes, I can. If you fail to show up when called, an arrest warrant will be issued. You'll be put on the no-fly list, and I understand that once on that list it's almost impossible to have your name removed."

"I don't have anything to say about your bloody murder trial!"

"Maybe you do and maybe you don't. We'll find out when you're on the stand under oath." She went to the sofa and sat down. "You've lied and lied," she said. "Do you lie under oath? How will Sir George react if his fair-haired boy is grounded or perhaps even in jail? Doesn't exactly add a fine luster to the finish, does it?"

As she spoke, she opened her briefcase and brought out the four prints of the paintings and placed them face down on the table. "I suggest, Mr. Worthington, that it would be a good idea for us to start over, for you to start over, from the real beginning, not some cock and bull story about a Rubens." Slowly, as if turning over fortune teller cards, she turned the prints face up, one by one, pausing between each one.

He made a strangled sound and bounded from his chair and across the office. "Where are they?" His voice was harsh, the words slurred, run together.

"They are safe," Frank said, coming around his desk. "Sit down, Mr. Worthington. Would you like a drink? Scotch, bourbon, gin?"

Worthington sank down into one of the easy chairs, his gaze fastened on the prints. "Is that all?" he asked hoarsely.

"That's all," Barbara said. She glanced at Frank. "Think Patsy could manage coffee? I have a lot of work to get to tonight. No alcohol for me now."

Frank buzzed Patsy for coffee, then opened his bar, much better stocked than Barbara's ever was. Scotch, he decided. Worthington looked like a Scotch man, a somewhat ill Scotch man, he thought as he poured the drink. Worthington had not said another word, and he was staring at the prints as if hypnotized. He was startled out of a trance-like state and jerked when Frank put the glass in his hand.

"What condition are they in?" Worthington asked after taking a long drink.

"Very fine," Frank said. He sat opposite Worthington. "It's in your court," he said.

Worthington did not move for several seconds, no longer in a near-paralytic state, but obviously thinking hard. Finally, he sighed, took another drink and set his glass down on the table. "Right," he said. "How it started. World War II, Mussolini had fallen and his inner-circle cohorts were scattering to the winds. One of those inner-circle men was Luigi DiGotto, a banker, close to Il Duce for a decade or longer, and director of a finance ministry. His assistant and translator was Anton Salzi, thirty-something, fluent in several languages. Anton's father was Italian, mother French, and they had lived in New York for years where his father was in business. Anton made his way back to Italy and became Luigi's right-hand man. After Mussolini's fall and death, DiGotto knew that he had to get out of Italy before the mobs with their pitchforks and torches came for him. He went to the Americans who were in Italy by then, and he made a deal. He knew the financial secrets of the highest of the high, the mightiest of the mighty, and he would tell all for a free pass to America, a job with the State Department as informal informer. Something to that effect."

There was a tap on the door, and Frank said to come on in. Barbara turned the prints face down and Patsy entered with a tray bearing the coffee carafe, cream, sugar, her nice cups instead of the usual mugs, and a plate of cookies. Teatime, Barbara thought sardonically. Patsy had fallen for the gorgeous Brit just like Maria and Shelley.

Frank thanked Patsy and no one else spoke until she was gone again. Barbara poured coffee for herself and Frank. He rose and took Worthington's glass, replenished it at the bar, and sat down without a word.

"Thank you," Worthington said. "It was arranged, diplomatic immunity for his possessions, no customs, no inspection, nothing. It was being done with a lot of people, scientists mostly, but also businessmen, bankers… Well, DiGotto was a real banker and he kept records of everything, a complete inventory of his residence and office, price paid, date acquired, everything. This came up later and was invaluable to us.

"He and Anton flew to New York in October 1944, and they were met by a state department flunky who was supposed to take them to a hotel that day and on the following day to Washington by train. They, and their trunk, headed for the city, and DiGotto and the state department man were both found dead days later. The trunk and Anton had vanished. When it became clear what had happened, the inventory came to light, filed among Luigi's papers that he had no use for in the new life he had planned."

Worthington paused and took another sip of his scotch. The first glass had been drunk as if it were medicine; he was sipping, tasting it now. "That's where it stood for a year or two. The company knew what had been taken, knew who the real owners were in most cases, and that's all they knew. DiGotto had not paid for any of the art, had not bought it at auction or from private parties. Confiscated, seized from opposition party members, gifts, bribes, extorted from refugees, safe passage out of Italy for a rich someone and family, it's all in the lists he made. There were those four," he indicated the prints, still face down, "and a Titian, a Caravaggio, a Matisse, and a Rubens. There were silver plates, and gold bowls, silver flatware, other miscellaneous silver and crystal pieces, two porcelain figurines. And there was a mirror with a carved ivory border. They put flags on all the items, of course, and over the next few years things began to show up. Not the Titian, not those—" he nodded toward the prints— "of course, and not the mirror. Anton was living high, no doubt, for more than ten years. The last thing that came to light was the Matisse, recovered in 1956. Nothing since. And then, after all those years an inquiry was flagged regarding the mirror."

Worthington took another sip of his drink, then put the glass aside and reached across the table to help himself to coffee. "I also have a lot of work to do tonight," he commented. "I can't give you details about the next phase because I wasn't involved. The San Francisco office sent detectives to track down the appraiser who had made the inquiry about the mirror and found that she had been murdered. They got files on all the appraisals for the past thirty days and checked them out; they got phone records and checked them; and finally they came to a name that gave the home office real concern. Another Italian family, named Valducci, and the pater nostra of the family, Robert Valducci, had been murdered. A Cosa Nostra connection? A new crime syndicate? Art theft ring? I was called in at that time."

He gave Barbara a sardonic grin. "You asked where I was when Robert Valducci was shot. I was in Sir George's office with several others, and we were trying to devise a scheme that had me on the scene in Oregon without raising suspicion. We came up with Reyes. A hint to him about small farmers, someone else waxing eloquent about the plight of small farms, an editor keen on the idea. Reyes is a genius photographer, no doubt, and a good writer, but he is also a vain, egocentric son of a bitch, totally uninterested in anything that doesn't have him at the center, and one who, moreover, is easily manipulated. All fired up about his new idea, he was thwarted when his assistant suddenly had a problem with his visa. Simon Alterman happened to be at a cocktail party that included Reyes, they had known each other for years, and Simon was at loose ends. He is usually at loose ends. He thought it would be a lark to be Reyes' temporary assistant, and Reyes agreed. We headed to Oregon. Reyes is pretty much fed up with Simon by now. Never around when needed, prowling about on his own, couldn't get a simple farm girl to allow the great Reyes to photograph her and her farm."

"That was the plan," Barbara said when he stopped talking. "Reyes was to keep Gina busy while you had a chance to get inside the house and find the paintings. Take them away if they were. And Gina never the wiser."

"One does not miss what one never had," Worthington said with a shrug. "I would have taken the paintings back to London, abandoning poor Reyes, but his assistant would have been informed that the difficulty with his visa had been cleared up. He and Reyes would have been reunited, and Gina would have looked forward to a very flattering article featuring her and her farm, spreading her messianic message far and wide. Everyone's happy; all ends well."

"It doesn't concern you that there have been two murders, that an attack was made on Gina's life, that an innocent man will go on trial next week for murder over art that he doesn't know a thing about? Yet, you went out of your way to protect Gina."

"That was because I didn't know the paintings had been removed," he said coolly. "I didn't want her dead and for her mother to reenter the scene, sell off the property. Murder does not concern me. My job is to find those paintings and take them to our home office in London. I knew from day one that Gina didn't have a clue, and I suspected they were still hidden away in that house. What I don't know is if anyone else still suspects that, or who killed the appraiser and Valducci, how the mirror ended up here, and the missing art as well, or if Valducci was part of a bigger group of art thieves. I'm certain, however, that you can fill in some of those blanks." He flashed his broad smile that showed gleaming, perfect teeth.

It surprised Frank to see Worthington or Alterman, whoever he really was, still trying to charm Barbara as if he had misread her close attention as she listened to him. By her body language, her expression, the timbre of her voice, Frank recognized that attention as a wary assessment of a repulsive and dangerous something slithering in the grass, something to be treated with caution and to be avoided as long as possible, and to be eliminated if that became necessary.

"I can fill in some blanks," Barbara said. "But first how did you end up coming here, to Dad's office?"

He shrugged. "The flags attached to those and the mirror—" he motioned to the prints—"were changed to track any visitor to the company website by anyone from Oregon. Now, your turn."

"Big Brother's alive and thriving," Barbara murmured. "Okay, the trunk." She told the story Gina had told her and finished by saying, "There were newspapers, *The New York Times*, dated December, 1956, and the *Chicago Tribune*, dated January 1957. The trunk was shipped from Chicago in January 1957. The sender never showed up."

"That's when the case went cold," Worthington said. "So now the puzzle is complete. As you can see, there is no reason to call me as a witness for your trial. I was not in the country, did not know any of the principals involved, had no interest in any of them, and know nothing about whatever happened. Ergo, nothing to testify to." He rose and straightened his tie, adjusted the sleeves of his sport coat, and smiled at Barbara, then turned a somewhat more restrained smile on to Frank. "What happens in a situation such as this," he said easily, "if a holder of property that is known to be stolen, that person is required to release it to the insurance company in order that it be returned to its legitimate owner. I'm confident that we can come to an equitable arrangement to bring about that result."

"Mr. Worthington," Frank said, just as easily as he had spoken, "in the United States, what happens in a situation such as this is that if someone has come across property known to be stolen, it is customary to contact the FBI as quickly as possible and let their investigators launch an enquiry concerning the legal owner of such property."

Worthington's eyes narrowed and he sat down again. Then, leaning forward, he said earnestly without a trace of a smile, "Mr. Holloway, that would be a grievous error. An investigation conducted by your FBI would take months, years even, to reach a conclusion, and meanwhile the rightful owners are deprived of their property. Justice delayed, as they say, is justice denied."

"Since they've been deprived of their property for over sixty years already, another few months should make no difference," Frank said.

"An FBI investigation would involve everyone here," Worthington said. "You, your daughter, her lover, people at his clinic, others at your office, Gina Valducci and her three friends, her mother and her associates, probably everyone at the farm… There would be the press, reporters, photographers, videographers. The disruption would be severe and continuous for a long time. What my company can offer instead is a quiet resolution of this problem within a week. No publicity, no FBI."

"We might be able to hold off with the FBI for a while," Barbara said thoughtfully. "But I'm afraid there could be some publicity following your testimony."

"I'm not going to testify at your goddamn trial!" He jumped to his feet and clenched his fists, glaring at her.

"Yes, you are, or face arrest and a spell in the county jail."

"Why are you doing this? You know I can't do anything for your client!" He was pale, furious, his words clipped and harsh.

"You're my most important witness," Barbara said. "You can furnish the missing ingredient, a motive for someone else to have committed murder. And you will take the stand and do that." She stood and faced him. "I'm calling it quits for today. Go away and think about it. Tomorrow, ten in my office, we can pick up where we've left off today. Go, stay, do whatever you want, but I'm done for today."

For a moment he didn't move, then swiftly he strode to the office door, yanked it open, and stalked out. When the door closed, Barbara sank back down on the sofa.

"Think he'll show tomorrow?" Frank asked.

"Sure he will. What time is it?"

"Six-twenty. Let's have Darren meet us at the Electric Station. What you want now is a tall frosty gin and tonic, or something in that neighborhood."

She nodded. "Dad, what I said is true, you know. He's my best chance to sway the jury away from Jeff. A snake in the grass, my best bet. God, what an insane world!"

At ten Maria buzzed to say that Mr. Worthington had arrived. Barbara was behind her desk, Shelley in a client's chair, and Frank in an easy chair across the office when Worthington entered.

"My associate, Ms. McGinnis," Barbara said, nodding toward her. "And you know my father. Please sit down."

Worthington was not smiling that morning. He looked grim and distant, and very English proper. He was wearing pale gray trousers with a knife-edge crease and a blue blazer. His dazzling white shirt was open at the throat. He bowed slightly to Shelley and Frank, arranged his clothes precisely, and sat opposite Barbara.

"Before you start," he said, "there is something I must tell you. Afterward you will understand more fully why I cannot testify at your trial."

He held up his hand as Barbara leaned forward. "Hear me out," he said in a peremptory manner. "I know every single thing there is to know about Simon Alterman, but Simon knows absolutely nothing about me, including my existence. When he was fifteen Simon was involved in a tragic automobile accident that left two of his companions dead, another so seriously injured that she is in wheelchair to this day, and he suffered a skull fracture plus multiple other fractures and lacerations. He had a forty percent chance to survive." He was speaking in a rapid fire, clipped manner, his British accent pronounced, every word distinct and hard edged. "His brain injuries were the most serious. Part of his skull had to be removed to accommodate swelling of brain tissue. But of course he did survive and was a year in convalescence, another year in physical therapy. He had absolutely no memory of the accident or of a two-hour period preceding it. Over the two years while Simon was convalescing, he had lapses of memory. Hours, minutes, even a whole day was sometimes forgotten. They finally diagnosed transient global amnesia."

Worthington was keeping his gaze steadily on Barbara as he talked. She had picked up a pencil and was rolling it back and forth in both hands, impatient for him to get to the point, thinking he was arrogant, condescending, even a bit ridiculous in talking about himself in the third person. She thought she would not be surprised if he began to use the royal "we." She rolled the pencil and did not interrupt.

"All right," Worthington continued. "He had this condition, rare for his age, but not too uncommon. More often, middle-aged people suffer from it, not adolescents, but there it was, and it persisted. Many people have it without awareness. A few minutes lost, an hour or two, even longer. The sufferer goes about business, does routine things, speaks, eats, in other words appears to be completely normal, but no memory of that period is retained. It wouldn't have been notable about him if he had not been under rather intense scrutiny, due to the head injury. A climax of sorts came about when he was twenty-two, seven years after the accident. He was at an auction where a friend's father was auctioning off some valuable paintings. Simon had become something of an expert in art, art history, old masters, contemporary artists, and he had an eye for forgeries. He had bypassed university, due to his condition, but he had tutors, and he immersed himself in art over the years. At the auction, he went into one of his fugue states, not noticeable to anyone not intimately familiar with him, and he placed a call to Sir George and told him that two of the pieces were forgeries. Sir George had his own investigators look into it, and it was discovered that the father of Simon's friend had sold other fake pictures, and that Simon was right about the two he named."

"That was the climax?" Barbara said coldly.

"Not yet," Worthington said, just as coldly. "The friend's father committed suicide, and the friend accused Simon of being responsible. Simon had no memory of his call to Sir George, no memory of naming the paintings as forgeries, no memory of any of it. He went into a tailspin and was institutionalized."

Barbara looked at her watch. Worthington smiled slightly for the first time. It was a fleeting smile.

"The best is yet to come," he said, as his expression returned to grim. "Once, before this incident, Sir George had offered Simon a job with the company, but Simon treated the insurance industry with revulsion and rejected the offer. Sir George, however, believed that Simon could be a valuable asset, that he could keep a lot of fake art out of circulation, keep a lot of art thieves locked up, the art world made safer, and insurance more profitable. He believed then and still believes that deep down Simon is in sympathy with his own belief system, or he would not have made that fateful call. There is a distant kinship, going back a few generations, multiple degrees of separation, but still family. Sir George believes in family connections, and believes even more that whatever is in his genes is also in Simon's. And he also believes, as I do, that most of us, no, all of us harbor a dark side that we mostly keep under control. The saintly Mr. Holloway, the angelic Ms. McGinnis, you, the ethical Ms. Holloway, all of us harbor that darkness. The original phone call to Sir George and Simon's amnesia regarding it set up a thought train that led to an interesting experiment."

He paused, regarding Barbara soberly for a moment, then continued. "Sir George believed that during that particular fugue state, the darkness in Simon was unleashed, that it manifested itself in a second persona, me. Simon had choices; he could have talked to his friend's father, could have talked to his friend, could have turned a blind eye to the auction to preserve a friendship, but he chose to do the one thing that was certain to destroy his friend's father. He called the insurance agency and caused an investigation that resulted in death. That's dark, Ms. Holloway. Damned dark. Sir George took it a step further. If that repressed persona could be unlocked unconsciously, could it also be induced to show itself deliberately? That he was determined to discover.

"After Simon's breakdown, Sir George brought in the world's finest psychiatrist and the best neurologist to be had. Dr. Caroline Whaite and Dr. David McNaughton. They had a number of meetings and in the end Sir George funded the Whaite McNaughton Psychiatric Neurological Facility. Simon was their original and primary patient and research subject, although they have continued to do important work that is lauded worldwide. But their original goal was to learn how to call up the other part of Simon, the dark side, a ghost in Simon's psychic machine. What Shakespeare said:

You can call them but will they come. That's what they set out to discover. They succeeded. Sir George can call upon me for my own expertise now and then, not too often, once or twice a year, and I can step forward as Stephen Worthington and work for the insurance industry. Simon knows nothing about it. He is unaware of my presence and has no memory of anything I do or say. He thinks he is having another of his transient global amnesiac interludes when I emerge."

Barbara's pencil snapped in half and she let the pieces drop. "What the hell does that mean?"

"Exactly what it sounds like," he said. "Simon has been living with transient global amnesia for years. There are no side effects, no pathology involved, no brain tumors or incipient psychoses to manifest. No cause is known—etiology unknown is the phrase—and the only after-effects generally are psychological or emotional distress over the fact that there is a blank space in the memory, a gap in awareness. There is no cure or treatment. During an episode no short-term memories are formed; when normalcy is restored, there is no way to recall what happened during that interlude since no memory of it was formed. His incidents were becoming further apart, and for years none has occurred, but he knew there was always the possibility of having the problem recur.

"He is well liked, popular in various groups, artists, gallery owners, museum directors, a certain social set. Wealthy people consult with him over possible purchases. He is consulted by Sotheby's and other auction houses. His expertise is unquestioned. He has money and family, important in the field of art for some reason, and he hates the insurance industry, also a plus in many quarters. He can get into places that an investigator can't, and that makes him important. Attending the private auction of his friend's father proved the point. If he would work openly with Sir George, his usefulness would be diminished; word would get out, he'd be shunned. As it is, he is considered an expert, somewhat naive, charming, and harmless. And at certain times, I can be brought in without his awareness. He believes such intervals are another manifestation of his condition, and he has come to accept that without undue concern. In this case of the stolen art from Italy, he doesn't have a clue about it, doesn't have a clue about why he's with Reyes. He doesn't remember offering to tag along, but when it came up in a subsequent conversation, he accepted it the way he accepted other incidents that happened during a fugue state."

Barbara picked up the pencil pieces and tossed them in a wastebasket. "Mr. Worthington," she said, "either you get to the point or please leave. I have a trial coming in a few days and I am extremely busy. I assume that all you've told us so far is prologue to whatever point you intend to make. I advise you to make that point now."

He nodded. "You are exactly correct. Prologue. Two points. Simon can't testify because you'd have nothing but blithering idiocy from a witness on the stand. He wouldn't know what you're talking about, why he was being questioned. He knows nothing about our search for the stolen art, nothing about my presence, nothing about anything of value to your defense."

He leaned back in his chair and continued, "You asked me if I would lie under oath, and in this situation I would have little choice. I am not a separate creature, a separate entity. The man called Worthington does not exist except on the books of a certain insurance company, and that is for financial accounting only. If I deny the name, I would have to reveal my dual identity, and that would end the career of a useful investigator. As soon as the mention of stolen art of such value became public, this area would sprout media attention to the extreme. Life stories, sob stories, the ancient accident dredged up again, questions about who was driving that day, Simon's years in an institution. It might destroy Simon Alterman. If he learned through newspaper accounts, television, any media that he had been used for more than ten years, that what he thought were legitimate fugue states of transient global amnesia were in fact induced amnesia brought about by his distant relative, Sir George, it no doubt would send him back to the institution, perhaps never to leave it again. What would you have accomplished? There is still the possibility that this is all a gigantic hoax, a long con, years in the making, only now reaching fruition. No expert has viewed the art."

He smiled a crooked smile that came and vanished fast. "If I say I'm Stephen Worthington, I lie under oath, with serious consequences for all. If I deny the name, I might destroy Simon Alterman, and since I admit to being the dark side of Simon, I commit a sort of suicide. The problem is that I enjoy my life as Simon, and I enjoy the work I do as Stephen. Rock and hard place, Ms. Holloway. My advice is to not put it to the test."

He stood, but before he could take a step away from his chair, Frank spoke. "Mr. Worthington, why don't you simply keep control and manage your dual identities to the advantage of all? I'm sure you have the ability to do that."

Worthington nodded. "We thought of that, of course, and even tried it. But Simon's transient global amnesia was and is unpredictable. There's no predicting when it will occur, or when it will end. There are triggers that he has learned to try to avoid—emotional distress, extreme temperature changes, a plunge into ice water, for example, a few others—but none has predictive value. Often there is no identifiable proximate cause. And it is the same with the cessation, when his psyche rejects the fugue state and wakes up. It happened twice with what could have been dire consequences if others had not intervened. The induced states are a different matter. I never try to keep control for more than a brief period. I tried once to extend it for more than a few hours, but sleep overcame us and when I woke up, he was in control again. I am very careful to return him to a familiar setting when I end the fugue state. He will be confused for a short time, but reassured that nothing remarkable has happened. More often he doesn't even notice it."

"One more question," Frank said. "You said when his psyche wakes up, he returns to a normal state. Is there a possibility that he'll wake up and reject you, his alter ego?"

Worthington paused for an extended period. "I don't know. I think it is possible. I could not maintain control for very long, as I have said. I'm little more than an echo to his whole being. We all know that without his quite real transient global amnesia syndrome this would not have worked. He's too strong. He should have died from his injuries as a youth. If we struggled for control, he could suffer another breakdown, and if he had to enter the institution again, there would I go. No, I would not fight him. And he could reject me. Dr. Whaite made that possibility clear to us in the beginning. In fact, she was expecting that to happen." He bowed again to Shelley and Frank and started to walk to the door.

"Mr. Worthington," Barbara said, still at her desk. "You said this could be a con game. What would it take to convince you that it isn't? Aside from the original art, of course."

He stopped and turned to regard her for a moment. "A look at the mirror that set off this enquiry might help," he said.

She nodded. "Thank you. I have a lot to think about."

After the door had closed behind him Shelley said, "Clark Kent and Superman to the rescue when things go wrong. Split personality or something."

"Or the Manchurian candidate," Barbara said. "Compartmentalism to the extreme, good Simon and rapacious, possibly evil Stephen taking turns at life." She was thinking of what he had said about protecting Gina as long as he had believed the paintings were still in the house, and no longer. Would Simon Alterman have said such a thing?

Frank stood and started for the door. "I think we need to double-check some of what he said. I've never heard of transient global amnesia, for one thing."

"I should go talk to Dr. Minnick," Shelley said. "If those doctors are world famous, he'll know about them. If the research is real, he'll know."

"I agree," Barbara said. "Dr. Minnick is the best bet. I sure don't have time to do a lot of research. Let me know what he has to say as soon as possible."

Frank frowned and shook his head. "I wish to God I could see a way out of this," he said. "It's a 'damned if you do, damned if you don't' situation. Any ideas?" he asked Barbara.

"Not yet. Goddamn that man and his double life!"

After the others left she sat at her desk drumming her fingers, hearing the words over and over: damned if you do, damned if you don't. "Right," she said and stood. She had to move, had to think. God, she thought vehemently, she hated paradoxes!

She drove to the riverside park and walked and walked, and then walked some more. It was too hot, she was too hot, but she couldn't not move. She was barely aware of the others in the park that hot afternoon; when she came to shade, she sat and cooled down, then got up and moved some more. Damned if you do, damned if you don't, kept a loop going in her head behind a jumble of plans thought of and discarded, rethought, discarded again. Other plans, discarded. Then, in a patch of shade she drew in a long breath.

"It will work, or it won't," she said under her breath, and she placed a call to Gina.

The store was more crowded than she had ever seen it. People were clustered around a large bin of corn, others crowded around a bin of Hermiston melons, mobs around heirloom tomatoes, and new potatoes…

Gina was at a checkout register. All six registers were in service that day, with lines at each one. Barbara stepped in front of a woman with an overflowing cart.

"I have to talk to you," she said to Gina. "It's important."

Gina looked at the line at her register, started to shake her head, and Barbara reached over the counter and caught her arm. "It's very important."

Some in line began to grumble when Gina left the register. She beckoned a young woman who was putting baskets of peaches on a bench. "Take over for me," she said when the woman got near.

"What's wrong?" she asked Barbara as they left the store.

"A new development, one I can't explain right now. I want you to permit Reyes to come out and start photographing the farm, whatever he wants. The fields, the store, greenhouses, everything except the house. Will you do that?"

"Why?" Gina cried. "I can't stand him and his assistant, that Alterman. Why now?"

"Gina, do you trust me?" Barbara asked, catching her arm, stopping her. "You have to trust me on this. Please, just trust me."

They stood for a moment, Gina, sweaty, with dirt on her hands and some smeared on her cheek, dressed in jeans and a tank top, and beautiful. And Barbara also hot and sweaty, also in jeans and a tank top and feeling anything but beautiful. Finally Gina nodded, and they resumed walking toward the house.

"I think you look great," Barbara said, "but if you'd be uncomfortable being photographed with a dirty face, maybe you can take a few minutes to tidy up. Think of the pictures for Reyes' book. I'll make a call."

Gina's hands flew to her cheeks, adding to the smears of dirt. She said something unintelligible and ran on ahead to the house. Barbara stopped on the terrace and called Geraldo Reyes.

Barbara and Gina were both on the terrace when Reyes and Alterman arrived. Reyes came rushing up to the line guarded by Rusty. Rusty was in a crouch, showing off impressive teeth, but not growling. "My dear, Ms. Gina," Reyes said, pleading, "please tell the brute I am a friend. I intend no harm. Does the dog bite?"

Alterman stopped short of the dividing line. He was carrying a large leather bag and a folding screen, a filter, Barbara guessed. She walked forward with Gina and, on the other side of the line, she nodded pleasantly to Reyes and Alterman. "I think Gina might want to hear your wishes about what to observe today, your plans for a future opportunity to photograph more, whatever you need."

"I am grateful, dear lady," Reyes said. "Yes, that is splendid. Today an introduction, a walk-through, a first impression kind of day. Ms. Gina, is that agreeable for you?"

As soon as Reyes turned his attention to Gina, Barbara studied Alterman. Or was it Worthington? He was smiling, and she realized the smile was different. Before, it had been a suggestive smile, a secret-shared kind of smile, somewhat lascivious, but now it was simply a good-natured smile. Alterman, she decided.

"Mr. Alterman," she said, "I thought that while Mr. Reyes and Gina make their preliminary tour, you might want to look at the house for possible future sites for photographs." Reyes and Gina were already walking away with him talking. For a moment it seemed that Alterman's expression changed, a flicker of light, a slight shadow, something crossed his features, but the moment was flashing, and he grinned and pointed at Rusty.

"Will he let me in?"

Barbara laughed. "As my guest, you are permitted. There's Greg. Perhaps he can sub for you with the gear. We won't be long, I'm sure." Greg had come from the house on cue and headed for them. Alterman handed over the gear he was carrying.

Then, with his hands free, and his pleasant smile in place, Alterman crossed the line and followed Barbara across the terrace and into the house. He gazed at the living room with approval, nodded at the fireplace, and walked to the far end to study the room from there. Barbara knew she couldn't rush him, knew she had to act as if this were what she had said it was, a preliminary tour to find good spots for pictures, but, on the other hand, she really didn't have much time to spare for this leisurely perusal.

Alterman didn't spend much time on the dining room, but in the hallway, he began to examine various pictures on the walls. "Nice work," he murmured several times, commenting on local artists' paintings.

"Is Reyes likely to be interested in local art?" Barbara asked, wanting only to hurry him on, to get on with it.

"Not at all," Alterman said with a shrug. "Only photography, and mostly his own."

Barbara laughed and led him to the stairs. "Gina's room is up here," she said. "It has some nice furniture from two or three generations ago."

Alterman smiled politely, but he followed along. Barbara had suggested that Gina tidy up the room a little, just in case, and she was pleased to see that her suggestion had been taken. She suspected that it would be a mistake to open a closet door and had no intention of doing so. "The pineapple poster bed is lovely," she said as she moved to the wall that held the mirror.

Alterman glanced at the bed, walked to the windows and glanced out, and finally looked at the wall where Barbara was standing. He drew in his breath and, walking fast, crossed the room to stand close to the mirror. He ran his hand over the carved ivory, then leaned in even closer and homed in on the lower right-hand section, where the minute flaw was.

He straightened up slowly and thrust his hands into his pockets, took a step backward, and stopped moving, his gaze fastened on the mirror in an unblinking stare. The seconds crept by and he didn't move or speak. Second after second, a minute, two minutes? It seemed to be hours.

Finally Barbara said, "Mr. Alterman, are you all right? Is something wrong?"

He roused with a start and shook his head. "No. Nothing. Do you know anything about that mirror?"

"Gina inherited it from her grandmother," Barbara said, choosing her words carefully. "Why?"

"A few years ago," Alterman said, still fascinated by the mirror, sparing her a quick glance only, "BBC did a series they called The Big Heist, all about big robberies. Bank robberies, museum pieces nicked, jewelry, and so on. One of the segments was about art thefts, major art thefts. One of the biggest occurred right after World War II, when someone smuggled a lot of paintings out of Italy. That mirror is associated with that theft. It was part of the haul. Some pieces have been recovered, some are still out there."

He turned his gaze to Barbara then and said in a low voice, "Whoever has that mirror might also have some of those paintings. That was the theory voiced by the BBC narrator, quoting a museum director." He moistened his lips. "Ms. Holloway, a very valuable art collection may be in this house."

"Stolen goods," she said faintly. "That's FBI business."

He cast a swift glance about the room, shaking his head. "Good God, no! Think! They'd come in with crowbars and axes and tear this nice house apart in their search. No, not the FBI, at least not yet. Let Gina and her companions make a search first. If paintings are found and are authenticated, then it will be time to consider the next move."

"We'd have to have experts to authenticate anything we might find," Barbara said.

"I can do it," Alterman said matter-of-factly. "That's the sort of thing I do now and then back home. For the initial authentication process my expertise would be sufficient. At least until a panel of experts could be put together."

"Would you?" Barbara asked. "Would you be willing to do that, if we find anything?"

His eyes were shining and he nodded vigorously. "It would be an honor."

"Let's go downstairs, have lemonade or something, and talk about all this," Barbara said. "I don't know what there is to drink in this house, but we'll find something."

A few minutes later they were sitting on the terrace with icy gin and bitter lemon drinks, and he was telling her what to look for. "They could be rolled, in a tube, even in a chair leg or table leg. Or in back of a regular picture hanging on the wall. You cut a couple of inches of the back dust cover, cardboard, cloth, whatever it is. Cut enough to lift it and you will be able to tell if another picture shares the frame. They could be sewn into the back of a sofa or easy chair..."

She made notes, and when he paused, thinking, she said, "Mr. Alterman, would it be a terrible imposition to ask you to testify for the defense in the upcoming trial? Just about today, not a long involved testimony or anything like that. Just why you're here, and what you discovered today, that's all I would ask."

"I doubt that Geraldo would sit still for that," he said with a rueful shake of his head. "And, besides, what good would that do your client?"

"It could establish a motive for someone else to have done murder," she said. "It's a long shot, but any little bit would be helpful. Someone else might have come to suspect the stolen art is here. Obviously Gina and her friends don't have any suspicions at all, or they would have located them, if they are here." She took a sip of her drink, leaned forward and said, "I have an idea. I can subpoena you and then Mr. Reyes can't object. Will you agree to that?"

He laughed and nodded. "Sure. Why not? But in exchange you have to let me know if the paintings are really located, and I have to have a close look at them."

"Fair enough," she said and raised her glass to tip his in a toast. "That sounds perfect."

A few seconds later he finished his drink and stood. "I'd better get back to my job," he said. "I'll tell Geraldo he has to include some pictures of Gina in the house, especially in the kitchen, and by the fireplace with a nice fire burning. Thank you, Ms. Holloway."

"It's been my pleasure," she said. She rose and, looking at him, she again saw the momentary flicker or shadow that subtly changed his expression.

"Well played, my dear Ms. Holloway," he said mockingly. "But be warned, you're playing with fire."

"Tell me about it," she murmured, and realized the lapse was already over.

Alterman shook his head and gave her a puzzled look. "I'm sorry. You were saying?"

"Nothing. I'll walk out with you. I have to get back to my own work. I'm afraid I've wasted too much time out here. Duty calls."

Sunday evening, the store closed, Barbara had come and gone, and her visit had really been just to give a final pep talk, and now Gina was showered and dressed in shorts and a T-shirt, thinking about what she had to do for dinner. She wanted a special dinner for Jeff, his last at home for a week or longer. She refused to think he might be convicted and never come home again. She had already stuffed a boneless leg of lamb with apricots, slivers of limes, a touch of honey, and sweet onions. It was on the counter, coming to room temperature, ready for the rotisserie. Vegetables were marinating in balsamic vinegar and olive oil: eggplant, red onions, zucchini, sweet red and yellow peppers… They would go on the grill. Slice tomatoes, she told herself, heading for the stairs, toss the salad…

She heard voices from the front of the house, Eric and someone talking, talking over each other. She hurried down a few more steps and was overtaken by Jeff. They both came to a halt at the bottom of the staircase, out of sight of the front door, and she caught his arm in a hard grip.

"I said for you to get your things and come with me." The stranger's voice was harsh and commanding.

Gina felt Jeff's arm stiffen under her grasp and she held him harder, took a step down to get between him and the rest of the staircase. "No!" she said in a low intense voice. "Don't move!"

"I said I'm not going anywhere," Eric said. "Why are you out here, Dad?"

"I told you. I've come to take you home. You're sick. You need medical care. You don't need to be out here in this godforsaken nowhere playing at being a farmer. Look at you! Thin, weak, a nervous wreck. I don't know what he has over you, what hold he has, but it won't stand. You hear me? It won't stand. Get your things!"

"Forget it, Dad. And you listen to me for once. If you testify against your own son, you won't only lose him, you'll lose me, too. I know what you did to him. Leemer told me a lot, and so did others at the academy."

"You don't know anything. He's been lying to you, hiding behind you, using you. He's a murderer! He's taking advantage of you because you're sick."

"Stop it, Dad! Just shut the fuck up. You had three sons, two you raised to be your little tin soldiers. One got killed, and one got broken, and one, the best and the bravest one, is his own man, doing his own thing."

"I'm ordering you to get your things together and come with me. Now!"

"You're not my commanding officer, and I'm not a little tin soldier anymore! You're a retired general who spent the last twenty years shuffling papers around on a desk, trying to relive your glory days in Vietnam, trying to relive wars you never saw. Trying to see Curtis in Afghanistan fighting off hordes of enemies, alone, facing them down until he was slaughtered. Trying to see Ramadi through my eyes. Tell me about it, you'd say over and over, salivating, drooling. Or you'd say, here's how it was in that jungle with those little fuckers swarming everywhere..." His voice dropped to a low note that didn't carry to the stairs. Then, still quietly, but audibly, he said, "Go home, Dad. Just go home. Leave us alone. Jeff is doing a good thing and I intend to help him. Go home. If you do, I'll come visit at Thanksgiving. We won't talk about war. We'll never talk about war again, but I'll visit. Just go home."

There was an extended silence, then the sound of footsteps retreating, fading away, and the front door closed.

Jeff's arm relaxed and he leaned against the wall with his eyes closed. Gina drew in a long breath and carefully removed her hand from his arm. Neither of them moved when Eric walked past the stairs on his way to the kitchen with the dog Rusty at his side. He looked at them for a moment and kept walking without a word.

"My God!" Barbara said in awe. "That's enough to feed an army." She was staring at a whole salmon that Frank had brought out of the refrigerator.

"Eight pounds," he said. "I ordered it a few days ago. Figured we'd eat what we can, and the rest will be salmon salad for the crew later in the week."

Darren laughed. "You're going to feed the lot of them every day of the trial?"

"That's the plan," Frank said. "Can't have them wandering off, forgetting the time, getting lost in the big city. Keep them under control, that's my plan."

"You kept me under control when I was in the hot seat," Darren said, smiling. "I remember it well."

"Do you remember our first dinner together?" Barbara asked, also smiling. "We argued for three hours, as I recall."

"Yep. At least three hours. Our waiter was unhappy with us."

They both laughed.

"So you're off in the morning," Frank said. "Any word yet when Todd will get in?"

"Wednesday, maybe. Friday, maybe. I'll be ready for him whenever it is."

Such easy, forced chat, Barbara thought, watching Frank do mysterious things to the giant fish. Stuffing it with lemons? Mushrooms? Shallots? It didn't matter. It would be perfect. His dinners were always perfect and he never got flustered. She thought that was the most incredible thing about his meals; he could do fantastic things to food, and he never seemed flustered, anxious, nervous in any way. She got nervous making toast, she sometimes admitted to herself.

He put vegetables on the grill, moved them around to make room for the salmon, and then sat down to have a glass of wine with her and Darren, watching the golden cats circle the grill. They continued the easy, forced chat for a time, then became silent until someone would remember to keep things light and say something that could be ignored entirely or treated with an undeserved seriousness.

When Barbara's phone sounded, they all became silent while she drew it from her pocket, saw that it was Bailey, and answered.

"What do you have?" she asked, dreading the answer.

"Tilsen's prints. He registered today at Valley River Inn. No match."

"Shit. Are you sure?"

"Come on, Barbara. See you in the morning." He disconnected.

She put the phone back in her pocket, tried to smile, and said, "Nothing. Just checking in."

Darren caught her hand and held it, and Frank went to do something or other to the salmon, or the vegetables, or the cats, or just to be doing something.

And there went what little case she might have tried to make, Barbara thought. She withdrew her hand from Darren's and tried again to smile. "And just why is it that my glass is empty?" she said, and promptly refilled it.

Dinner was superb. Barbara barely tasted it. The wine was very good and she drank a lot of it. And eventually she and Darren went home and made wild, passionate love for a long time.

Then, in the dark, with Darren sleeping next to her, she stared into the darkness of the bedroom and tried to recall the exact Nietzsche quote. Something about staring into the abyss until it stared back at you. She stared, it stared back, and then it was pulling her into itself inexorably, inescapably.

Jury selection had gone smoothly without drama or undue delays, which Judge McNulty had warned against sternly. Gil Weymouth, the prosecutor, had given his opening statement with a lot of talk about greed, opportunism, sex, how the defendant had set up a corporation with himself as vice president, how Gina had inherited an estate worth millions while she was vulnerable, still in the throes of grief following the death of her beloved grandmother and her father. He talked about murder and attempted murder, and said the state would prove that the same gun was used in both instances, and that the gun had been hidden by the defendant. He did not say anything that Barbara had not anticipated.

Barbara had talked at some length about what a circumstantial case meant. There was no forensic evidence, no hard evidence, no fibers, no fingerprints, no eyewitnesses, no DNA. Being in the approximate vicinity of a crime did not indicate guilt. Lack of a credible motive was enough to cast a reasonable doubt of guilt. Being the colleague and friend of a woman did not automatically make a man guilty of maneuvering for a romantic relationship. She talked briefly about the aspirations of the four corporate members, who, she pointed out, had been working ten-hour days, twelve-hour days, even longer for months to establish an organic farm with the intention of providing wholesome food for the valley community.

Now she was in the small interrogation room in the county jail where clients and attorneys could confer. When Jeff was brought in, he looked tired and depressed.

"I warned you that it would be boring today," she said, seating herself opposite his chair. He slumped down into it without a word. "Tomorrow they'll start the real trial," she said. "I want you to pay close attention to what the various detectives and deputies say, and if anything deviates from what you remember, make notes. Can do?"

"I didn't see the general in court today."

She had already decided not to tell him that his father had come into the courtroom, had remained seated for no longer than ten minutes, and departed. Knowing that his father intended to testify against him was devastating enough; he didn't need to know how disinterested his father appeared to be. Instead, keeping it light, she said, "I think he knew it would be a bore. Debra Valducci wasn't there, or Tilsen. I expect we'll be seeing all of them tomorrow or the next day. Can I bring you anything? Will you be able to sleep okay?"

He shrugged, as if to say it didn't matter.

"He isn't helping his case," she said to Frank that evening over dinner at Martin's. "He sits there looking guilty as hell. But what he's guilty of is anyone's guess. Certainly not Valducci's murder." She moved a snap pea aside, searching for a last tidbit of halibut. With a sigh she pushed her plate back then. "He has a secret recipe for that sauce," she said. "And he'll never reveal it under any torment his competitors might apply."

"About Jeff," Frank said, but he stopped as the waiter came to remove their plates. That done, he resumed, "I think he's guilty of making his father hate him. Just a guess, you understand."

"But he never did anything to make—" She paused, thinking, and finally nodded. "I would feel guilty if you turned on me," she said. "No matter if I'd done anything to deserve it or not."

"Guilt, hatred, yearning for acceptance, a young man hungry for his father's approval. The human condition is not an easy one." He looked up in surprise when the waiter returned with two dessert dishes. "We didn't order anything else."

"Martin told me to bring them," the waiter said with a smile.

Moments later Martin approached their booth with a tray. He set it down on the table. "Loganberry tart," he said. The tart was topped with ice cream. He held a tiny glass cup over a lighted candle for a moment, then poured the contents on the tart and lighted it. A smile so big that it seemed to cover his entire face erupted as the flame burned blue. "You never know if it's going to work. Sometimes the cognac just sits there," he said when the fire died, leaving a brown glaze on the ice cream and the tart crust. Deftly then he cut the tart in halves and placed them on the two dessert plates.

"Martin, this is too much," Barbara said. "Beautiful theater, but too much."

"Binnie said I had to do it," Martin said with an abashed grin. "You know when she tells me to howl, I set up a real racket. Just the way it is. Enjoy." He walked away.

Barbara half rose from her seat and leaned out over the booth to see the kitchen door, where Binnie was standing, Martin's diminutive, beautiful wife, who blew her a kiss. Barbara kissed back and Binnie vanished into the kitchen.

Frank sighed. Those three had a secret, one he would never learn; he accepted that. It showed in the way Martin treated Barbara, always the best wine priced like the least expensive, special desserts that never appeared on the bill, a never-empty coffeepot when she held court in the restaurant. Early on he had said the meal was on the house and Barbara had told him that if he tried that, they could never come back, and she would hate him for depriving her of the best restaurant food in the state. Meanwhile, there was the loganberry tart. He took a bite and nodded his appreciation. Binnie had an angel's touch with desserts, and she had outdone herself with this one.

Today it was a full house, Barbara mused the next morning, taking her place at the defense table. The group that Frank called Jeff's cheering section was already seated: Gina, Gregory, and Daniel, along with Eric. In the back row of seats the general sat alone. He looked hung over and wretched. As rigid as a flagpole, with his buzz cut, he silently screamed military even in his lightweight summer suit. Tilsen was there and he looked bored and fidgety already. Jeff was brought in and took his seat by her. He didn't respond when she pressed his hand, and she wanted to shake him, shake loose that hangdog look of guilt. She passed him a legal pad and pen, and he nodded silently.

The jury was led in, and finally the judge appeared; all stood, all sat again, and Weymouth called his first witness of the day. The real trial began.

Deputy sheriff Wayne Travis was forty-two, heavily built, jowly, with scant brown hair and a big nose. He had a deliberate manner of speaking as he recounted his actions of the night Robert Valducci was murdered.

"We got the dispatch and went straight to the house," he said. "Me and José Juarez. Ten minutes after nine. Mr. Tilsen let us in and I determined that Robert Valducci was dead. I told José to check the house and see if anyone else was there. Mrs. Valducci and Mr. Tilsen were in the living room with her on the couch, and I stayed near them until the sheriff came."

Weymouth drew him out for some details. There were few. "All right. And after the sheriff arrived, what else did you do?"

"He told me and José to take a look around outside, see if anyone else was there, and to see who was in the greenhouse that had lights on. We went out to the greenhouse and saw that it was the defendant, working on plants or something. I told him there had been a shooting, asked if he heard a shot, and took down his name and address. He said he didn't hear a shot. Then we looked over the other outbuildings and other greenhouses, but there wasn't anyone else there and we went back to the house."

Again Weymouth got a few more details that added nothing. When Weymouth nodded to Barbara to start her cross-examination, Travis looked relieved, reminding Barbara of a boy who had just passed a dreaded examination with a satisfactory grade.

Barbara rose and addressed Judge McNulty. "Your honor, at this time I would like to introduce an aerial map of the area in order to allow the jury to see the buildings and the distances we are discussing here."

"Stipulated," Weymouth said with a wave of his hand, as if to add that it really didn't make any difference.

Judge McNulty nodded, and Barbara set up her tripod and the map. She turned to Deputy Travis then and nodded to him.

"When you arrived at the Valducci house that night, who let you in?"

He looked blank for a moment, then quickly said, "Him, Mr. Tilsen. He was standing with the door open waiting for us."

"A minute ago you said he was in the living room," she said.

"That's after we got there. He let us in first."

"You mean this entrance?" she asked, pointing to the door at the covered portico, the one that opened to the hall. When he said that was the one, she asked, "And what exactly did you do when you went inside?"

"He said the body was in the room they called the study, and I went in and made sure the victim was dead, and then we went to the living room where Mrs. Valducci was."

"Was the light on in the study?"

"Just on the desk. It was pretty dark in there."

"Were other rooms dark?"

"No, ma'am. It was lit up pretty much in most rooms."

"When the sheriff arrived, you and your partner looked around the property and the greenhouse that had lights on. Is that correct?"

After his affirmation, she went to the map and, using a pointer, traced a path from the house to the greenhouse. "Is this the way you went, in a pretty straight line to the sixth greenhouse?" He said yes, and she continued, "At what point along that path could you actually see inside the greenhouse?"

"I never could see in," he said. "I mean, it's plastic, but not a clear kind of plastic. I just seen that it was lighted and there was a figure or something, but not enough to say I really seen a person."

"When you entered the greenhouse, what could you see?"

"Him, the defendant. Standing by a bench with plants. He had his back to the door."

"How was he dressed?"

The deputy shook his head. "Nothing special. I don't remember just how."

"All right. Then what did you do?"

"I said something to him, like what was he doing, or something like that. But he didn't answer and I had to go all the way to him and touch his arm before he seen me. He had those little earpieces in his ear, like he was listening to music. And he jerked around and pulled them out, like he was really surprised to see anyone."

"When you touched his arm, do you recall if he was wearing a jacket?"

"I don't remember."

"Was he wet to the touch?"

"I don't think so. I would have noticed that."

"Were you wet?"

"Yes, ma'am. It was raining outside. I had a rain jacket and it was wet."

"All right. When you told him there had been a shooting, what did he say?"

"He said he didn't believe it. He looked like he didn't believe it and he shook his head hard. He said, you mean Mr. Valducci? Robert Valducci?

Like that. I said yes, and me and José went back out to look 'round, like we were told."

"Deputy, before you left the greenhouse, did you see a poncho anywhere? Or a raincoat?"

"No, ma'am."

Barbara now pointed to the door of the greenhouse and asked, "From here what could you see of the rest of the property?"

He looked confused and she said, "For instance, could you see the residence?" She pointed to the house.

"No, ma'am. Just lights down that way."

"And around the rest of the buildings, the store, the other greenhouses, could you see anything from here?" She kept the pointer on the door of the greenhouse.

"There were a few lights on some of the buildings," he said after a moment. "Really dim, though, just enough to see that there was a building or something."

"All right. Now where did you go in order to ascertain if anyone else was there?

"The next greenhouse," he said. "I opened the door and flashed my light around and seen that no one was there."

"Did you actually enter that greenhouse?" she asked, pointing to it.

"No, ma'am. It was enough to see from the door that it was empty."

"Did it have a lot of benches, plants, pots?"

"Yeah. But no one was there."

She asked him about each greenhouse the same way, asking the same questions each time and getting the same answers. She then led him through his investigation of the several outbuildings and the barn. The answers were the same: If the door was unlocked, they shone their flashlights inside. Some were locked, some weren't, he said. They had not entered any of the buildings, nor the store itself.

"Do you know if any of those buildings can be locked from the inside? she asked.

He glanced at the prosecutor's table and away before he said, "No."

"What is this space? she asked then, pointing to the truck access road that led to River Road.

"It's where trucks can get in and out. The driveway where the workers can park, and trucks can turn around and such."

"Did you look over that area?"

He had not. Nor had he and José looked inside the garage at the residence.

"Deputy Travis," Barbara said slowly then, "do you know for a fact that no one was in the barn, in any of those outbuildings, on that access road, or in any of the other greenhouses?"

His hesitation was prolonged before he said, "No, ma'am."

Weymouth called Sheriff Dave Sprecht. He was forty-eight years old, had worked for ten years as sheriff of Lane County. Tall and lean, thin faced, with graying black hair, an incipient beard, and crease lines above his nose, at his eyes, he looked as if he would be badly wrinkled before he hit sixty.

"Sheriff Sprecht, in your own words, tell the jury how you proceeded when you arrived at the Valducci house the night of the murder. You may use any notes you took that night." Weymouth stood behind his table to say this, and then promptly sat down, as if anticipating a lengthy response.

The sheriff cleared his throat. "I got there at twelve minutes after nine, and two of my detectives were right behind me in another car. We entered the house through the main door under the covered section of the driveway. That door was open with Deputy Travis waiting for us. I went into the study to ascertain the death of the victim, but I didn't touch anything there because I wanted my forensics team to go over the room first. We proceeded through the hall to the living room where Mrs. Valducci and Mr. Tilsen were. Mr. Tilsen told me he and Mrs. Valducci had arrived at nine at the same time although they had not been together. Mr. Tilsen discovered the body and took Mrs. Valducci to the living room and then called 911. Mrs. Valducci was white as milk and shaking hard. Mr. Tilsen asked if he could go find a blanket for her because he said she was in shock and might pass out. I told him to do that and he left to find a blanket. The big French doors to the porch were open and the house was real cold. I had my detectives make a search of the house for a weapon. There was no sign of a struggle or a forced entry. I couldn't tell if anything had been stolen since Mrs. Valducci was not able to answer questions. The forensic team came and collected what they could in the study and tried to lift fingerprints from the French doors. They and the other detectives continued to search the house and the porch and the back patio for a weapon. They didn't find one. While they were doing that Ms. Gina Valducci showed up with the defendant at the

French doors to the patio, and I let her in to take care of her mother. She asked if she could make hot tea for her mother, and I sent a deputy to the kitchen with her for her to do that. A few minutes later I had a deputy drive her and her mother to the hotel where Mrs. Valducci was staying. And Dr. VorHees, the coroner, came and made his examination of the body."

Weymouth produced photographs of the study with the body of Robert Valducci lying on his back on a red and blue Oriental rug that hid any blood.

Weymouth had few questions to ask the sheriff concerning the night of the murder, content apparently with the narrative already given. He moved on to the night someone shot at Debra Valducci.

"Was that the only time you were in that house, Sheriff?"

"No sir. On the night of April 10 there was a 911 call about a shooting at that residence. I drove straight over there. Two cars of deputies were already there. I found Mrs. Valducci in the living room with Gina Valducci and Mr. Anthony Mirano. Mrs. Valducci was hysterical. She said someone had shot at her in her car on Green Briar Road. Mr. Mirano came along on his way home a few minutes after that and he took her to the house. The car was off the road. Fortunately Mrs. Valducci had not been hit."

"Sheriff, exactly what did Mrs. Valducci say that night?"

The sheriff looked straight at Jeff and said, "She said that the defendant had called her to come to a meeting with him and Ms. Gina Valducci to settle a property dispute."

"She named him, the defendant?"

"Yes sir. She said Jeff Cobbe called her."

"What was the result of your investigation of that incident?" Weymouth asked.

"We located the spot where the shooter had stood in ambush, concealed by shrubbery. We found four spent bullets, three in the field across the road, and one in the car itself. We found a revolver, a Smith & Wesson .38 caliber gun, hidden in a hedge outside the defendant's apartment building the next morning. The gun was the same one that had been used to murder Robert Valducci, and it was used that night to shoot at Mrs. Valducci."

"When you found where the shooter stood, were you able to find footprints?"

"No. There's bark mulch and it was scuffled and depressed, and some branches of a bush were broken, some bent, but there weren't any recoverable footprints."

Weymouth introduced photographs of the car and had the sheriff point out where a bullet had grazed the window frame on the driver's side of the backseat, breaking the window, had hit the window frame on the passenger side, and had fallen to the floor. Then, using the aerial map, Weymouth had him locate the position of the car off the road, where the bullets had been found, and where the shooter had waited.

Weymouth nodded to Barbara. "Your witness."

There was a stir in the spectators behind Barbara. She turned in time to see General Ballantine leave. A second later Eric got up and walked out also. She faced the sheriff again. "When Gina Valducci arrived with Jeff Cobbe, did you assume that they were together?"

"Objection," Weymouth said quickly. "The question is ambiguous, subject to different interpretations."

"Sustained," Judge McNulty said.

"Sheriff, what exactly did you mean when you said Gina Valducci showed up with Jeff Cobbe?"

He shrugged and said, "I meant they were standing side by side at the door."

"How was he dressed?"

"What do you mean?"

"It's a simple question, Sheriff. What was he wearing?"

"I don't know. I was interested in her, not him, not at that time anyway."

"Try to refresh your memory, Sheriff. It was raining. Was he wearing a rain jacket like the one your deputy wore? A raincoat like Mr. Tilsen's? Just a denim jacket? A poncho?"

"That's it," he said. "A poncho, down to his knees, with a hood. Black. He looked like a walking tent."

"Did you notice his shoes?"

"No. Why would I?"

"What did Gina Valducci do after she was admitted to the house?"

"She ran over to her mother and hugged her, and tried to pull the blanket around her some more. I asked her for her name and address and she told me."

"Where was Mr. Tilsen at that time?"

"He was there, in the living room."

"Was he wearing an overcoat, a raincoat?"

"Yes. A raincoat. Like I said it was cold in the house. No one took off their jackets or coats."

"When he went to get the blanket, how long was he gone?"

The sheriff looked annoyed and shook his head. "I wasn't paying much attention to how long," he said. "Minutes, I'd guess."

"Do you know it was minutes?"

"I said I wasn't paying much attention to how long. I don't know how long."

"When Gina Valducci asked permission to make tea for her mother, you sent a deputy with her to the kitchen. Is that correct?" When he said it was, she asked, "Why?"

"It just seemed like the thing to do," he said sharply. "I didn't have a reason."

"When Gina Valducci returned with the tea, was Mr. Tilsen with her?"

"Not really with her. They just came back at about the same time."

"Did he ask for permission to leave the living room the second time he left?"

"No."

"Do you know how long he was gone the second time he wandered off?"

"He didn't just wander off. He said he needed to use the restroom."

"Did he mention that before leaving, or after returning?"

"When he came back, I asked where he had been."

"How long was he gone that time?"

"I don't know. A couple of minutes, long enough to use the restroom and come back."

"Do you know when he left the second time?" He didn't. "How do you know he was gone for a few minutes if you don't know when he left?"

"Objection," Weymouth said finally. "Counsel is simply badgering the witness."

"I agree," Judge McNulty said. "Sustained. Move on, counselor."

"Sheriff, you said that the house was cold, the big French doors wide open, and that Deputy Travis was at the front entrance with that door open when you arrived. Did you look at the thermostat at any time?"

"No."

"You stated that you did not immediately search or investigate the study, that you were waiting for your forensic team to do their work. Is that what you would call the crime scene?"

"Yes. It's the primary crime scene."

"You also said you left the French doors open, as you found them. Would that be considered part of the crime scene?"

He hesitated, then said, "In a way it was. Like a secondary part of the crime scene. The whole house was."

"Including the hall where the thermostat is located?"

"Yes, in a way it was."

"Did you authorize Gina Valducci to turn up the thermostat that night?" She asked sharply, crisply, half expecting Weymouth to object that it was improper cross-examination.

The sheriff shrugged and said no.

"Did you know she was going to do that?"

His answer this time was as sharp as her question. "No, I did not. It was not important. The house was very cold. We were all cold."

"Did your forensic team lift fingerprints from the thermostat?"

He looked at Weymouth before answering. "No."

"Because you decided it was not important?"

"Objection!" Weymouth said in a slightly higher voice register than he had used before. "Counselor is again badgering this witness, voicing opinion instead of proper questions. I ask that the court strike counsel's comment."

"Sustained. Miss Holloway, move on." Judge McNulty sounded as annoyed as Weymouth. "The comment will be stricken. Miss Holloway, do not try the patience of this court with improper comments. Do you understand?"

"Yes, Your Honor." Under her breath she added: *She replied meekly.* She turned again to the sheriff. Using the photograph of the car, she asked, "Can you tell the order of the shots that were fired that night?"

"No."

"All right. If the shooter had stood here," she said, pointing to the place in the bushes he had indicated before, "he would have had some branches of this bush between him and the road, possibly obscuring his line of sight. Is that correct?"

"Yes. We think he took a step or two forward before he shot so that he was in front of that bush, not behind it. Likely that's when that branch got broken."

"I see," she said, pointing to a spot two feet closer to the roadway. "Did you find the bark mulch disturbed in this spot as well as the other one?"

"Yes. But no recoverable footprints," he added hastily.

"So, now we have the shooter about a foot away from the pavement, and the road, according to your figures here, is about twenty feet wide at this point. A driver in a car heading toward the Valducci residence, if she kept in the right lane, would have been about eleven or twelve feet from the shooter. Is that correct, Sheriff? Did you make those calculations?"

"Yes, we did. That's about right."

"We don't know, of course, if she stayed in the right lane. She might have been in the center of the road. Is that correct?"

"It's possible," he said.

"Yes, it is. And that would put the shooter even closer to the car and to her behind the wheel. Would you agree to that conclusion?"

"It's speculation, but it's possible. We don't know."

Barbara turned to Shelley, who handed her a model car and a wooden skewer. Taking these items with her, Barbara walked to the witness stand. "This is a model of an Accord sedan, like the one Mrs. Valducci was driving that night," she said, handing him the model. "Please examine the model car, Sheriff. Notice that there is a small hole drilled in the rear window frame on the passenger side, and that there is an area of the window frame on the driver's side that has been replaced with modeling putty. Do you see them both?"

He looked it over carefully and nodded. "I can see them both," he said. He was looking at Weymouth again as if seeking instructions.

"Sheriff, according to your photographs of the actual car, the bullet that grazed the window frame hit one-third the way up, and the place where it hit the opposite side window frame was also one third the way up. On the model, the hole and the putty are both one third up on the window frames. Straight across the car. Do you agree that that is correct?"

He nodded, cleared his throat, and said yes.

Barbara took the model from him and placed the skewer in the car in the drilled hole, and the tip pressed into the putty, where it held fast. "This gives us the trajectory of that bullet," Barbara said, holding up the car with the skewer sticking out of the rear window. She went back to the aerial map of the area and put her finger on the spot where the shooter had stood to take his shots. Then, holding the model with one hand and pointing to the map with the other, she said, "He stood here and fired the first shot through the rear window. The car swerved and ran off the road, seven feet from where that shot hit. We know where the car was when it was hit, demonstrated by the straight trajectory of the bullet from the gun to the interior of the car; we also know where it was when it came to a stop, turned halfway around from the skid. Now," she said, "we also know where the shooter was standing when the other three shots were fired." She put the model car down on the defense table and picked up a length of twine. Using it, she held one end at the spot where the shooter had been and stretched the twine straight to one after another of the marked spots where they recovered three bullets that had missed. They were all within a few feet of one another.

"Sheriff, does that indicate that the shooter continued to shoot almost straight ahead even though the car had driven past him, swerved, and skidded off the road?"

"I don't know when the shots were fired," he said.

She regarded him silently for a second or two, then said, "Sheriff, can you suggest any way that the shooter could have fired that shot straight through the car after the car swerved and skidded off the road? Where would the shooter have had to be standing to take that shot?"

"He could have fired a shot or two and missed, then hit the car and fired again."

"If he missed the car altogether three times, would you say that the hit that made it to the car was simply good luck?" She didn't try to hide the sarcasm in her question.

The sheriff flushed slightly and his eyes narrowed. "I don't know the sequence of the shots, and it could have been luck or not."

She picked up the model car again with the protruding skewer. Walking slowly the length of the jury box, she showed it to the jurors.

She had it added to the evidence table, smiled at the sheriff, and asked, "Did you examine Jeff Cobbe's shoes after you arrested him?"

"Yes, that's routine."

"Of course. Did you find any trace of bark mulch?"

"No, but he had plenty of time to clean them or he could have thrown shoes away."

"Your Honor," Barbara said, "I ask that all his remarks after 'No' be stricken."

Judge McNulty nodded. "They will be stricken. Just answer the question, Sheriff."

"Did you examine his car after you arrested him?"

"Yes," he snapped.

"Did you find any traces of bark mulch?"

"No, but— No!"

"No more questions," Barbara said taking her seat.

Weymouth rose and asked, "Sheriff, when you arrived the night that someone shot at Mrs. Valducci, what did she say to you?"

"She said that the defendant called her, asked her to come to the house because they, him and Gina Valducci, wanted to talk, to settle a property dispute."

"No more questions," Weymouth said.

The judge tapped his gavel and said court would recess until two o'clock.

Geraldo Reyes and Simon Alterman were waiting for Barbara outside the courtroom door. Reyes rushed to her with an ecstatic smile. "It is beautiful, exciting, thrilling! We must talk. I simply must take photographs inside the courtroom. There must be exceptions to the rules, which are primitive and arbitrary."

She tried to ignore him, tried to determine if it was Stephen Worthington with him or Simon Alterman. Simon smiled and she knew.

"It is exciting," he said. "And I admit I'm a little nervous about my role here."

"Don't be," she said. "You're the proverbial innocent bystander. Now, please excuse me. There's something I have to see to."

She didn't wait to hear Reyes' protest when she left them to hurry across the corridor where Eric was beckoning her.

"What?" she asked, drawing close to him. The rest of the cheering gallery had gone ahead to the end of the corridor and the stairs.

"It's Dad," Eric said. "He told me he's going home. I think he means it, Barbara. He isn't going to testify."

"Did he say why, anything more than that?"

Eric shook his head. "But I think it means that he doesn't believe Jeff did it. He knows as well as I do that if Jeff had wanted to shoot her, he could have done it easily."

‡

At first Jeff was disbelieving. "Why would he duck out now? He has his chance to get me for good finally. Why pass on it?"

"I don't know. Eric will come at visiting hour. Maybe he'll have details. But, to the point now, Weymouth probably will call the medical examiner for the autopsy report, and likely he'll call Debra Valducci this afternoon."

"About the general, did he say he was going home today? Or just some time?"

"I think today." The change in his demeanor was remarkable. From listless and almost nihilistic, he had become alert and hopeful for the first time. When they say a burden was lifted, she thought, they meant it. An anvil had been pressing on his mind and now it was gone. He even grinned briefly.

"That was good, about the bullets, the trajectory," he said. "No one who knows anything about gunfire could doubt that you nailed the sequence of the shots. But what difference does it make?"

"Not sure yet," she said. "Anything else on your mind, anything I'm overlooking?"

There wasn't, and she didn't linger. When she retrieved her car from the parking lot, she drove straight to her office. "No calls, no interruptions," she told Maria as she passed her desk. Inside her office Shelley had already arrived with sandwiches, and arranged the coffee carafe and mugs on the round table. Barbara sat on the sofa, pulled out her cell phone and her notebook, where she had jotted down the phone number of the Italian embassy in Washington. She dialed the number and waited for an answer as Shelley unwrapped two sandwiches, spread napkins, and poured coffee.

A nicely modulated woman's voice answered the ringing phone. She sounded friendly, saying, "Good afternoon. You have reached the Italian Embassy. To whom shall I direct your call?"

"Hello," Barbara said. "My name is Barbara Holloway. I want to speak with someone who has the authority to discuss art works that were stolen in Italy in 1944. I am an attorney in Eugene, Oregon, and my associate Frank Holloway and I represent a client who has possession of some works of art, which include a Caravaggio and two sketches by Leonardo da Vinci."

"Ms. Holloway, please, will you hold while I direct your call to the office of the cultural affairs director?"

"Of course," Barbara said. Music came on. Maria Callas? She was singing an aria from Cosi Fan Tutte. Barbara pressed the speaker button on her phone and put it down on the table. "This might take a while." She picked up her sandwich and took a bite.

"I read that a Caravaggio titled Nativity with St. Francis and St. Lawrence was stolen in 1969," Shelley said dreamily. "It was valued at twenty million dollars. Do you have any idea of what that would be in today's dollars?"

"Nope. A bunch."

Shelley laughed. "A great big bunch."

Barbara had time for several more bites before her phone stopped playing opera and a man's voice came on. She assumed that more than one person would be listening to the call, and that a high-quality recording would be made. She was making such a recording herself.

"Ms. Holloway, I'm Servio Giovanni, assistant to the director Roberto da Silva. I understand that you have a client who may have come across some stolen paintings. As unlikely as that is, we are interested in learning more. What else does your client claim to possess?"

He sounded more amused than excited. He would enjoy explaining things to a woman, Barbara thought, listening to him. "You must understand that we can't take action on such scant information," he advised her in a patient, good-natured tone.

"I've disclosed all I'm at liberty to say at this time," Barbara said. "The Caravaggio depicts a nude youth with a bowl of fruit. He is very beautiful. The Leonardo sketches are in ink on parchment, figures, perhaps those in the Last Supper. My father, Mr. Holloway, and I are exploring several options presently. We feel that the Italian government is one of the foremost of the different paths we can take, and for this reason we have not contacted any of the others as of this date. As I said in the beginning of my call, our client has works of art that were smuggled out of Italy in 1944, and we are eager to return them to the proper owners. Of course, your people will have to consult about this and make a decision as to how to proceed. I shall be in court most of the week, but Mr. Holloway will be available at any time in the next few days to talk further about this. He will give you a few additional details about the paintings to demonstrate that we do in fact have what I have claimed. Meanwhile, the art is safe and protected in a bank vault."

"Ms. Holloway, please, you must know that Mr. da Silva is a busy man. I can't go to him with this story with no verification as to its legitimacy. If Mr. Holloway has more details, I assume you also know them, and I urge you to disclose all now in order for me to proceed in a proper manner." His tone had gone from the kindly avuncular to the put-upon father whose patience was running out.

"Mr. Giovanni," Barbara said, "I have told you all I can reveal at this time. I prefer to speak with someone who has the authority to act on this matter, and I can assure you that when you take this information to the proper authority, there will be immediate action." She didn't pause for him to speak, but gave Frank's phone number and her own. "As I said, I'll be in court where phones are not allowed. Mr. Holloway will be available. Good day, Mr. Giovanni."

She disconnected and picked up her sandwich. "The ball," she said with an expansive gesture, "she is in the air."

Barbara waited for Gina and her guys to arrive before she entered the courtroom. She drew Gina aside. "This is going to be very difficult for you," she said. "Impossible for you to take in and remain composed. It's always ugly and today is no different. Please, wait in the coffee shop, or in the hall."

Gina shook her head. "I think I need to know it all," she said in a low voice. She had paled with Barbara's words and her voice was shaky, but she looked at Barbara with an unflinching gaze.

Barbara patted her arm and entered the courtroom to start the afternoon of day two. Frank was not there, nor had she expected him to be. She took her seat at the defense table.

Dr. VorHees was an admirable witness. He answered questions succinctly, precisely, in technical terms and never embellished a statement or offered an opinion unless pressed to do so. He was a tightly knit man, on the down side of middle age, wiry and self-contained without gestures or mannerisms. And, Barbara thought, listening to his testimony that afternoon, he never played favorites or picked sides in any way. She liked that.

Now Weymouth said, "Dr. VorHees, thank you for that technical report. For the benefit of all of us without your expertise, will you please state for the jury in layman's terms exactly what your findings were?"

Dr. VorHees nodded genially. "Of course. The victim was shot in the back from a distance of about four feet, a non-fatal injury, but one that caused him to fall heavily face down. He was shot a second time, possibly fifteen to twenty minutes later, a fatal shot to the back of his head. This shot was from no more than two feet away. Minutes after that he was turned over to his back for up to an hour, when he was returned to the face-down position. At nine o'clock, when Mr. Tilsen discovered his body, he was again moved to lie on his back. His death occurred between six p.m. and eight-thirty."

Weymouth thanked him and bowed slightly to Barbara before resuming his seat.

"Dr. VorHees," she said, "what was the temperature of the room when you examined Robert Valducci's body?"

"Fifty-six degrees Fahrenheit."

"Mr. Valducci was in shirt sleeves when he was shot and killed. Would that indicate to you that the temperature had been a more normal seventy or even a bit higher in the room at that time?"

"I would assume as much."

"If the room had maintained that temperature, would your estimate of the time of death have been different?"

"Objection," Weymouth said. "This is speculative, in no way factual. And it's irrelevant."

"Your honor," Barbara said quickly, "the thermostat being turned down all the way might well have been an attempt to obfuscate the time of death. It is not irrelevant."

Judge McNulty pondered this for a few seconds, before saying, "Overruled."

Dr. VorHees did not need the question repeated. "I have no way of knowing how cold the room got before the thermostat was turned up, and not knowing that did in fact have a bearing on my not being able to be more precise in the time of death. The temperature of the body and the ambient temperature are both important in determining when death occurred."

"And the fact that the body was moved at least two times, was that a factor in your determination?"

"Yes."

"Will you explain why that was?"

"Yes. The victim fell face down, bruising his cheek, and he continued to bleed, possibly for twenty minutes. No artery was compromised, or he would have bled out, bled to death in that amount of time. After the fatal shot, there was no further bleeding, but the lividity of the blood was a factor in my determination. Blood flows to the lowest parts of the body after death, and that pooling of blood demonstrated that he had been on his back for at least an hour. There was very little blood flow after he was turned once again to a face-down position, and none after he was turned over the last time."

"Was he conscious, in your opinion, during the period between the first and second shot?"

"No. There was no sign of consciousness. He didn't move about or make an effort to rise. His fingernails had no carpet fibers under them, and the blood pattern did not suggest any movement. The first shot induced unconsciousness."

"Dr. VorHees, according to your analysis of the times of the shots and the moving of the body, is it accurate to say that the person who shot Mr. Valducci remained in the vicinity for at least an hour and twenty minutes?"

"Assuming the same person shot the victim and moved his body two times, that is correct."

"Thank you, Doctor. I have no further questions."

When she turned to go back to her table, she saw that Frank was once again in the courtroom in the seat behind her own. He nodded to her. It was done, that nod meant. He and Bailey had put the paintings in the bank safe deposit vault. She nodded back. Her statement to Giovanni had been premature, but now it had become legitimate. The art was safe and protected.

Weymouth dismissed Dr. VorHees and called his next witness: Donald Tilsen.

Besides having his nose too close together, Barbara thought, watching Tilsen shift about to get comfortable in the witness chair, he was fidgety. A thin man, it could have been that his bones rubbed against the seat, making him twitch a few times before settling down to state his name and occupation.

"Mr. Tilsen, what was your relationship to Robert Valducci?" Weymouth began.

Tilsen talked at some length about his friendship with Valducci, about their positions in the company, how closely they had worked together for the past eight years. "Our mission in Oregon was to find a tract of ground suitable for our company to develop for future use in our ongoing effort to provide sufficient food for an expanding world population. When Robert's mother died tragically in an accident and he became the owner of the Valducci estate, we realized that his own property was ideal for our purposes.

We were reaching the final agreement to transfer ownership of the property to the company when he was murdered."

"What brought you to Eugene on the night of March 8?"

"I had a memorandum of agreement regarding the upcoming sale. It could not be concluded until his mother's estate was settled, but our company needed a formal agreement before investing in various aspects of the arrangement. Robert and I agreed that I should bring the MoA, the memorandum of agreement, for him to sign that night. I had a reservation at Valley River Inn for the night, and on the following day I planned to return to Chicago. And he had a great many things to do to settle the estate. That evening at nine o'clock was convenient for both of us."

"Tell the court about that night, when you arrived at the Valducci residence."

Tilsen cleared his throat and shifted his position. "I drove down from Portland," he said, cleared his throat again, and continued. "I checked in at the hotel a little after eight, ten, fifteen minutes after eight, and I left the room a little after eight-thirty. As I drew near Green Briar Road another car turned in there, and I followed the other car to the driveway of the residence. Mrs. Valducci was ringing the doorbell when I arrived behind her and introduced myself. She didn't have a key, she told me, and there was no answer when she rang the bell. She said maybe Robert was upstairs taking a nap. I went around the house to see if the kitchen door might be unlocked, and I saw the open French doors to the living room and entered. I admitted Mrs. Valducci, and she decided to go upstairs to see if Robert was asleep. She went to the staircase and I stepped into the study intending to go back to the living room that way. I got several feet into the room before I saw him on the floor. I thought he might have fallen, or even had a heart attack and I hurried to him and rolled him over. Then I saw that he was dead"

Interesting, Barbara thought, watching Tilsen. All that long story and not a single twitch. He had gone into his presentation mode apparently. As a corporate attorney, he was well accustomed to giving presentations, removing himself, leaving a near-robot well rehearsed in what it was to do and say. He even looked at ease.

Weymouth was standing by the rail of the jury box as Tilsen recounted his story. Now he moved closer to his table and asked, "What did you do next, Mr. Tilsen?"

"I nearly fainted. I backed away all the way to the hall door and remembered Mrs. Valducci. I went to the stairs and called her. She came down and I told her that her husband had been shot, that he was dead. She pulled away from me and ran to the study and screamed. I took her by the arm and forced her on through the study to the living room sofa, and when she was seated, I called 911."

"Was there a light on in the study?" Weymouth asked.

"A desk light, that's all. Most of the room was quite dark. Robert's body was in the shadow of the desk."

"Was there anything else that you observed that night?"

"Yes, but I didn't think of it until the next day or two. I heard footsteps running on the wooden porch floor while I was coming around the house to gain entry. And when Mrs. Valducci's car turned onto Green Briar Road, her headlights illuminated the store, and I recalled seeing a pale car parked there. I simply didn't think of that on the night it happened. I was too shaken to think clearly."

Weymouth had all that he wanted from Tilsen and soon nodded to Barbara that he was her witness.

Deliberately she asked for the photographs of Valducci's body, and holding two of them she turned to Tilsen. "Mr. Tilsen, how did you know that Robert Valducci had been shot?"

"I assumed it. I didn't know."

"I see." She held up one of the photographs and showed it to him and then to the jurors. "There is so much blood on his shirt, front and back, and so much on his head, again front and back, it is impossible to see anything that looks like a bullet wound. Why did you come to that conclusion?" She put down the first photograph and displayed the other one in the same way, first to him, then to the jury.

"I don't know why," he said. "I just thought he probably was shot."

She returned the photographs to the evidence table and from there asked, "Was the project to come to Oregon and acquire property for your company your responsibility?"

"Yes."

"Were the other three members of your group all subordinate to you?"

"Robert was hardly subordinate," he said. "We were actually partners. My other two associates were subordinate."

"Could any of them, including Robert Valducci, have made an offer to a land owner without your permission?"

"Objection!" Weymouth called out. "This is improper cross, and it is irrelevant to the murder of Robert Valducci."

"Your Honor," Barbara said, "I believe Mr. Tilsen misspoke in his direct testimony. I am trying to clear up a mistake."

Judge McNulty frowned at her, made a show of looking at his watch, then said, "Overruled. You may answer the question."

"No." Tilsen said it fast, as if hoping the question he was responding to had been forgotten by the jury.

His first twitch, Barbara thought, and she repeated the question, this time as a statement. "So, it would have been cleared with you first, before Mr. Valducci made an offer to his mother to purchase the property. Did she reject the offer, Mr. Tilsen?"

"Yes."

"Mr. Tilsen, in your direct testimony you stated that after Mr. Valducci became the owner of the property you realized that it was ideal for your purposes. But almost immediately after arriving in the area an offer was made to Mrs. Magda Valducci. Did you know you wanted to buy that particular farm the day you arrived in the state?"

"Of course not. I had never even seen the property before. It was a tentative offer, testing the water."

"Was the offer for a premium price, well above the estimated value of the property?"

"Objection!" Weymouth's voice was rising, the way it did when he became angry. That day his necktie sported what looked like peacock feathers. They appeared to be dancing as he gesticulated, using both hands. "This is totally irrelevant! It has nothing to do with the case we are trying."

"Sustained," Judge McNulty said before Barbara could say a word.

She bowed her head slightly. Let the jurors wrestle with it, she was thinking. One of them was a retired real estate salesman; he would know a kickback scheme when he smelled it. "Mr. Tilsen, you spent a good deal of time with Robert Valducci following the funeral of his mother, didn't you?"

"Yes. We had many details to work out."

"You were with him the day an appraisal video was made of the residence. Is that correct?"

He cast a swift glance toward Gina before he said, "Yes." And it seemed that his bones and the chair were at odds again. He was shifting his weight more often.

"At that time your deal with him was concluded enough that he was planning auctions and a final estate sale. Yet you didn't produce the memorandum of agreement until days later. Why was that?"

"As I said, we had details to work out. I wasn't here all that much. I was back and forth between Eugene and Portland. I had to send my other two associates back to Chicago, and review the reports they had turned in considering other properties. I was quite busy, and Robert was preoccupied with settling his mother's estate."

"Were you in Eugene on March second, the day of Magda Valducci's funeral?"

"Yes. I attended the funeral."

"And you were here on March fourth, the day Mrs. Chadwick made the video for her appraisal. When did you return to Portland that week?"

"Objection!" Weymouth called out. "Immaterial, irrelevant, and improper. Mr. Tilsen is not on trial here!"

"Sustained."

"On Saturday, March seven, did you take a call from Mrs. Chadwick on the landline in the Valducci residence?"

"Objection!" Weymouth was on his feet this time. "Your honor, may I approach?"

McNulty motioned for him and Barbara to come forward.

"She's pulling one of the oldest tricks in the book," Weymouth said. "Confuse the jury, cast suspicion on the outsider, the guy with the thousand-dollar suit and spit-polished shoes, divert attention from the defendant, the poor guy behind the plow. Pulling class..." He sputtered to a stop.

"Your honor," Barbara said in her most reasonable voice, "Mr. Tilsen has said several contradictory things. I'm trying to unravel his testimony."

"She's fishing!" Weymouth said, his voice nearly treble by then.

"Quiet, both of you. Miss Holloway, you know your cross-examination is improper. If you continue in this fashion, I'll find you in contempt of court. Do you understand?"

"Yes, your honor."

"Now get on with it. Be careful, Miss Holloway. Be very careful." He waved them away.

"The motion is sustained," he said when they were back at their tables.

Barbara regarded Tilsen for a moment, then asked, "According to the sheriff's testimony it took you several minutes to find a blanket for Mrs.

Valducci the night you discovered her husband's body. You had been all over the house when Mrs. Chadwick took the appraisal video. You must have known where the linen closet was. Why did it take so long?"

"I wasn't thinking clearly. I forgot the linen closet location."

She nodded. "I see. On the several occasions when you were either alone in the house, or out of sight of others, did you ever have occasion to handle any of the many pictures hanging on the walls?"

"Objection!"

"Your honor, I apologize. Withdraw the question," Barbara said quickly. She didn't want a verbal answer; she wanted a twitch or two. She got them.

"No more questions at this time," she said. "I request that the court advise Mr. Tilsen to make himself ready to retake the stand at a future date as a hostile witness for the defense."

Weymouth was practically screaming his objection this time. She waited him out calmly. When he subsided, she said, "I believe Mr. Tilsen has information vital to the defense of my client. It is well within my right to demand that he be recalled as my witness."

Judge McNulty looked murderous, but he turned to Tilsen and told him he would be notified by the court when he would be required to return to the stand. Tilsen twitched, and twitched, and the look he turned toward Barbara was even more murderous than the judge's.

Weymouth didn't leave his table when he asked, "Mr. Tilsen, did you and Robert Valducci reach an accord with the offer you proposed to him for your company?"

"Absolutely."

"Was the amount agreed upon satisfactory to him?"

"More than satisfactory. He was very pleased, as I was."

Weymouth let it go at that.

Judge McNulty called for a ten-minute recess and stalked from the courtroom.

"He's pretty pissed," Frank said. "Might want to have a little talk with you in his chambers."

Barbara nodded. "Did you tell Bailey to sic Alan on to Tilsen?"

"He'll keep tabs," Frank said. Just then the bailiff approached and Frank grinned. "To the woodshed."

‡

Barbara and Weymouth entered the judge's chambers together. McNulty was standing behind his desk, a massive piece of furniture with curved, carved legs, a turned top, and a clutter of papers and books. McNulty was spinning a globe next to his chair. On the wall behind him was a map that might have been used by seventeenth-century sailors. There were no personal photographs, no diplomas or any other framed papers signifying achievements or awards, nothing to reveal the man himself, except for the fact that he was fond of maps. An oversized topographical map of the United States took most of one wall. There were several easy chairs arranged before the desk; they were covered with gold damask fabric. The judge did not invite them to be seated.

"This won't take long," he said. He gave the globe a final spin and sat in his own chair. "Miss Holloway, I did not appreciate your last ploy, getting in one more question after I admonished you. I warned you. That little stunt will cost you one hundred dollars. Now, it has been suggested that you might have influenced a witness for the state to renege on his pledge to testify. Did you speak to General Ballantine, persuade him to refuse to testify?"

Barbara could not control a gasp of indignation and surprise. "Of course not," she said. "I never even met the man, never spoke to him." She turned to Weymouth, who avoided her eyes. "That's crossing the line," she said furiously.

"Miss Holloway, it has also been suggested that you are packing the defense witness list with irrelevant witnesses who cannot possibly have anything to do with this case. Who is Simon Alterman?"

"Mr. Alterman has a great deal to do with my defense," she said. "I furnished his name to the state in due time for them to make their own investigation if they chose to do so. I am not required to preview my defense case to the prosecutor."

"He's nothing but a rich British playboy, an art dabbler. He wasn't even in the area until a couple of weeks ago," Weymouth said. "This is another attempt to obfuscate the facts with irrelevant material. The idea is to confuse the jury with so much outside the parameters of the matter at hand that they don't know what to believe."

"Be quiet," McNulty said sharply to Weymouth. "Miss Holloway, if counsel proves to be correct, if you are indeed introducing irrelevant issues in an attempt to derail this trial, the one hundred dollar fine I just imposed will seem a pittance. Do you understand?"

"Yes, of course I do."

"Now, both of you leave. I want this case wrapped up this week."

Barbara did not wait for Weymouth to open the door even though he reached past her in an attempt to do so. She pulled it open and started to walk.

"Barbara," Weymouth said, coming to her side. "I had to know if you talked him into jumping ship."

She gave him a withering glance. "You crossed the line."

Back at her table, she saw that Frank had brought coffee. She sipped it, then told him what had happened. His mouth tightened at the thought that Weymouth had accused her of witness tampering. The fine was nothing, but that was not nothing.

The jury was marched back in, Jeff was returned to his seat, and McNulty resumed his. Weymouth called Debra Valducci. Barbara smelled her perfume before she made it halfway to the witness stand.

Don't take it out on her, Barbara warned herself. She was furious and that was not good. Get mad and fight cool, Frank had counseled years before. She repeated it to herself: Fight cool.

Barbara watched Debra Valducci with great interest as she was sworn in and took her seat in the witness stand. Judge McNulty drew back a bit when her scent cloud reached him.

Debra was monochromatic that day. Pantsuit, blouse, shoes all dusty rose. Even her dangling earrings were the exact same rose color, as were her fingernails and her lipstick. If Weymouth was envious of Tilsen's thousand-dollar suit and spit-polished shoes, and he was, what was he making of Debra's designer outfit? How much time and effort, to say nothing of price, had such an outfit and accessories cost? Barbara had no clue about the price of such a display, but she knew that Debra had not grown up with wealthy parents, that she had not had wealth of her own until recent years, and now she was determined to demonstrate to the world that she had done it herself, and this was the reward. Shelley passed Barbara a note, and as she read it she had to cover a giggle with a cough. Bet her underwear is mauve. Not dusty rose. Mauve. Something new every day, Barbara thought, pocketing the note.

Weymouth asked several questions to establish that Debra was a successful businesswoman from Los Angeles, and the widow of the murder victim. Now, leaning toward her, close to the witness stand, he asked in a sympathetic voice, "Mrs. Valducci, on the night of March 8, did you have an appointment with Mr. Robert Valducci?"

"Yes. He asked me to come at about nine that night. He said there was someone I should meet and that we had things to discuss."

"Did he name the person he wanted you to meet?"

"No. Later, Mr. Tilsen said he was the one, that he also had a nine o'clock appointment. We arrived almost simultaneously."

"All right. Now let's move forward to the night of Friday, April 10. Please tell the court what happened on that night."

Debra drew in a long breath and looked at the jury box. "I received a phone call a few minutes after nine o'clock. I'm not certain of the time. Mr. Jeffrey Cobbe called. He said that he and Gina, my daughter, had been talking and wanted to settle a property dispute. He asked if I could come out to the farm before Gina had time to change her mind. He knew I had a reservation to fly out of Eugene the next morning, and if we were going to talk it had to be that night. I told him I'd leave my hotel immediately, as he asked."

She shuddered and pressed a tissue to her eyes for a moment, then straightened her shoulders and drew in another long breath. Weymouth looked as if he wanted to pat her and murmur, "There, there. You're safe now." He even made a tentative motion toward her, but backed off when she spoke again.

"I drove to the farm," she said. "After I turned in at Green Briar Road, someone began to shoot at me." she said. "The car jerked a little bit and there were so many shots and glass everywhere. I threw myself down across the passenger seat thinking he would come and finish the job, or maybe he thought he had hit me. I didn't cry out or scream. I didn't move, could hardly even breathe, and then Tony Mirano came. I heard his truck, heard it stop, and at first I thought it was the shooter, but it was Tony. He's a neighbor who lives on Green Briar Road. He took me to the house in his truck and called 911."

Well done, Barbara thought at her. Well rehearsed, well played out.

"Where were you when this phone call came?" Weymouth asked.

"I was alone in my hotel room. The Hilton. I always stay there when I'm in town. I was packing my things so I could leave in the morning."

Debra appeared to be pleased with herself, pleased at how well things had gone, how fine her performance had been. Her glances at the jurors were confident; she was relaxed.

"Were you at all anxious about such a meeting, alarmed, or feeling threatened in any way?"

"No. Why would I be? In fact, driving out there I was feeling relieved that we would finally settle things, that it was going to work out. I hoped that Mr. Tilsen was still in Portland, that we could go through with our deal at last."

Barbara didn't smile, but inside she was smiling. "Objection," she said. "We are getting into a lot of things here without any preparation at all. What deal? Things work out? How? What things?"

"Sustained. The answer will be expunged from the record. Rephrase the question or withdraw it, counselor."

Your call, Barbara thought, watching Weymouth struggle with it. Open the door, she urged him silently. You have a befuddled jury panel as of now, one witness who wore a thousand-dollar suit, and another one outfitted by Vogue magazine, both outsiders, exotic, both hinting at mysterious deals, a possible conspiracy.

"Withdraw the question," Weymouth said. "Did you mention to anyone that you were going out to the farm that night?"

Buying time, Barbara thought. Debra's brief answer, a single No, bought very little.

Weymouth glanced at the jurors, attentive, too attentive, too curious; he glanced at Barbara, who let him glimpse a slight smile before she ducked her head and began scribbling nonsense on her legal pad: the owl and the pussycat…

He opened the door.

"Mrs. Valducci, will you please explain to the jury the nature of the dispute you wished to settle with your daughter that night?"

Debra was surprised by the question, as if it had not been in the script she had rehearsed. Her self-satisfied expression changed to one of mild disapproval and uncertainty now that they had gone off-script into unrehearsed territory. "The dispute? Oh, you mean the mix-up about the will? I contested my mother-in-law's will, and the probate judge made a serious mistake and said that Gina had inherited the farm, not Robert. Probably this was the first will dispute of this kind that she'd ever had, a great big farm and millions at stake, I mean. Anyway, I was relieved that we could talk it over and I wouldn't have to hire a lawyer and appeal the decision. That's why I was happy to go out to the farm that night."

Barbara cast a swift look at Judge McNulty, whose default frown deepened and became a scowl as he regarded Debra.

Weymouth sounded resigned as he asked the next question. "What was the deal with Mr. Tilsen that you mentioned?"

"I mean, nothing in writing yet, but a verbal arrangement. A verbal is binding, you know. He was kind when I went to Chicago to close out my late husband's condo and take care of various matters about his personal possessions, and a vacation cottage. Things like that. Mr. Tilsen recommended an attorney in Chicago who would take care of things for me so I wouldn't have to stay there. I have a business in Los Angeles, you know. I couldn't spend a lot of time in Chicago. At lunch Mr. Tilsen told me about the deal he and Robert had agreed on about the farm. He made the same offer to me. Actually a better offer, because I wouldn't have to stay around for auctions and things like that. He said furnishings, farm equipment, and all probably would bring in another hundred thousand dollars, and he added that to the sale price. He would simply take care of everything, after Gina collected the things she wanted. That was a great relief to me, not to have to spend a lot of time to do it all. I accepted his offer, of course. Then, when the will business came up and the probate judge made her mistake, there was no deal any more. I hoped after talking things over with Gina, I would be able to get back to Mr. Tilsen and move forward again."

God bless you, Mrs. Valducci, Barbara thought. She could almost pity Gil Weymouth, who knew very well the Christmas stocking he had delivered to her. He had little more to ask Debra; likely he was fearful of asking many more questions, afraid of adding more goodies to the stocking.

Barbara rose from her chair and walked around her table. "Mrs. Valducci, how well do you know Mr. Cobbe?"

"Objection! Improper cross-examination."

"Sustained."

"Let me put it this way," Barbara said, "did you recognize the voice on the phone that night of April 10?"

"No. I've never even met the defendant, never said a word to him or heard a word from him."

"Can you recall exactly what he said?"

Debra had drawn herself together and was sitting upright, almost rigidly upright. Ah, Barbara thought, Debra had been warned about the dangers lurking in a cross-examination; she had girded her loins. She straightened her shoulders even more against the imminent attack that she must brace herself for.

"I remember it very well," Debra said. "He said he was Jeff Cobbe and he and Gina had been talking over our problem and wanted to come to an agreement about it, settle it. He said that since I was leaving the next morning, I should come to the farm then, at that moment, before Gina had time to change her mind. I said I would be happy to settle things and I would be out right away. We hung up." She glanced at the jury triumphantly and gave Barbara a disdainful look.

Barbara nodded. "Can you describe his voice? I mean, was he shouting, stammering, high-pitched sounding? Anything out of the ordinary?"

Debra looked puzzled, then impatient. "I don't remember anything strange about his voice. He was speaking low, kind of whispery, like he didn't want to be overheard. That's all."

"How did he get your telephone number if you didn't give it to him?"

"I don't know. I never gave it to him. I never spoke to him, like I already told you. He must have gotten it from Gina."

"If he got the number from Gina, why speak in a low voice, trying not to be overheard, if she gave him the number and knew he was calling?"

"I don't know how he got the number," Debra said. "Anyway it was the hotel phone, not my cellphone. Anyone can call a hotel room."

Barbara moved slowly to stand at the jury box rail. "Did you know that Mr. Valducci had made an offer to buy the farm from his mother?"

"Yes. I heard about it."

"You knew that she rejected the offer?"

"That was a serious mistake. It was a very generous offer."

"Did you know she turned it down?"

"I said I knew it and it was a mistake."

"Did you know that two days after that offer Magda Valducci wrote a new will that left the farm to her granddaughter, Gina Valducci?"

"That's the will I contested. Of course, I knew about it. She was completely under Gina's thumb, unduly pressured to change her will."

"Is it correct that under the new will, accepted by probate court, your late husband, Robert Valducci, was never the owner of the property?"

"Of course he was the owner. I told you that will is fraudulent. I intend to appeal the opinion."

"As matters stand now, the will is valid. Since Mr. Valducci was never the legal owner of the estate, he could not have bequeathed it to you. Is that correct?"

"No! He left it to me!"

"Did you know that your daughter Gina opposed any sale to the Halsey

Enterprises group, the company Mr. Tilsen works for, and that Robert Valducci worked for?"

"I know that. It's his doing, Cobbe's influence. He wants the farm for his own use. He told Gina to say no if an offer was made."

Barbara looked at the judge then. "Your Honor, I request that everything after the words 'I know that' be stricken, and that the witness be directed to answer the questions without further commentary."

Judge McNulty looked as if he would be willing to gag the witness if requested to do so. He simply said, "The remark will be stricken. Mrs. Valducci, just answer the questions."

"Mrs. Valducci," Barbara said, "as a real estate consultant, with a Realtor's license, you know how to research land prices, don't you?"

"That's my specialty," she said sharply.

"Did you assess the value of the Valducci farm?"

"Objection. Irrelevant."

"Sustained."

"Let me put it this way," Barbara said agreeably. "You've said several times that the offer Mr. Tilsen made, first to Mr. Valducci, then to you, as well as the offer Mr. Valducci made to his mother, was very generous. The question is: Without going into actual numbers, was it substantially above what an outside appraisal might have suggested?"

Debra hesitated for a long moment, looking thoughtful, as if she was trying to find the downside of answering. She shrugged slightly and said, "Yes it was."

"Did the figure surprise you?"

Her answers were slower with this new line of questions, as if she had to weigh each one individually. "Yes," she said.

"Did you ask Mr. Tilsen what the company plans for the farm were?"

"No. That was none of my business."

"Did it surprise you when Mr. Tilsen said he would do the actual liquidation of the furnishings, the farm equipment, everything?"

She had to think about it before she finally said, "At first. But not later after we talked it over. It was easier for both of us that way."

"When he mentioned adding a hundred thousand dollars to the purchase price, did he refer to a professional appraisal that had been done by a Mrs. Chadwick?"

She shook her head. "He never mentioned an appraisal. He said he just pulled a number out of the air, what he called a nice round figure."

A change had come over her as she answered the last few questions. Barbara suspected that earlier she had banished doubts about the Tilsen offer, but those doubts had now resurfaced and were troubling her. She was successful, Barbara reminded herself, and that meant she understood her own business of real estate. No doubt she was canny, wary of deals too good to be true, yet she had accepted such a deal and lashed out at those who had thwarted it. Greed and cautious self-interest made for compatible bedmates.

"Thank you, Mrs. Valducci," Barbara said. "I have no more questions."

Weymouth wanted only to reinforce the important parts of her testimony. Did the defendant call her to a meeting on the night of April 10? She said yes. Was she alone when the call came and did she tell anyone where she was going? She said she was alone and she told no one. He dismissed her. She walked out stiffly looking neither to the right nor the left. Her scent lingered in the air, like the Cheshire cat's smile, Barbara thought.

The bailiff handed Judge McNulty a note. The judge nodded and said there would be a ten-minute recess. He stalked from the courtroom. Maybe he welcomed time to clear the air, Barbara thought, but she said to Jeff, "Someone wants a potty break. Do you want coffee? A cold drink? He said ten minutes, but it's going to be half an hour." She watched the jury shuffle out.

"Draft beer?" Jeff said.

"Yeah, right."

"I'll settle for iced tea," he said. Then his guard came to escort him from the courtroom to a holding cell.

Shelley, Frank, and Daniel left to get drinks, and Gregory sat frozen in his seat. His name was on the prosecution witness list, and he was terrified. Eyes wide open, he was staring straight ahead, probably seeing little or nothing. Gina leaned in close to Barbara and whispered, "His parents are in the courtroom watching."

Jesus! What was it with parents and their grown children? Barbara resisted the urge to turn around and find the parents. According to Gina, they were the only two people on earth who didn't know that Greg was gay, and he lived in fear that his father would learn the truth about his only child. Was Greg terrified that Weymouth would out him on the witness stand?

The recess was for twenty-seven minutes. Close enough to her estimate, Barbara thought as the various players resumed their places. Weymouth called his next witness: Kay Saltzman. He wanted to wrap up the shooting incident, Barbara knew, and she pitied poor Greg, who would have to live in torment another night. It was five minutes after four, too late for an additional witness after Saltzman.

Kay Saltzman was thirty-two years old, a round-faced, bottle-blonde woman, a little overweight. She had married right out of high school when she was eighteen, and divorced five years later, and had been single since then. After her divorce she had attended classes at the community college, LCC, and wound up as a dental hygienist for a downtown dental practice. Independent, relatively well paid, self-assured, she smiled a lot, displaying dimples in both cheeks, and well aware of how charming she was when smiling. The only thing unconventional about her were her hands: She wore rings on every finger. Compensation? With her hands in other people's mouths every day, did she feel she had to reclaim them, adorn them when off work?

Weymouth led her through the preliminaries quickly before getting to the point. "Please tell the court about what happened on the night of April 10."

"Well," she said, smiling at the jury, "I went to the movie with a friend, Brice is his name. We saw an old Buster Keaton movie at the Bijou. The General. They were doing a retrospective of silent movies. It ended at ten minutes after nine and we put on our coats, and I had to find my umbrella. You leave them out front at the Bijou. It took maybe five minutes before we actually left the theater. Then we walked to my apartment on Jefferson. It's about a ten-minute walk, maybe fifteen. I stood out on the walk to the front door while Brice got the door unlocked and open. While I waited, I happened to be looking up the street, and I saw a man walking on the other side of Jefferson. I saw him bend over like he was putting something down in some bushes. Then he turned around and walked back the way he had come. By then Brice had the door open and I didn't see anything else."

"What else can you tell the court about that night?" Weymouth asked.

"Not about that night," she said, dimpling prettily. "But the next day I saw in the news that a man had been arrested up there on Jefferson, and the police had found a gun in a row of bushes, and I thought, that's what I saw. I saw him putting the gun there, trying to hide it or something. So I called the police, and a detective asked me to come to the station to make a statement. That's what I did. I made the statement and signed it and that was that."

"Are you acquainted with the defendant?"

She shook her head, then quickly said, "No. I never heard of him until I read about it in the news."

"Can you tell us what time you saw him?"

"Not really," she said, looking sad, shaking her head. "After nine-thirty, but I don't know how much after."

"Did you get a look at the man's face?"

Her sadness deepened and she shook her head harder. "It was too dark and misty, you know, mist and fog, a little light rain, the way it gets sometimes. I just saw a figure of a man."

Weymouth produced a map of downtown Eugene, including that section of Jefferson Street. He put an X on a spot near Twelfth. "Is this where your apartment is located?"

She studied the map carefully before saying it was. He put another X on Jefferson about half a block away on the other side of the street. "Is this where you saw the man put something in the bushes?" She studied the map again, nodded, and said it was.

"Thank you, Ms. Saltzman. No more questions."

Barbara regarded the witness with a friendly smile. "Ms. Saltzman, did your friend Brice have a key to your apartment?"

Kay Saltzman blushed and shook her head. "No. It was my key. See, I was holding my umbrella in one hand and a bag with chips and cheese and salsa in the other hand. I told him he had to hold the umbrella, or else fish my key out of my coat pocket. We were joking about it, that men don't like to use umbrellas. He got out the key."

Barbara smiled again at her and walked to her table where Shelley handed her papers clipped together. On her way Barbara glanced at the jury. They had been impassive, without expression for the most part when Debra testified; two of the women had pursed their lips, and one man had a network of frown lines then. Now they were relaxed and even smiling at this candid, open-faced young woman and her pretty dimples.

She showed the papers to Weymouth, then to the judge before returning to the witness stand. "You said you went to the station to make a statement that you signed. Is this that statement?" She handed the papers to Kay Saltzman.

After looking them over, she said that was her statement.

"Do you see the two sections that I have highlighted?" When Kay said yes, Barbara asked her to read the first one.

She read: "'We were talking about the movie, and I said I had a collection of the Marx Brothers movies, that maybe we could watch one of them. Brice said great. He'd make nachos and he asked which movies I had. I told him I didn't have any chips or salsa. I had a little cheese. But we could pick up stuff. And I said I'd like to watch *A Night at the Opera*.'"

She finished with that section and looked at Barbara. "You want me to read the next part that's highlighted?"

"Yes. Please."

She flipped the papers to the last one. "'After Brice got the door open we went inside and he made nachos, and we watched the Marx Brothers.'"

"Fine," Barbara said. "You said you were carrying a grocery bag while he unlocked the door. Where did the chips, salsa, and cheese come from?"

"Oh, that. We went over to the New Frontier Market and bought some stuff."

"Where is that store? Can you locate it on the map?"

Kay Saltzman squinted at the map and after a few seconds shook her head. "It isn't on that map. It's farther over."

"Your honor," Barbara said, turning to the judge, "may I replace this map with a larger one of the same area with more of the streets included?"

"Objection," Weymouth called out. "Irrelevant, and it's wasting time. It doesn't make any difference where the witness bought groceries." He grinned at the jury as if to ask them to understand a stall when they witnessed it.

"It matters," Barbara said coolly. "We are trying to establish a more accurate time of night when Ms. Saltzman saw someone place something in the hedge."

Judge McNulty sounded weary when he overruled.

Barbara produced her bigger map and now Kay Saltzman pointed to a spot on Eleventh at Van Buren. "That's where it is," she said. "New Frontier Market. It's been there forever. I think it was the first grocery store to open in the city and they have organic stuff, a good wine selection and beer, good cheeses. I go there all the time. It's five or six blocks from my apartment, a ten- or fifteen-minute walk."

"You know the people who work there?"

"Oh, yes. Probably all of them. Wesley was working that night. He and Brice got into a discussion about what was better with nachos, wine or beer. They decided on beer, and that's what we got."

"How long do you think you were in the store that night?"

"I don't know. Maybe ten minutes."

"Now, back at your apartment, you were holding the umbrella and the grocery bag, and you saw the figure down the street. Are you certain it was a man?"

"Yes. You know, the way he walked. Dark coat, even a hat. Maybe a raincoat. I couldn't tell that much. A car came along and I could see him with the light from the headlights. I probably wouldn't have seen him if the car hadn't come along. I'm sure it was a man."

"How long do you think you observed that figure?"

Kay Saltzman looked thoughtful for a second or two. "He was near the hedge when the headlights shown on him. The car passed on and he took three or four steps before he bent over. I thought he had dropped something. Then he straightened and turned to walk back the way he had come. That's all I saw. Ten, fifteen seconds, maybe a little longer, but not much longer."

Barbara thanked her and sat down. Weymouth didn't have much, and it ended for the day. The judge admonished the jury not to talk about the case, not to watch anything about it on television, or listen to any radio...

"Good day's work, Bobby," Frank said, squeezing her shoulder.

"I have to get out and walk," she said.

He nodded. "I know you do. We'll have a bite when you show up. You take off. I'll speak to Jeff and try to answer the questions he must have by the dozens."

At that moment a staff member of Weymouth's office approached Barbara and handed her a manila envelope. "Mr. Weymouth has added another witness," he said. He turned and walked away quickly.

Barbara glared at him, then at the envelope he had handed her. She pulled out a cover letter, loose from pages paper clipped together. It wasn't a real cover letter, just a note with a single line of type under the heading. The new state witness was named Dr. Sidney Overton. She had never heard of him.

"Eleventh-hour expert witness," Barbara muttered after looking at the papers clipped together. "This is some kind of cockaminny personality test. There have been cases... Dad, I'll have to get into the office library later tonight."

"No you won't. I know damn well there have been cases. Does that damn fool think he's playing with amateurs? You and Shelley get along to your office, do your thing there. I'll have a word with Jeff, then find a few cites. And I'll rustle up some food in a little while." He left them gathering up their things.

Half an hour later, in her office Barbara and Shelley looked over the test briefly. "Okay," Barbara said. "This is going to take some time. You start on Sidney Overton, and the other three names connected to the test, but concentrate on Overton. I'll start with the test itself."

Both offices became quiet with erratic bursts of printers spitting printouts now and then breaking the silence. At ten minutes after seven Barbara's phone sounded.

"Hi," Darren said when she answered. "Are you at home?"

"Office. Are you settled in somewhere?"

"Ah," he said after a slight pause. "Got it. I'll email you the hotel name. And I'll call tomorrow night. Try to get in some sleep time. Love you. Miss you. Good night."

She closed her eyes hard for a moment, then went back to the last section she had been reading on the Internet. Minutes later Shelley came in with a note. "Dr. Minnick's password for APA and a couple of the journals," she said. "Coffee," she added, putting a mug down on Barbara's desk. At fifteen minutes after eight Frank walked in carrying a large brown bag in one hand and a bulging tote bag in the other. "Dinner," he said. "Chinese. And five cites so far. I synopsized them for you." He patted the tote bag. "Books. I could round up a couple more, but that's probably plenty."

They ate in silence for the most part, until Barbara said, "That isn't a personality test. It's a test for psychopathology. Jeff failed."

"He told me he never took a personality test in school," Frank said.

"He signed off on it. His signature and date. When he was a junior at Penn State."

No one spoke again until the food was gone and Frank gathered up the containers and put them in the brown paper bag. "I guess it wouldn't hurt to have a few more cites, in case the judge has a bad night and takes it out on whoever stands in front of him."

No one smiled. He waved to them and left with the paper bag. At ten-thirty Barbara told Shelley she had done enough, to go home. She had printed out many pages, had summarized some articles, and that was more than Barbara could get to overnight. Given a week or two, Barbara thought, then shook her head. She didn't have a week or two.

At fifteen minutes after eleven Frank left his own office carrying another tote bag with three more books, three more cites, three more summaries. He drove to Barbara's office, pulled in at the parking lot and sat for a minute brooding. Shelley's car was gone, and that was good, but Barbara's car was still there and her lights were on. That was not good. Finally, he shook his head, backed out of the parking slot, and drove home. He would hand over the books in the morning. There were only so many hours in a night, and there wasn't a damn thing any of them could do about that.

Barbara regarded the test booklet with loathing. A photocopy, four pages stapled together. The front and back of each page had five brief scenarios, with six questions. Forty scenarios in all. She opened it at random and read the topmost scenario again:

You can hear your neighbors, Janet and Bill, having a terrible fight with things breaking and Janet screaming. What do you do?

1. Leave by the back door, get in your car, and drive away. You don't want to get involved.
2. Turn up the television to drown out their noise. They've done this before, and it's none of your business.
3. You know he's jealous and has a terrible temper. You get out your gun and have it handy in case he bursts in on you in a rage.
4. You go to the kitchen door and listen. You hope he doesn't kill her this time, but she shouldn't have provoked him.
5. You make a tape recording of the fight, hoping to sell it to Bill after he cools off.
6. Call Janet's brother, tell him to bring his gun.

Jeff had filled in the oval by number 3. You get out your gun…

"No!" Barbara said. "Just no! I don't believe it!"

She flipped through the test, stopping now and again to check his answers to impossible situations with no good answers. Number three again: The scenario was that an elderly woman across the street staggered, dropped her groceries and purse, and was leaning against a fence. Answer: You cross the street, pick up the purse, and walk away fast.

Barbara shook her head. No way! She put the test down and rubbed her eyes. More coffee. She rose and crossed to the round table where the carafe was. Dregs, and cold, but it was coffee, caffeine. She poured it into her mug and drank some. There was something, she thought then, something about the test. Something she had seen/not seen, something wrong. Taking the terrible coffee with her she returned to her desk and looked over the first page, the answers 1, 3, 6, 1, 3; the next page 6, 1, 3, 6, 1…

"Oh my God," she whispered. She hurried to the closet with office supplies and found a pad of graph paper. Back at her desk she numbered down from 1 to 6, and from one to ten across; she put an X for each test answer for the first ten scenarios.

She took a long breath, drank more of the foul coffee, and considered her next move. The whiteboard, she decided. Turn it into a graph, half-inch squares, forty across, six down… There was still more reading to do, but first the graph.

At two-thirty, at home, she pulled off some of her clothes, enough, and dropped into bed. Nappy, no doubt lonesome, came to keep her company, and she didn't finish the first comforting stroke down his back before she plunged into sleep.

"Where is she?" Frank asked Shelley in the courtroom. It was five minutes before nine.

"Chambers," Shelley said. "She called me a few minutes ago to let me know."

Frank nodded. She just might get to use some of the cites he had found dealing with eleventh-hour expert witnesses.

In Judge McNulty's chambers the judge glowered at Barbara and Weymouth, then, surprising them both, nodded to a coffee service on a side table. "Help yourselves, if you're inclined." He had coffee and a pastry on his desk.

Barbara was holding a bulging tote bag in one hand, and her briefcase in the other one. She put them both down by a chair and went to help herself to coffee. Weymouth shook his head and muttered that he was fine.

"Well, sit down. It's your call, Miss Holloway. What do you want?" the judge asked. He pulled the pastry into small pieces and ate one.

She moved to the chair she had more or less claimed with her belongings, put her coffee down on the end table by the chair, and began. "I've been researching the various ways to handle a situation where a last-minute expert witness is called without first notifying defense counsel. There are several cases where defense simply demanded that the witness and his or her testimony not be allowed. But difficulties arose when leaks somehow found their way to the jury and made them sore. They convicted. In other cases, leaks to the press made it appear that the state lost due to a slick defense technicality. The defendant was besmirched, another reputation ruined, and so on."

Weymouth looked grave and almost regretful and did not say a word. Now he sat in the chair indicated by the judge.

"Another way it has been handled," Barbara continued, "was by having defense demand a delayed cross, and continuation of a week to ten days, time enough to round up its own expert. The judge acquiesced and ordered the state witness to remain in the area, prepared for cross-examination. That meant per diem expenses for days and days, plus another day in court with full compensation, and the costs mounted dreadfully, I'm afraid. Also, everyone was angry, judge, jury, both counsels, just everyone."

She glanced at Weymouth, who was looking angry himself at the moment. She shrugged, looked back to the judge, who was continuing to eat his pastry and sip coffee.

"I have several cites for those solutions to a vexing problem," she said, nudging the tote bag with her foot. "But there are a couple more ways to deal with it that don't need cites. Defense can call a witness back as a hostile witness, of course. Since he is still the state witness, the burden of expenses will be on the state. And since defense already has a procedural plan, this witness will be added to the end of its witness list, several days in the future."

She smiled at Weymouth then. "You can readily see that with so many options, my decision can't be hastily made."

"Judge, she's threatening this court, blatantly threatening to drag this case out to an indefinite length of time."

"I didn't bring in a last-minute surprise witness," Barbara said coolly.

"You brought in an English man who has nothing to do with this matter!"

"You've had his name for over a week. He certainly wasn't an eleventh-hour two-by-four to the head."

"Quiet! Both of you. Stifle it."

Judge McNulty leaned back in his chair wiping his fingers on a large damask napkin. Barbara drank some of her own coffee. It was surprisingly good. She wished she had a pastry to go with it.

"She has a point," McNulty said to Weymouth. "And she has options." He leaned forward again and picked up his coffee cup. He drank, set the cup down and, still regarding Weymouth with his frowning gaze, asked quite mildly, "Are you willing to give up this last-minute witness?"

"Absolutely not! He's a renowned psychologist who, along with colleagues, developed a test for psychopathic behavior. The defendant took his test about ten years ago and was singled out as a definite psychopath!" His voice rose to a higher octave as he rushed through the words, and he was red-faced when he became silent again.

The judge nodded and turned his gaze to Barbara.

"Do you recall that at our pretrial meeting we agreed that this trial would be done in a week? And based on that assumption, that agreed-upon time frame, I so informed the jury? And do you acknowledge that in all the options you have outlined, that time frame will most assuredly be false?"

"I do, Your Honor," she said. "Of course, I had no way of knowing that Mr. Weymouth would pull this Hail Mary on me. Be assured that I want this trial to be over as much as anyone. My client is languishing in jail, his supporters are in court every day neglecting their work at the farm, bringing hardship to others there who have to work harder or risk losing valuable produce. This expert witness poses a problem that must be dealt with, however, if justice is to be served. I do have one additional proposal to make that will see the witness dismissed today so that we can get on with the matter at hand."

Weymouth made a strange sound in his throat, a growl, a rasping noise, a strangled curse. It was hard to tell. Judge McNulty glared at him and said to Barbara, "What is it?"

"If I am allowed to cross-examine the witness as if he were my hostile defense witness, I could wrap up my cross fairly quickly."

"Character assassination? You want me to agree to that? Let you crucify my witness, ad hominem attacks, innuendo! Absolutely not!"

"None of that is my intention," Barbara said, keeping her gaze on the judge, who looked thoughtful and interested. "I want the opportunity to thoroughly examine the test material, everything about the test itself. I haven't had time to look into his past to ferret out any undergraduates he might have been overly friendly with. Nor do I care about his past. I am interested in his test. I'm confident that Mr. Weymouth's direct will be narrowly focused on the test result itself, leaving little leeway for me to probe more deeply into methodology, for one example. I expect that my questions will draw one objection after another if I take a wider approach to the test than that afforded by direct."

"Judge, don't you see what she's done? Threats, then what looks like a reasonable solution to forward her own agenda."

"It does appear to be a reasonable solution," Judge McNulty said. He gave Barbara a stern look. "You understand that if you stray from the test material, from that point forward your cross will be according to the book and any other option will have been waived."

"I would expect that to be the case, Your Honor."

"Judge, I protest this decision. I take exception to it."

"Noted," Judge McNulty said. "Now, get back to your tables. We've wasted too much time on this already."

Frank could not tell a thing about how the meeting in McNulty's chambers had gone from Barbara's expression. As soon as she appeared in the courtroom she huddled with Eric and Shelley. Barbara handed Eric paper-clipped sheets of paper, had a few more words with him, and only then turned to Frank.

"It's okay," she said. "I'll fill you in later. I asked Eric to take Major Farleigh's part in that deposition. You might get a phone call today and you have to be free to beat it out of here and answer. More later. Here they come."

Jeff was brought in; the jury filed into their box, and the judge strode in promptly when they were seated. Weymouth called his witness.

Straight out of central casting, Barbara thought, studying Sidney Overton. Someone put in a call for the amiable college professor, and here he was, a good-natured, pleasant-faced dude with a bemused expression, wearing a slightly wrinkled sport coat, Docker slacks, loafers, open shirt, no tie. He had a neatly trimmed brown beard, brown hair with a slight wave, a little long, but not too long. A week, two weeks overdue for a haircut, that's all, she thought sardonically. A bit absentminded, but not seriously forgetful.

Weymouth led him through his introductory questions and answers: former psychology professor at Purdue, research funded by a grant from NIH, now CEO of Human Diagnostics, married, no children, author of four books on psychology and the science of testing...

"Your company is in the business of creating different tests for different purposes. Is that correct?"

"Yes, it is."

"What we're interested in today is the test administered in November ten years ago to a junior class at Pennsylvania State College. This test." Weymouth held up the test labeled Personality Test. "Is this your test?"

"Indeed it is," Overton said smiling.

"Please tell the court how it came about and what it intended to test for."

"Fifteen years ago while at a symposium I met Dr. Bella Gravitch, Dr. Leonard Weinstein, and Dr. Benedict Seth. We were at dinner, discussing various problems in dealing with people who had not yet done anything to warrant suspicion or medical treatment, but who we believed were destined to act in antisocial ways due to their psychological makeup. Almost simultaneously two of us came up with the idea of constructing a test to determine the degree of psychopathology a subject might harbor. Over the following years we were in steady contact with one another and the idea was fully developed. All in all we spent over four years writing the test, perfecting it, testing it rigorously again and again, until we were ready to apply it. That was five years from the time we first thought of it."

"Please tell the court how the test works, what it entails, how it is administered," Weymouth said. He was almost as smooth as Overton.

"Of course," Overton said with a flashing smile. His teeth were dazzling white. "The test is timed. It takes exactly two hours. Before the timer is set, instructions are given: Each question must be filled in, there is a penalty if a blank is left, for example. And there is a brief questionnaire, name, age, gender, how many credit hours the student is taking, if working part-time how many hours, general information of that sort. There are forty short situations described, followed by six choices of action to take. The student fills in a circle by the action he selects. Each answer is weighted by the degree of psychopathy it reveals. The most benign answers are given 1 point, the worst choices are given 6. The overall score can be as low as 40, and the highest is 240, but we've never had a pure 40 or 240."

Weymouth nodded thoughtfully. "Can you demonstrate that your analysis of the test results is valid?"

"We definitely can do that. We tested patients in hospitals for the mentally ill, and we tested convicts serving time after being found guilty of heinous crimes that are psychopathic in nature. The correlation is proof enough. The most psychopathic patients and criminals all scored above 220." He referred to an article written by Dr. Bella Gravitch that had been published in *Psychology Today.*

Weymouth produced the magazine and showed it to the jury, then asked, "This article details the test and shows how the test scores match scores of diagnosed psychopathic patients and convicts. Is that correct?"

"That is absolutely correct."

Barbara hoped that someone on the jury would know that an article in *Psychology Today* was not exactly a peer-reviewed article.

"What was the defendant's test score?" Weymouth asked.

"Two hundred twenty-five."

Weymouth thanked the witness, nodded to the jury, and mock bowed to Barbara with a small smile on his face.

She rose leisurely and walked around her table. "Dr. Overton, exactly how was the test handled when it was administered? From start to finish."

"It was handed out to the students on arrival along with the information sheet. The students were required to arrive fifteen minutes before the test began in order to fill out the information sheet. Promptly at the time stamped on the test, they started. When the time was up, a bell sounded and they put down their pencils. They turned the test and information sheet in to the person giving the test, and that person stapled the information sheet to the test and put on the end time stamp. The tests were then sent to our offices for evaluating, which is done by computer. The information on the top sheet was digitized and added as a small running line on the top of the test."

"Then what? Were the results sent to the students?"

"No."

"Were they sent to the university?"

"No."

"Has anyone outside your company seen those test results before today?"

"No."

"Were the students volunteers?"

"No."

"Were they even psychology students?"

"I don't know."

"Was it a psychology class that you tested?"

"No."

"Did you or anyone else inform the students that the test was not altogether what it was called, a Personality Test?"

"It is a personality test, with emphasis on psychopathic tendencies."

"Were they told that?"

"No. It might have skewed the results."

"Did you go through the university administration to get permission to test a class of students?"

"No. Dr. Gravitch went straight to the instructor. He was happy to assist in our research."

"Did you pay him?"

For the first time the answer was slow in coming. Overton glanced at the jury, then at Weymouth who was remaining absolutely still. "We did pay him," he said. "Our five-year grant was nearing its end and we were anxious to test young adult students. It was the easiest way to gain access to them without having to wait for months for administrative bureaucracy."

"Is this the cover of your test?" Barbara asked, showing him the cover she had downloaded and printed.

"Yes, it is."

"Was it on the tests when they were handed out?"

"Yes, of course."

"It says here Human Diagnostics, and on the back it gives an address for the company Human Diagnostics. Why is that, Dr. Overton?"

"I had left academia to start our company that fall," he said in a patient-sounding voice. "By the time the test was administered and sent in for evaluation, that address was active and the company incorporated."

"You said that Dr. Gravitch approached the instructor with the proposal to use his class for your test purposes. Had Dr. Gravitch also left academia to join your new company?"

"Yes, she did."

"Was that the last time you actually paid someone to administer the test?"

"Yes. Our grant money was gone."

"Do you now sell the tests and the evaluations?"

"Yes. We are a for-profit corporation."

Barbara nodded. She was pacing back and forth slowly between her table and the jury box. Now, with her hand on the rail of the jury box, she said, "You testified that there was a penalty if the students left a question unanswered. Was there also was a penalty if a student refused to take the test?" When he said yes, she asked, "What was the penalty?"

His hesitation was a bit longer this time. "The instructor was responsible for the class participation. He proposed a slight reduction in grades for failure to take the test."

"Was that the penalty for not answering a question?"

"Yes. It was an insignificant reduction, not meaningful."

She regarded him levelly for a moment, then returned to her table. "Let me be clear about this," she said. "The instructor whose class you used was paid, and the students were coerced into submitting to a test not listed in the syllabus; no one saw the test results, no counseling or any other action was recommended. Are those all true statements, Dr. Overton?"

"They are true statements, but this was pure research—"

"Your Honor, please strike the comment following 'they are true statements.'"

"The comment will be stricken."

Barbara picked up the test Weymouth had introduced. She handed it to Overton. "Please tell the court what that running line across the top means."

He looked at it and shrugged. "His name, Jeffrey Cobbe, age, nineteen, credit hours 18, part-time work 15 to 20 hours a week, 4 to 5 hours' volunteer work in the conservatory, grade point average 3.8." He had read it in a fast monotone. Then, raising his voice and emphasizing the words, he said, "Test score 225." He looked smug and self-satisfied at getting in his point again.

Barbara retrieved the test and opened it. She said, "Let's have a look at one of the test questions, Dr. Overton. This one." She read the scenario, and the possible answers:

You can hear your neighbors, Janet and Bill, having a terrible fight with things breaking and Janet screaming. What do you do?

1. *Leave by the back door, get in your car, and drive away. You don't want to get involved.*
2. *Turn up the television to drown out their noise. They've done this before, and it's none of your business.*
3. *You know he's jealous and has a terrible temper. You get out your gun and have it handy in case he bursts in on you in a rage.*
4. *You go to the kitchen door and listen. You hope he doesn't kill her this time, but she shouldn't have provoked him.*
5. *You make a tape recording of the fight, hoping to sell it to Bill after he cools off.*
6. *Call Janet's brother, tell him to bring his gun.*

Barbara looked at the jury when she finished reading the possible answers. Frowns, worry lines, distress, but for the most part impassivity registered on their faces. Again regarding Overton, she said, "There is no way to say none of the above, is there?"

"No. That's the point of the test. People are faced with terrible situations all the time and they have to make decisions. Sometimes there are no good choices. You choose the lesser of evils."

She nodded. "I see. The test has forty scenes, situations you call them, and it takes two hours to complete. That means that each situation with six possible courses of action allows no more than three minutes, first to grasp the situation, then to deliberate on the action. That gives the student less than thirty seconds to consider each answer and its implications. How long did it take you and your coworkers to determine which answer was better of these two? To get in the car and drive away, or to turn up the television to drown out the noise?"

"We spent hours discussing, debating, sometimes arguing about the actions and the scores. It was arduous work over a period of several years." His voice was tight, the words clipped, his expression one of dislike. "The nonprofessional has no understanding of what goes into a comprehensive test such as this."

"You spent hours on the answers that the students had thirty seconds to grapple with. Is that true?"

"Yes. As far as it goes."

She turned to the judge and asked that the comment be stricken. He nodded and it was done. Overton's expression of dislike looked more like hatred for a moment. He shrugged and regained a more neutral look as if with some effort.

She held up the test again and asked, "The time stamp when Jeff's test was completed and turned in indicates he took eighteen minutes. Is that correct?"

"It is."

"That means that he had forty-five seconds to read each situation and the six possible answers. Is that right?"

"Yes. May I add something?"

"Please do," she said.

"It indicates that he didn't consider any of the implications of his choices, that he saw the most vile choice and selected it without more thought." Smug again, triumphant, he looked at the jury and shrugged.

"Is it possible that coincidence accounts for the number of bad choices selected?"

"No. I would say the odds against coincidence are infinitesimal."

Back at her table Barbara pulled out a large carrier bag with the whiteboard and tripod. She set up the tripod and the board so that it was visible to the judge and the jurors. Then, pointing to it, she said, "You can see that this is marked off to chart the test answers, forty situations across and lines numbered one through six down for the possible answers."

"Objection," Weymouth finally called out. "Your Honor, we have beat this matter of the test to death. This is another delaying tactic of the defense counsel."

"Your Honor," Barbara said, "this chart, when filled in, is essential to the defense."

"Overruled," Judge McNulty said. "Proceed, counselor."

"Thank you," she said. Walking again to Overton, she handed him the test. "This is Jeff Cobbe's test. Please tell the court the first answer he filled in."

Bored, he said, "One."

She moved to the whiteboard and put a big X in the first circle under Scenario One. "And the next?"

"Three."

She drew another X and asked for the next one, and then the next and the next.

The chart was showing the same sequence again and again until the fourth 1, 3, 6 turned into 6, 3, 1, and continued that way for another four answers.

Overton's voice became raspy as he continued giving the proper numbers for her to fill in with Xs. Soon however his voice faltered and grew fainter, and by the time they were at number 21 across he no longer waited for her prompt to give the next number in a low, strained voice. There was no other sound in the courtroom as she filled in one X after another. When she reached the end of the line at number 40, she drew back and regarded the chart. Very deliberately she began to draw lines connecting the numbers.

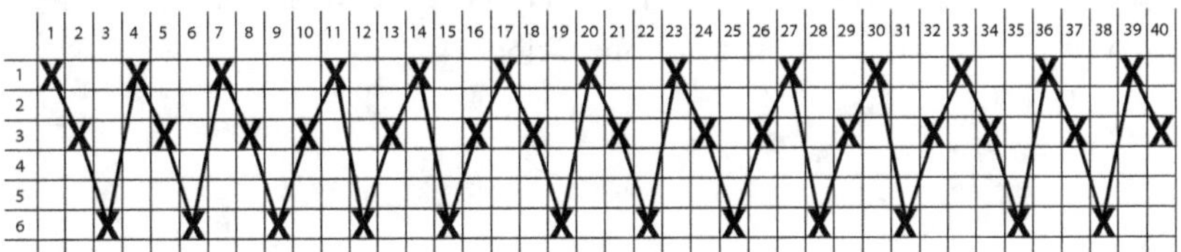

She studied the result for a moment, then moved aside and turned to watch the jurors react to the pattern she had revealed. Curiosity, renewed interest, with some of them looking from the board toward Jeff, then back to the board. Got their attention, she thought as she faced Overton and asked, "Did you ever examine his test or did you simply see the number 225, and accept it as his final score?" She walked to him and retrieved the test.

"It was his score," he said.

"Did you or anyone else ever examine his test?"

"No, not directly. We relied on the computer score."

She pointed to the whiteboard. "Can that pattern be coincidence, Dr. Overton?"

"I can't account for it," he said. "I don't know how it came out that way. It may be coincidence."

"Consider this," she said. "An A student looks over your test and realizes it is not a proper test for this class, not even a school test, but that of a private company that has nothing to do with him. He doesn't have time for this kind of nonsense but, relying on scholarships, he can't risk having his grade average lowered, so he answers every question in eighteen minutes. And in doing so he makes a mockery of the whole thing. Is that a more likely chain of reasoning than saying he deliberately selected the worst of six bad answers time and time again?"

"It's more likely that my partner and I failed to notice the arrangement of the answers, and failed to scatter them more randomly."

Barbara shook her head and looked him over, then said, "No more questions for this witness."

Weymouth simply had him repeat that a score above 200 indicated a psychopathic personality, that Jeff's score was 225, and that the validity of the test had undergone rigid scrutiny and had checked out.

Then to Barbara's surprise Weymouth said that the state rested.

It was twenty minutes after eleven, a little early for lunch, but an awkward time to start the defense. Judge McNulty called for the luncheon break anyway. Court was in recess until one o'clock.

"Listen up, people," Frank said to the gang entering his house. "There's corn to shuck, onions and tomatoes to slice, lettuce to wash and drain, pickles, mustard, and so on to haul out to the back porch. "For me, there are hamburgers to grill. Hop to it."

He took out the hamburger and started to make patties as the others milled about getting organized. He was smiling slightly as he watched Gina take charge and give orders that the others accepted without hesitation or question.

Within half an hour they were eating.

"I don't understand why Barbara didn't tear into that creep," Gregory said. "What a fake, what a fake test, and she let him off the hook. I don't get it."

"I thought she was going to join us," Daniel said. He had butter from the corn on his chin.

"She will. She needed to walk out some kinks," Frank said. "She'll be here presently." He considered Gregory for a moment, then said, "What you don't know is that Weymouth threw her a foul ball when he brought in the expert at the last minute. What happened was a pretty good example of the test the professor was promoting. A situation and several bad choices.

"See, she could have demanded that the state simply not use him, and that meant the judge had a choice of two bad decisions: Kick him out, knowing the matter would be leaked to the jury and that they would be sore and probably decide that it was a strong indication of guilt. The test proved he is a psychopath, you see. If they didn't find him guilty, the state could claim that the defense in desperation and by a technicality denied the state a chance to prove guilt. One decision could lead to an appeal and the other might ruin the reputation of the defendant and damage the defense attorney. Puts the judge in the hot seat.

"Or she could have asked for a continuation, a pause in the proceedings while she finds her own expert and eventually let them go at it, expert versus expert. Time consuming, expensive, keeps the jury for an extra week or two, and everyone's sore. An irate jury tends to convict. Or keep the expert to be recalled as a hostile defense witness, costly to the state, and again, time consuming, running over the week the judge said the trial should take. She would have torn him to shreds, of course, but meanwhile the jury had a week or longer to absorb that a test found him to be a psychopath. What she did, instead, was get an arrangement that let her question the witness in a single area without interference from the prosecutor. She gave the judge an out and he grabbed it."

He was making another hamburger as he spoke, loading a bun with lettuce, onion, and tomato, adding mustard to the other half, and finally lifting the last hamburger from the grill to finish it.

"And here she is now, if I'm not mistaken," Frank said. He had seen her just inside the screen door as he described the choices she'd had. She stepped out onto the porch and he put the hamburger on a plate and handed it to her. "Great job today. Congratulations. I didn't see that coming."

"It wouldn't have worked without all those cites. The judge blanched at the thought of reading them, and Weymouth looked positively sick. And it wouldn't have worked if Jeff had not been a genius the day of the test. How he thought through that in so little time is a miracle. He's a whiz," she added to Eric.

"The smartest one in the family," Eric said, grinning.

Frank looked at his watch. "Okay, gang, ten minutes to clean up, and then leave. Bailey, a word." He walked back into the house with Bailey, and the others began to gather up things to put away.

At twenty minutes after one Frank was at the entrance to his bank. He had to wait only a few minutes before Bailey appeared with Simon Atherton and Geraldo Reyes.

Bailey had a more than usual morose expression. He jerked his thumb toward Reyes and said, “Only way I could keep him out was if I slugged him.”

“What’s happening?” Reyes asked. “What are you up to with secret meetings, keeping my assistant and me away from the trial?”

Alterman shrugged. “I haven’t told him a thing,” he said, almost apologetically. “But I think we should tell him. Let him take pictures even.”

Frank considered it a second or two. He had to believe that it really was Alterman, not his alter ego, Worthington. Shelley had reported back that Dr. Minnick had verified everything Worthington had said about transient global amnesia, and about the continuing research being done in England. He nodded. “Mr. Reyes, you’ll have to pledge secrecy for the time being. Are you willing to do that?”

“Of course, I never reveal sources or secrets. I would not have the awards I’ve garnered if I did.” He puffed out his chest and stood straighter. “I am a man of honor, Mr. Holloway. You have my word.”

“And I’ll want copies of pictures,” Frank said.

Reyes agreed. “Now, can we get on with it? I’m all aquiver to see this big secret.”

In the courtroom Barbara was questioning Leona Whorley, who was the owner of the house where Jeff had had an apartment until his arrest. She was sixty-four, a compact, sturdy woman with hair the color of champagne, pale lipstick, and no other makeup. She was wearing her best pantsuit, Barbara felt certain. A cobalt-blue tailored jacket, slim-legged pants, with a bright pink shirt.

“How would you describe Mr. Cobbe?” Barbara asked.

“He was the best tenant you could have,” Mrs. Whorley said. “Always prompt with his rent and helpful. If he saw that a light bulb needed replacing, like it did on the porch, he’d just go ahead and do it. Or take out the trash for me when I was laid up with a cold, little things like that. Just real helpful and cheerful.”

“Did you have conversations with him, chat with him?”

“Some. I always wished he’d talk more. He has such a nice accent, not the deep south kind, or Texas. Almost like a British accent, but not quite that either. I asked him once about it, and he said it was Virginian. That’s how they talk in Virginia.”

"Now, about the night of April 10, do you recall that night, Mrs. Whorley?"

"Yes, I do. I wrote it all down in a notebook the next day so I could tell my sister about it. I remember it very well."

"Please tell the court what you remember about that night," Barbara said.

"Well, it was my sister's birthday and I made a casserole to take to her party. Scalloped potatoes. About nine or a few minutes after, I saw that fog was coming in, and I decided to leave early and get home before it got bad. She lives out on Fox Hollow Road, you see, and it gets foggier out there than here in town a lot of times. So I left and drove home. I had the empty casserole with me, and I'd left a few dirty dishes in the sink, so I decided to wash them up and be done with all that before ten. You don't want to leave a potato and cheese dish overnight, you see. It gets real hard to scrub out if you do. There was a program on at ten that I wanted to watch. One of those reality shows. That's what I was thinking when I got to my place and put the car in the garage. I saw the lights in Jeff's apartment were on, so I knew he was home, and when I put the casserole in the sink and turned on the water I knew he was taking a shower. We have a problem with water pressure when someone's running a bath or taking a shower, you see. So I decided to let the dishes go for a while. It was only nine-thirty and there was plenty of time before the show came on. Then, when I went back to the kitchen to do the dishes, I saw that his lights were off, and the pressure was all right, so I washed the dishes. I made a cup of tea and had a piece of birthday cake that my sister insisted I bring home with me, and then I watched my show."

"You say you saw his lights. How was that possible if he had the upstairs apartment?"

"You see, his apartment was the one in the back, over my kitchen, and when his kitchen lights or bathroom lights are on, the light hits my garage out back. It was lighted up when I got home, but after a few minutes it was all dark. So I knew."

"Mrs. Whorley, are you sure that it was nine-thirty when you had low pressure in the kitchen and the lights were shining on your garage?"

"Yes, I am. At the sink, I'm looking right at the garage out the kitchen window over the sink. I just walked in the door, took off my coat, and started to wash things up and I looked at the kitchen clock to see how much time I had. It was nine-thirty."

"What did you do after you discovered the water pressure was low?"

"I took my purse to the bedroom and hung up my coat, and by then it was dark out back."

"How long do you think you took to make tea and eat the birthday cake?"

"Maybe ten minutes or a little longer. I know that when I was done with the dishes it was a ten minutes to ten. I only had the few, you see, the casserole and a little plate for the cake and a cup, a glass or two. Anyway, I checked and saw that I had time to change my clothes, put on a robe and slippers, and then sit down to watch television."

"Mrs. Whorley, you said you wrote down everything about that night. Why did you do that?"

"Like I said, so I could tell my sister about it. I thought it was odd that the police detective came and asked me about Jeff, how he was as a tenant, if he had a drinking problem, did he do drugs, all kinds of questions like that. I just didn't have anything bad to say about him. The detective asked me if I saw him that night and I said no. I didn't, you see. I just saw his lights, and knew he was there because of the water pressure, but no one asked me more than that. Just did I see him? And when I started to say something more, he just said thank you and walked away. I thought that was a strange way to do an investigation. I watch detective and mystery shows, you see, and they always ask more than that. So I wrote it all down."

Barbara thanked her and said no more questions.

Weymouth tried to shake her, but she didn't budge. She knew what she knew and besides she had written it all down. He asked if she had had wine with dinner and she stiffened and said no. She never drank anything alcoholic. Never.

She was soon dismissed and Barbara called Mr. Carl Paceck.

He was a wiry man, fifty-nine years old, gray haired, and wearing black-framed glasses that magnified his eyes, made them appear too large for his lean face. He was an electrical engineer and had worked for the Eugene Water and Electric Board, for seventeen years. His manner of speaking was slow and deliberate as if he had to weigh each answer twice before uttering a word.

"Where do you live?" Barbara asked.

He gave his address and located it on the map for her. It was across an alley and one house down from the Whorley house.

"Do you know Jeff Cobbe?"

"No, ma'am. I've seen him a few times, but not to speak more than to say hello."

"Do you recall the night of April 10?" Barbara asked.

"Yes, I do."

"Please tell the court what you recall from that night."

"We were watching television early on," he said slowly, "my wife and I. News, and then a movie. At ten she wanted to watch a reality show and I didn't. I never watch them. I went upstairs to the room we call our hobby room. She does sewing in there and I have a stamp collection. I'd been eating chips and I didn't want to get grease or salt on my stamps so I went to the bathroom to wash my hands before I handled stamps. I happened to look out the window and saw a car in the alley. Not moving or anything, and no lights on, as if someone had just parked it there."

He paused, his forehead creased with lines, and he shook his head. Then even more deliberately than before he said, "The problem was the car was blocking my access to the alley. If there's an emergency with the electricity anywhere in the district, I'm on call. But with that car down there I wouldn't have been able to get out. I watched it for a couple of minutes thinking what I should do. I didn't want to go down and confront anyone who might be in the car. Too many crazy people with guns these days. That's not a good idea to confront them. And if I called 911, was that really an emergency? I mean an emergency might come up any time day or night with electric power, but there wasn't one yet. So I didn't know if that was a good idea, to call 911. They'd have to get a tow truck out, and it could be an hour or more before the alley was clear. But on the other hand it could have been blocked all night. So I decided that's what I should do, call 911, just in case. I had to go to the bedroom to get my phone and by the time I got back to the window, the car was moving down the alley."

"Could you make out what kind of car it was?"

He shook his head. "No, ma'am. It was dark at my end of the alley and I was on the second floor of my house looking down at it. It was black, and a sedan, four-door, I think, but that's all I could tell about it. When I saw it on down the alley driving away all I could see were taillights, and I didn't pay much attention to them. I closed the drapes and got out my stamp books."

He had nothing more to add and Barbara thanked him and said no more questions.

"Did you see the driver?" Weymouth asked when Barbara sat down.

"No. I didn't see anyone."

"Was the driver inside the car when you saw it?"

"I don't know. I didn't see anyone in or out of the car."

"A driver could have been sitting there, perhaps consulting a map, or making a phone call, couldn't he?"

"Objection," Barbara called. "Speculative. He said he didn't see anyone."

"Sustained."

"Do you know how long the car had been there before you saw it?"

"No."

"Is that a typical way for you and your wife to spend the evening? To watch a movie, then you work with your stamp collection while she watches something else?"

"Lots of times that's how it is."

"So it might have been any night in April, not one in particular that you saw that car while preparing to work with your collection?"

"It was April 10."

"Can you be certain of that?"

"Yes."

"But the routine you followed that night is one you follow many nights of the year. Isn't that correct?"

"It is."

Weymouth shook his head and waved to Barbara. "No more questions."

She rose and said, "Mr. Paceck, how can you be certain that incident with the car happened on April 10?"

He took his time gathering his words. "Edith, my wife, and Leona Whorley get together the next day and talk about that reality show they're addicted to. But this time all they talked about was the gun the police found and the arrest of Jeff Cobbe, how they searched his apartment and towed his car, and that's all Edith talked about when I got home from work. That was the day after I saw that car in the alley. Edith kept saying I should call the police and tell them what I saw, but I said they had all they needed or they would have come around and asked questions. They never did."

When he left the courtroom, Barbara stood and asked, "Your Honor, may I approach?"

He beckoned her and Weymouth and leaned over to say, "What now, counselor?"

"I have a deposition to present to the court," she said. "However, it is quite long, twenty pages, and if I may, I'd like to use only a small portion of it, in order to expedite this trial. Mr. Weymouth has a copy with the sections I wish to present highlighted, and I have another copy for you."

"Just the parts that put a halo around the head of the defendant," Weymouth said bitterly.

"The whole deposition does that," Barbara said. "It is quite revealing in that respect."

"And you want to cut out most of it? Why?" McNulty asked, scowling at her.

"It isn't needed for the defense," she said. "The part I'll present is enough to represent the whole."

"Give it to me," McNulty said. "We'll recess for ten minutes and I'll look it over and decide."

She handed him the folder she was holding and he shooed them away and announced the recess.

"I think this will wrap it up for today," she told Jeff back at her table. "I have to see you later, though. As soon as we are done here. How are you holding up?"

He shrugged. "The bed is hard, the food is awful, the noise in town here is intolerable, this trial is insufferably boring, the jury keeps trying to see inside my head, but aside from all that, I'm doing great."

Barbara laughed, and it seemed almost in spite of himself, he grinned at her. "I'm okay," he said. "You're the one doing great. I just wish it meant more than I think it does."

"It does," she said. "Jeff, take my word for it, it really does."

When they resumed, the judge gave her the go-ahead and she stood and said, "At this time, the defense will present a deposition taken by my associate Ms. McGinnis who will read the questions asked, and Mr. Eric Ballantine, who will read the responses. Mr. Ballantine will be seated in the witness chair in order to speak into the microphone so that his voice will be heard clearly by the jury. Mr. Ballantine, I might add, is Jeff Cobbe's brother."

Eric rose and went to the witness stand, and Shelley stood in front of the defense table. In her clear distinct voice she read the opening section detailing the date and where the deposition was taking place, in an office in a law firm in Hilton, New York, and who was present: a local attorney who represented Major Farleigh and never said a word, a stenographer, Major Avery Farleigh, and Shelley McGinnis.

Shelley: Major Farleigh, for the record please state your full name and where you were last employed.

Farleigh: Avery Farleigh. Until three years ago I was an instructor at the Ridge Academy for boys, aged twelve to eighteen. The academy is situated seven miles from Hilton, New York.

Shelley: How long were you an instructor at the academy?

Farleigh: Eighteen years.

Shelley: Please tell us something about the academy.

Farleigh: It's rated among the top five percent of similar boarding schools for academic excellence, and as high as the top three percent in physical fitness. There are many areas of physical education from swimming to various team sports, track, diving, firearms, rock climbing…

As he talked Barbara kept her eyes on the jury. Restless at first, they had become attentive; Mrs. Martin, a retired nurse, glanced from Eric to Jeff and back several times, and one of the men, the retired construction worker, also looked from one to the other more than once, nodded, and concentrated then on what Eric was reading. It was uncanny, listening to him, how like Jeff he sounded. Not a true southern accent, but a way of softening vowels, softening and lengthening slightly some combinations of vowels and consonants. No dropped g's in *ing* words, nothing that definite, but a softness, almost a gentle-sounding accent that was pleasing to the ear. She heard Shelley's next question.

Shelley: You were the instructor for track and firearms. Tell us about the firearms program.

Farleigh: When the boys are fifteen years old, they are put in the firearms program. It has two parts. In the first they learn about safety, how to clean and care for all kinds of weapons, sidearms, shotguns, rifles, assault rifles, automatic and semiautomatic weapons, and so on. They learn to disassemble them, and to reassemble them, how to pick out parts from a bin of unlabeled parts, to assemble weapons in moving vehicles, in the dark. When they are sixteen they start target practice. No boy under sixteen is allowed to fire a gun. The target practice starts with stationary targets for all the weapons, then advances to moving targets, and finally to moving targets with a variety of obstructions, like it would be for an animal running in among rocks and trees or bushes. That is the most difficult part of the course. Not all the boys make it to that level.

Shelley: Was Jeff Cobbe in your firearms classes?

Farleigh: Yes.

Shelley: How did he do?

Farleigh: Excellent in both sections. He achieved the highest possible scores. We devised more difficult tests for him, made the target smaller, and sometimes made the movements more erratic, faster, then slowing down, for instance. He still excelled. To achieve that level of precision requires more than simply excellent hand and eye coordination, but also a rapid calculation of where the target will be in the next second or two, not just where it is when you see it, but where it is likely to be when you fire your weapon.

Shelley: Was he given any recognition, a reward or anything like that for his proficiency as a marksman?

Farleigh: The highest honor was an invitation to join what they call Sharpshooters Incorporated. It's a group of older boys who showed great skill as marksmen. They are given some extra privileges, excused from some of the tasks required of all students. Jeff declined the honor. He told me that he'd had to take the firearms course because it's mandatory, but the Sharpshooters Incorporated group is voluntary, and he never intended to touch a gun again as long as he lived.

Barbara knew the deposition continued for another page or two, detailing the various penalties and punishments Jeff had suffered for not going along with the militaristic training forced on him. That had been a possible refutation of his father's anticipated testimony. She had pondered a long time on whether to include any of it, and decided not to. She had gone to Shelley's final question.

Shelley: Major Farleigh, how much of that training persists over the years if it isn't reinforced by regular practice?

Farleigh: It's a matter of what we like to call muscle memory. Once you learn to ride a bicycle, ride it well, it doesn't matter how many years pass before you ride one again. You remember. Your muscles remember, and you can still ride. Or swim, same thing. If you were ever a decent swimmer, you can always swim even after years of not being near water. Or skate. Almost anything that involves real training. If you're still physically fit, you can do it after years pass. He was a shooter of the first class; he'll always be that.

Shelley nodded to Eric. "Thank you, Mr. Ballantine. That concludes the deposition." Eric rose and walked back to the defense table, handed Barbara the folder with Farleigh's responses, and resumed his seat behind the table. Shelley sat in her chair.

Before Barbara spoke, Judge McNulty tapped his gavel. "The court will be in recess until eight-thirty tomorrow morning." He stood and stalked out of the courtroom.

It was five minutes before five.

33

"I'm losing my mind," Jeff said in the small interrogation room with Barbara. "Crazy. Or you're crazy. Or both of us. I can't believe that! Million-dollar art hidden away for decades?" His eyes were wide, his hands on the table fisted so tight the tendons stood out.

"Believe," Barbara said. She had just told him about the stolen art, what had led her to it, its past history. "I did some research on Alterman and it turns out that he's an authority on art, all aspects. Today he looked at the pictures, and in his opinion that's the art stolen back in the forties."

"You've known this for more than a week, and not a word? Why not tell us?"

"I wanted to make sure it was the stolen art. Trial coming up, no time to round up an expert, no leaks to the press about the possibility even or the trial would have been toast. Anyway, now it will come out. And it's going to be chaotic. Jeff, you have to be prepared to face questions. A lot of people will want to ask you questions, and I don't care who they are, not a word. Not a single goddamn word!"

He had relaxed his hands and was leaning back in his chair, eyeing her shrewdly.

"That's what that was about, all those odd questions to Tilsen. You think he knows. That's why he didn't reduce the offer even after Valducci was shot." His face tightened and his eyes narrowed. "My God," he whispered. "He did it himself! He shot Valducci!"

Barbara rose. "I have to go. Tonight Dad will tell Gina, not spring it on her in court. You're my client; she's Dad's client. See how that works out? Remember, no talking about it to anyone. See you in court tomorrow."

She knew he wanted to ask questions. He was too stunned to think of the right questions now, and she did not want him to gather his thoughts enough to demand answers that she did not intend to give.

After leaving Jeff she drove to Frank's house. They had agreed that he would whip up something to eat, and together they would go to the farm, be there by eight. She had said it should be early enough for Gina to settle down afterward so she would be able to sleep, but not before they had time to have some dinner. She suspected that Gina would not eat that night after hearing this news, and it was likely that she would not sleep no matter what hour they got there. But they had a plan, she told herself as Frank opened the door for her.

"Lamb chops, baked potato, and salad," he said, leading the way to the kitchen, pretending he didn't see the two golden cats darting in and out ahead of him. He never kicked one, and he never looked to see where they were. Barbara thought that was a sign of telepathic communication between them. She had to sidestep, pause, nudge one or the other now and then.

"How did he take it?" Frank asked when she was seated at the table with wine.

"He said that one or both of us had lost our mind. Then he said Tilsen was the killer, and then he sat with his mouth a little open and nothing coming out. That's when I left."

Frank nodded. "I had a chat with the ambassador from Italy after I let Alterman and Reyes pop their eyes out over those pictures. Alterman was shocked that we handled those pictures with our bare hands. He wore white gloves, and Reyes didn't touch them because Alterman snapped at him when he started to. Reyes will print out copies of the photographs he took, and Alterman will bring them to court tomorrow. Alterman brought special acid-free padded envelopes to put them in. On Friday we'll have a visit from people high enough up to make decisions, plus an art expert. I invited Alterman to come also. Two art experts, like two heads, are better than one."

They ate what Frank called a scrappy dinner, washed the few dishes, and were at the Valducci house by eight. "Your show," Barbara reminded him as they waited for someone to open the door.

The one to greet them was Gregory. He was examining Barbara's face intently as he stepped aside for them to enter. "He didn't call me," he said. He still looked like a frightened little boy. "Can he still call me?"

"No way," she reassured him. "He's had his shot and you're in the clear. Where's Gina?"

Gregory put his hand on her arm, hastily withdrew it, and asked, "Are you going to call me?"

"Nope. You can relax. About Gina?"

He exhaled a long breath, making her wonder how long he had been holding it, even while speaking. He shook himself, and finally answered her question. "Oh, in the living room. Scared, like we all are. Has something gone wrong, a new problem?"

They were walking through the hall toward the living room, with Frank in front. He entered first. Gina, Daniel, Eric, and now Gregory just a step behind him, were all present. He raised his eyebrows at Gina. "This should be private," he said.

Ignoring him, Gina rushed to Barbara and clutched her arm. "Has something happened to Jeff? What's wrong?"

"It isn't about the trial," Barbara said, disengaging her. "Let's step into the study and talk a few minutes."

Gina looked helplessly at the others, who all appeared ready to take up a fight if necessary. She nodded, and walked to the study door. "Back in a minute or two," she said and went into the study. Barbara and Frank followed and he closed the door and indicated the chairs grouped in front of the television. They moved to the seating arrangement, but Gina remained standing by one of the easy chairs.

"Please, sit down," Frank said.

"Just tell me," she said. "What's wrong?"

"Nothing's wrong," Frank said. He seated himself in one of the comfortable chairs and leaned forward, keeping his gaze on her. "Gina, that trunk your family's been keeping for someone contained a few million dollars' worth of art that was stolen back in the forties."

She stared at him with wide eyes, shook her head, and started to turn toward the door. "No. There wasn't anything but junk in it. I looked when I was a kid."

"It's true, Gina," Barbara said. "The pictures were hidden behind the horses. I found them, and today Simon Alterman verified that they are pictures smuggled out of Italy before the war ended."

Gina looked from her to Frank, back to Barbara. Abruptly she sank down into the chair behind her. She had gone pale, even as her expression still registered disbelief. "What do you mean? How did you find them? When? Why didn't you tell me? Why Alterman? I don't understand any of this."

Briefly Frank told her the story of the Italian finance minister and his secretary. "Simon Alterman recognized the mirror and told Barbara about the stolen art, and she remembered your story about the trunk and put two and two together. We couldn't tell you until we knew that was the original art, and today we got that confirmation."

Gina jumped up from her chair and nearly ran to the window, back, gesticulating wildly. "Millions of dollars! Are you sure? Can I sell the pictures? What do I do now?"

"You can't sell anything," Frank said. "On Friday I'm meeting with an envoy from Italy and another art critic, an expert, just as Simon Alterman is an expert. We'll decide how to handle this. There will be a reward, Gina, and with your permission I'll represent your interests in his matter."

"God yes! Oh, my God, a million dollars and it just sat down there in that trunk! All my life, down there…" She was still moving fast around the room, but suddenly came to a stop, staring at the floor in the shadow of the desk, the spot where her father had died. Her face had a stricken, drawn expression. "He did it, didn't he? Tilsen did it! He knows about the art. That's why he was desperate to get this one particular farm. How did he find out? You can't let him get away with it!"

Barbara and Frank exchanged quick glances and she said, "We won't let him get away with it, Gina. I promise you."

"Now, there are some practical things we have to talk about," Frank said. "Come, sit down, Gina. Calm yourself."

With what appeared to be a great effort Gina returned to the chair she had vacated. She perched on the edge of it, as relaxed and calm as a rabbit cornered by a snake.

"When this hits tomorrow, it's going to be a madhouse in these parts. I don't want you to have to deal with the press, any of the media, and they will swarm. Anyone gets close enough to ask a question, all you should say is no comment. Or nothing at all. You don't have to answer anyone's questions, no matter who they are, or claim to be…"

At a few minutes before nine Barbara tapped her watch and rose from her chair. "I want one favor," she said, going to the door to the hall. "May I borrow one of the prints hanging in the hall for tomorrow? I'll return it, of course."

Gina nodded helplessly, and Frank said, "I know you have many questions, but we have to leave. Barbara has to prepare for tomorrow and try to get in some sleep. What you tell your fellows is up to you. I just didn't want a committee in here while we made our plans. Try to get some sleep..."

Barbara walked out into the hall and looked over the various paintings and prints that she had admired months earlier. She pulled one far enough from the wall to inspect the backing. There were two slits, each about three inches long. One horizontal at the bottom right corner; the other vertical up the same side. It would do fine, she decided, and removed it. She returned to the study door, but didn't enter.

"Ready, Dad?"

"You bet." Frank joined her at the door and looked back at Gina with a grin. "Try to keep the noise level down when you tell them. We'll see you tomorrow." With a wave, he joined Barbara and they let themselves out.

"How they'll handle it in court is anyone's guess," he said when they got in his car. He was chuckling. "It's going to give Weymouth an attack of ulcers or something to see them all hopping with excitement." He started the engine.

When they reached his house, she refused to go in with him. "Work," she said. "Lots of work." She got out of the car and headed for her own.

"I know. Wait a minute, though. I have something for you." He hurried to the door and entered.

She was behind the wheel of her car when he came out. He handed her a thermos. "Coffee, good thermos, hot now, hot for the next several hours. Don't make it too late, Bobby. Tomorrow's going to be bedlam."

"Right," she said. "Thanks, Dad. See you in court."

He stood at the door and watched her back out of the driveway, watched until her taillights vanished around the corner. He scowled at the two coon cats that were at the open door as if ready to make a dash outside. "You do it and you spend the night out there," he warned them. They retreated and turned to chase the house ghosts only they could see.

‡

At home again, Barbara made sure that Nappy had food and fresh water, and then sat on the sofa in the living room with her briefcase on the coffee table. She didn't open it yet. She leaned back tiredly, waiting for her phone to ring. When it did, a few minutes later, she snatched it up and said hello.

"Are you home?" Darren asked in his softest, most seductive voice. She swallowed hard and said yes. She leaned back with her eyes closed, prepared to talk, to listen, to be with him however remotely.

Everything had been done that needed doing, she thought the next morning when she took her place at the defense table. The judge had sent out the message to Tilsen that he was to be recalled to the witness stand that day, and Barbara had seen him in the corridor staring at her large tote bag that wasn't large enough to completely conceal the picture she had brought from Gina's house. She was certain that he had also seen the candelabra that Shelley had moved when she reached inside her bag to give Barbara a folder. The jury was in place, Jeff at her side at the defense table, and the judge in his big chair.

Gina and her guys were all in a state of barely controlled high excitement, flushed cheeks, flashing eyes, making them all seem ready to stand up and dance or sing or simply yell out. Jeff was more contained, but his color was high and he had grinned at the guys and Gina, and raised his thumb in the okay sign. Several jurors were regarding him with renewed interest and curiosity. Court was called to order and the real day began.

She called Simon Alterman. As soon as he spoke, the jurors were enlivened by his accent, his presence, his charm. One, Gladys Giles, thirty-something, a bit plump with a pretty face, and hair down to her waist, leaned forward watching him avidly as he spelled his name and said he lived in London.

"What is your occupation?"

"I'm a fine art consultant."

"Please explain to the court what that entails."

"I do consulting for museums, for auction houses such as Sotheby's and Christie's and others to authenticate art pieces. I often am asked to appraise art that an owner wishes to sell, and to suggest a floor bid if the art is to be auctioned."

"Have you discovered forgeries, copies of famous art?"

"Yes. That's one of the things I do."

"What brought you to this part of the country, Mr. Alterman?"

He smiled and shook his head. "Serendipity, happenstance. I was in New York and ran into Geraldo Reyes, the photojournalist, who is an old friend. He was fuming because he has a contract to write an article about small farms in your country, and his assistant was tied up with some technicality over his visa. I offered to accompany him until his regular assistant straightened out the matter. I thought it would afford me insight into your country in a way that tourists seldom manage."

"Mr. Alterman, please tell the court what happened in the Valducci house eleven days ago."

He smiled more broadly. He was enjoying this, Barbara realized. He was almost as elated as Gina and her gang over the found art. Any fears that he might be reticent, withdrawn, cold, all faded, and she felt something relax just a little bit in her own stomach as he began to recount that day. Glancing at the jury, she also realized that they loved him, at least most of them did. A couple of the men were regarding him with suspicion if not hostility.

"We were at the farm, Geraldo and I, in order for Ms. Valducci to take Geraldo on a walking tour of the entire farm. Meanwhile, you, Ms. Holloway, offered to show me through the residence to determine if there were likely places inside for photo shoots. There were several, as I recall. What made the day outstanding, however, was a unique mirror on one of the walls. It is about this big—" He held his hands up to show the size, then continued. "The frame is intricately carved ivory, and it has a minor flaw that only a few people know about, people in the business of art thefts and insurance. That mirror was included in one of the major art thefts at the close of World War II."

He stopped, well aware of the almost preternatural silence in the courtroom, the intensity of the interest shared by the jury, the judge, everyone.

"Please continue," Barbara said.

"Yes, of course. I told you about the theft, the smuggling out of Italy of a number of paintings, other items, and the mirror. I told you that some of the items had been recovered, but several were still at large, and that if the mirror was in that house, there was a chance that the other items could be there, also. And I advised you in the matter of locating hidden art, where it could have been concealed."

She pulled out the borrowed print from Gina's house and held it up for Weymouth, then the judge to see. She asked Alterman if he recognized it.

"Yes. I saw it in the Valducci house."

"Is this one of the ways original art may be concealed behind other pictures?" She turned the picture to show him, then the jury, where the picture backing had been cut making a flap. She lifted it to show the back of the framed print.

"Exactly like that," Alterman said. "Such a cut would not be noticeable unless a real examination of the picture was made, but it would give the one searching the opportunity to see if another picture was concealed there. A hidden picture could stay in that position for years, decades without drawing suspicion."

"What followed your tour of the residence?" Barbara asked, after putting the picture down.

His eyes were shining and his smile was wide as he regarded her, then turned his bright gaze to the jury box. "Yesterday, I went to a bank with Mr. Frank Holloway, and there I saw four of the stolen paintings: a Rembrandt, a Picasso, a Caravaggio, and two sketches by Leonardo, considered to be one piece since they belong together. It is my opinion that the art smuggled out of Italy in 1944 has been located. I brought pictures of the paintings and the Leonardo sketches with me today."

There were gasps from onlookers behind Barbara when he mentioned the paintings, and a commotion caused by the hurried exit of several people. There was a murmur of voices. There had been few people in attendance every day of the trial; it had not attracted much attention, little press coverage. Some court junkies were always in attendance, a stray passerby now and then dropped in, and there was usually one or two who knew that with a phone call they could pocket a few dollars if anything interesting happened. Something interesting had just happened. She watched them exit, Tilsen among them. Judge McNulty tapped his gavel, and the courtroom settled into silence again. Barbara faced Alterman once more.

He produced an envelope from an inside pocket of his coat and handed it to Barbara. They were five-by-seven prints, sharp and clear, good photographs.

Barbara showed Weymouth and the judge the photographs and then handed them to the jury foreman to examine and pass around. When they'd had a chance to view the photographs Barbara retrieved them and entered them into evidence.

That done, she asked, "Mr. Alterman, in your professional capacity, if you were asked to put a floor bid on those paintings, what would you suggest?"

He was nearly laughing as he said, "As a group, although that would never happen, I would suggest one hundred million dollars. Individually, I would suggest fifty million dollars for each piece."

The courtroom erupted with excited cries, and another man rushed out. Gina and her guys were all talking to one another; Jeff was turned in his seat joining in with them, and even the jurors were whispering to one another. Judge McNulty tapped his gavel to no avail, then banged it hard a few times and yelled for order.

"This court will come to order, or I'll have it cleared!" He looked at Barbara with a ferocious scowl. His face was cherry red, his eyebrows drawn almost together across the bridge of his nose. If he snorted fire, Barbara thought, it would not be surprising. He looked as if he could do that. He said, "Proceed."

"Mr. Alterman," Barbara said, "how was it that you remembered the story about the mirror and the theft that happened decades before you were even born?"

"About three or four years ago," he said, "the BBC did a series titled 'The Big Heist'; it was about major burglaries and robberies, grand thefts of the past hundred years. Bank robberies, train robberies, the theft of jewelry, things of that sort. One of the episodes concerned itself with art theft, and the story of the mirror and the other items was featured prominently. There was a photograph of the mirror that highlighted the series. It stuck in my mind. My field, don't you see?"

She nodded. She stood before the jury box to ask, "If someone wanted an appraisal of the mirror, how would that lead to the story of the stolen art?"

He looked thoughtful for a moment, then said, "If that person wanted to appraise the mirror for its possible monetary value, he or she would go to a database that might list it. That database would provide a link to stolen art, if the mirror had been tagged as stolen by an insurance company or other entity with an interest in the art. Following the link would reveal the whole story of the theft and list the pieces still missing. All stolen fine art, valuable art, is listed as an aid in recovering it. Auctioneers, the better pawn shops, appraisers all avail themselves of the service from time to time. Knowingly dealing in stolen art is a serious crime."

Walking back toward her own table, Barbara paused and asked, "Have you ever met anyone connected to this trial, to the Valducci family before this trip to Oregon?"

He shook his head. "Never. I've never been in Oregon before, but if I might add, I find this area charming, and I will recommend it highly to friends as a destination spot for a visit."

Barbara smiled at him and said, "I have no more questions. Thank you, Mr. Alterman."

She glanced at Weymouth and was not at all surprised to see that he was struggling with anger. He stood and said, "Your honor, may I approach?'

McNulty beckoned both of them, turned off his microphone, and turned to the side of his bench with a sour expression. "What?" he snapped at Weymouth.

"I request that this witness and all of his testimony be expunged from the record. He was nowhere near Oregon at the time of the murder; his testimony has nothing to do with the murder of Robert Valducci; and this whole tactic is nothing but extreme obfuscation."

"It has everything to do with the murder," Barbara said angrily. "And you know it as well as I do."

"Quiet," McNulty ordered in a manner that brooked no argument.

He was furious, as she had known he would be. How that anger would be channeled was the only part of this equation she had not been able to predict. He had been put in the position she had avoided giving him earlier, but this time it was Weymouth who had put him there. Bad choices, and a decision had to be made. If there was any justice—

Her speculation was cut short when he snapped at Weymouth, "Denied. Now get on with it."

She and Weymouth walked back to their respective tables silently, without a glance at each other. She took her seat. Weymouth stood at his table and said, "I have no questions for this witness."

He was going to bluff it out, pretend the art didn't exist in the universe that had Jeff being convicted of murder, his universe where he would get another gold star, another notch in his belt, another step closer to the next office he decided to run for. Good luck with that! she silently flung at him. Simon Alterman was dismissed and she called her next witness, Lucy Harris.

She was a tidy, little woman, small-boned and delicate looking, with masses of curly hair that had been red and now was fading and streaked with silvery white. Her eyes were a sharp, clear blue, her complexion fair with pink cheeks. In her early sixties, she had been widowed six years earlier, and had been in business with Mildred Chadwick for nearly that long, until Chadwick's murder.

Barbara took her through a brief summary of her history before asking, "When Ms. Mildred Chadwick was so brutally murdered, where were you?"

"I was in Bellingham, staying with my daughter who had given birth to a child in February. She had a two-year old and one going on five and needed help for a few weeks. Of course, when they called me about Mildred's death, I took the first flight home that I could get."

"What did you learn when you returned to Portland?"

She drew in a long breath, but her voice was steady when she said, "Mildred had been attacked and killed during the night on Saturday, March 7. The officers wanted to know if anything was missing. Her laptop, the camcorder we both used, her cell phone, another camera, two flash drives, things like that. Her purse was in the house with forty-four dollars and her credit cards were still in it."

"Were you and Ms. Chadwick in touch during your absence?"

"Oh my, yes. Two, three times a week we talked, and we emailed back and forth a lot."

"Did she mention a large estate sale she had been commissioned to handle?"

"Yes. She had told me she was going to an estate that week, Wednesday, I think. She told me she got the commission. The last time we talked, she was excited and said there was something big, but it could wait until I got home. My granddaughter was making a fuss and we didn't talk more than a minute."

"When was that?"

She swallowed hard, but her voice continued steady as she said, "That Saturday afternoon, the day she died."

"Objection!" Weymouth called out. "Your honor, all of this is irrelevant to the case being tried here."

"It is not irrelevant," Barbara said quickly. "I can tie this testimony directly to the trial before us."

"I advise you to do so quickly," Judge McNulty said. "Overruled."

"Ms. Harris," Barbara said, "did you have to go through various records, including telephone records, to bring your accounts up-to-date after Ms. Chadwick's death?"

"Yes. We were careful to keep our accounts separate, and to label everything either personal or business related. We had to for tax purposes, of course. When I looked over the telephone records, sometime in June, I found a call made to a 541 number, and I didn't know if it was personal or business. I put it aside for a time, but then Gina Valducci called me to ask about an appraisal Mildred had planned to do for Robert Valducci. I had no record of it because all the computer material was missing. But I realized that accounted for the 541 call, and I marked it business."

"When exactly was that call made, Ms. Harris?"

"Saturday, March 7, at eleven in the morning. It lasted two minutes."

Barbara walked to her table where Shelley handed her a copy of the phone bill for March. Barbara showed it to Weymouth and the judge, and then asked Lucy Harris if that was a copy of her phone bill. She said it was.

"Do you know whose telephone number that is?"

"I didn't. But I called it and whoever answered said it was Valducci's. I didn't speak or anything. I just wanted to know."

Barbara thanked her and turned to say to Weymouth that she had no more questions.

And neither did he, she knew, as she watched him fumble around to find something to discredit Lucy Harris and her damning testimony.

He finally asked the question she thought he should have started with: "Ms. Harris, do you know who Ms. Chadwick talked to on March 7 when she called the Valducci residence?"

"No, I don't."

"Do you know what they talked about?"

"No."

"I have no more questions," Weymouth said.

Shelley touched Barbara's arm, then handed her a note. T on I-5, heading north. Barbara glanced at Frank and nodded. He returned her nod and quietly left his seat and walked from the courtroom.

Barbara thanked Lucy Harris and she was dismissed. Barbara called her next witness: Donald Tilsen.

Barbara was standing at her table and when Tilsen didn't appear at the summons, she sat down after a swift survey of the courtroom. There were no empty seats. Two of the regulars, informers, she assumed, had returned, and there were many newcomers, several looked like reporters or bloggers with notebooks already open, pens ready. Word must have gone out that this judge would confiscate any electronic device found activated in his court. Reyes was in the back row, looking insanely happy. She watched a suited man hurry in and rush to Weymouth, hand him a note. He read it, then crushed it in his hand and rose.

"Your Honor," Weymouth said, "may I approach?"

Judge McNulty beckoned them both and at the sidebar, he snapped at Weymouth, "Where is your witness?"

"Your Honor," Weymouth said, "I have a note from my office. A reliable source has called in a tip to inform us that Mr. Tilsen was seen driving north on Interstate 5 a few minutes ago."

Color flooded McNulty's face and his jaws tightened, making rigid, bulging cable-like lines from his ears to his chin. He didn't speak instantly, but glared at Weymouth. Finally, he said in a low rasping voice, "I charge your office with bringing Mr. Tilsen to this court. I shall issue a bench warrant immediately. Bring him in, Mr. Weymouth. I advise you to find that man and deliver him to court ASAP. Do I make that clear enough for you?"

"Yes sir. Very clear."

"We'll recess for ten minutes. After that, Miss Holloway, call your next witness."

He motioned them away. Weymouth's mouth was a thin, nearly lipless line when he turned to go back to his table. He gave Barbara a cold, bitter look, but did not say a word to her. At his table he consulted with the note bearer, who left in a trot. From the bench Judge McNulty said there would be a brief recess. He stalked out and the courtroom was instantly filled with the buzz of conversations.

Barbara turned to Frank and said, "Bench warrant." Frank grinned and nodded.

Frank leaned past Gina to say to Gregory, "I want you to take down sandwich orders. And drinks. Here's the number to call when you have the orders. His name is Martin and he'll be expecting the call. That's where we go for lunch today. Martin can keep the media maniacs out so we can eat in peace. Okay?" He handed Gregory a notepad and pen. "Make mine ham and Swiss, tomato, onion, lettuce, on rye. Coffee."

Gregory nodded, evidently pleased that he had been asked.

"What's happening with Tilsen?" Gina asked.

"A bench warrant has been issued. He's on I-5 and the cops will haul him back. It's contempt of court, for openers, so he can't run anywhere again. We'll go on from there."

"Just contempt of court," Jeff said with a touch of bitterness. "He'll have high-priced lawyers at his side instantly, and they'll stretch it out for months."

"I said for openers," Barbara reminded him. "That's what I mean. Openers, starting position. Settle down." She looked at Gregory. "Tuna, tomato, lettuce, whole wheat, coffee."

Minutes later Gregory went out to place the lunch order. When he returned he said in a hushed whisper, "I went to the main door and had a look outside. It's a mob already: TV vans, guys with cameras, camcorders, cell phones, and more coming every minute it looks like. And cops. Lots of cops."

"Circus time," Frank said with a nod.

They all remained in their seats during the brief recess. When the jurors returned, and the judge was at the bench, Barbara called Gina.

She led Gina through the preliminaries, then asked, "What is your relationship to Jeff Cobbe?"

"He's my friend and colleague. He's the vice president of the Valducci Corporation, and I'm the president."

"From the time you met him until the present has there ever been a romantic relationship between you?"

"Never," Gina said.

"How did you meet Mr. Cobbe?"

"I was working toward my master's degree at Oregon State, and he was in the doctoral program. Dr. Tideman, the head of the department, held seminars for six or eight of us to talk about our plans, how we would use our degrees. Jeff and I both attended. I talked about turning the farm into an organic farm to serve the surrounding community, and he said it was as if I had read his notes for his dissertation. He already had a name for farms around cities such as Eugene. Satellite farms, he called them. Small and mid-sized farms dedicated to providing local produce for a local population. We had a common goal, to feed the world, one community at a time."

"Did your grandmother approve of your plan for her farm?

"Absolutely. She was very concerned about climate change, extreme weather, floods, and droughts, and feared for the future if small farms keep being driven away by conglomerates and agribusiness interested in industrial farming and exporting, with no regard for the community around them."

"Objection," Weymouth said. "I object to an irrelevant lecture on farming practices and hearsay prophecies."

"Sustained. Move on, Miss Holloway."

"Were you present when Mildred Chadwick was commissioned to do an appraisal of the Valducci residence?"

"Yes."

"Who was present during her visit?"

"My father, Mr. Tilsen, and I."

"Did Mr. Tilsen stay with you and your father the entire time she was there?"

"Yes."

"Did she take special note of the mirror that Mr. Alterman mentioned?"

"Yes. She examined it carefully. She said since it wasn't signed, she would have to do some research on it."

"What arrangement was made when her tour of the house was finished?"

"My father gave her a Valducci card and told her to send her appraisal to the address on the card."

"Did Ms. Chadwick send her appraisal?"

"No. It never came."

"Do you know why?"

"Yes. I didn't think of it again for weeks, but in June I called her business number and reached her partner, Ms. Harris. She told me Ms. Chadwick had been robbed and killed in March, the Saturday after she came to the farm, and that all of her electronic devices were stolen, all her records were gone, and there was no record of her appraisal or even of her visit."

"What do you mean a Valducci card?"

"It's the business card for the farm, the store, and nursery. Some old customers and friends still use the landline, the phone number on the card."

"On the Saturday following Ms. Chadwick's visit, did you see your father?"

Gina's voice had been firm and steady until that question. Now her voice dropped and faltered for a moment when she said she had seen her father that late afternoon.

"Tell us about that," Barbara said.

"I was moving things from my old room to my apartment in town. It was about five-thirty. I had gathered some clothes and was heading for the stairs to take them out to my car when I saw him… He looked almost ready to cry, he was so sad."

Barbara nodded and moved to stand at the jury box. "Did you see him the following day, March 8?"

Gina ducked her head and swallowed before she answered. "Yes. About the same time of day, closer to six o'clock. Again, I was taking things to my car and I saw him in the study. There were drawers stuffed full of things, miscellaneous bits of this and that. He was looking through them. That was the last time I saw him." Her eyes glistened with unshed tears, but her voice remained steady if low pitched.

"How was he dressed?"

"In his shirt sleeves. The house was a little too warm and he had taken off his coat and draped it over his chair."

"In your own words please tell the court about the next few hours."

Gina cleared her throat. "I put things in my car and drove out and around to the back of the greenhouses where we usually park. I worked there for a couple of hours. We were certain we could bring ripe tomatoes to market weeks before our usual time in August. We were nursing a hundred along with extra light, repotting them before they became stressed—"

"Objection!" Weymouth cried angrily. "Another lecture."

Before McNulty could call, "Sustained," Gina flushed, ducked her head, and said in a near whisper, "I'm sorry." There was a moment of silence.

"Please continue, Ms. Valducci," Barbara said gently. "After you worked for a couple of hours, then what?"

She told it succinctly, work, home, a sandwich, starting to run a bath when Jeff's call came. Barbara stopped her when she said she drove to the truck access road.

"Why didn't you drive to the house?"

"I started to, but there were so many cars there, police cars, other cars, flashing lights. I didn't think I could get close, so I went to the truck access road and on to the truck loading area. It's directly across from the house. Then I saw Jeff and I ran to him to ask what happened. All he knew was that the officer had told him my father had been shot dead. We went on to the house together."

"How was Jeff dressed when you saw him that night?"

"In his poncho. We all wear them. We keep them on a clothes rack inside the greenhouse door."

"Does he usually listen to music when he's working in the greenhouse?"

"No. He was listening to a symposium that night. Dr. Tideman had attended a meeting at UCLA about what to expect due to climate change. He gave Jeff a recording of the papers presented and some panels. The whole symposium was about how climate change will affect many areas of life: transportation, the migration of disease vectors, migration of plant and animal species, probably extinction of many life forms, and how it would affect agriculture, our food supply chain."

She stopped abruptly and gave a quick look at Weymouth as if anticipating his objection. When he remained silent, she returned to her narrative about what she had done after entering the house: She made tea, turned up the thermostat, and had seen Tilsen in the hall near the kitchen door.

"Was the thermostat turned low or all the way off?"

"It was off, all the way down. I turned it up to seventy again, where we usually kept it in cold weather."

"On the night that shots were fired at your mother's car, were you working in the greenhouse?"

"Yes. Daniel and Gregory had left at about seven, and Jeff and I worked a little longer. I was very tired and I left at nine. I walked to the house and took off my poncho and boots on the porch outside the kitchen door. Then I walked through the house to make sure the doors were all locked. When I got to the living room doors, I could see that the greenhouse lights were off. Jeff had gone home. It was about five minutes after nine. I had a sandwich, a bath, and was ready to go to bed when Tony Mirano came to the house with my mother. When I heard the doorbell I looked at the clock because I was thinking that no one comes at that hour, ten o'clock. Tony called 911 and we waited for the police in the living room."

"Ms. Valducci, if Jeff Cobbe called you on the phone, would you recognize his voice?"

"Absolutely."

"Why?"

"His accent primarily. Virginia accent, and the fairly deep tone. But mostly by his accent."

"Subsequent to the shooting incident, what measures did you take?"

"We talked it over, the four of us who are the Valducci Corporation, and we decided to live together in my house. We were thinking safety in numbers, and I shouldn't live there alone any more. We would all save money if we pooled our resources. It's a big house with enough bedrooms for all of us. And we got a watchdog."

"So no one has been able to enter the residence without permission ever since that night of the shooting. Is that correct?"

"That's right."

"From testimony we know that Mr. Tilsen and your father made a proposal to your grandmother to buy her farm, that the same offer was accepted by your father, and following his death it was made to your mother, who also accepted it. Was such an offer made to you?"

"Yes. Two times. I rejected the first one directly to him. Then the second offer came through my attorney and I rejected it through him."

"Do you know why Mr. Tilsen thought you might be amenable to such an offer made a second time?"

"Only what I heard from my attorney. He said Mr. Tilsen didn't believe I could manage the farm alone after Jeff was found guilty of murder and sent to prison."

"Objection! Hearsay!"

"Privileged attorney/client discussion which Ms. Valducci is free to disclose," Barbara said.

McNulty shook his head and said, "Sustained."

Barbara shrugged slightly. The jury heard what the jury heard. They couldn't unhear it. Even if in his instructions the judge told them to disregard it, that bit of information was in their heads.

"When did you learn about the stolen art that was discovered in your house?" she asked.

Gina appeared startled at the change in subject. "Last night," she said. "At ten minutes after eight. I looked at my watch to make sure I was awake and not dreaming."

Barbara smiled at her. Then, standing by the jury rail she asked, "In your opinion, knowing your father as you did, is it possible that he took a phone call from Ms. Chadwick and learned about the possibility of the stolen art from her?"

"Objection! Speculation, conjecture."

"Not just speculation. Ms. Valducci knows very well how her father reacted to different scenarios. She would have known if he reacted to such a call."

Judge McNulty frowned at them both but, possibly more angry with Weymouth at the moment than with Barbara, he said, "Overruled. You may answer the question, stating that it is not a fact, but your opinion."

"In my opinion, because I know how he reacted to almost everything that came along, he would not have been able to hide his excitement at such a possibility. No more than I could last night, when my friends and colleagues knew instantly that something big had happened. I was up most of the night just thinking about those priceless paintings hidden away in my house."

She looked at her guys then with a big smile on her face. Some of the jurors even smiled slightly.

"Ms. Valducci, several times you've indicated that you and your colleagues worked until nine o'clock or even later. Please tell the court about your days, and Jeff Cobbe's days at the farm."

Gina looked surprised at the question. She said, "We were all working regular eight-hour days on the business of the farm, getting ready for the coming season, planting, potting up plants, and so on. There's so much to do at that time of year. We were making the same wages as other workers, and applying much of our money toward the expense of using the greenhouse. And we were trying to get in anywhere from four to six hours or even more on our own project, for which there was no pay, of course. We were working anywhere from twelve to sixteen hours every day, all of us."

"Why did you keep up such a schedule when you knew your father intended to sell the farm and dismantle everything?"

She ducked her head again and said in a low voice, "We had to abandon some of our work, some of our plans, but Jeff had found several other farmers who were willing to let us move tomatoes to their property. Five here, ten there. Tony Mirano said he could accommodate up to twenty. We were making certain that they had every possible advantage until the last day, late in April, when we knew we had to move them. That's usually too early to plant them outside, but we were also planning on cloches and other covers to protect them, and we knew we would be kept busy going from one planting to another to maintain them. But it was important to us to see if some of our experiments with the seeds and seedlings would pay off. We had put in too much time and effort to just give up on that much of our project."

Barbara turned toward her table then, but stopped and faced Gina once more to ask, "Did you have unusually early tomatoes this past summer?"

Gina smiled broadly and nodded. "Sixteen days earlier than ever before. It's a start."

Barbara thanked her and said she had no more questions.

Weymouth stood at his table, glanced at Jeff, then at Gina and smiled, the kind of smile that Barbara connected to men in a mixed group when they told dirty jokes. A telling smile that hinted that you were in on a secret, that you and the smiling man had a relationship that you didn't talk about. "Isn't it true that you and the defendant were thrown together a lot when you were at Oregon State?"

Gina looked puzzled for a moment, then said, "We were on a few projects together with several other students from time to time. And we attended Dr. Tideman's seminars with other students."

"Not just the two of you on some of those projects?"

"No."

"Ms. Valducci, you're a lovely young woman, the defendant is a handsome young man, you share a common goal, a dream you might call it, wouldn't it make sense to get together with him to discuss that dream?"

"Objection," Barbara said. "Is that a question? Or a suggestion that Ms. Valducci engage in speculative conjectures?"

"Sustained," Judge McNulty snapped. "Ask your question without conjectures, counselor."

Weymouth's voice tightened slightly as he asked, "Did you and the defendant get together to discuss your common dream?"

"Just the two of us? No."

"Can you really claim that there was no physical attraction between the two of you?"

"Yes," she said angrily. "I was attracted to someone else and he wasn't interested in me. We were colleagues from the start, not romantics."

Weymouth shook his head in disbelief. "Were you furious with your father when you learned he planned to sell the farm?"

"No. I was angry and frustrated not furious."

"Did you have a violent quarrel with him about it?"

"No. We argued. We argued all our lives over everything. It was no different than it always had been."

"Did you express your anger to the defendant? Tell him about your frustration?"

"I didn't have to. We were all frustrated."

"Did you live in the residence when your father first came back to the area?"

"Yes."

"And did you move out and return to your apartment when you learned he planned to stay a few days?" When she said yes again, he said, "On Saturday, March 8, were you living in the residence?"

"No."

"Did you hear the telephone ring that morning?" She said no. "Do you know who answered the telephone?"

"No."

"On the night shots were fired at your mother's car, you said you left the greenhouse at nine o'clock. Did you see the defendant leave that night?" She said no. "Do you know what time he left?"

"No."

Weymouth tried again to get Gina admit to a relationship with Jeff, and Barbara let it go on longer than usual because Gina was fielding his questions with dignity and grace, and had the sympathy of the jury. When it continued too long, Barbara finally objected.

"Counselor is badgering and bullying this witness."

Testily McNulty said, "Sustained. Move on, counselor."

"Ms. Valducci, you testified that you learned about the art last night. Who told you?"

"My attorney."

"You mean, Ms. Holloway?"

"No. She isn't my attorney."

"Were you told how the paintings had been found?"

"Objection. Improper cross."

"Sustained."

"Do you know when the paintings were found?"

Barbara objected again and it was sustained. The only point in direct testimony that could be addressed was the fact that Gina had learned about the art the night before. Barbara had not left that door open for cross-examination to reveal any more than that.

Weymouth knew this as well as she did, but he persisted, no doubt hoping to get the jury to side with him because he had been blindsided by the introduction of stolen art late in the game, or because he knew the jurors were chock full of questions themselves about the discovery. She knew how it frustrated jurors when they thought the attorney failed to ask the next obvious question.

"Do you know who found the paintings?" Weymouth asked, leaning nonchalantly on the jury box rail.

"Objection. He's fishing, Your Honor. Improper cross."

"Move on, counselor. Sustained."

Frank watched and listened intently. Barbara had been playing Weymouth like a two-dollar fiddle, he thought, and he was surprised at how unnerving he found that idea. He had seen her fight cool before; she was a master at it, but this was more than just that. She was implacable and almost cold, not just cool. She had sized up Weymouth and found his weaknesses, and she was homing in on them again and again. Like now, nurturing the jury's growing resentment of his treatment of Gina, whom they had found attractive and appealing, especially after her faint apology for what Weymouth had sarcastically called another lecture. Barbara had let Weymouth go on long enough to demonstrate that he was a bully, and then Barbara had stepped in to shut him up. Was it all playback for his insinuation that she might have tampered with a witness? She had been furious, Frank knew; he had shared that fury. Later that night, he suspected, Weymouth would have a drink or two and try to reconstruct how it happened that he kept stepping in it up to his hips before he even knew it was there. But for now he was not up to any constructive thought process. He continued to pound on Gina. He was back at her days at OSU, trying to get her to admit to something that never had happened between her and Jeff. This time Barbara wasn't having it.

"Objection! Your Honor, he has asked that same question in half a dozen different ways, and she has answered it the same way each time. Isn't that the definition of insanity, doing the same thing again and again, expecting a different result?"

"I object!" Weymouth yelled. "She's resorting to ad hominem attacks! I demand an apology here and now."

Judge McNulty banged his gavel and motioned them both forward. At the sidebar he looked first at Barbara and snapped, "You will not resort to personal attacks again in this court! And as for you," he said to Weymouth, "if you have anything new to ask, I advise you to get to it. I'll not tolerate any more badgering of that young lady. Now, both of you get back to your places and let this trial continue in a civilized manner."

When they were at their tables again, Judge McNulty said, "The objection is sustained. Mr. Weymouth, proceed."

Frank let out a long breath. He had been afraid Barbara had gone too far this time, but it seemed that she was reading Judge McNulty as well as Weymouth. And her reading skills were in good order.

Weymouth didn't have anything to add to what he had already asked, and Barbara stood again.

"Ms. Valducci, you said you and your father argued a lot over the years. What kind of arguments did you have?"

"The definition of Scrabble words, sometimes the rules. Or whether I had filled the car with gas after I drove it. If it had rained on a certain day in the past. If a politician had or had not said something or other. Silly things, inconsequential things. He liked to argue, and I guess I did too. The most recent argument last year was when he offered me a job at his company and I said it was nepotism and turned it down. I didn't want to work for a corporation, and that led to another argument. He believed the future of agriculture is in chemistry and I believe that isn't sustainable, that we have to nurture the earth as we farm and not poison it."

Barbara thanked Gina, who was then dismissed. It was twelve-fifteen. Judge McNulty said court would be in lunch recess until one forty-five. Frank's phone was muted, but it was tingling, and he walked out as soon as the judge left the courtroom. When Barbara joined him a minute later, he said, "The judge is having the jury eat lunch in a dining room off the café, out of reach of the media. Good thinking. I should have thought of it for our gang."

"You'll be fine at Martin's," she said. "I don't think I'll go with you. I have to move more than Martin's place will let me. I'll hang out here and prowl the various halls and corridors. I don't think I've ever been all over this place."

Frank nodded and said, "Well, I'll be the bulldozer and get our guys through the mob out front. See you later." He gave her cheek a peck and she walked away as Gina and her guys emerged from the courtroom.

Barbara could no longer say she had not roamed throughout the courthouse. She passed the café twice and each time told herself that she had to eat something, but kept moving on. Wide corridors, narrow halls, closed doors, no admittance signs, personnel-only signs on doors, guards, other random walkers, purposeful walkers, hurrying clerks and other office workers going about their days…

She was jolted by a hand on her arm and surprised to see Frank at her side. "What?"

"Fifteen minutes left," he said. He propelled her along toward the café and through the doorway to a table, where he placed a wrapped sandwich down. "Eat. I'll get coffee."

She unwrapped the sandwich and took a bite, but found that she didn't want it. When Frank returned with coffee, she welcomed that.

"Scuttlebutt," he said, moving the sandwich to the side. "They hauled Tilsen back and he's being processed. A real arrest and all the works. McNulty isn't playing around with him. He's sore, I reckon, and means to throw the book. It also seems that Tilsen had a boarding pass on a flight to Chicago this evening. Bad moves. Really bad moves. Contempt of court big time."

"Good," she said in satisfaction.

She finished the coffee, found a restroom, and washed her face and applied new lipstick, and was ready to face McNulty, Weymouth, and Donald Tilsen. Her earlier fatigue was forgotten.

Court proceedings did not commence immediately, however. She and Weymouth were called to chambers first.

"Miss Holloway," the judge said, "Mr. Tilsen will be delayed a few minutes. Meanwhile, we have some procedural matters to consider. How many more witnesses do you intend to call?"

"Depending on what I get from Mr. Tilsen, perhaps no one else," she said. "Or perhaps a character witness or two. Nothing of great length."

"Good. Mr. Weymouth and Miss Holloway, I want your closing statements in the morning. Be prepared to give them before noon. No multi-hour monologues, I warn you. I shall be brief in my instructions to the jury. There are not that many points to cover and they should not take long. I want the jury to have this case immediately after the luncheon break."

Weymouth half rose from his chair. "Judge," he said. McNulty turned a cold, nearly malevolent gaze toward him, and he subsided. "Nothing," he muttered. "I'll be prepared."

"Miss Holloway, when court is again in order, call Mr. Tilsen, as you planned earlier. That is all. You may both go."

Barbara and Weymouth walked out side by side, not speaking a word to each other. At her table, she turned to tell Frank about the meeting. "Tonight, up for closing statement?"

"You know I am," he said. She always tried out her closing statements on him, exactly the way he had always tried his out on her mother. It might be a late night, but one he would not have given up for anything he could think of.

It was a wait of another ten minutes before the jury filed in, and finally Judge McNulty took his seat. He nodded to Barbara and she rose and called on Donald Tilsen.

Barbara watched Tilsen enter the courtroom and walk toward the front section, closely followed by a tall, broad man in a suit. Another man sitting in an aisle seat rose and left and the tall man took his place. Tilsen passed through the swinging gate and went directly to the witness stand. He did not look at Barbara, or the jury, or anywhere else as far as she could tell. His gaze was straight ahead.

When he was seated, Judge McNulty said, "Mr. Tilsen, you are still under oath. Proceed, Counselor."

Barbara watched Tilsen squirm, the way he had done earlier, as if he had trouble finding a comfortable fit for his bony bottom. He was stiff and awkward, and his strange straight-ahead gaze was disconcerting. He looked like a sleep walker, or a hypnotic subject who had no awareness of his surroundings.

"Mr. Tilsen," she started, speaking crisply, "when you and Mr. Valducci plus two associates first arrived in Oregon in your pursuit of a farm to purchase, did you arrive by a company-owned jet?"

His gaze did not shift to her. An infinity point seemed to hold his fascination. "Yes," he said.

"Was the date you arrived in Oregon February 17?"

"I think so. About then."

"Did you lease a house for three months, and a car for three months?"

His yes answer was flat; his gaze still on something beyond the courtroom.

"When you explore various areas with the plan to buy a plot of farming land, do you do a diligent search for land values, fair market prices?"

"Yes."

"Did you do such a search for the value of the Valducci farm?"

"Yes."

"Did you approve of the offer Mr. Robert Valducci made to his mother on February 19?"

"Yes."

"The offer was made two days after you arrived in Oregon. When did you do that research, Mr. Tilsen?"

"Mr. Valducci had already done the necessary research."

"Was the offer he made significantly higher than the research revealed the market price to be in this area?"

He shifted his position as if the chair was becoming more and more uncomfortable. "It was a fair offer in my opinion."

"Mr. Tilsen, did you and Mr. Robert Valducci come to Oregon with every intention of buying his mother's farm? Was that the plan from the start?"

"We had discussed it," he said after a pause. "I had to inspect it personally, but I had Robert's assurance that the land was worth the price we were offering."

"Are your superiors aware that you made that same offer, or one higher, to several different people? For instance, first to Magda Valducci, then to her son Robert Valducci, to Debra Valducci, and finally to Gina Valducci?"

"I have autonomy in pricing properties," he said, speaking to the air in front of him.

"After Magda Valducci rejected Robert's offer, did you investigate other properties for sale in the area?"

"I looked at several," he said after a moment.

"Did you make an offer for any other property?"

"No. None was suitable for our purposes."

"In fact, have you even considered any other properties since last February?"

He shifted in his chair again, and, although she could not see his legs, she felt certain that he was crossing and recrossing them over and over. He said no, he had not considered any other property.

"After Gina Valducci rejected your offer, why didn't you give up on acquiring the Valducci property and look into other farms that were available?"

He took several moments before he answered. "I believed that she would change her mind," he said finally.

"Did you tell her attorney that you thought she would change her mind after Jeff Cobbe was convicted of murder and sent to prison?"

"I don't remember what I said exactly."

There was a clatter behind Barbara and she turned to look. Shelley had been fumbling with the large picture from the Valducci residence. She had taken it from a big carrying case and in the process had pulled out the candelabra in a plastic evidence bag. It had fallen to the floor. She looked embarrassed and hastily picked up the candelabra and stuffed it back into the case. She mouthed a "Sorry," and folded her hands on the tabletop. The framed picture was now leaning against the side of the table, the case beside it.

Barbara turned again to Tilsen. His posture had changed; he was leaning forward, his eyes focused and narrowed, staring at the framed picture and the carrying case that held the candelabra.

"Mr. Tilsen," she said, "you were present when Ms. Chadwick made an appraisal of the Valducci residence, were you not?"

"Yes," he said after a moment or two.

"You heard her plans for the disposal of the furnishings of the residence, the auctions, estate sales, and so on. Is that correct?"

"Yes."

"Was it the understanding between you and Robert Valducci that the sales would commence as soon as the appraisal was complete?"

His hesitation was perceptibly longer before he said yes.

"Was it also the plan for the property to be vacated entirely and the key given to Mrs. Chadwick in order for her to conduct the various auctions and sales?"

He said yes again and she pressed on. "Were you also in the house on the morning of Saturday, March 7?"

"Yes. Robert and I had much to discuss."

"Did you answer the landline telephone that morning at eleven o'clock?"

He didn't hesitate a second. "No."

"Did you leave the house soon after eleven o'clock that morning?"

"I don't know what time I left. I wasn't paying much attention to the clock."

"On that same day, Saturday, March 7, did you take a candelabra to the place of business of Chadwick and Harris on Burnside in Portland?"

She could almost see the wheels spinning in his head. He must not have expected such a direct frontal attack and was unprepared for it. Had he left a partial print on the candlestick, a drop of sweat, a hair, fiber, anything a forensics team could connect to him? Had someone seen him entering with the candelabra? He didn't think so, but could he be certain? How much did they know, guess, assume? He fidgeted, recrossed his legs, then found that infinity spot to focus his eyes on.

"I am invoking my constitutional right granted under the Fifth Amendment to remain silent and refuse to answer the question."

There was complete silence in the courtroom for a second or two, not a bustle, not a whisper, nothing, until two men in the back jumped up and hurried out, and then, as if on cue, there seemed to be a collective sigh, an exhaled breath, and a murmur like a gentle tide filled the air. Judge McNulty tapped his gavel and the soft noise subsided.

"Mr. Tilsen, did you ever look up stolen art files on the Internet?"

Again, he hesitated for a second or two, then said, "I am invoking my constitutional right granted under the Fifth Amendment to remain silent and refuse to answer the question."

Barbara could guess what was going through his mind: He knew they could seize his laptop, flash drives, hard drive, computer, and find out. Possibly they had already seized the laptop when they arrested him and brought him to court. He had probably deleted any search results, but he also knew that deleted files could be found.

Barbara gazed at Tilsen a moment, then asked, "At various times when you were alone in the Valducci residence or had a few minutes out of sight of others, did you take the opportunity to examine pictures on the walls throughout the house?"

Again she watched his struggle with the problem of not being certain he had not left evidence that could tie him to the pictures. He was now looking at the painting leaning against the defense table. After a prolonged silence, Barbara said, "Mr. Tilsen, would you like me to repeat the question?"

"No. I am invoking my constitutional right granted by the Fifth Amendment to remain silent and refuse to answer the question."

Okay by me, Barbara thought, prepared to ask a great many questions that would evoke the same answer. To her surprise, Tilsen turned toward the judge and said, "Your Honor, this is a witch hunt! It's a blatant vicious attempt at entrapment! I refuse to answer any further questions until I have had the opportunity to consult with my attorney. I plead the Fifth Amendment to any and all questions until such a time."

Your call, Judge, Barbara thought and waited for his response. He was furious with the twist this case had taken, the delay it threatened, and with both attorneys for complicating a simple case beyond reason. Now he could allow Barbara to continue to ask questions, let the jury hear them all and speculate about why Tilsen refused to answer, or he could stop all questioning immediately. He glared at Barbara, angry that she had put him in the position of having to make a choice between bad and worse, and at Tilsen for running out, and now for taking the Fifth. At last, after what seemed a very long time, he nodded.

"That is your right, Mr. Tilsen. However, you are in contempt of court for failing to appear when called, and for attempting to leave the county when you were still sworn in as a witness in this trial. You will be presented with an invoice of the costs the state, the county, and the city have incurred and will incur as a result of your ill-advised action. Accordingly, you will be remanded to the county jail until such an invoice is presented to this court. There will be no bail or appeal since you have demonstrated a willingness to disregard the orders of this court and flee." He tapped his gavel as if to signify that no further word was permissible. "At this time the court will be in recess."

"Your honor, I object to this treatment!" Tilsen cried, jumping up from his chair. "I forgot I was to be recalled. It was a lapse of memory, not a deliberate attempt to flee."

Judge McNulty didn't even glance at him. He nodded to the tall man who had escorted Tilsen to court, then rose and left the bench as that man strode forward to escort Tilsen out of the courtroom, this time with his hand on Tilsen's arm.

Barbara knew that if it was to be a short recess, Jeff would be allowed to remain in his seat; if it was to be a long recess, he would be taken to the holding room. As the court erupted in tumult as soon as the jury was hurried out, she watched for Jeff's guards. Weymouth rushed out with his assistant, both of them on their cell phones.

"Listen up," she said to Jeff. "I'll come speak with you as soon as possible, but for now, we go with the flow. They're coming for you. Remember, this is just one more hurdle to jump."

"It's Kabuki theater," he said. "The judge is sore because his wife ran away with the mailman. Weymouth just wants another notch on his gun. Half the jury is stupefied with boredom, and the other half is salivating over a fortune in lost art. And the media is mad with story-lust to break the monotony of day-by-day nothingness."

His guards reached his side, and he rose and left with them without another word.

That settled it, Barbara decided, watching them leave. Others in the courtroom were busy texting, talking on their cell phones, talking to each other. For a minute or two she had considered putting Jeff on the stand, in spite of her previous reluctance, thinking that he must realize the jury really wanted to hear him talk, to listen to his side of the story. And his side was fine, good as gold, but he was its worst messenger.

"The judge is probably educating the jury about the meaning of taking the Fifth," Frank was explaining to Gina. "Not necessarily a confession of guilt, but rather a cautious approach to self-preservation, not knowing what questions are to come once you start down that avenue. And he probably wants to dictate to his clerk his orders regarding Tilsen's incarceration. Make it official, more than just his oral decision. It has to be something on paper to hand over to the attorneys Tilsen will produce in due time, and to hand out to the media. It's going to take a little time."

He rose and stretched. "As for me, time to take a little walk. You folks can go get something to drink in the café, if you're so inclined, or just to move a little bit. Moving's good."

He would find out what was going on, Barbara knew. He had so many acquaintances, friends, allies, he was always able to hear what was going on, and she doubted that many of the people he gathered information from realized that he was like a honey bee gathering pollen. Did the flower know what was happening? She shook her head and stood.

"I'm going to get a walk in," she said. "Don't worry about missing anything. When the judge is ready to restart the circus, the bailiff will get out the word. They won't start without us."

She left them in a huddle, paid no attention to a few others who tried to speak to her, to ask her a question, and strode out to the corridor where clusters of people were gathered, all talking to one another or on their cells.

Kabuki theater, she kept thinking, hearing the words in her head. A ritual, a farce, fake trial, fake everything meant only to impress. A Kafka trial? She shook her head hard and walked faster. Weymouth had a shitty case, and he knew it but was making the most of it. And she had an even shittier defense, and she knew it. No I didn't, was not a good defense. There was no good defense in such a circumstantial case. If the stolen art had not turned up, had not upended everything, it would have been a coin toss about guilty or innocent. It still could be that if he convinced the jurors that the art was a separate issue, that Chadwick was a separate issue. It could well be a coin toss.

She still had Dr. Tideman, the Oregon State expert, Jeff's mentor, instructor, advisor, and friend who would testify as to Jeff's honesty, integrity, strength and honor of his purpose, his future role in ameliorating the coming problem with food supply… Character witness, she added to herself. And there was Mike Krusich, Valducci's general manager, who would happily testify about Jeff's work ethic and his meticulous care in tending to his plants… Another character witness.

She walked and walked until Gregory caught up with her and said they were going back into the courtroom. She thanked him and looked about to see where she was and how to get to where she belonged again, and they made their way back to the courtroom that was fast filling with spectators. Full house, she thought, elbowing her way to the defense table.

As the jury was filing in, Frank touched her shoulder. He leaned in closer and whispered, "They're running a DNA on him."

That clinched her decision. Judge McNulty took his seat and tapped his gavel lightly, looked at Barbara, and said, "Proceed, Counselor."

She rose. "The defense rests, Your Honor."

The tide of general noise rose; the judge banged his gavel, hard this time, and he began to instruct the jury about not talking about the case, not watching television or any electronic device regarding the case.

Afterward Barbara had few coherent memories of the next several hours. She knew that, with Frank leading, the group had made its way through the mob of reporters, other media people with recorders and cameras, out to the SUV driven by Bailey. Frank made his way through a crowd like that the same way he walked through the cats at home, straight ahead without a glance to see if the path was clear. And the path always cleared before him. They had driven to Frank's house where she had gone inside and to his office to start work on her closing statement. She knew that Frank had foreseen, or had been tipped off, that Portland forensic detectives would show up at Gina's house with a warrant to inspect various pictures on the walls, and that they had departed with two pictures. Frank had stayed long enough to get a receipt for them. Portland had reopened Chadwick's murder case. She had eaten, but she couldn't remember what. Some time that evening Darren had called and, laughing, had said she had made national news with stolen art heist stories. She remembered distinctly the sound of his voice when he said in a different tone altogether that Todd would fly in late Saturday night or Sunday, and that Todd had sounded dead tired and depressed. There had been a fatality in his group of scientists.

She had tried out her closing statement on Frank, had tinkered a little with it, and at one in the morning Frank had driven her home.

And now it was Friday and she was in court again, and this was the end game.

She focused on what Weymouth was saying.

"A desperate man, a mountain of debt, over fifty thousand dollars of debt, and a young woman who lived with her grandmother who could deny her nothing, and who owned a very valuable piece of property that would suit his purposes exactly. Everything was going well for him, but then Robert Valducci appeared. And the doting grandmother suffered a fatal accident. Suddenly the farm was at risk, his future was at risk…

"On the night of the murder Gina Valducci left at eight, and he had to stick around until nine and not draw attention by leaving earlier than he had been doing. He had an hour to carry out his plan. In that hour he shot and killed Robert Valducci, turned off the thermostat and left the French doors wide open to cool down the house and make the time of death uncertain by chilling the body of his victim. He even thought to move that dead body twice in order to confuse the time of death, hoping it would appear that Robert Valducci had been shot while he, the defendant, was still working with Gina Valducci in the greenhouse. And for a while it worked, ladies and gentlemen."

He talked briefly about the dispute over the will and the decision of probate court.

"It seemed to be settled then. Gina Valducci was the heir, and he had free rein to carry out his plans and write his dissertation, get his doctorate, with no more problems. Within days of that court decision the Valducci

Corporation was formed, and the defendant was named vice president. A farm worth millions is the only asset of the corporation, and he is second in command. But Mrs. Debra Valducci threatened to go to a higher court to get the probate decision overturned. Whether she would be successful, he had no way of knowing, but it was a threat and it had to be dealt with."

He used Debra's testimony to make the case about the telephone call she received, and the shots fired at her. "As soon as he was alone that night, he placed that call, and he waited in ambush for her. And he tried to kill her. We found the gun, ladies and gentlemen, outside his apartment hidden in shrubbery. Ballistics proved it was the same gun that was used to shoot and kill Robert Valducci."

He turned to give Jeff a long, hard stare, shook his head, and faced the jury again. "That is the state's case, ladies and gentlemen. But the defense counsel has chosen to enter an extraneous matter into it, a distraction, in an attempt to bring confusion and disarray into a simple murder trial. All we know or can know at this time is that a call was placed to the landline telephone in the Valducci residence. We don't know and can't know who took that call. It could well have been Mr. Valducci, responding to a benign question of Mrs. Chadwick's, something on the order of did he want separate appraisals for the several items Gina Valducci had indicated that she wanted. It could have been something else, but the fact remains that we don't know the content of that call. Mr. Tilsen testified under oath that he did not answer the telephone that morning.

"We don't know at this time if the artwork that was examined by Mr. Alterman is indeed the same art that was stolen decades ago. As he testified, his opinion is not enough to confirm the legitimacy of the paintings. That will require laboratory specialists, and it will take weeks or even months to determine.

"We know nothing about the death of Mrs. Chadwick, and her only connection to this case is the fact that she was a businesswoman who had been commissioned to do an appraisal of the Valducci residence. It is tragic and regrettable, but it is a fact that innocent people do get assaulted, sometimes killed, during a burglary. And it is a fact that electronic devices of all kinds have a street value. But that has nothing to do with the trial we are hearing."

He added little or nothing that was new, and in his wrap-up he returned to the points he had made earlier about motive and opportunity.

"No one else was around at that time of night," he said. "Robert Valducci was alone in the house, and the defendant was alone in the greenhouse from eight o'clock on. He had the opportunity. The night shots were fired at Mrs. Valducci, the defendant again was alone, unobserved, and again, no one else was around except her daughter who was taking a bath. Again, opportunity and motive. No one else could have hidden the gun in the shrubbery at his apartment. No stranger could have known about the dispute between mother and daughter, no stranger could have known where the defendant lived. Robert Valducci would not have admitted a stranger to his house. Mrs. Valducci would have not agreed to a stranger's request for a meeting at night."

When he finished and sat down, it was 10:40. He had talked for an hour and forty minutes. Judge McNulty called for a short recess, and this time no guards came to collect Jeff. He looked depressed, almost defeated, the way he had started the week. Barbara patted his arm. "Believe me, Jeff, I'll undo a lot of that."

"You'd better," he said. "As of now, if I were on the jury, I'd probably vote guilty."

"Darkest hour, sunrise, you know the saying," she said. "Just don't look so hangdog when they come filing back in. At least give it a try," she added. "Imagine them all naked."

He grinned. "You know I won't be able to get that out of my head, don't you?"

She laughed.

"The trial we are deciding here is one of a circumstantial case, ladies and gentlemen," Barbara said, standing near the jury box. "That has a meaning in law. It is a case where there is no direct, factual evidence linking the accused to the crime. There is no eyewitness, no fingerprints on a weapon, no DNA evidence, no fiber evidence—in short, nothing concrete points to the accused. It is a case where the state tries to find a narrative that uses evidence and facts to reach a possible explanation. It is the defense attorney's job to examine that narrative minutely, to determine if there are facts brushed aside because they don't fit the narrative put forth by the prosecutor, and possibly point to a different narrative that is equally plausible, or sometimes more plausible than the state's. And it is the defense attorney's job to indicate where the facts as presented by the prosecutor point to more than one possible explanation, or in some cases to no explanation. And it happens now and then that the defense attorney may present facts or evidence that the prosecutor chose to ignore, or perhaps never even grasped.

"Starting with the night that Robert Valducci was murdered, the state claims that no one was in the area at the time of the shooting except Jeff Cobbe. There are several problems with that contention. First, the time of death was not determined exactly. Gina Valducci last saw her father alive at six o'clock, and his body was found at nine o'clock. The medical examiner put the time of death between six and eight-thirty, a two and one-half hour period. We know from testimony that Jeff Cobbe was with Gina Valducci until she left at a few minutes after eight. We know from testimony that Mr.

Tilsen said he heard running footsteps on the wooden floor of the porch when he went around the house to find an open door at a minute or two after nine o'clock. We don't know who was running, and it couldn't have been Jeff because his rubber-soled boots would not have made that sound. Mr. Tilsen also testified that he saw a light-colored car parked in front of the store that night. We don't know whose car that was, when it was parked there, or when it left.

"Although the prosecutor stated as fact that no one else was on the premises that night, we don't know that. Two deputies went to see who was in the lighted greenhouse where they found Jeff Cobbe. They did not search a single building or greenhouse. Those were not vast empty spaces. There were benches of plant starts, thousands of starts of all sizes; there were plants in tubs, shrubs and trees; there were stacks of pots, hand tools, grocery carts, and farm machinery in some of those buildings, plows, trucks, other equipment. Imagine how much you could see in your own home at night if you stood in the doorway with only a flashlight to illuminate the interior of the dark house. That's what they did. They did not walk out to the truck access road. Some of the outbuildings were locked, and we do not know if they were locked from the inside. The officers didn't even look in the garage. So it can't be stated as a fact that no one else was around that night. The most that can be said is that the investigators did not see anyone other than Jeff Cobbe.

"The prosecutor said that preventing the sale of the farm, and manipulating Gina Valducci to allow Jeff to pursue his plan was a possible motive for the murder, but it is no more than a narrative in an effort to explain some of the facts. Before Gina Valducci earned her master's degree, she was offered a job with her father's company, a lucrative job, starting high up on the ladder instead of the first rung. She rejected it. She is the fourth generation of the Valducci family to own and farm that piece of ground, and she wanted to keep it that way. She already knew what she wanted to do before she and Jeff Cobbe discovered a mutual cause; a dream is how she put it. Make a good piece of land better and provide healthy, pesticide-free food for the local community. Jeff didn't have to talk her into it.

"Knowing they would have to vacate the greenhouse as Robert Valducci's deal to sell the farm progressed, Jeff already had made plans to set out tomatoes on several different farms. He had earned the trust and approval of neighboring farmers. It was important to see one hundred plants through to fruiting, and he was busy arranging that. As Gina stated, their tomatoes ripened sixteen days earlier than usual. They proved their point."

She walked slowly from the end of the jury box to the other end, back, keeping her focus on the jury members, speaking almost conversationally, holding their attention.

"When Gina was asked why they formed the corporation, she said it was to make certain that her plan would go forward if something happened to her. She had seen her beloved grandmother die in a tragic accident, and she had seen her father alive at six and dead before nine. She realized how an instant in time could change not just lives, but also plans.

"Robert Valducci was murdered before a second, more recent will was found, and under the old, invalid will Robert was heir to the estate, and according to his will his widow was his heir. No one knew about the new will at the time of his death. It would have made no sense to murder him in order to keep the farm, because Mrs. Valducci was even more eager to sell it than he had been."

She stopped moving at the center of the rail, then spread her hands palm up at her sides, shaking her head.

"What we are left with, ladies and gentlemen, is one single fact: Jeff Cobbe was working about a quarter mile away from the house where Robert Valducci was murdered. There has been no testimony, no evidence to support more than that one fact."

She started her deliberate pacing up and down the rail again. "There was no motive for Jeff to kill Mr. Valducci. Gina inherited nothing from her father, and her mother, who did inherit his estate, was eager to sell the property. We also don't know if there was anyone else around the property that night. We don't know whose footsteps Mr. Tilsen heard. We don't know whose car was parked in front of the store. We don't know who turned down the thermostat or why. Robert Valducci was in shirt sleeves at six that night, and he was still in shirt sleeves when his body was found at nine o'clock, but someone turned off the heat. The fact that the house had become so cold that the temperature was 56 degrees when the medical examiner arrived suggests that the heat had been turned off for several hours, but we don't know for how long because no attempt was made to determine that. We do know that Gina Valducci turned the heat on after ten o'clock. It must have been colder than 56 degrees before that. It could have been turned off before eight-thirty, before seven-thirty, even earlier, possibly six-thirty. It is possible to assume that the heat was turned off by the killer to confuse the time of death, but we don't know that as a fact. We do know that Jeff Cobbe's fingerprints were not found in the house."

She paused her slow pace back and forth before the jury box, then shrugged and said, "Now let's move to the night that someone fired shots and hit the car Mrs. Valducci was driving."

This time when she began to speak, she moved to stand closer to the defense table, and she talked a little faster, less conversationally, more as a lecturer.

"I'll go over the facts that we have, starting with Gina Valducci's testimony that she left Jeff in the greenhouse at nine o'clock that night, and that five minutes later she saw that the greenhouse lights had gone off. At about ten minutes after nine, Mrs. Valducci received a telephone call in her hotel room. The call was placed to the hotel line, not her cell phone. She said a whispery voice claimed to be Jeff Cobbe and that he and Gina wanted a meeting with her to settle a dispute."

Barbara looked over the jurors, who were all following her closely. "Mrs. Valducci did not recognize the voice, and when she was asked if there was anything about it that she could recall, she said no. Just a whispery voice, as if he didn't want to be overheard. Two people have testified that Jeff has a southern accent, and he corrected them both and said it was a Virginia accent." She smiled slightly and added, "Maybe to us here in the northwest, Virginia and southern accent is one and the same thing. But however that goes, it is a noticeable accent that draws attention. You heard that Virginia accent when Eric Ballantine read the deposition responses of Major Farleigh. Mrs. Valducci did not hear it. And if the caller had been Jeff, why was he whispering, since he was alone after Gina left the greenhouse? No such call was recorded on his cell phone, and the hotel doesn't keep a record of incoming calls. So there is a problem with that phone call. The problem is that we know only this: Mrs. Valducci received a phone call, a whispery voice said he was Jeff Cobbe, and he asked her to go to the Valducci residence."

She shook her head. "Ladies and gentlemen, I could call anyone and claim to be Queen Elizabeth, but that does not make it so."

She set up the easel with the overhead shot of the scene at Green Briar Road. Pointing to it she said, "This is where the shooter waited for Mrs. Valducci. Concealed by shrubbery, in wet bark mulch, he waited until she turned off River Road, and then he stepped out closer to Green Briar Road.

The trampled bark mulch tells the story of his wait and his final position." She retrieved her little car and the dowel that went through the window, grazed the opposite window frame and stopped. "We know where this bullet was fired from, straight from his position on the side of the road. What is strange, however, is the fact that the car had almost cleared this area. The bullet hit the rear window. The car swerved and ran off the road. The question is why the shooter waited until the car was almost past him to fire. And why he kept firing in the same direction. Three more bullets were recovered in the field here, almost in the exact line of fire as the first bullet that hit the car." She pointed to the spots marked on the map. "Why didn't he aim at the car when it swerved and came to a stop? Why didn't the shooter cross the road and shoot Mrs. Valducci as she lay across the seat? If he shot Mr. Valducci in cold blood from two feet away, why not do the same to her?"

She removed the car and set up the street map of the Jefferson Street apartment, the alley behind the apartment house where Jeff had lived, and the apartment of Kay Saltzman. "On that night, we heard testimony from Ms. Saltzman stating that she and her friend left the Bijou theater at about nine-fifteen to walk to her apartment on Jefferson. That would have taken ten to fifteen minutes, but they detoured and continued to the New Frontier Market, another ten to fifteen minutes. They spent up to ten minutes in the grocery store, then continued to her apartment, arriving there at about ten o'clock. That was forty-five minutes from the time they left the theater until they entered her apartment." She was pointing to the various places she mentioned as she talked. "While her friend opened the door, she stood on the front walk and she saw a man on the other side of the street about half a block away. He was dressed, she stated, in a coat and hat. He walked to the hedge at the front of the apartment building here, stooped as if putting something down, then turned and walked back the way he had come. She saw no more than that."

Barbara faced the jurors again and held up her hand. "There are several important bits of information in that statement, ladies and gentlemen. It was ten o'clock when she saw the man put something in the hedge. He was dressed in a coat and hat not a poncho, which offers a different silhouette—a walking tent is how the sheriff described it. Jeff Cobbe had no overcoat or raincoat and no hat. He had a poncho. The gun was not hidden, not covered with soil or dirt. It was simply lying there, as you saw in the photographs. No attempt had been made to hide it."

She now pointed to the back of the house where Jeff had rented an apartment. “Here is the rear of the house,” she said, “and the garage where Mrs. Whorley parked her car. That night she arrived home from a birthday party at nine-thirty. She could see the lights in Jeff’s apartment. When she started to wash a few dishes, the water pressure was low, which meant that he was taking a shower. Many of us have faced that dilemma, ladies and gentlemen. The change in water pressure when an appliance is started, a dishwasher, washing machine, even the flushing of a toilet, if a shower is being used. She knew her own plumbing problems and knew the cause. He was taking a shower. In a few minutes the pressure was restored, and his lights went out. She said she assumed he had gone to bed. From nine-thirty until ten o’clock, she had time to change her clothes, wash some dishes, have a bit of birthday cake, and make tea before a particular television show came on. She was certain of the time she arrived home, what she had time to do between then and when her television show came on at ten. She was sure that he was in his apartment already when she got home.”

She pointed again to the map, this time to the house across the alley. “And here Mr. and Mrs. Paceck had watched television until ten o’clock. He went upstairs and he happened to look out the back window. He saw a black sedan parked in the alley blocking his exit from his garage. He decided to call the police to have the car towed away. He had to leave to get his cell phone, but when he returned to the window, the car was moving away down the alley and he did nothing about it. That was a minute or two after ten o’clock.”

Barbara moved away from the easel, and Shelley rose and removed the map and returned it to the evidence table. Barbara walked the length of the jury box waiting until Shelley was done. Then she said, “All I have said about that night, ladies and gentlemen, is supported by statements of witnesses; it is all factual. I asked several questions as I outlined the events of that night.

“Now I want to propose some possible answers, starting with the time Gina saw the light from the greenhouse go out, five minutes after nine. If Jeff left at that time, he would have been home before nine-thirty, time to remove his wet poncho, his boots, other damp clothing, and be in the shower. Minutes later he would have been in bed. Remember, he and the others in his group had been working twelve to fourteen hours a day, and that night was particularly nasty with intermittent light rain, mist, and fog. He would have been cold and tired.

"The arresting officers did not find any traces of bark mulch on his boots or in his car. His other two pairs of shoes had no bark mulch. Anyone who walks in wet bark mulch knows how it clings. He had no record of the call on his cell phone. His fingerprints were not on the gun. He did not have a coat and hat. And the gun was not hidden; it was simply placed in the hedge where anyone passing might have seen it."

She paused, then continued, again in the conversational tone she had used earlier. "As for the call that Mrs. Valducci received, why was the speaker's voice whispery? I suggest, ladies and gentlemen, that it was to disguise that voice. She had never spoken with Jeff; she would not have recognized his voice, and in fact she didn't notice an accent. But it was a voice she possibly would have recognized if he had spoken in a normal way.

"Why didn't the shooter cross the road and finish the job if his intention was to kill her? I suggest that he had no intention of killing her, or that he was indifferent about the matter and simply didn't care if he killed her or not. According to Jeff's instructor at a military academy, Jeff excelled in all matters dealing with firearms; he was a crack shot with handguns and long guns, using both stationary and moving targets, so good that he had been invited to join an elite upper-classmate shooters club, which he declined. He stated that he would never touch a gun again. A crack shooter could have hit Mrs. Valducci from across the road; any shooter could have crossed the road to shoot her at close range.

"I suggest that murder was not the intent of the shooter that night. Having recoverable bullets that could be traced to the gun that was used to murder Robert Valducci was the sole intent of that incident. And planting the gun where it was sure to be seen was the second act of that particular scenario." She paused again, frowning, then shook her head and continued.

"Whoever was the shooter, if he left the scene as soon as the shots were fired, he would have arrived back in town, back to Jeff's apartment building by ten o'clock. And that's when Ms. Saltzman saw him, and when Mr. Paceck saw the car parked in the alley."

She glanced at Jeff who looked frozen in his seat. She hoped he was breathing. Facing the jurors again, she said, "The prosecutor said that the motive for Jeff was that he perceived a threat from Mrs. Valducci regarding the farm. That is at best a mistake, and at worst a narrative twist that will not stand examination. Mrs. Valducci had contested the will, and probate court had decided the matter in favor of her daughter Gina. That matter was settled. Done. Mrs. Valducci does not like that decision, and she may rail about it, but it is a fact. She posed no threat then, and poses no threat now about ownership of the farm, and Jeff, Gina, everyone else knows that."

She walked to her table and stood by it with her arms folded across her chest for a moment, then said with a slight smile, "There are many ways we teach children numbers. Remember? 'Red fish, blue fish. One fish, two fish.' Other rhymes: 'One two, buckle your shoe. Three, four, shut the door.' Learning numbers and how to use them is a very complex matter, ladies and gentlemen. From simple nursery rhymes and songs, a child has to progress to understand sequence. You aren't born knowing that seven follows six, or that ten comes before eleven. One way or another the lessons are learned, and one of the ways that seems to delight children is by connecting dots, a few dots on a page, each numbered. The child has to draw a line from one to two, on to three, and so on, until as if by magic a box appears on the paper. As the child becomes more proficient, more dots are added until a complex picture is the result.

"When this is done correctly, the child is learning sequence, and abstraction, although neither word will appear on the paper. The dots alone mean nothing, just random dots, and if the sequential system of numbering is not followed, connecting multiple dots randomly will not result in anything identifiable. It will be an incoherent scribble, chaos. The rule is that meaningful dots on a given page must be connected, even if it violates a prematurely assumed outcome."

She stopped again, this time for a longer pause as she gazed at the jurors. Some of them obviously had had more than enough of dots and abstractions. Time to move on.

"We can't simply brush aside any facts that we can't account for in a given scenario as a distraction. There are too many unconnected facts left on this page. There are no real lines connecting Jeff in the greenhouse to the death of Mr. Valducci. And there are no real lines connecting him to that phone call and that found gun. Artificial lines are tenuous and fall apart under examination, and the result is chaos. We have to examine some of the other facts remaining unaccounted for. Mrs. Mildred Chadwick is unaccounted for and she is not a distraction.

"What we know about Mrs. Chadwick is that she spent several hours in the Valducci residence on Wednesday making a video for an appraisal. We know that she said the routine she and her partner used to dispose of the contents for closing out an estate was to have fine-used-furniture dealers come in first, go on down the line to other used furniture dealers, an open estate sale, and a final donation to a charity. During this time the house would be empty and she would have the keys. She also said that her company would post a night watchman to prevent vandalism. We know that she showed a great deal of interest in a unique mirror with an ivory frame. She said it would take some research to evaluate it. We know that she spoke with her partner, Ms. Harris, on Saturday following her visit to the residence, and that she was excited. Her excitement would not have been about closing an estate; that was her business, routine for her. Something else had excited her. We know that Mrs. Chadwick placed a call to the landline of the Valducci residence at eleven o'clock on Saturday, and that she spoke with someone for two minutes. We know that she was killed that Saturday night, and all her electronic devices were stolen, but forty-four dollars in cash was still in her purse. Not a note or memorandum, not a trace of evidence about her visit to the Valducci residence was found after her death. Two months later her telephone bill revealed the call to the Valducci residence. And that's all we know about Mildred Chadwick."

She stopped by her table for a sip of water, and then, standing by it, she said, "Now let's examine some of the facts regarding another important person in this case, Mr. Ronald Tilsen."

"Objection," Weymouth called out.

"On what grounds?" the judge asked.

"Counselor is muddying the entire case with extraneous material, casting aspersions on people not connected to it, implying conspiracies even, all in an attempt to totally confuse the jury."

"I don't believe stating the facts in the case can in itself be confusing. I'm simply arranging facts in an orderly fashion since that was not done originally when they were presented," Barbara said mildly, as if bewildered by the accusation.

"Stick to the facts, counselor," Judge McNulty said. "Overruled."

"Back to Mr. Tilsen," Barbara said. "He and Robert Valducci and two other associates arrived by means of a company plane in late February. Mr. Tilsen leased a house and a car for three months in Portland. He and Mr. Valducci came down to Eugene, where Mr. Valducci moved into his mother's house for a short stay, and Mr. Tilsen rented a suite at the Valley River Inn. The day after they arrived in Eugene, Mr. Valducci, with Mr. Tilsen's approval, made an offer to buy his mother's farm, quoting a price significantly above its market value. Mr. Tilsen testified that it had not been predetermined to buy the property on arrival. Ostensibly he and the two associates in Portland were on a scouting trip to find a satisfactory property for his company's purposes. However, the offer was made before Mr. Tilsen had the opportunity to look over the property, to pass judgment on it, or for anyone even to research land values in this area. If he and Mr. Valducci had an arrangement about the price, we don't know what it was. Mrs. Magda Valducci rejected the offer.

"After the funeral of Robert Valducci's mother, Mr. Tilsen was on the scene. He was present the day Mrs. Chadwick made her video. He was there when Mrs. Chadwick displayed a keen interest in the mirror with the ivory frame and said it would take research to evaluate it. That was on Wednesday. On Saturday morning he was present when Mrs. Chadwick placed a call to the Valducci landline. He and Robert Valducci were the only ones in the house at that time. One of them took the call. He left for Portland that day. He stated that he went back to Portland to write a memorandum of agreement regarding the purchase of the property. He could not give a good reason why he had not done that earlier, in the past weeks when it was assumed that Robert Valducci owned the property."

She paused again, this time regarding the jurors soberly. They were still engaged, still attentive. "Mr. Tilsen stated that he returned to Eugene on Sunday, March 8, and that he registered at the Valley River Inn at eight-twenty. At nine o'clock he drove into the driveway of the Valducci house right behind Mrs. Valducci, and he entered and discovered the body of Robert Valducci.

"The next information we have regarding Mr. Tilsen's movements was provided by Mrs. Valducci. She stated that when she went to Chicago to take care of her late husband's affairs, Mr. Tilsen was attentive and very helpful. He also made the same offer to buy the property that he had proposed before, above market price, and with an added incentive. He added one hundred thousand dollars to the purchase price, ladies and gentlemen. Mrs. Valducci said it was to cover the liquidation of all the furnishings, everything so that she would not have to bother with the appraisal, the dealers, the estate sale, and so on. All she had to do was receive a check and walk away, he would take care of everything. She accepted.

"But after probate court found in favor of Gina, the sale fell through. We can ask questions about an extravagant offer that was made first to Magda Valducci through her son Robert, and we can assume that Robert Valducci and Mr. Tilsen had discussed it before it was made. But why such an extravagant offer was made again, and then again, is an open question.

"Meanwhile, little or no progress had been made in the investigation of the death of Robert Valducci. Jeff was not a prime suspect. He gave a statement as did everyone: his associates, Gina, neighbors, Mr. Tilsen, Mrs. Valducci, others. The investigators had no reason to be more suspicious of him than of anyone else.

"And then there was the strange shooting incident, the apparent ambush of Mrs. Valducci, and the subsequent arrest of Jeff Cobbe. Following that, Mr. Tilsen made his final offer to buy the property through Gina's attorney. Mr. Tilsen said he could not recall what reason he gave for persisting after being rejected."

Barbara shook her head and glanced at Gina, who seemed as paralyzed as Jeff. She regarded the jurors again and said, "You would think that Gina would have been terrified enough to move out of the big house, isolated as it is, and take an apartment in town. Instead, she and her associates turned the residence into the headquarters for the Valducci Corporation, where all four of them could live, save money, be safe in numbers. They bought a guard dog, and from then on no one could approach the house without permission. And that's when Mr. Tilsen made his final offer to buy the property, to no avail."

Barbara glanced at Weymouth, who was listening as intently as the jurors. She knew he was waiting for her to go beyond what had been testified to, and she had no intention of doing that. The facts speak for themselves, buster, she thought at him and turned her attention again to the jury.

"It should be noted, ladies and gentlemen, that although Mr. Tilsen and Mr. Valducci first arrived in the area in late February with the mission to acquire a farm for their company, no such purchase has been made. Now, nearly seven months later no suitable property has been bought. Mr. Tilsen said he had not made an offer on any other property." She shrugged, then added, "It's hard to believe that in seven months no farm has come on the market that meets their needs, except the Valducci farm."

She glanced over the attendees and spotted Geraldo Reyes, who looked beside himself with joy. He gave her a thumb's up and she acknowledged it with a nearly imperceptible nod. Simon Alterman was not with him. She had not expected him to be there.

Turning again to the jury, she said, "Finally we come to the issue of stolen art and Mr. Alterman." The jurors had been attentive, but there was a difference in their attitudes now, a renewed and greater show of interest, even a general movement as if they collectively were sitting up straighter, quieting their breathing. She was aware of a movement at Weymouth's table and glanced at him. He had started to rise, and was half way up when apparently he changed his mind and sank back into his chair. His expression was unreadable. She suspected he knew the judge would not sustain an objection, not stop her in the middle of the stream, not with the jury so eager to hear more. She hoped her suspicion was correct and that, furthermore, Judge McNulty knew exactly where her dots led, what picture was being revealed.

"Mr. Simon Alterman, a renowned art critic, consultant, and investigator, by happenstance came to the area a few weeks ago as an assistant to his old friend Geraldo Reyes, an award-winning photojournalist.

"While touring the Valducci residence, Mr. Alterman saw a certain unique mirror with an ivory frame. He recognized it as an item stolen along with priceless art, stolen and smuggled from Italy to the United States more than seventy years ago. He stated that anyone knowledgeable about art, about antiques, estate closings would have been able to research the mirror and follow links to the art theft story. An experienced appraiser would know how to go about the research. He gave suggestions on how to search for the art if it was actually in the house. Four paintings were found. When Mr. Alterman inspected the paintings, he stated that they are genuine, authentic, but that with such priceless art, laboratory tests would also be made to confirm his opinion. He put the floor price at an auction at one hundred million dollars for the group as a whole, or fifty million each if offered individually."

Barbara smiled slightly at the jurors, who were rapt with attention. "Mirror, mirror on the wall," she said. Then, soberly she continued. "It intrigued Mrs. Chadwick on a Wednesday. On Saturday evening she was in a state of excitement when she spoke to her partner. On Saturday morning she placed a call to the Valducci residence and had a brief conversation, two minutes, with someone. And on Saturday night she was murdered. Her house was burgled, all electronic devices were taken, but cash was left in her purse." She shook her head. "No, ladies and gentlemen, Mrs. Mildred Chadwick is not a distraction in this trial. And neither is Mr. Alterman and priceless stolen paintings."

She stood some feet away from the jury box now and addressed them as a group, focusing on one after another of them as she summed up.

"Jeff Cobbe did not murder Robert Valducci. He had nothing to gain from such a crime. He had nothing to fear from Mrs. Valducci, and he did not shoot at her car. It might even be said that he would not have shot at her if he had wanted to harm her. He would have shot her. He remains an isolated dot, a fact, a quarter of a mile away from the murder and nowhere near the shooting incident.

"The state even tried to indicate that Jeff is psychopathic. And that is ludicrous on the face of it. Jeff did not take a test to demonstrate psychopathy. He made a mockery of the test, revealing it to be pseudoscience at best.

"There are dots to be connected, facts to be linked, however. Anyone who became aware of a fortune in stolen art had a sufficient motive to do murder. No one in the Valducci family knew of such artwork hidden in their house. If Gina or her colleagues had known of such a fortune, they would not have been working fourteen-hour days to make a dream become a reality. If Robert Valducci had suspected priceless paintings were concealed in his house, he would not have contemplated having a liquidation as proposed by Mrs. Chadwick, having the house stripped to the bare walls while no family member was present. If he had learned of such a possible fortune, wouldn't he have been tearing his house apart searching for the paintings?

"As you begin your deliberations, ladies and gentlemen, the foremost question you must ask yourselves is whether the state has proved its case beyond reasonable doubt. I submit to you that the state doesn't even have a case. There is nothing factual to link Jeff Cobbe to murder and attempted murder.

"It has become a figure of speech almost: Follow the money. If you want to investigate any crime, follow the money. Who benefits, who stands to gain what? I suggest that the state failed to do that. In your deliberations ask those questions. Who might benefit, who might gain what? To make their narrative work, the state had to make a faulty connection between Jeff and Gina, and even that tenuous connection fails under scrutiny. To have a common dream is not necessarily to have a romantic relationship. Gina had nothing to gain from her father's death. When the new will came to light, it was established that her grandmother had left the property to her, to Gina. Robert Valducci would have had to accept that exactly as Mrs. Valducci has had to. No death was necessary to achieve that end.

"If in your opinion the prosecutor failed to prove beyond a reasonable doubt that Jeff Cobbe shot and killed Robert Valducci, you must find him not guilty. He is not guilty. He was an isolated fact a thousand feet away from the act of murder. Thank you for your attention."

She made a slight bow to the jurors and walked to her table. When she sat down Jeff put his hand on hers and squeezed it.

Immediately after Barbara sat down Judge McNulty called for the luncheon break recess until one o'clock, an hour and ten minutes from then.

"He'll have the bailiff escort them to the café downstairs," Barbara said to Jeff. "No time for more than that, and to keep them out of the hands of the media outside. We'll do the same thing. When we come back, he'll give his instructions to the jury, and then the hellish waiting starts."

"Barbara, whatever happens, you were great. Thanks. I don't know what I expected, but I got a lot more than whatever it was. Just thanks." His guard came to take him out.

In the café a few minutes later Barbara outlined the afternoon to the others. "We'll go back after lunch, instructions for the jury, and the waiting begins. Where we wait is problematic right now, with the media thick as flies on honey out there. We'll figure it out. The judge will tell us to be back around five-thirty or even six, unless they reach a verdict before then; if that happens we'll be called back to court. And that's how the end game is played."

At their table minutes later, Frank watched both Barbara and Gina push salad greens around on their plates and regretted that. It could be a very long afternoon and more food now might help later. His phone rang and he talked to Patsy, then motioned for Barbara to move away from the table.

"What's up?" she asked, joining him.

"Laudermilk, at the office, willing to wait for me. Can't take that crew over there."

Laudermilk was one of the best-looking men and by far the snazziest dresser she had ever known. His suits had hand-sewn buttonholes. And he was the district director of the FBI. If he was at Frank's office, she suspected that someone a grade level below him was at hers, also willing to wait. She frowned in thought, then said, "Martin's. I'll give him a call."

"And I'll mosey over to the bank and see about a private meeting room there."

It had gone exactly as Barbara had said it would. Back to court, instructions to the jurors, recess. "We'll go with them to Martin's," Barbara told Shelley. "But I won't stay. A pity you don't have your care package."

"I do have it." Shelley pointed to a tote bag. "I brought it, just in case. Just no ton of snacks, but taking pastries to Martin's would be coals to Newcastle."

She often provided some games, playing cards, even jigsaw puzzles, along with a ton of edibles to help while away the time for those waiting out the longest day.

"I'll give you a buzz when it's time to go back," Barbara said. "So, heigh ho, away we go through the madding crowd." She turned to the others. "We'll just elbow our way through, and not a word. Not a single word."

They elbowed their way through the media crowding the steps of the courthouse, yelling questions, camcorders in action, cell phones held high getting pictures, on down to the van. Bailey, behind the wheel, whizzed away, with several cars following closely. That didn't matter; Martin would keep them out of his restaurant. When they arrived, they hurried inside; Barbara kept walking through the kitchen with a wave to Binnie, and out the back door to the alley. No one was back there yet, but they would be soon.

She walked fast until she was a block away from Martin's, then slowed her pace. Not her office, not home, not Frank's… The Rose Garden, where it was peaceful, quiet, unless the humming bees counted as noise, no reporters, no family picnics, no bicycles, and within easy walking distance.

It was as peaceful as she had anticipated. She felt it was almost sinful to bring her turbulent thoughts to such a peaceful haven. The roses were spectacular, as if aware that the time for flowers was swiftly passing; the bees were extraordinarily busy, possibly with the same instinctive awareness of time, the air so heavy with fragrance it was almost narcotic. Sorry, she thought at it all. Sorry.

She sat on a bench and began to sort out her swirling mind storm. Was it time for her to quit, to take one of the teaching jobs she had been offered, to be a stay-at-home stepmother? She had to smile at that one. Todd would be off to Stanford by the end of the month, and she and Darren were not even married. But the thoughts of possible futures were there; her anger had turned into something else, something oppressive, depressing and dark. She felt like an ant trying to move a mountain a grain at a time, only to have an ill wind blow in drifts of airborne dirt that kept piling higher. Dirt, she thought, that summed it up. It was dirty. Filthy. Too much to try to deal with and remain sane. Should she just quit?

Frank was humming as he waited in a conference room at the bank. The room was relatively small, but comfortable with a long polished table, good chairs well padded, covered with dark red leather. A backroom for deals to be discussed and arbitrated in gentlemanly words that belied sharp knives. There was a large, closed art portfolio case on the table in front of Frank.

Simon Alterman was the first to arrive. He was happy, smiling. "I'm officially done with Geraldo," he said. "It seems that his regular assistant, friend, SO is due almost any minute. Geraldo is beside himself." He stopped speaking, frowned. "What the hell does that even mean? How can one be beside oneself? Language is mysterious, isn't it?" He eyed the case. "The paintings?"

"Yes."

Almost reverently Alterman touched the case. He chose a chair next to Frank's. Minutes later the bank manager ushered four other men into the room, nodded to Frank, and discreetly left again.

The tallest of the arrivals nodded to Frank and said, "Roberto Corsi, assistant to Ambassador Vecchi. Mr. Holloway?"

"I am," Frank said, extending his hand. Corsi was tall and handsome, movie-star material, thick black hair with a wave, good bones, good teeth, a public figure, figurehead?

It seemed that they knew who Alterman was, and no handshakes were necessary. He nodded to two of the newcomers and they nodded back.

"Herman Bartolli," Holding out his hand was the man Frank suspected was in charge. He was trim, his handshake a not-too-obvious test, and his dark eyes were shrewd, his face expressionless. He had more black hair than any one man needed, helmet-like, bullet-proof thick. "And this is David Angelini," he said.

Angelini was no more than five feet three inches tall, broad, and bald. He and Alterman had not simply nodded to each other, but had greeted each other as old friends with embraces and air kisses and many exclamations from Angelini in rapid Italian, which Alterman apparently had no trouble following.

"Gabriel Dalman," Bartolli said nodding toward the fourth man, who was obviously security. A big man, not quite as well dressed as the others. He had quickly surveyed the room, Frank, the case on the table, the door. He did not step forward to meet Frank and he did not offer to shake hands.

"Gentlemen," Frank said, "please forgive me for changing our meeting place. I was informed that the district director of our Federal Bureau of Investigation is in my office waiting for me. But I think for our purposes this will suffice, will it not?"

There were rapid glances and a few words in Italian exchanged among the others. "This is excellent," Bartolli said. "Excellent."

Frank nodded toward the case on the table. "Mr. Alterman, if you would be kind enough to show what I have here."

Alterman and Angelini were already drawing on white gloves. Carefully Alterman opened the case and pulled out the paintings in their separate envelopes. No one made a sound as he spread the paintings on the table until Angelini broke the silence with a gasping intake of air, followed by an explosive rush of Italian words. He swung away from the table to embrace Alterman again, speaking excitedly, almost hysterically. Both art experts produced magnifying glasses from their pockets, and bent over the paintings, talking to each other in Italian, touching each other to point out something. Bartolli watched them for a minute or two without speaking, and Corsi was also silent, evidently waiting for Bartolli to make the next move. Frank stood aside and watched them both, watched Alterman and Angelini, and watched the security man move closer to the door.

"Mr. Holloway," Bartolli said finally, "perhaps we can leave our two critics at this end of the table and discuss matters at the other end? You will, of course, want reassurance that we are fully authorized by our government to initiate arrangements concerning the artwork, that whatever agreement we might reach will be binding. I take it that if we reach an agreement, you will represent Ms. Valducci."

"That is exactly right," Frank said. "I don't think they'll hear a word we say. Or care." He smiled at Alterman who was pointing to something on the Caravaggio. Both men were examining the Rembrandt, the burgher with his luminous eyes and cheeks. Alterman looked up and said, "He paid homage to Caravaggio. The same pattern in the drape as in the fruit the boy is holding. That's why they were so often paired." Angelini spoke in his rapid Italian, and Alterman laughed and turned back to the paintings.

"School boys with a new and wonderful discovery," Bartolli said with a shrug. He pulled out a chair and sat, and Frank and Corsi took seats, Corsi opposite Bartolli and Frank at the head of the table.

Frank opened his briefcase and brought out his laptop and printer, and Bartolli opened his own briefcase and brought out another laptop and a folder of papers. "Our authorization," he said, passing a printout to Frank.

"And my authorization to represent Ms. Valducci."

They nodded at each other, and read the documents carefully before putting them aside.

"I have made a tentative agreement regarding the paintings," Bartolli said taking another document from his briefcase.

"As I have done, also," Frank said. They exchanged documents. "As you can see I have left blank certain items."

"Yes, of course. We are prepared to offer Ms. Valducci a million dollars, American, for the art, which, of course, belongs to the Italian government for the time being."

Frank's smile broadened as he shook his head. "Come now, Mr. Bartolli. I heard Mr. Alterman state under oath that a floor of fifty million for each piece would be his recommendation at an auction. Twenty million."

Bartolli stiffened and his genial smile vanished. "Impossible! That is impossible!" He was waving his hands, and he closed his briefcase with a loud snap.

Frank leaned back in his chair. "It seems that a Sir George Croft-Acton has called my office several times, yesterday and again this morning. And Mr. Laudermilk is waiting in my office. The FBI has a keen interest in stolen property. They've been known to take what we call a SWAT team in to private offices and residences to recover stolen property."

"Five million."

"Fifteen."

"Ten."

"After taxes."

Bartolli and Corsi exchanged words. "About some of these other items," Bartolli said. "The time limit for laboratory examination is unreasonable."

Frank looked at Alterman and Angelini, who appeared oblivious to the conversation taking place. He smiled. "Let's talk about it."

Barbara was sitting on her favorite bench near the giant cherry tree that was almost as old as the city itself when her phone rang.

"Hi, Dad. How did it go?"

"Not bad," he said, the words belying the tone of amusement and satisfaction in his voice. "They left with the stuff, heading for a private jet out at the airport. Alterman went with them."

She knew he was smiling, that he had laughed before placing the call to her, that he most likely would laugh again after they disconnected. Not bad indeed.

"What about Laudermilk?"

"Oh, we had a nice little chat over a fine brandy. We discussed diplomatic immunity, how annoying it can be at times. He sends you his best wishes." The laughter was in his voice again. "The coast is clear now. A black limo with a tail of followers, like a comet passing through town, cleared the way. I aim to walk home and pick some tomatoes. I told Bailey I'd be there when it's time to go back. How are you holding up?"

"Great," she said, speaking to the tree as much as to him. "See you later."

Great, she repeated under her breath, pocketing her phone. Just great. Relieved, tired, anxious, depressed, and even a little bored. But great.

The call came at twenty minutes after five. Barbara called Frank, then stood and regarded the ancient tree regretfully. "You let me down," she whispered to it, and began to walk to the garden parking lot. Always before, this respite changed something, resolved something, but not today. She was leaving in exactly the same way she had arrived, mired in a deep pit of depression.

The SUV rolled in and she climbed aboard to sit next to Gina, who was pale and haggard looking, her eyes too big and too bright. Unshed tears? Barbara said nothing to her, patted her hand, and let it go at that. Nothing to say right now, not until the verdict came down. Reassurance without insurance meant nothing. They stopped at Frank's office building; he came aboard, and they rolled on to the courthouse in silence.

It was strange, Barbara was thinking as they took their places in the courtroom, all choreographed, normal, routine, curtain-up time, places everyone. Silence in the court. She was there and she was watching herself there, watching everyone else: the judge taking his place, the jurors neatly spaced, comfortable, inscrutable; Jeff silent with a strong tendon showing in his jaw, staring ahead, probably seeing nothing. And she, Barbara, there and not there.

"Ladies and gentlemen, have you reached a verdict?"

Lines down pat, response down pat: "Yes, Your Honor."

The folded verdict handed to the bailiff, his stiff walk to the judge's bench, handing over the sheet of paper. The judge reading it, then looking at the jury again.

"Not guilty, Your Honor."

A gasp from Gina, intake of a breath from Jeff. The judge thanking the jury for their service, addressing Jeff: "Mr. Cobbe, you are free to go. Court adjourned."

As he exited, the court erupted. Jurors coming forward, Jeff hugging Barbara, Gina weeping, hugging everyone, Frank shaking hands here and there, being embraced by Daniel and Gregory, even Jeff. Eric hugging Barbara, jurors shaking hands, patting Jeff, reporters with cellphones taking videos, still pictures, and Barbara removed, watching.

"Barbara," Weymouth said, coming to her. He held out his hand. "No hard feelings, I hope. Good job."

She ignored the hand and turned to say to Shelley, "Go on home. We'll pick up the bits and scraps next week." They embraced as Weymouth walked away.

"Look, I brought my own car this morning," Eric said. "I had faith," he added to Barbara. "They told Jeff to come by the jail to pick up his belongings. I'll take him and bring him on out to the farm as soon as he signs something, gets formally released, I guess."

"Barbara," Frank said, coming to her side. "I'll go on out to the farm and tell Gina where she stands with the art business. You want to come along?"

She shook her head. "No. Tell her we'll catch up next week. I'll walk over to your house."

He examined her face, bothered, but it was not the place or time, he decided. He nodded and said to the rest of the crew. "Let's get out of here."

He started to march toward the door and the others fell in line like obedient ducks, Barbara thought with a slight smile flickering on and off. She waited until they were well on their way before she started out, only to be met by Geraldo Reyes and a man whom she assumed was his real assistant, and his lover.

"Ms. Holloway! Please, a moment. You were magnificent! A goddess in complete control! I must talk with you, an interview, photographs. I am in awe, your servant—"

"Next week," she said without slowing her pace. "Not now. Next week." She hurried to enter the elevator.

In the SUV Frank sat in the passenger seat next to Bailey. They exchanged amused glances as the kids in the back babbled happily.

"Two pizzas. Maybe three. And beer."

"Ice cream. A gallon at least, two half gallons, one chocolate chip and nut."

"As soon as they get back. I want to be there when Jeff comes home."

Gina leaned forward and touched Frank's shoulder. "Mr. Holloway, will Barbara explain it all to us? Tell us how she knew so much, how she found out so much."

"She said next week. Give us all time to unwind a little, then talk."

"I'll make you and Barbara a dinner to kill for," Gina said. "A real Italian celebration dinner."

"Maybe we should grill steaks, not go for pizza."

Frank thought it was Daniel speaking, but he didn't turn to look. He settled back in his seat and let the ongoing talk flow past him.

At the house both he and Bailey entered. Rusty greeted them all with an enthusiastic wagging of his tail. "I'll be a few minutes with Gina," Frank said and Bailey nodded toward the kitchen.

"I'll get a drink of water and wait."

As the crew headed for the living room, Frank caught Gina's arm. "We should talk a few minutes while you wait for Jeff."

"I know," she said, leading him into the study. She closed the door and crossed the room to close the living room door. "There's something I wanted to bring up as soon as the trial ended. I want to make a payment arrangement, monthly or whatever you think is best. For your services in setting up the corporation and handling the probate problem. I know it's a lot, but I can make monthly payments. And I want to arrange the same kind of thing with Barbara and cover Jeff's expenses for the trial. I can't even imagine how much that's going to come to. But if you both are willing to take monthly payments, fine. If that's not what you do, I'm pretty sure I can get a mortgage on the farm and just pay you."

She looked earnest and even solemn, like a child playing grownup, Frank thought. He took her arm and guided her to one of the easy chairs. "Sit down, Gina. We'll discuss our fees next week, not this evening. You are going to need a little time to assimilate what I have to tell you."

She sat as stiffly as a kid in the principal's office. He sat opposite her. "Gina, today I had a conference with a representative of the Italian government and the chief assistant to the ambassador from Italy. They agreed to a reward for locating and turning over the stolen artwork. You're about to become a very rich young woman, Gina."

When he told her the amount of the reward, at first she was disbelieving. She shook her head. "It's Barbara's," she said. "I didn't find the paintings, she did."

"Your family kept them safe for over fifty years. Your reward. Please understand that it will take a few weeks, possibly more than a month for money to materialize."

"All at once? Not in payments or something?"

"All at once. You'll need a financial advisor. I can put you in touch with one of ours and guarantee good service."

She had jumped up, sat down, jumped up again, and now she was pacing, or even racing, around the room, gesticulating wildly, not hearing a thing he said. He sat back and waited.

Abruptly she stopped moving, her head cocked to one side. "He's home," she said. She didn't run to the door leading to the hall, but went to the one to the living room, where she came to a stop with her head pressed against the door. Frank rose and walked to her side. The shouts from Gregory and Daniel were loud, exuberant, victory cries. Rusty had broken training, had been caught up in the excitement and was adding to it with frantic barking.

Gina continued to wait another minute, then opened the door and paused a second before running across the room to where Jeff was standing, laughing with Gregory and Daniel. Eric stood a little apart, watching with a broad smile. Gina ignored everyone else as she ran to Jeff, threw her arms around him, and kissed him hard. For a moment he was immobilized, then he responded in kind. It was a long kiss.

Gina drew back and gazed at his face. "I love you. I've loved you too long, and you love me. Will you marry me?"

She was grasping his arms, holding his gaze with her own.

"Jesus!" he whispered. "Jesus Christ! Yes!"

Slowly Frank turned and walked through the study to the hall. He glanced toward the kitchen where Bailey was leaning against the doorframe. Frank motioned for him to come along. It would take some time for anyone to realize he had left, he mused, walking out to the SUV. He shook his head in admiration of Gina for the little dramatic scene. First the commitment with witnesses, then the revelation. By the time he was seated and Bailey was heading back to town, he was chuckling.

What?" Bailey said.

"Nothing. Just thinking about Gina. She'll do." It was high praise.

Barbara heard Frank return, listened to the closing of the front door, his quiet footsteps in the hall. "In here, Dad. Your study." More footsteps and he entered. She had turned on the desk light, leaving the rest of the room shadowed. Pale light was coming in from the window behind her, but she was deeply shaded. Frank hesitated momentarily, then went to his old, decrepit chair that he refused to give up or recover. It was the first piece of furniture he had ever bought and he claimed the most comfortable chair in the house. Thing One jumped on his lap when he sat, and Thing Two tried to follow, but was batted away by his brother, and with a flick of his tail he crossed the room to jump on Barbara's lap. Automatically she began to stroke him.

"How Pavlovian," she murmured. "They get near, we respond. You've spoiled them rotten."

"Probably," he said. "I told Gina—"

"Wait. Me first. I have to tell you something."

Frank felt an iciness form somewhere in his center. He continued to stroke Thing One without speaking again.

"It's filthy, disgusting, rotten to the core," Barbara said. "The system. If Gina had not come to you with the will business, Jeff would have been forced to go with a public defender. Poor, deep in debt, no real job. They do great work, public defenders, but none of them would have found the holes in the prosecutor's bag of tricks. They don't have time to read and reread hundreds of pages of discovery, to find the discrepancies and follow up. They don't have you and Shelley, Bailey and his guys. They don't have the resources to send someone across the country for a deposition. Sometimes they don't even have time to get acquainted with their clients, know them, remember their names. And the prosecutors know all this. A little lie of omission here, lie of commission there, phony baloney expert witnesses, not asking the next question when it's so apparent that a child would have asked it. They didn't think I'd notice that a woman said she didn't have nacho ingredients, then at the end of her testimony said they went inside and made nachos. An inconvenient detour to the grocery, let's just pretend it didn't happen. Or when a woman said she knew someone was home because she saw the lights and understood her water pressure problems. They asked her if she saw him; she said no. That was enough, done with her. Or the other guy who saw the car. They didn't even bother to canvas the neighborhood. Pretending to search the farm area. Just a little stroll through, enough.

"The paintings would not have come up at all, if Gina had gone to someone else about the will. The prosecutor, the investigators weren't interested in Chadwick's phone call to Valducci's, or her murder, or in Tilsen's obsession about getting the house. Just not interested. They had their man. It was a travesty of a trial, a farce, a Kafka trial. And with a public defender they would have won.

"It's completely broken, the whole system. And it isn't fair to Shelley for me to keep her in her position. She should be with a firm that will let her fly solo. She's plenty good enough, but I can't turn her loose. I need her for cases like this one. And I can't simply bring in more help. Not enough office space, not enough income for another hungry mouth."

Not enough high-paying cases, or even paying cases Frank thought and did not say.

She had been speaking fast, hardly pausing for breath. Now she did pause and lifted her glass to take a long drink of wine. Thing Two stirred, shifted. She resumed petting him.

"But most of all," she said, putting down her glass. "I'm just tired of it all. Tired of the lies, the plea deals that catch the innocent with the guilty, just to avoid the expense of a real trial with an involved attorney. Then to have Weymouth practically accuse me of witness tampering, insinuate that I was responsible for his witness bowing out. To bring in that lousy psychologist with his lousy test score. I wonder if he even read through any of the questions, if it mattered to him that it's phony, that it hurts people, hurts kids. It could have been the determining factor for a conviction if the jury took their word that the final score was all that mattered. Jeff was psychopathic, obviously the killer. It's just so sick, so evil."

She drank again, and this time when Thing Two protested, she dumped him off her lap. In a dull voice she said, "I didn't save Jeff. The paintings did. It was touch and go without them, and I believe the jury would have tilted toward Weymouth. Judge McNulty knew what was happening, he was a prosecutor for years. He knew and didn't care."

"Not his job," Frank said mildly.

"Then whose the hell is it?"

"Yours. You and the prosecutor present the case, he makes sure it's all legal. He doesn't go sifting through the evidence."

"Right," she said bitterly. "And another innocent guy gets sent to prison. They would have found him guilty without the paintings."

"We can't know that," Frank said. But he believed she was right. Juries tended to go along with the prosecution unless given a good reason to doubt, and it was possible that they had not seen a reason strong enough to overcome their natural inclination. He knew it would be a mistake to try to argue with her, to try for reason. She was too angry. He also knew he had to stop her before she took the next step, because if she took it, she might be reluctant or even unable to retract it. "Is there any more of that wine? Or should I open a new bottle?"

"There's enough. I'm afraid I might have pulled one out that you were saving for a special occasion. It's good."

This was as special as occasions were likely to get, he thought, standing. Thing One protested in a piteous voice. "Be right back," Frank said. "But there's something you should know. I made a deal with the Italians. Ten million, after taxes."

"It will all go right into the farm project," Barbara said, uninterested. "Return on investment: more tomatoes and carrots. Good for them."

"To be divided into two parts," Frank said. "Eight million for Gina, two million for you. I'll get myself some wine now." He walked out fast.

He didn't pour wine for himself. He opened the refrigerator and pulled out ham, Swiss cheese, lettuce, mayonnaise, and mustard. At the counter he put together a large sandwich, added sliced tomato to it and a slice of Walla Walla onion. He worked methodically, in no hurry. She needed time to grasp what he had told her. He cut the sandwich in halves and wrapped it in plastic wrap. He found a bag for the sandwich and the half full bottle of wine, which was indeed a nice pinot noir from the King estate. Her care package for later. He knew it would be a futile gesture to ask her to stay for dinner, or to offer a meal out. She needed time.

Five minutes later she walked into the kitchen, went to the sink to rinse her glass and put it on the counter. "I have to go home," she said.

"I'll drive you. Seems any day now we'll all be driving our own cars again."

She picked up her briefcase and purse and he picked up her care package. They walked out to his car. The drive was short, and silent until he pulled into her driveway. Neither mentioned her impassioned outburst, or the two-million-dollar reward coming her way.

"Don't get out," she said, opening her door. "I'm going to the coast tomorrow, back Sunday late afternoon or evening."

"Sounds good," he said. "Bobby, I know you need a little time, just add a vacation to your bucket list. You haven't taken any real time off for years. And if you find it in your heart to shop a little, bring home a couple of pounds of fresh clams. I'll provide the wine, garlic, and bread. This is for you." He handed her the sandwich bag.

She leaned over to kiss his cheek, and then she was out of the car, on the walkway, opening her door, and gone. He waited until a light came on in the house before he backed out of the driveway.

Barbara stood by her car on the last viewpoint of her trip home. The ocean was glass smooth, incredibly blue, pacific, the way it had been the previous day, all morning. She had walked miles on beaches, had slept ten hours, to her surprise, had thought about Gina and her pals, feeding the world, one community at a time; thought about public defenders and the impossible tasks assigned to them time and again; thought about the Juans and Juanitas; the leaking roofs and old women in head scarves who didn't know who to call to get a roof patched; the girls with swollen bellies and no men in sight; the renters being kicked out of houses; fences falling down with no landowner willing to repair them; the sometimes petty, sometimes serious crimes that could send a kid away for ten years, twenty, life, with little or no distinction in the courts. And now it was time to go home. Another car pulled off the road and a couple got out, young, in love, holding hands, laughing. She nodded at them, got in her own car, and started driving.

After turning inland, she slid a CD into the player without looking to see what she had chosen. She smiled when the sound-track started from *Oh, Brother Where Art Thou?* It dated her, she thought, but it was one of her favorites.

Frank was putting finishing touches on potato salad. He had blanched broccoli and steamed green beans to a tender, crisp stage, and added them along with diced sweet onion to the potatoes. Then his own mayonnaise, and it was done. He covered it and put it in the refrigerator. On the stove, minced garlic was sautéing gently in a butter-olive oil mix. If she brought the clams, he was halfway there in the preparation. If she didn't, the garlic would keep in the fridge. He wandered out the backdoor to his garden, which was winding down. Another week or two, come October, he would start cleaning it all up. Start a new compost pile...

He sat on the back porch, considering Barbara for a long time. She had done a hell of a job with a hopeless case. A toss of the coin verdict, however. A shitty case, a shitty no-defense case. He had recorded it all, and he had the discovery package if he wanted it. A new chapter for the book he was writing. There were plenty of other cases as badly screwed. He could dig out some of them. The system was badly screwed, he thought then. Royally screwed. A systemic problem. Maybe a separate article aimed at a mass audience...

He reentered the kitchen and turned off the burner. The garlic oil was done to perfection. He went to his study and picked up a yellow legal pad, his notebook. He smiled as he thought of Bailey's notebook, a three-by-five spiral pad, and those in the twenty-first century who used tablets and laptops, or even their smartphones. He preferred his oversized legal pad. "Old habits," he murmured, and took the pad out to the porch to make a few notes.

He heard Barbara's car when she pulled into the driveway. He was surprised at the hour, only four. When he opened the door, he examined her face quickly, then took a Styrofoam cooler from her.

"Clams," she said. "And a nice piece of halibut. I figured that since I'm going to be rich one of these days, I might as well live it up. It's twenty-two dollars a pound. Caught this morning. And I thought that since it's happy hour time, we might do the clams and swill wine, and have the halibut later. I haven't eaten since dawn or something like it."

"Sounds like a plan," he said. "We'll let these guys soak a bit and do up happy hour in style. Half an hour. Can you hold out that long?"

"I'll try not to start gnawing the furniture. I'd better wash up a little bit. Sand, salt spray, bringing the beach home with me as usual." She left for the bathroom.

So they were not going to talk about her rant or her dark mood, and that was probably good, he thought as he put the clams in a large pot, added cold water and a bit of sea salt. He turned on the burner again and added half a bottle of decent champagne to the garlic oil. He had a good Soave chilling.

Later, seated at the kitchen table across from him, she picked up another clam and said, "Darren said Todd will get in around midnight tonight. He'll let him sleep twenty-four hours or however long he needs and start home probably on Tuesday. He said he sent off a boy on an adventure, and a man is coming home. I'm not sure how either of us feels about that."

"I sent a girl off to college and a damn smart woman came home," he said after a moment, remembering how eerily quiet the house had become when she had left that time. They ate without speaking again for a few minutes. The clams were delicious.

Barbara broke the silence. "My lease is up the first of January. Decisions, decisions." She dipped a piece of baguette into her bowl, ate a clam, followed by the bread, and sighed deeply.

He waited. And they both continued to eat clams, dip bread, sip wine, and finally she continued what she had started.

"I'm thinking of buying my building."

"Buying it? Why?"

"Smithson wanted to sell it last year, but the deal fell through. I need more space. I'm going to make Shelley a full partner and she'll need a bigger office, and we are desperate for storage space for file cabinets and supplies. Also, Shelley's replacement will need a room, and a receptionist will free up Maria, and she'll need an office working as secretary for Shelley and me." She eyed him thoughtfully. "You mean, why buy, why not a new lease?"

"Something like that," he said.

"Well, I'll be able to make a good down payment, and a mortgage won't be more than rent for that much space. Also, there will be income from the other tenants. Blackmun, you know, the accountant across the hall from me? He's leaving when his lease expires, January 1. He's going in with a bigger firm over on Garden Way, a more refined neighborhood, more elegant address or something. I'll want his space. And I'll have to do some remodeling, get an architect in to help plan, things like that. Can't do that in someone else's building. I'll keep the building manager, Mort Thurston. He's a good guy and does a good job."

She continued to talk out the plan she had already made as she and Frank continued to eat. Finally she leaned back in her chair and regarded the last few clams with regret. "I really want to eat them, but I can't. God, they were good! I just remembered something you said once. I asked you why you worked so hard at the office and in court and yet you worked really hard on your garden, too."

She grinned at him. "Do you remember what you told me?"

He shook his head.

"You told me that doing something altogether different was as good as a vacation. For the next few months, I'll be doing something different that involves carpenters, plumbers, electricians. I'll verify your answer, or not, when it's done."

"To your new establishment," he said, raising his glass in a toast. And he was thinking of her return on investment: more space, more crew, more work than ever, and likely not a cent more than she was already making. They touched glasses and finished off the wine.

About The Author

Kate Wilhelm's first short story, "The Pint-Sized Genie," was published in Fantastic Stories in 1956. Her first novel, *More Bitter Than Death*, a mystery, was published in 1963. Over the span of her career, her writing has crossed over the genres of science fiction, speculative fiction, fantasy and magical realism, psychological suspense, mimetic, comic, family sagas, a multimedia stage production, and radio plays. Her works have been adapted for television, theater, and movies in the United States, England, and Germany. Wilhelm's novels and stories have been translated to more than a dozen languages. She has contributed to *Redbook, Quark, Orbit, The Magazine of Fantasy & Science Fiction, Locus, Amazing, Asimov's Science Fiction, Ellery Queen's Mysteries, Fantastic Stories, Omni* and many others.

Kate and her husband, Damon Knight (1922-2002), also provided invaluable assistance to numerous other writers over the years. Their teaching careers covered a span of several decades, and hundreds of students. Kate and Damon helped to establish the Clarion Writer's Workshop and the Milford Writer's Conference.

Kate Wilhelm lives in Eugene, Oregon.